Liza Marklund is an author, publisher, journalist, columnist, and goodwill ambassador for UNICEF. Her crime novels featuring the relentless reporter Annika Bengtzon instantly became an international hit, and Marklund's books have sold 12 million copies in 30 languages to date. She has achieved the unique feat of being a number one bestseller in all five Nordic countries, and she had a number one bestseller in the USA with *The Postcard Killers*, the novel she co-wrote with James Patterson. She has been awarded numerous prizes, including a nomination for the Glass Key for best Scandinavian crime novel.

The Annika Bengtzon series is currently being adapted into film.

Neil Smith studied Scandinavian Studies at University College London, and lived in Stockholm for several years. He now lives in Norfolk.

www.transworldbooks.co.uk

Also by Liza Marklund

RED WOLF
EXPOSED

and published by Corgi Books

By Liza Marklund and James Patterson

POSTCARD KILLERS

THE BOMBER

Liza Marklund

Translated by Neil Smith

CORGI BOOKS

TRANSWORLD PUBLISHERS
61–63 Uxbridge Road, London W5 5SA
A Random House Group Company
www.transworldbooks.co.uk

THE BOMBER
A CORGI BOOK: 9780552160926

First published in Great Britain in 2005 by Pocket Books
Corgi edition published 2011

Addresses for Random House Group Ltd companies outside the UK
can be found at: www.randomhouse.co.uk
The Random House Group Ltd Reg. No. 954009

Typeset in 11/13pt Sabon by
Kestrel Data, Exeter, Devon.

6 8 10 9 7

Penguin Random House is committed to a sustainable future for
our business, our readers and our planet. This book is made from
Forest Stewardship Council® certified paper.

Printed and bound in Great Britain by Clays Ltd, Elcograf S.p.A.

Contents

A Note on the Currency

Calculated at a rate of 10.3 Swedish Krona to the pound, the monetary figures in this book would convert approximately as follows:

10kr = 97p	500kr = £48.50
50kr = £4.85	1000kr = £97
100kr = £9.70	2000kr = £194
200kr = £19.40	3000kr = £291

STOCKHOLM

N

Lidingö, 2 miles

DJURGÅRDEN

Saltsjöbaden, 3 miles

NACKA

Värmdö Road

OLYMPIC TRAINING GROUND

VICTORIA STADIUM

Hammarby Harbour

Sickla Canal

Southern bypass

Hammarby canal

Tungelsta, 14 miles

Lumagatan

Bangata

Katarina

Folkungagatan

Götgatan

Vintertullstorget

GAMLA STAN

SÖDERMALM

Ringvägen

SÖDERMALM HOSPITAL

Southern bypass

CITY HALL

Kungsholmstorg

Hantverkargatan

KUNGSHOLMEN

STADSHAGEN

RUSSIAN EMBASSY

Essinge motorway

Sätra Hall, 3 miles

1 mile

miles

0

Prologue

The woman who was soon to die stepped cautiously out of the door and glanced around. The hallway and stairwell behind her were dark; she hadn't bothered to switch on the lights on her way down. She paused before stepping onto the pavement, as if she felt she were being watched. She took a few quick breaths and for a moment her white breath hung around her like a halo. She adjusted the strap of the handbag on her shoulder and took a firmer grasp of the handle of her briefcase. She hunched her shoulders and set off quickly and quietly towards Götgatan. It was bitterly cold, the sharp wind cutting at her thin nylon tights. She skirted round a patch of ice, balancing for a moment on the kerb. Then she hurried away from the street lamp and into the darkness. The cold and the shadows were muffling the sounds of the night: the hum of a ventilation unit, the cries of a group of drunk youngsters, a siren in the distance.

The woman walked fast, purposefully. She radiated confidence and expensive perfume. When her mobile phone suddenly rang she was thrown off her stride. She stopped abruptly, looking quickly around her. Then she bent down, leaning the briefcase against her right leg, and started searching through her handbag.

Her movements were suddenly irritated, insecure. She pulled out the phone and put it to her ear. In spite of the darkness and shadows there was no mistaking her reaction: irritation was replaced by surprise, then anger, and finally fear.

When the conversation was finished the woman stood for a few seconds with the phone in her hand. She lowered her head, clearly thinking hard. A police car drove slowly past her; the woman looked up at it, watchful, following it with her eyes as it went away. She made no attempt to stop it.

She had clearly reached a decision. She turned on her heel and started to retrace her steps, going past the wooden door she had come out of and carrying on to the junction with Katarina Bangata. As she waited for a night-bus to pass she looked up, her eyes following the line of the street to the square, Vintertullstorget, and beyond to the Sickla canal. High above loomed the main Olympic arena, Victoria Stadium, where the summer games were due to start in seven months' time.

The bus went past, the woman crossed the broad sweep of Ringvägen and started to walk down Katarina Bangata. Though her face was expressionless, her fast pace let on that she was freezing. She crossed the pedestrian bridge over Hammarby canal to reach the media village of the Olympic Park. With quick, slightly jerky movements she hurried on towards the Victoria Stadium. She decided to take the path beside the water although it was further, and colder. The wind from the Baltic was ice-cold, but she didn't want to be seen. The darkness was dense, and she stumbled a few times.

She turned off by the post office and pharmacy towards the training area and jogged the last hundred metres towards the stadium. When she reached the main entrance she was out of breath and angry. She pulled the door open and stepped into the darkness.

'Say what you want to say, and be quick about it,' she said, looking coolly at the figure emerging from the shadows.

She saw the raised hammer but didn't have time to feel any fear.

The first blow hit her left eye.

Existence

Just beyond the fence was a huge anthill. When I was a child I used to stand there and study it intently for hours. I would stand so close that the insects ran over my legs. Sometimes I would follow an individual ant from the grass down in the courtyard, over the gravel drive, and up the bank of sand to the anthill. I was always determined not to lose sight of it at that point, but I always did. Other ants caught my attention. When there were too many of them my interest fractured in so many different directions that I ran out of patience.

Sometimes I would put a sugar-lump on the anthill. The ants loved my gift, and I would smile as they swarmed over it and pulled it down into the depths. In the autumn, when the cold came and the ants got slower, I would poke a stick into the anthill to wake them up again. The grown-ups got angry with me when they saw me doing that, and told me I was spoiling the ants' hard work and destroying their home. To this day I can still remember the sense of injustice, because I didn't mean any harm. I just wanted to have a bit of fun. I wanted to get them moving again.

My games with the ants gradually started to infiltrate my dreams. My fascination with the insects turned into an inexpressible horror at their creeping and crawling.

Now that I'm grown up I can't stand the sight of more than three insects at any one time, no matter what species they are. I start to panic when I lose sight of them. My phobia developed at the moment I realized the parallels between myself and the little insects.

I was young, still actively trying to find answers to my life, building up theories in my head, testing them against each other in various ways. The fact that life could be capricious wasn't part of my world view. Something had created me. I had no idea what that might be: coincidence, fate, evolution, maybe even God.

But it did seem to make sense that life could be meaningless, and this made me angry, and sad. If there wasn't any point to our time on the planet, then our lives were simply an ironic experiment. Someone put us here to study the way we fought, crawled, suffered and struggled. Occasionally this Someone would distribute random rewards, a bit like putting a sugar-lump on an anthill, and watch our joy and despair with the same emotionally detached interest.

As the years passed, a sense of reassurance grew. Eventually I realized that it doesn't matter if there's no great purpose to my life. And even if there is, there's no point in me knowing it here and now. If there were any answers, then I'd already know them, and because I don't, then it doesn't matter – however much I might think about it.

This has given me a certain sort of freedom.

Saturday 18 December

1

The sound reached her in the middle of a bizarre sexual dream. She was lying on a bed of glass on a spaceship; Thomas was on top of her, inside her. Three presenters from the radio programme *Studio Six* were standing alongside them, watching expressionlessly. She was desperate for the loo.

'You can't go to the toilet now, we're on our way into space,' Thomas said, and, looking through the big panoramic window, she saw he was right.

The second ring tore the cosmos to shreds, leaving her sweaty and thirsty in the darkness. The ceiling loomed above her in the gloom.

'Answer the bloody thing before it wakes the whole house,' Thomas grumbled from the mess of pillows.

She twisted her head to see the time: 03.22. The excitement of the dream vanished in a single breath. Her arm, heavy as lead, reached for the phone on the floor. It was Jansson, the night-editor.

'The Victoria Stadium's gone up. Burning like fuck. Our reporter's out there for the night edition, but we need you for the next edition. How soon can you get there?'

She took several breaths, letting the information sink in, feeling adrenalin rolling like a wave through her body and up into her brain. The Victoria Stadium, she thought. Home of the Olympics. Fire, chaos. Bloody hell. South of the city centre. Should she take the southern bypass or the Skanstull bridge?

'How are things looking in town? Are the roads okay?'

Her voice sounded rougher than she would have liked.

'The southern bypass is blocked. The exit by the stadium has collapsed, but that's all we know. The Södermalm tunnel is shut off, so you'll have to go above ground.'

'Who's doing pictures?'

'Henriksson's on his way, and the freelancers are already there.'

Jansson hung up without waiting for a response. Annika listened to the dead crackle on the line for a few seconds before hanging up and letting the phone drop to the floor.

'So what is it this time?'

She sighed silently before replying.

'Some sort of explosion at the Victoria Stadium. I've got to go. It'll probably take all day.'

She paused before adding: 'And all evening.'

He muttered something inaudible.

Carefully she extricated herself from Ellen's slightly damp pyjamas. She breathed in her daughter's scent, her skin sweet, her mouth sour, her thumb firmly lodged between her lips, then she kissed the child's soft hair. The girl stretched happily, then rolled up into a ball, three years old and utterly content, even in her sleep. She dialled for a taxi with a heavy hand, climbing out of the numbing warmth of the bed and sitting on the floor.

'A car to Hantverkargatan 32 please. Bengtzon. It's

urgent. To the Victoria Stadium. Yes, I know it's on fire.'

It was bitingly cold outside, at least ten degrees below zero. She turned up the collar of her coat and pulled her woollen hat down over her ears, her toothpaste breath hanging in a haze around her. The taxi pulled up just as the front door clicked shut behind her.

'Hammarby Harbour, the Victoria Stadium,' Annika said as she landed with her bulky handbag on the back seat.

The driver glanced at her in the rear-view mirror.

'Bengtzon, the *Evening Post*, eh?' he asked with a hesitant grin. 'I always read your stuff. I like what you said about Korea, my family come from there. I was up in Panmujom as well – you caught the atmosphere really well, the soldiers standing there facing each other, never allowed to talk to one another. That was a really good report.'

As usual she heard the praise but didn't take it in, couldn't take it in, because that might make the magic ingredient, the thing that made her texts work, vanish.

'Thanks. I'm glad you liked it. Do you think the Södermalm tunnel is okay or should we stick to the streets?'

Like most of his colleagues, he had a perfect over-view of the situation. If something happened anywhere in the country at four in the morning, there were only two calls you had to make: one to the police, and one to the taxi service. That was enough to guarantee you an article for the national edition: the police could confirm what had happened, and the taxi-drivers were almost always able to give some sort of eye-witness account.

'I was on Götgatan when it went off,' he said, performing a U-turn. 'God, the street lamps were swaying like hell. Christ, I thought, a bomb's gone off. The Russians are here. I radioed in, wondering what the fuck . . . They said the Victoria Stadium had blown up. One of our guys was right next to it when it went up, he had a call-out to an underground club in one of the new blocks out there . . .'

The car raced down towards the City Hall as Annika fished her notepad and pen out of her bag.

'Was he okay?'

'Fine, I think. A lump of metal came through the side window, missed him by a couple of centimetres. Just a cut on his face, so they said over the radio.'

They passed the metro station in the old town, heading towards the big junction at Slussen.

'Where did they take him?'

'Who?'

'Your colleague – the one with the bit of metal?'

'Oh, him, his name's Brattström. Södermalm Hospital, I think; that's the closest one.'

'First name?'

'Don't know, but I can check over the radio . . .'

His name was Arne. Annika pulled out her mobile, put in the earpiece and dialled Jansson's desk in the newsroom. He knew from the number on the phone's LCD-screen that it was her calling before he answered.

'A taxi-driver's been injured, Arne Brattström, he was taken to Södermalm Hospital,' she said. 'We might be able to get up there and see him; we can do that in time for the first edition . . .'

'Okay,' Jansson said. 'We'll find out what we can about him.'

He put the receiver down and yelled to a reporter: 'Look up an Arne Brattström, then check with the police to see if his family's been told, then call his wife if he's got one.'

Back on the line he said, 'We've sorted an aerial shot. When will you be there?'

'Seven, eight minutes, depending on what they've closed off. What are you working on?'

'We've got the bare facts, comments from the police. I've got reporters ringing people in the buildings facing the stadium for their comments, and one reporter's already there but is about to go home. And we're re-running the earlier Olympic bombs, the bloke who let off fire-crackers in the old Victoria Stadium in Stockholm and New Ullevi in Gothenburg when the Stockholm bid went in—'

Someone interrupted him, and Annika could feel the buzz of the newsroom all the way down the line to the taxi. She said quickly, 'I'll be in touch when I know more.'

'Looks like they've closed off the warm-up area,' the taxi-driver said. 'We'd better take the scenic route.'

The taxi swung onto Folkungagatan and down towards the Värmdö road. Annika dialled the next number on her phone. As the call went through she watched the last stragglers going home from their night out, raucous and stumbling. There were a lot of them, more than she would have imagined. It was always the same these days: the few times she was out at this time of day were always because a crime had been committed somewhere. She had forgotten that the city could be used for more than just crime or work, had somehow suppressed the fact that there was an entirely different life that only emerged at night.

A stressed voice picked up her call.

'I know you can't say anything yet,' Annika began. 'Tell me when you've got time to talk. I'll call whenever suits you. Just say when.'

The man sighed down the line.

'Bengtzon, I don't fucking know. I don't know. Call later.'

Annika looked at her watch.

'It's twenty to four. I'm writing for the early edition. What about half past seven?'

'Okay, fine. Call at half seven.'

'Okay, we'll talk then.'

Now that she had a promise, it would be hard for him to pull out. The police hated journalists who called as soon as something happened and wanted to know everything. Even if the police had managed to gather any information, it was hard to know what they could go public with. By half past seven she would have had time to formulate her own observations, questions and theories, and the detectives would know what they wanted to say. That would work okay.

'You can see the smoke now,' the taxi-driver said.

She leaned over the front passenger seat, peering up to the right.

'Bloody hell.'

Thin and black, it stretched up towards the pale half-moon. The taxi swung off the Värmdö road and onto the southern bypass.

The motorway was blocked off a few hundred metres from the mouth of the tunnel and the stadium itself. A dozen other vehicles were already lined up behind the roadblock. As the taxi pulled up alongside them, Annika handed over her taxi account card.

'When do you want to go back? Shall I wait?' the taxi-driver asked.

Annika smiled weakly. 'No thanks, this is going to take some time.'

She gathered up her pad, pen and mobile.

'Happy Christmas!' the taxi-driver called as she shut the car door.

20

Oh God, she thought, there's a whole week to go yet. Are we going to start that already?

'Thanks, same to you,' she said to the taxi's rear window.

She wove through the cars and pedestrians until she reached the roadblock. Not set up by the police. Good. She usually respected their cordons. She didn't even slow down as she jumped the barrier and started to run.

2

She didn't hear the angry shouts behind her as she stared up at the immense construction in front of her. She had driven past often and each time had been fascinated by the scale of the job. The Victoria Stadium was being built into the rock itself, excavated from the old Hammarby ski-slope. The environmentalists had made a fuss, of course; they always did whenever a few trees were cut down. The southern bypass carried on right through the rock and beneath the stadium itself, but the opening had been shut off with concrete blocks and emergency vehicles. The flashing lights on the roofs of the vehicles reflected off the wet tarmac. The north side of the stadium leaned out above the opening of the tunnel like a great chanterelle mushroom, but now it was torn in two. That must have been where the bomb went off. The curved shape was torn apart, spiking up into the night sky. She ran on, but realized that she wasn't going to get much further.

'Oi, where do you think you're going?' a fireman shouted.

'Up there,' she shouted back.

'It's shut off!' the man yelled.

'Oh, is it?' she muttered. 'So arrest me!'

She carried on, then turned off to the right as far as she could. Beneath her the Sickla canal was frozen solid. On the far bank, on the other side of the ice, there was a sort of concrete plinth, where the roadway plunged into the rock. She heaved herself up onto the railing and dropped down, falling a metre or so. Her bag thudded against her back as she landed.

She stopped for a moment and looked around. She had only been this close to the stadium a couple of times, once for a press tour back in the summer, and then one Sunday afternoon in the autumn together with Anne Snapphane. To her right was the site of the Olympic village, the half-finished blocks of Hammarby Sjöstad, where the competitors would live during the games. The windows gaped blackly, every pane of glass in the area seemed to have been blown out. Immediately ahead of her the training ground glimmered in the darkness. To her left was a ten-metre-high concrete wall. Up above it was the plaza and the main entrance to the stadium.

She started to run along the wall, trying to make sense of the sounds she could hear: a siren in the distance, muffled voices, the noise of a water cannon, or maybe a large ventilation unit. The red lights of emergency vehicles played across the wall. She reached the end of the wall and set off up the stairs towards the entrance just as a policeman began to unroll a reel of blue and white tape.

'We're blocking this entrance off,' he yelled.

'My photographer's up there,' Annika shouted back. 'I'm just going to get him.' The policeman waved her through.

God, I hope I wasn't lying, she thought.

The stairs were divided into three even flights. By the time she reached the top she was out of breath. The whole plaza was full of flashing emergency vehicles and people running. Two of the pillars holding up the northern stand had collapsed and were lying crumpled on the ground. Twisted green seats were scattered everywhere. A television camera-team had just arrived. She caught sight of a reporter from the other evening paper, and three freelance photographers. She looked up, into the hole made by the bomb. Five helicopters were circling above, at least two of them media choppers.

'Annika!'

It was the photographer from the *Evening Post*, Johan Henriksson, a twenty-three-year-old part-timer who had moved down from a local paper in Östersund. He was both talented and ambitious, the second of these being the most important. As he ran towards her his two cameras jolted against his chest, his bag hanging off his shoulder.

'What have you got?' Annika asked, pulling out her pad and pen.

'I got here thirty seconds or so after the fire brigade. I managed to get a shot of an ambulance taking a taxi-driver away, seems he was hit by something. The fire crews are having trouble getting water up to the stand; they ended up driving an engine right into the stadium. I've got pictures of the fire from the outside, but I haven't been inside. A couple of minutes ago something must have happened – the cops started running around like mad. I'm sure something's happened.'

'Or else they've found something,' Annika said, putting her pad away.

Holding her pen like a relay baton she started to jog towards the entrance at the far side of the plaza. If her memory was right, it ought to be somewhere over to the right, under the part of the stadium that had collapsed.

No one stopped her as she crossed the plaza, there was too much chaos. She wove her way between lumps of concrete, twisted metal and green plastic seating. Four flights of steps led up to the entrance; she was out of breath when she reached it. The police had blocked the entrance, but that didn't matter. She didn't need to see more. The doorway was untouched, it seemed to be locked. Swedish security companies evidently couldn't resist putting stupid little stickers on the doors of buildings they guarded, and the Victoria Stadium was no exception. Annika pulled out her pad and noted down the name and phone number.

'Please evacuate the area. There is a risk of collapse! I repeat . . .'

A police car glided slowly across the plaza, its loudspeaker on. People started to hurry off towards the warm-up area and the Olympic village down below. Annika jogged along the outer wall of the arena, and managed to avoid having to go back down to the plaza. Instead, she followed the ramp that curved gently round the whole edifice. There were several entrances; she wanted to check them all. None of them had been damaged or forced open.

'Sorry, madam, it's time to leave.'

A young policeman put his hand on her arm.

'Who's in charge?' she asked, holding up her press card.

'He hasn't got time. You've got to leave. We're evacuating the whole area.'

The policeman started to guide her away, he was clearly shaken up. Annika pulled away and stopped in front of him. She took a chance: 'What did you find inside the stadium?'

The policeman ran his tongue over his lips. 'I'm not sure, and I'm not allowed to say either,' he said.

Bingo!

'So who can tell me, and when?'

'I don't know, check with the duty officers. But you have to get out of here now!'

3

The police positioned their cordon on the far side of the training centre, several hundred metres from the stadium. Annika bumped into Henriksson close to where the restaurants and cinema were being built. A makeshift media centre had started to form on the broadest part of the pavement, in front of the post office. More journalists were arriving by the minute, a lot of them wandering about with smiles on their faces, greeting colleagues. Annika found this sort of comradely back-slapping difficult, people hanging around accident scenes boasting about which parties they'd been to. She shrank away, pulling the photographer with her.

'Have you got to get back to the paper?' she asked. 'The first edition's about to go to press.'

'No, I emailed my photos over. I'm okay to stay.'

'Good. I've got a feeling things are going to happen here.'

An outside-broadcast truck from one of the television stations pulled up beside them. They walked away from it, past the bank and pharmacy, down towards the canal. She stopped and looked across at the stadium. The police and fire brigade were still in the plaza. What were they doing? An icy wind was blowing from the water, further out a broken outlet pipe formed a dark gash in the ice.

She turned her back to the wind and warmed her nose in her glove. Through her fingers she suddenly saw two white vehicles gliding over the pedestrian bridge from Södermalm. Bloody hell, it was an ambulance! And paramedics! She looked at her watch: it had just gone twenty-five to five. Three hours until she could call her contact. She inserted the earpiece and tried the duty desk instead. Engaged. She rang Jansson.

'What do you want?'

'There's an ambulance on its way up to the stadium.'

'My deadline's in seven minutes.'

She could hear the sound of tapping from his keyboard.

'What are the agencies saying? Any reports of casualties?'

'They've got the information about the taxi-driver, but they haven't spoken to him. The destruction, comment from the police, they're not saying anything yet, that sort of thing. Nothing special.'

'The taxi-driver was taken away an hour ago, this is something else. Is there anything on police radio?'

'Nothing remotely controversial.'

'Anything scrambled?'

'Nope.'

'What about radio news?'

'Nothing so far. There's an extra television news broadcast at six.'

'Yes, I saw the OB unit.'

'Well, keep an eye on things. I'll call you once we've got the first edition to press.'

He hung up. Annika ended the call on her mobile, but left the earpiece in place.

'Why have you got one of those?' Henriksson said, pointing at the wire running down her cheek.

'Your brain gets fried by radiation from mobiles,

28

didn't you know?' She smiled. 'I just think it's practical. I can run and write and talk on the phone at the same time. And it's quiet, there's no noise when I make a call.'

Her eyes were watering from the cold; she had to squint to see what was going on over by the stadium.

'Have you got one of those big telephoto lenses?'

'Doesn't work in the dark,' Henriksson said.

'Well, use the biggest lens you've got and try to catch whatever's going on over there,' she said, pointing with her glove.

Henriksson sighed gently, put his photographer's bag on the ground and peered through the lens.

'I could do with a tripod,' he muttered.

Various vehicles had driven up the grass bank and were parked outside one of the entrances. Three men got out of the paramedics' car, and were standing behind it talking. A uniformed policeman walked over to them. There was no movement by the ambulance.

'Well, they're not in any hurry,' Henriksson said.

Another two police officers went over, one in uniform, the other in plain clothes. The men were talking and gesticulating, one of them pointed up towards the hole made by the bomb.

Annika's mobile rang. She clicked to take the call.

'Yes?'

'What's the ambulance doing?'

'Nothing. Waiting.'

'So what have we got for the next edition?'

'Did you get anything on the taxi-driver in hospital?'

'Not yet, but we've got people there. Unmarried, no partner.'

'Have you tried to get hold of the Olympics boss, Christina Furhage?'

'Haven't been able to get through.'

'What a bloody nightmare for her, after all her work . . . We'll have to run the whole Olympic angle as well: what's going to happen to the Games now, all that. Can the stadium be repaired in time? What does the President of the International Olympic Committee say? That sort of thing.'

'We've thought of that. We've got people working on it.'

'Then I'll do the story of the explosion. This has to be sabotage. Three articles: the police hunt for the bomber, the crime scene this morning, and—'

She fell silent.

'Bengtzon?'

'They're opening the door of the ambulance. They're taking out a trolley, they're going up to the entrance. Bloody hell, Jansson, there's another victim!'

'Okay, Police hunt, I-was-there and Victim. You've got pages six, seven, eight and the centrefold.'

The line went dead.

4

She watched intently as the men walked up to the stadium. Henriksson was looking through the pictures he had taken. None of the other journalists had noticed the new vehicles.

'Fuck, it's cold,' Henriksson said as the men disappeared into the arena.

'Let's get back to the car and call from there,' Annika said.

They walked back up to the media circus. People were standing about freezing, the television crews were unrolling their cables, a few reporters were trying to blow some life into their pens. Why don't they ever learn to use pencils when it's below freezing? Annika wondered with a smile. The radio reporters looked like big insects with their broadcast equipment strapped to their backs. Everyone was waiting. One of the freelancers who worked for the *Evening Post* had come back from his trip to the office.

'There's going to be some sort of press conference at six o'clock,' he said.

'Right on time for a live broadcast on the television news, how convenient,' Annika muttered.

Henriksson had parked his car on the other side of the tennis courts and health centre.

'I ended up there because of the roadblocks,' he said apologetically.

It was quite a walk; Annika could feel her feet getting numb. A few snowflakes had started to fall, not good if you wanted to take night-shots with a telephoto lens. They had to clear the windscreen of Henriksson's Saab.

'This is fine,' Annika said, looking over at the stadium. 'We can see the ambulance and the paramedics, this is a great view.'

They got in and ran the engine to warm up the car.

Annika started phoning round. She tried the police duty desk again. Engaged. She called the hospital's incident control room and asked who had first sounded the alarm, how many calls they had received, whether anyone had been injured in the flats when the windows blew in, and if they had any idea of what the material damage was. As usual, the hospital staff were able to answer most of her questions.

Then she called the number she had taken from the stickers at the stadium entrance: the security company that was supposed to be guarding the Victoria Stadium. She reached an emergency room in Stadshagen, over in Kungsholmen. She asked if any alarms had gone off in the Victoria Stadium during the early hours of the morning.

'Any alarms we receive are confidential,' the man at the other end said.

'Yes, I realize that,' Annika said. 'I'm not asking about an alarm you received, but about one that you probably didn't receive.'

'Erm,' the man said, 'we can't answer any questions about the alarms we receive.'

'Yes, I understand that,' Annika said patiently. 'I

32

was just wondering if you received any alarms from the Victoria Stadium at all?'

'Okay,' the man said. 'Are you actually listening to me?'

'Right,' Annika said. 'How about this: what happens when you get an alarm?'

'Well, it comes through here.'

'To the emergency room?'

'Of course. It goes onto our computer system, and comes up on our screens along with a plan of action.'

'So if there was an alarm from the Victoria Stadium, it would come up on your screens?'

'Well, yes.'

'And it would tell you exactly what to do about that particular alarm?'

'Yes, that's right.'

'So what has your security company been doing at the Victoria Stadium tonight? I haven't seen a single one of your vehicles here.'

The man didn't answer.

'The Victoria Stadium has been blown up, we can agree on that, can't we? So what's your company supposed to do if the stadium is on fire or damaged somehow?'

'It's in the computer,' the man said.

'So what have you done?'

The man didn't answer.

'Because you haven't had any alarms from the stadium at all, have you?' Annika said.

The man was silent for a few moments before replying: 'I can't comment on the alarms we've received or haven't received.'

Annika took a deep breath and smiled. 'Thank you.'

'You won't write anything about what I've said, will you?' the man said anxiously.

'Said?' Annika said. 'You haven't said anything. All you've done is tell me it's confidential.'

She ended the call. Great, now she had her angle. Breathing deeply, she stared out through the windscreen.

5

One of the fire engines drove off, but the ambulance and paramedics were still there. The bomb squad had arrived; their vehicles were spread out over the plaza. Men in grey overalls were pulling things out of their vans. The fire was out now; she could hardly see any smoke.

'How did we get the tip-off?' she said.

'From Smoothy,' Henriksson said.

Every newspaper has a number of more or less professional tip-off agents who keep an eye on what's going on in their areas of interest, and the *Evening Post* was no exception. Smoothy and Leif were their best sources for police news; they slept with the police radio on beside their beds. As soon as anything happened, no matter how big or small, they called the paper. Other sources kept an eye on judicial records, and reporting from various public bodies.

Annika sank deep into her own thoughts, her eyes roaming across the rest of the site. Immediately in front of them was a ten-storey building where the technical aspect of the Games would be controlled. A footbridge led from the top of the building right across to the rocky hillside. Weird, who on earth would want to go over there? She looked along the path of the bridge.

'Henriksson,' she said, 'there's one more picture we need.'

She looked at the time. Five thirty. They still had time before the press conference.

'If we climb up beside the Olympic flame, right at the top of the hill, we ought to get a pretty good view.'

'You think so?' the photographer said sceptically. 'They've put up huge walls to stop people looking in.'

'The centre of the arena is probably blocked, but we might be able to see the north side of the stadium, and that's the interesting bit right now.'

Henriksson checked his watch.

'Will we have time? Haven't we got those shots from the helicopter? And don't you want to keep an eye on the ambulance?'

She bit her lip.

'The chopper's gone now; the police have probably banned them. And we can ask one of the freelancers to watch the vehicles. Come on, let's get going.'

The rest of the journalists had discovered the ambulance and the air was thick with questions. The television crew had moved their truck down to the canal to get a better view of the stadium. A frozen reporter was preparing his piece for the six o'clock bulletin. There were no police nearby. Once Annika had spoken to the freelancer they set off.

Climbing the hill took longer and was much harder than she had expected. The ground was slippery and stony. They clambered up through the darkness, stumbling and swearing. Henriksson was carrying a large tripod. But they didn't encounter any barriers and made it to the top in time, only to be met with a two-and-a-half-metre-high concrete wall.

'Oh, no,' Henriksson groaned.

'Oh, yes, and maybe it's for the best,' Annika said.

'Climb up on my shoulders and I'll try to push you up. Then you can climb up onto the torch itself. You should be able to see something from there.'

The photographer stared at her.

'You want me to stand on the Olympic torch?'

'Yes, why not? It's not lit, and it isn't cordoned off. I'm sure you can get up there; it's only a metre or so from the top of the wall. If it's strong enough to carry the eternal flame, I'm sure it can carry you. Up you go!'

Annika passed the tripod and camera bag up to him. Henriksson clambered up the metal frame.

'It's full of tiny holes!' he yelled.

'For the gas,' Annika said. 'Can you see the stand?'

He stood up and looked out at the stadium.

'Can you see anything?' Annika called.

'Bloody hell, yes,' the photographer said. He slowly raised his camera and started shooting.

'What can you see?'

He lowered his camera without taking his eyes from the stadium.

'They've got floodlights on part of the stand,' he said. 'There's about ten of them. They're picking things up and putting them in small plastic bags. The paramedics are there. They're joining in too. Looks like they're being pretty thorough.'

He raised the camera again. Annika felt the hairs on the back of her neck bristle. Fuck. Could this really mean what she thought it did? When Henriksson had finished taking pictures, they slithered and scrambled back down the hillside, shaken, slightly nauseous. What do medics put in small bags? Fragments of explosive devices? Unlikely.

A couple of minutes before six they were down in the media throng again. Blue-tinted television lamps lit up the scene, making the snowflakes sparkle. The television crew was set up; the reporter was powdered and ready. Led by the officer in charge, a group of policemen was heading towards them. They lifted the cordon, but got no further.

The wall of journalists was impenetrable. Silence fell as the lead officer blinked in the glare of the lights. He looked down at some sheets of paper, then raised his eyes and started to speak.

'At three seventeen this morning an explosive device detonated at the Victoria Stadium in Stockholm,' he said. 'We do not yet know what caused the explosion. The explosion resulted in severe damage to the north stand. It is not yet clear if the damage can be repaired.'

He stopped and looked at his notes again. Cameras clicked, microphones were poised. Annika was standing off to the side so that she could see if the ambulance left, while at the same time following the press conference.

'The stadium caught fire after the explosion, but the fire is now under control.'

Another pause.

'A taxi-driver was injured when a piece of debris went through the window of his car,' the officer went on. 'He was taken to Södermalm Hospital where he is in a stable condition. The windows and façades of approximately ten properties on the other side of Sickla canal have been damaged. The buildings are still under construction and not yet inhabited. No other casualties have been reported.'

Another pause. The officer looked tired and solemn as he went on.

'This is an act of sabotage. The device that damaged the stadium was clearly extremely powerful. The police are in the process of securing evidence left by the culprit. We will use all the resources at our disposal to catch him. That's all we have to say for the time being. Thank you.'

He turned to retreat behind the cordon. A torrent of voices stopped him.

'. . . anyone under suspicion . . .'

'. . . other victims . . .'

'. . . paramedics on the scene?'

'That's all we have for now,' the officer repeated, and walked away. He and his colleagues went off quickly, their shoulders hunched. The media circus dissolved, the television reporter stood in the light from the lamps and ran through his text before handing back to the studio, while everyone else was busy with their mobile phones or trying to get their pens to work.

'Hmm,' Henriksson said, 'that wasn't much use.'

'It's time to go,' Annika said.

Leaving one of the freelancers on duty they walked off towards Henriksson's car.

'Let's go via Vintertullstorget and get a few witness statements,' Annika said.

6

They rang the doorbells of those living closest to the stadium: young families and pensioners, alcoholics and Goths. They all spoke about the bang that woke them up, how shocked they were and how awful it was.

'That's enough,' Annika said at quarter to seven. 'We've still got to pull this together.'

They drove back to the paper in silence. Annika was writing introductions and captions in her head, Henriksson was going through the images in his mind's eye, sorting and organizing them, printing and fixing the light-levels.

It was snowing properly now. The temperature had risen considerably and the road was dangerously slippery. On the Essinge motorway four cars had gone into each other. Henriksson stopped to check that no one was hurt.

They reached the paper just before seven. The atmosphere was tense, focused.

Jansson was still there, at weekends the night-editor looked after the second edition as well. Most Saturdays only one or two articles were switched between editions, but there was always the option of resetting the whole paper. Which was precisely what was happening now.

'Will it hold?' Jansson asked, jumping to his feet the moment he saw them.

'I think so,' Annika said. 'There's a body in the north stand. In tiny pieces, but I'm sure it's a body. Give me half an hour and I'll know for certain.'

Jansson rocked back and forth on his heels.

'Half an hour, no sooner?'

Annika fired him a look over her shoulder as she shrugged off her coat, grabbed a copy of the early edition and headed off to her room.

'Okay,' he said, sitting back down.

First she wrote the news article itself, which was really just an expansion of the work already done for the early edition. She added quotes from the neighbours and the fact that the fire was now under control. Then she started her I-was-there piece, complete with details of the sights and sounds. At two minutes to eight she called her contact.

'I can't say anything yet,' he began.

'I know,' Annika said. 'I'm going to do the talking, and you can either stay quiet or tell me I'm wrong—'

'I can't do that this time,' he interrupted.

Shit. She swallowed and decided to go on the attack.

'Hear me out first,' she said. 'I reckon this is what happened: someone died in the Victoria Stadium last night. Someone is in tiny pieces in the north stand. You're there right now trying to find the remnants. It's an inside job; all the alarms were turned off. There must be a hundred alarms in a stadium like that: burglar alarms, fire alarms, motion detectors – they were all switched off. Someone let themselves in with a key and disarmed them, either the victim or the culprit. And right now you're trying to work out which one it was.'

She fell silent and held her breath.

41

'You can't go public with that yet,' the policeman on the other end of the line said.

She breathed out quickly.

'Which bits?'

'The suspicion that it was an inside job. We want to keep that to ourselves. The alarms were working, but had been switched off. And yes, someone did die. We haven't got an ID yet.' He sounded exhausted.

'When will you know?'

'No idea. It's going to be hard to identify the body visually, if I can put it like that. But there's other evidence. I can't say more about that right now.'

'Male or female?'

He hesitated.

'Not yet,' he said finally, and hung up.

Annika rushed out to Jansson.

'They've confirmed one death, but they don't know who the victim was.'

'Mincemeat?' Jansson said.

She gulped and nodded.

Helena Starke woke up with the mother of all hangovers. As long as she was lying in bed it was okay, but when she got up to fetch a glass of water she threw up on the hall rug. She kneeled on all fours panting for a while before she felt able to stagger into the bathroom. She filled the toothbrush glass with water and drank it greedily. Bloody hell, she would never drink again. She looked up at the mirror and saw her bloodshot eyes through the spatters of toothpaste on the mirror. Would she never learn? She opened the bathroom cabinet and pressed two paracetamols from the pack, and swallowed them with plenty of water, offering up a silent prayer that she would be able to keep them down.

She stumbled out into the kitchen and sat down at the

table. The seat of the chair was cold against her naked thighs, and she had a pain in her groin. How much had she actually drunk? There was an empty cognac bottle on the draining-board. She lay her head on the table-top and tried to remember anything about the previous evening. The bar, the music, all the faces – everything was a blur. Christ, she couldn't even remember how she got home! Christina had been there, hadn't she? They left the bar together, didn't they?

She groaned, stood up and filled a jug with water, then went back to the bedroom. On her way back she pulled up the mat and threw it into the washing basket in the hall cupboard. She was on the verge of throwing up again as the smell hit her nostrils.

The clock radio beside the bed said five to nine. She groaned. The older she got, the earlier she woke up, especially when she had been drinking. Once upon a time she had been able to sleep off the alcohol over a whole day. But not any more. These days she woke up early, feeling like death, then lay awake sweating for the rest of the day. She might drift off for a few brief moments, but she couldn't sleep properly. With an effort she reached for the water and drank straight from the jug. She arranged the pillows against the headboard and settled down. Then she saw the clothes she had been wearing last night, neatly folded on the chest of drawers by the window, and a shiver ran down her spine. Who the hell had done that? Probably her. That was the worst thing about losing your memory when you drank: you could go round like a zombie and do a load of completely normal things without having any idea of what you were doing. She shuddered and switched the radio on; she may as well listen to the news while she waited for the pills to work.

The lead item on the news made her throw up again.

And she knew at once that there would be no more rest for Helena Starke that day.

Once she had flushed her vomit away down the toilet she picked up the phone and called Christina.

7

The paper's news agency flashed up Annika's findings at 09.34. Which meant the *Evening Post* was first out with the news about anyone being killed in the explosion at the stadium. The front-page headlines shouted: ONE DEAD IN OLYMPIC BOMBING and BOMBER WANTED FOR MURDER.

They were taking a chance with the second one, but Jansson was convinced they had enough to support the claim. The cover was dominated by the picture Henriksson had taken up on the Olympic torch. It was a striking image: the circle of light below the hole made by the bomb, the men crouching over, the dancing snowflakes. It was deeply unsettling, but somehow not macabre. No blood, no body, just an awareness of what the men were doing. They had already sold it to Reuters. The ten o'clock television news was quoting the *Post*'s information, while the radio news bulletin was pretending that it was their story.

Once the next edition was printed the crime reporters and news-editors gathered in Annika's office. Boxes of her files and old cuttings were still piled up in the corners. She had inherited the sofa, but the desk was new. Annika had been in the office for two months, ever since she became head of the crime team.

'We've got a lot to get through, and a lot of work to divide between us,' she said, putting her feet up on the desk. As soon as the paper had gone to press and she had stopped to catch her breath, tiredness had hit her like a brick to the back of the head. She leaned back, reaching for her coffee.

'One: who's the body in the stand? That's tomorrow's main story, and it may turn into several stories. Two: the hunt for the killer. Three: the Olympics angle. Four: how could this happen? Five: the taxi-driver; no one's spoken to him yet. Maybe he saw or heard something?'

She looked at the people in the room, trying to read their reactions to what she had just said. Jansson was half asleep, he was about to go home. The news-chief, Ingvar Johansson, was staring blankly at her. One of the reporters, Nils Langeby, at fifty-three the oldest member of the crime team, was having his usual trouble concealing his hostility. Another one, Patrik Nilsson, appeared to be listening attentively. The third reporter, Berit Hamrin, was sitting quietly.

The only person missing was Eva-Britt Qvist, who was both researcher and editorial secretary.

'I think the way we go about things like this is appalling,' Nils said.

Annika sighed and thought: Here we go again.

'How do you think we should go about it, then?'

'We spend far too much time on this sort of opportunistic violence. What about all the environmental crimes we never cover? And all the crime in schools?'

'Obviously, it would be good if we could give more coverage—'

'Of course it fucking would! This paper's drowning in a swamp of tragic old ladies and bombs and motorbike gangs.'

Annika took a deep breath and counted to three before she replied.

'You're raising an important point, Nils, but maybe now isn't the right time to discuss it . . .'

'Why not? Don't you think I'm capable of working out the right time to raise an issue?'

He shifted in his chair.

'Nils, environmental and school crimes are your brief,' Annika said calmly. 'You spend all your time on those two issues. Do you really think we're tearing you away from your particular area if we call you in on a day like today?'

'Yes, I do!' he thundered.

She looked at the furious man in front of her. How on earth was she supposed to handle him? If she didn't call him in he'd go mad at being left out of their coverage of the Bomber. If she gave him a job he would first refuse, and then mess it up. If she let him stay in the office on standby he would complain about being frozen out.

Her train of thought was interrupted when the editor-in-chief, Anders Schyman, came into the office. Everyone, including Annika, said hello and sat up in their chairs.

'Congratulations, Annika! And thank you, Jansson, for a phenomenal effort this morning,' Schyman said. 'We beat everyone. Excellent! The front-cover picture was brilliant, and we're the only ones who got that view. How on earth did you get it, Annika?'

He sat down on a box in the corner.

Annika told them, to general acclaim: of course, the Olympic torch! That was one to get the Press Club talking.

'So what are we doing now?'

Annika dropped her feet to the floor and leaned over

the desk, ticking off points on her list as she read them out.

'Patrik, you can cover the murder hunt and forensic evidence, and stay in touch with the police. There's bound to be some sort of press conference this afternoon. Find out when, and get a photographer ready to go. We should probably all go along to that.'

Patrik nodded.

'Berit, you're doing the victim – who and why? And there's our old Olympic bomber, the Tiger, of course. He has to be a suspect, even if his little bombs were child's play compared to this. What's he doing now, and where was he last night? I'll try to get hold of him; I interviewed him at the time. Nils, you can take the security aspect of the Olympics, how the hell could something like this happen seven months before the Games, and what are the security arrangements like from now on?'

'I think that's a pretty irrelevant line of inquiry,' Nils Langeby said.

'Really?' Anders Schyman said. 'I don't. It's one of the most important general questions we've got on a day like this. Getting to grips with that proves that we're putting this sort of violence into a social and global context. What impact will this have on sport generally? It's one of our most important articles today, Nils.'

The reporter didn't know how to react – should he feel honoured to have been given one of the most important jobs or upset at being corrected? As usual, he chose the option that made him look best, and puffed out his chest.

'Well, of course, it all depends how you do it,' he said.

Annika cast a grateful glance at Schyman.

'And maybe the evening crew can deal with quotes from the Olympic officials and the taxi-driver?'

Ingvar Johansson nodded. 'My lads are taking the taxi-driver to a hotel in the city as we speak. He lives in a one-room flat out in Bagarmossen, so everyone else will be trying to get hold of him there. We're keeping him hidden at the Royal Viking Hotel until tomorrow morning. Janet Ullberg is trying to get hold of Christina Furhage, a shot of her in front of the hole made by the bomb. Students from the journalists' college are answering the phones for Have Your Say . . .'

'What was the question?' Anders Schyman said, reaching for a paper.

'"Should the Olympics be stopped? Call us tonight between five and seven o'clock." It's pretty obvious that this must be another attack by the Tiger or some other group that doesn't want the Games held in Sweden.'

Annika paused for a moment before saying, 'That's one line we have to look into, of course. But I'm not so sure that's actually the case.'

'Why not?' Ingvar Johansson said. 'We certainly can't ignore the possibility. Apart from the victim, the terrorism angle is our main focus tomorrow.'

'I think we need to be careful not to push the sabotage angle too far,' Annika said, cursing her promise not to say anything about insider involvement. 'As long as we don't know who the victim was, we can't really speculate about what the bomb was meant to do.'

'Of course we can,' Ingvar Johansson said. 'Obviously we'd have to get the police to comment on the theory, but that shouldn't be too hard. They can't deny or confirm anything right now—'

Anders Schyman interrupted. 'I don't think we can rule anything in or out at the moment. We'll keep all our options open until we have to make up our minds about our angle tomorrow. Anything else?'

'No, not with what we know at the moment. As soon

as the victim's been identified we'll get onto the relatives.'

'Okay, but be careful,' Schyman said. 'I don't want to hear any complaints about us harassing the family.'

Annika smiled. 'I'll be looking after that myself.'

8

When the meeting broke up Annika called home. Kalle, her five-year-old son, answered.

'Hello, darling, how are you?'

'Good. We're going to McDonald's, and Ellen spilled orange juice on the *One Hundred and One Dalmatians* DVD, which was stupid because now we can't watch it any more . . .'

The boy fell silent and let out a few small sniffs.

'Oh, that's a shame. How did she manage to spill juice on it? What was the film doing in the kitchen?'

'It wasn't, it was on the floor in front of the television, and Ellen kicked my glass over when she got up to go to the toilet.'

'But why was your juice on the floor in the television room? You know you shouldn't take your breakfast into the television room.'

Annika could feel herself getting angry. Surely she could do something as simple as going to work without their domestic routine falling apart and things getting broken?

'It wasn't my fault,' the boy yelped. 'It was Ellen! It was Ellen who broke the film!'

He was crying properly now, and dropped the phone and ran off.

'Hello? Kalle!'

Bloody hell, how had this happened? She had only called home to hear their voices and ease her conscience a bit. Thomas came on the line.

'What on earth did you say to him?' he said.

She sighed and felt the beginnings of a headache.

'Why were they eating breakfast in front of the television?'

'They weren't,' Thomas said in a controlled voice. 'I let Kalle take his juice in there, that's all. Turns out that wasn't a smart move considering what happened, but I'm bribing them with lunch at McDonald's and a new film. Stop thinking we can't cope for a minute without you! Concentrate on your big story. How's it all going?'

She gulped.

'One dead, really messy. Murder, suicide, maybe just an accident, we don't know yet.'

'Yes, I heard. You're going to be late, aren't you?'

'That's putting it mildly.'

'I love you,' he said.

For some reason she felt tears welling up.

'I love you too,' she whispered.

Her source had been on the night shift and had gone home now, so she had to make do with the usual police channels. Nothing new had happened that morning, the body hadn't been identified, the fire was now completely out, and the forensic work was still going on.

She decided to go out to the stadium again with another photographer, a part-time temp called Ulf Olsson.

'Actually, I don't think I'm dressed right for this sort of assignment,' Ulf said in the lift on the way down to the garage.

Annika looked up at him.

'What do you mean?'

The photographer was wearing a dark grey wool coat, a suit and smart shoes.

'I thought I was going to be covering the red carpet at the National Theatre tonight. You could have told me sooner that we were heading out to a murder scene, you must have known for a couple of hours.'

He gave her a pathetic look. Something clicked inside Annika's head, and her tiredness got the better of her.

'Don't tell me what I should or shouldn't do. You're a photographer, so you ought to be able to cover anything from a traffic accident to a gala premiere. If you don't like taking pictures of mincemeat in an Armani suit, you should have some overalls in your camera case.'

She kicked the lift door open and marched into the garage. Fucking amateurs.

'I can't say I like the way you're talking to me,' the photographer said.

Annika blew up, spinning to face him.

'Stop being so fucking pretentious,' she snarled. 'There's nothing stopping you from finding out for yourself what's going on in the paper. Do you really imagine that I – or anyone else, for that matter – has time to organize your fucking wardrobe?'

The photographer gulped and clenched his fists.

'Now you're just being unfair,' he muttered.

'For God's sake,' Annika groaned, 'stop whining! Just get in the car and drive to the stadium. Or do you want me to drive?'

The tradition was always for photographers to drive when a team went out on a job, even in vehicles from the paper's car-pool. A lot of papers had actually given their photographers company cars, but there'd been such a fuss about the impact on people's tax status that the *Evening Post* had stopped that.

This time Annika got behind the wheel and headed out onto the Essinge motorway. The atmosphere in the car was tense all the way out to Hammarby Harbour. Annika decided to try the road through the old industrial area, but it didn't help. The entire Olympic site was blocked off. Much to her annoyance, Annika could feel herself getting frustrated, while Ulf Olsson looked relieved at the possibility of not having to get his shoes dirty.

'We have to get a picture of the stand in daylight,' Annika said, and did a U-turn by the roadblock on Lumavägen. 'I know a couple of people who work for a television company based out here. If we're lucky they might let us onto the roof.'

She pulled out her mobile and dialled her old friend Anne Snapphane, a producer of daytime chat-shows for a cable channel.

'I'm up to my neck in editing,' Anne snarled as she took the call. 'Who is it and what do you want?'

Five minutes later they were up on the roof of the magnificent old light-bulb factory next to Hammarby Harbour. The view of the damaged stadium was fantastic. Using a telephoto lens, Olsson quickly took a whole sequence of shots.

They said nothing as they drove back to the office.

9

'The press conference starts at two o'clock,' Patrik shouted as she walked into the newsroom. 'The photographer's all set.'

Annika waved in reply and went into her office. She hung up her coat, tossed her bag onto the desk, and plugged her mobile phone in to charge.

She felt exhausted and inadequate after her outburst at the photographer. Why had she reacted so strongly? Why had she let it bother her? She hesitated for just a moment before dialling the editor-in-chief's internal number.

'Of course I've got time to see you, Annika,' he said.

She walked through the open-plan newsroom towards Anders Schyman's office in the corner of the building. There was almost no sign of any activity. Ingvar Johansson was holding a phone to his ear as he ate a tuna salad. The picture editor, Pelle Oscarsson, was trying something in Photoshop, and one of the layout team was setting up the next morning's pages.

As Annika closed the door behind her she heard the theme tune of the lunch news bulletin on Anders Schyman's radio. They were going with the sabotage angle, claiming that the police were hunting a madman who hated the Olympics. So they hadn't got any further than that.

'The madman theory is all wrong,' Annika said. 'The police think it was an inside job.'

Schyman let out a shocked whistle.

'Why?'

'There was no sign of a break-in, and the alarms were switched off. Either the victim turned them off or the Bomber did. Either way, it means that someone on the inside is responsible.'

'Not necessarily; the alarms could just have been broken,' Schyman said.

'They weren't,' Annika said. 'They were all in working order, just switched off.'

'Someone might have forgotten to turn them on,' the editor-in-chief said. Annika thought about this for a moment, then nodded: that could have happened.

They sat down on the sofas in one corner of the office, listening to the radio. Annika looked out at the Russian Embassy. The daylight was starting to fade even though it had only just arrived, and a grey haze outside made the windows look dirty. Someone had made a belated attempt to decorate the office for Christmas with a couple of potted poinsettias and some Advent candles in the windows.

'I had a go at Ulf Olsson today,' Annika said quietly.

Anders Schyman waited for her to go on.

'He was moaning about wearing the wrong clothes for the Hammarby job, making out that it was my fault – he said I should have told him earlier that we were heading out there.'

She fell silent. Anders Schyman looked at her for a moment before replying.

'Annika, you don't decide which photographer gets allocated to which job. The picture editor does that.

56

And anyway, reporters and photographers alike need to wear clothes that work for any job, no matter where. That's part of the deal.'

'I swore at him,' Annika said.

'Well, maybe that wasn't a good move,' the editor-in-chief said. 'If I were you I'd apologize for swearing and give him a bit of general advice on what to expect. And keep an eye on how we cover the sabotage angle – I don't want us pushing too hard on terrorism if that isn't what happened.'

Schyman stood up, indicating that the conversation was finished.

Annika felt relieved, partly because she had some support for her coverage of the Olympics story, and partly because she had told Schyman about her outburst herself. Of course people got angry with each other every day at the paper, but she was a woman, and she hadn't been in a position of authority for long, so she had to be prepared for extra scrutiny.

She walked straight over to the picture editing section, picking up one of the big bags emblazoned with the paper's logo on her way. Ulf Olsson was on his own, leafing through a glossy blokes' magazine.

'I'm sorry I swore at you,' Annika said. 'Here, use this for winter clothes. Keep a change of thermals, some winter boots, and a hat and scarf in your locker or in the back seat of your car.'

He glared sourly at her.

'You should have told me sooner that we were going—'

'You'll have to take that up with the picture editor or the editor-in-chief. Have you uploaded those pictures?'

'No, not yet . . .'

'Could you get onto it, then?'

She walked away, feeling his eyes on her back. As she

approached her office it struck her that she hadn't eaten anything all day, not even breakfast. She headed off to the canteen instead and picked up a meatball sandwich and a Diet Coke.

The news of the explosion at the Victoria Stadium had made headlines all round the world. All the big TV stations and international papers had sent people to the press conference in police headquarters at two o'clock. CNN, Sky News, BBC, and all the Nordic channels, as well as reporters from *Le Monde*, the *Herald Tribune*, *The Times*, *Die Zeit*, and many more. The approach to the building was full of outside-broadcast trucks.

Annika was there, together with four others from the paper: Patrik and Berit, and two photographers. The room was packed with people and equipment. Annika and the two reporters found chairs close to the door, while the photographers elbowed their way closer to the front. As usual, the television crews had parked themselves right in front of the podium, blocking the view for everyone else. Their cables snaked all over the floor, and everyone would have to remember to let them ask their questions first. Their lights seemed to sweep all over the room, even if most of them were focused on the makeshift platform where the police would soon be making their appearance. Several of the news teams would be broadcasting live, among them CNN, Sky and Swedish television news. Their reporters were practising their pieces to camera and scribbling notes, while the radio reporters checked their recording equipment with repeated chants of 'one two, one two'. The hubbub of voices was like a waterfall. The room was already unbearably hot. Annika groaned and dropped her outdoor clothing in a heap on the floor.

The police emerged from a side-door close to the

podium. The voices fell silent and the click of cameras took over. There were four of them: a spokesman for Stockholm Police, Chief Prosecutor Kjell Lindström, a detective from the violent crime unit whose name Annika couldn't remember, and Evert Danielsson from the Olympic organizing committee. They sat down at the table and dutifully sipped from their glasses of water.

The police spokesman began, running through the facts that had already been made public: that there had been an explosion, that one person had died, the extent of the damage, the fact that forensic work was still going on. He looked tired and drawn. Annika wondered what on earth he would look like after several more days of this.

Then the Chief Prosecutor took over.

'We haven't yet identified the victim at the stadium,' he said. 'Our work has been complicated by the fact that the body is severely damaged. We do, however, have a number of leads which may help us to confirm identity. The explosive material itself is being examined in London. As yet we haven't received confirmation, but preliminary reports indicate that the explosives were not of military origin.'

Kjell Lindström took a sip of water. The cameras clicked.

'We are also looking for the man who was convicted of the bombings that damaged two sports stadiums seven years ago. The man is not suspected of any involvement, but he may be able to help with our inquiries.'

The Chief Prosecutor looked down at his notes, almost as if he were hesitating. When he started to speak again, he was looking right into the camera of the Swedish television news team: 'A person wearing dark clothing was observed close to the stadium shortly before the explosion. We appeal to anyone who may have any information about the explosion at the Victoria Stadium to come forward. The police would like to talk to anyone who was in South Hammarby Harbour between midnight and three twenty this morning. Even if your information does not seem particularly relevant, it could be vital in helping the police piece together the sequence of events.'

He listed some phone numbers that would soon be rolling across the bottom of the screen of the television news.

When the Chief Prosecutor had finished, Evert Danielsson cleared his throat.

'Obviously, this is a great tragedy,' he said nervously, 'both for Sweden as host of the Olympic Games, and for sport in general. The Olympic Games stand for fair competition, regardless of race, religion, politics or gender. And that is why it is so distressing when someone commits an act of terrorism against a global symbol like the Victoria Stadium.'

Annika craned her neck to look past the CNN camera. She wanted to see the reactions of the police and the prosecutor to Danielsson's Olympic angle. Just as she had expected, they flinched when the Olympic chairman mentioned both a motive and a summation of the attack: the explosion was an act of terrorism aimed directly at the Olympics. Although they still didn't know who the victim was. Or did they? Maybe the Olympic chairman didn't know as much as she did – that the attack was most likely an inside job?

The Chief Prosecutor interrupted, trying to get Danielsson to shut up, but he hadn't finished yet. He went on, 'I urge anyone who thinks they may have seen anything to contact the police. It is vital that the culprit is caught— Yes, what is it?'

He looked in surprise at the Chief Prosecutor, who must have kicked or nudged him.

'I would just like to stress,' Kjell Lindström said, leaning towards the microphones, 'that we have no information about a possible motive at this point.' He glanced at Evert Danielsson. 'There is nothing – I repeat: nothing – to indicate that this is an act of terrorism against the Olympics. No threats have been made against either the facilities or the Olympic Committee itself. We are currently considering various different lines of inquiry and various possible motives.'

He straightened up.

'Any questions?'

The television reporters were ready. As soon as the invitation came they yelled out their questions. As usual, the first questions were about things that had already been mentioned, but either too slowly or in too much detail for the television news. So the reporters always asked about the same things again, in the hope of getting a clearer, simpler answer.

'Do you have any suspects?'

'Is there a clear line of inquiry?'

'Have you identified the victim?'

'Was this an act of terrorism?'

Annika sighed. The only reason for coming to press conferences like this was to watch how the police behaved. Everything they said was covered in the media, but the facial expressions of those not in shot were usually more revealing than the often rather obvious answers. Now, for instance, she could see how furious Kjell Lindström was with Evert Danielsson for talking about 'an act of terrorism'.

If there was anything the Swedish police would want to avoid, it was the idea that there was a link between terrorism, Stockholm, the Olympic Games and this

61

explosion. Besides, the terrorism angle was probably wrong. But, for once, they had actually revealed some new information.

Annika scribbled a few questions in her notebook. There was information regarding a person in dark clothes close to the stadium: when, and how? That meant that there was a witness – so who was that, and what were they doing there? A sample of the explosives had been sent to London: why? Why wasn't the national forensics unit down in Linköping conducting the analysis? When would the tests be finished? How did they know the explosives weren't military? What did that mean for the investigation? Did it limit it, or stretch its boundaries? How easy was it to get hold of civil explosives? How long would it take to repair the north stand of the stadium? Was the stadium insured, and, if so, who by? And who was the victim? Did they know? And what were the lines of inquiry that might help them identify the body that Kjell Lindström had referred to?

She sighed again. This story showed every sign of spiralling out of control.

10

Chief Prosecutor Kjell Lindström was marching down the corridor outside the press room, white in the face and clutching his briefcase hard. If he wasn't careful, he was likely to strangle Evert Danielsson. The other participants in the press conference followed in his wake, with three uniformed officers. One of them closed the doors behind the little procession, shutting out the last and most persistent reporters.

'I don't see what's so controversial about saying what everybody's thinking,' the chairman of the Olympic Committee said defensively. 'It's obvious to all of us that this is an act of terrorism. We on the Olympic Committee think it's vital to control public opinion from the start, to build up support against this attempt to sabotage the Games—'

The Chief Prosecutor spun round, stopping inches from Evert Danielsson's face.

'Read my lips: There Is No Evidence To Suggest That This Is An Act Of Terrorism. Got that? The last thing the police need right now is a bloody great debate about terrorism and how to stop attacks. Anything like that would mean a total overhaul of measures to protect the Olympic venues and public buildings, and we just don't have the resources for that . . . Do you have any idea how many venues are linked into the Olympics, one way or another? Of course you do. Just remember the fuss when the Tiger was causing trouble. He let off a couple of little blasts and every single fucking reporter in the country started crawling round unguarded stadiums in the middle of the night and shrieking about what a scandal it was.'

'How can you be so sure that this wasn't a terrorist attack?' Danielsson said, taken aback.

Lindström sighed and started walking again.

'We have our reasons, believe me.'

'Such as?' the chairman of the committee persisted.

The prosecutor stopped again.

'This was an inside job,' he said. 'Someone inside the Olympic organization did it, okay? It was one of your lot. Which makes it pretty bloody awkward that you're going around blabbing about terrorism, don't you think?'

The colour drained from Evert Danielsson's face.

'That's impossible.'

Kjell Lindström started walking again.

'No, it's not,' he said. 'If you go upstairs to the crime unit, you can tell them exactly who has access to all the pass keys and alarm codes for the Victoria Stadium.'

The moment Annika walked into the newsroom after the press conference, Ingvar Johansson beckoned her over to look at his computer screen.

'Come and see if you can make anything of this!' he yelled.

Annika went into her room first to drop off her bag and outdoor clothes. Her top was sticking under her arms and she was suddenly very conscious of the fact that she hadn't showered that morning. She pulled her jacket tight around her and hoped she didn't smell.

Ingvar Johansson was leaning over one of the news-room's more powerful computers with Janet Ullberg, the young temp.

'Janet hasn't been able to get hold of Christina Furhage all day,' he said. 'We've got a number that's supposed to reach her, but there's no answer. According to the Olympics office she's in town, presumably at home. We checked her out on the national database, so we could go and pay her a visit. But when you put in her details nothing happens. She's not there.'

He indicated the search results on the screen: *no Christina Furhage*. 'There are no results for that name.' Annika slid behind Janet and sat down in front of the screen.

'She must be there; everyone is,' Annika said. 'You just made the search too narrow, that's all.'

'I don't get it,' the young temp said in a thin voice. 'What are you trying to do?'

Annika explained as she typed.

'The national database is the official list of names and addresses. It's got a new name these days, Sema Group or something, but everyone still calls it Dafa Spar. It's not even run by the government any more, but by some Anglo-French company . . . Anyway, every single person in the whole country is listed, along with their identity number, address, previous addresses, place of birth – every Swede, and any foreigners who've been given ID numbers. You used to be able to see family connections as well, whether people were married or had children, but they stopped that a couple of years ago. You can get into the system online these days, through a site called "Info Square". That lets you choose between different databases, such as the vehicle registration site, or the register of limited companies, but we want dear old Dafa Spar. There!

You just put "spar" in the search box at the top . . .'

'I'm going back. Call me later,' Ingvar Johansson said, heading over towards the news desk.

'. . . and you're in. Then you decide how to search. You see? By ID number, date of birth or name. *Voilà!*'

Annika pressed enter and a questionnaire appeared on screen.

'So, we're looking for a Christina Furhage who lives somewhere in Sweden,' she said, filling in the necessary details: gender, first name, last name. She didn't bother to fill in the boxes for approximate year of birth, council district or postcode. The computer hummed and after a few seconds three lines of information flashed up on the screen.

'Okay, we'll take one thing at a time,' Annika said, pointing at the screen with a pen. 'Look at this one: "Furhage, Eleonora Christina, Kalix, born 1912, hist." Which means that the information is historical, so that one's probably dead. They keep dead people on the register for a year or so. But it could also mean that she's changed her name, so she might have married some old bloke in the home. If you want to, you can check by highlighting her name and clicking historical detail, but we won't bother with that right now.'

She moved her pen to the last of the three entries.

'"Furhage, Sofia Christina, Kalix, born 1993." Just a child; probably related to the first one. Strange surnames almost always occur in just one place.'

She moved the pen again.

'This one's probably our Christina.'

Annika clicked on the name and the screen flashed up more details, but not the ones she had been expecting. Annika gave a start.

'Bloody hell,' she said.

She leaned closer to the screen, as if she didn't believe her eyes.

'What is it?' Janet asked.

'The information's protected,' Annika said. She printed the page, then hurried over to Ingvar Johansson with it.

'Can you remember us ever writing about Christina Furhage having bodyguards? Or about any threats against her?'

Ingvar Johansson leaned back and thought for a moment.

'No, not as far as I know. Why?'

Annika held out the printed page.

'Christina Furhage is under protection, serious protection. No one but the head of the tax office in Tyresö knows where she lives. And there are only – what? – a hundred or so people in Sweden who have that sort of protection.'

She gave Johansson the printout. He stared at it uncomprehendingly.

'What? Her details aren't protected – her name's on here.'

'Yes, but look at the address: "Head of tax office, Tyresö".'

'What the hell are you going on about?' Ingvar Johansson said.

Annika sat down.

'The authorities use different types of protection when someone's been threatened,' she explained. 'The least serious are covered by a block in the census results. That's not unusual; there are something like five thousand people in Sweden covered by that level of secrecy. Then the screen just flashes up "personal details protected".'

'Okay, but that's not what it says here,' Johansson said.

Annika pretended she hadn't heard.

'To get your details protected there has to be some sort of concrete threat. The decision to block access is taken by the head of the local tax office where the person is registered.'

Annika tapped her pen against the printout.

'But this, on the other hand, is really unusual. It's a much stronger form of protection than just getting your details blocked in the database so that they can't be viewed. Furhage isn't in the database at all, apart from this, a referral to the head of the tax office in Tyresö outside Stockholm. He's the only person in authority who has any idea where she is.'

Ingvar Johansson looked sceptically at her.

'How do you know this?'

'Do you remember those articles I wrote on the Paradise Foundation? About people living under the radar in Sweden?'

'Of course I do. And . . . ?'

'That's the only time I've ever come across this response before. When I looked up people the authorities wanted to hide.'

'But Christina Furhage isn't hidden, is she? What's that number we're supposed to have for her?'

They looked up the contacts database shared by all the newspaper's computers. Under the name Christina Furhage, job title Head of Olympics, was a mobile number. Annika dialled the number. The mobile company's automated answering service picked up the call immediately.

'The phone's switched off,' she said.

She called Directory Inquiries to ask who was listed under that number. The information was confidential.

Ingvar Johansson sighed.

'Well, it's too late now for my picture of Christina

Furhage in front of the stadium,' he said. 'We'll try again tomorrow.'

'Okay, but we still need to get hold of her,' Annika said. 'I mean, she has to make some kind of comment about all this.'

She stood up and headed off towards her office.

'What are you going to do?' Ingvar Johansson asked.

'Call Olympic headquarters. They must know what the fuck's going on,' Annika said.

11

She sank heavily onto her chair and leaned her head on her desk. Her forehead hit a dried-up pastry from the day before – she took a bite, swallowing it with the remnants of the Diet Coke from lunchtime.

Brushing the crumbs away, she dialled the number for the Olympics office: engaged. She dialled again, but changed the last digit from a zero to a one, an old trick to get past reception and straight to someone's desk.

Sometimes you had to dial a hundred different combinations, but you almost always reached some poor overworked sap in the end. No need for that this time, it worked straight away, and no less than Evert Danielsson, chairman of the Olympic Committee, answered.

Annika paused to think for a second before deciding to skip the niceties and get straight to the point.

'We want a comment from Christina Furhage,' she said, 'and we want it now.'

Danielsson groaned.

'Look, you've tried a dozen times already today. We've said we'll pass on your questions.'

'We want to talk to her in person. She can't stay out of the way on a day like this, surely? Think about how it looks. These are her Games, for God's sake! She isn't usually so shy about speaking up, is she? So why's she hiding this time? Get her to come forward, right away.'

She could hear Danielsson breathing down the line.

'We don't know where she is,' he said quietly.

Annika felt her pulse race as she switched on the tape-recorder that was sitting beside the phone.

'So you haven't been able to reach her either?' she said slowly.

Danielsson gulped.

'No,' he said eventually. 'We've been trying all day. We haven't been able to reach her husband, either. Look, you're not going to print this, are you?'

'I don't know,' Annika said. 'So where might she be?'

'We thought she was at home.'

'Which is where?' Annika asked, thinking about the national database.

'In the centre of the city. But there's no answer there, either.'

Annika took a deep breath and asked quickly, 'What sort of threats have been made against Christina Furhage?'

The man gasped. 'What? What do you mean?'

'Oh, come on!' Annika said. 'If you don't want me to write about this, you're going to have to tell me what's going on.'

'How . . . ? Who told you . . . ?'

'Her details are blocked on the national database. That means that the threat is serious enough for a judge to issue an injunction against whoever is making the threats, preventing them from contacting her. Is that what's happened?'

'Good God,' Danielsson said. 'Who told you this?'

Annika gave a silent groan.

'It's all in the database, if you know how to read

71

between the lines. Is there an injunction preventing anyone from contacting Christina Furhage because of threats made against her?'

'I can't tell you anything,' the man said in a strained voice, and hung up.

Annika listened to the silence for a moment before putting the phone down with a sigh.

Evert Danielsson looked up at the woman standing in the doorway.

'How long have you been there?' he said.

'What are you doing in here?' Helena Starke asked, folding her arms over her chest.

The chairman got up from Christina Furhage's chair and looked around, apparently confused, as though he had only just realized that he was sitting in her office.

'Well, I . . . needed to check something . . . Christina's schedule, to see if she'd put anything in her diary, about going away or anything . . . but I can't find it.'

The woman stared hard at Danielsson. He met her gaze.

'You look terrible,' he said before he could stop himself.

'What an incredibly chauvinistic thing to say,' she said, her face contorted by her distaste as she walked over to Christina Furhage's desk.

'I got very drunk last night and threw up on the hall carpet this morning. If you say that was unusually un-feminine behaviour, I'll punch you in the mouth.'

Danielsson felt his tongue run involuntarily along his front teeth.

'Christina is supposed to be at home with her family today,' Helena Starke said, pulling open the second drawer of her boss's desk with a practised hand. 'That

72

means she was planning to work from home instead of here in the office,' she clarified.

The chairman watched as Helena Starke took out a heavy diary and opened it up towards the back. She turned a few pages noisily.

'Nothing. Saturday the eighteenth of December is completely empty.'

'Maybe she's doing her Christmas cleaning,' Evert Danielsson said with a smile, and this time Helena Starke joined in. The thought of Christina putting on an apron and going round with a duster was absurdly funny.

'Who was that on the phone?' Helena Starke asked as she put the diary back in the drawer.

The chairman noted that she shut it firmly and turned a key to lock all the drawers.

'A journalist, from the *Evening Post*. A woman. I don't remember the name.'

Helena put the key in her jeans pocket.

'Why did you tell her we haven't been able to get hold of Christina?'

'What was I supposed to say? That she doesn't want to comment? That she's in hiding? That would only make things worse.'

Danielsson held out his hands.

'The question is,' the woman said, standing so close to him that he could smell the alcohol still on her breath, 'the *real* question is, where on earth *is* Christina? Why hasn't she come to the office? Wherever she is, it must be somewhere where she isn't able to get any news at all, mustn't it? And where the hell could that be? Any ideas?'

'Her place in the country?'

Helena Starke looked pityingly at him.

'Oh, please! And that terrorism stuff you were going

on about at the press conference wasn't very smart, was it? What do you think Christina's going to say about that?'

Evert Danielsson suddenly flared up: the huge sensation of failure felt suffocatingly unfair.

'Well, that's the conclusion we reached, isn't it? You were there. I wasn't the only one thinking it – quite the opposite. We agreed that we had to take the initiative and try to shape public opinion from the start.'

Helena turned and started walking towards the door.

'It was just a touch embarrassing when the police were so eager to refute everything you said. You came over as hysterical and paranoid on television, and that wasn't particularly attractive.'

She turned round, her hand on the door-handle.

'Are you staying, or can I lock up?'

The chairman of the Olympic Committee left Christina Furhage's office without a word.

12

The editorial meeting that evening took place round the editor-in-chief's conference table. The main television news would be on in fifteen minutes and everyone apart from Jansson was present.

'He's on his way,' Annika said. 'He's just . . .'

'He's just' was the accepted way of explaining delays caused by all manner of problems: reporters who didn't know what they were doing, or a reader who insisted on expressing their opinion over the phone right there and then. It could also mean going to the toilet or getting a cup of coffee.

The others sat round the table and waited. Annika went through her notes of the things she wanted to raise during the meeting. Her list wasn't as long as Ingvar Johansson's, who was handing round a sheet detailing all the jobs currently underway. The picture editor, Pelle Oscarsson, was on his mobile. The editor-in-chief was rocking on his heels and staring blindly at the silent television screen.

'Sorry,' the night-editor said as he rushed into the room with a mug of coffee in one hand and a mock-up of the paper's layout in the other. He looked as though he'd only just got up, and had only had time for one huge mug of coffee so far. Predictably, he spilled some of the second one as he closed the door. Anders Schyman watched him with a sigh.

'Okay,' he said, pulling out a chair and sitting down at the table. 'We might as well start with the Bomber. What have we got?'

Annika started talking before Ingvar Johansson leapt at the chance. She knew the news-editor was more than happy to run through everything, including the subjects she was responsible for. And she wasn't about to let that happen this time.

'As I see it, there'll be four articles from us in the crime section,' she said. 'We can't get away from the terrorism angle entirely. Evert Danielsson raised the issue at the press conference, even if the police are trying to tone it down. That's really a story in itself. Because we've found out that Christina Furhage, the head of the Olympics, has received some sort of threat. Her only details on the national database list her via the tax office in Tyresö. And no one knows where she is right now, not even the people she works most closely with in the Olympics office. I'll be writing that one.'

'What's your headline?' Jansson asked.

'Something like "Olympic Boss Threatened", and a subheading quoting Danielsson, "This is an act of terrorism".'

Jansson nodded approvingly.

'Then we've got the basic story itself, of course; we'll have to do that in detail. We could do that with arrows and text boxes round a picture of the damage. Patrik's got that one. We've got shots of the stadium in daylight, both from the air and from the roof of the old light-bulb factory, haven't we, Pelle?'

The picture editor nodded. 'Yes, but I think the helicopter shots were better. I'm afraid the pictures from the roof are just too dark. I've tried to lighten them digitally, but the focus isn't great. I think we'll go with the aerial shots.'

Jansson wrote something on his mock-up of the layout. Annika could feel herself getting angry: useless bloody amateur Armani-photographer, incapable of getting the exposure *or* the focus right.

'Who took the roof shots?' Anders Schyman asked.

'Olsson,' Annika replied bluntly.

The editor-in-chief made a note.

'What else?'

'Who's the victim? Male, female, old, young? Coroner's report, forensic evidence from the police, what are the lines of inquiry mentioned by the Chief Prosecutor at the press conference? Berit and I will do that one together.'

'What have we got so far?' Schyman asked.

Annika sighed. 'Nothing much, I'm afraid. We'll give it a real go this evening. We'll get something.'

The editor-in-chief nodded and Annika went on, 'Then we've got the murder mystery, the hunt for the Bomber, the trail, the theories, the evidence. Who was the dark-clad man outside the stadium just before the explosion? What does the witness have to say about him? Patrik's writing that. We haven't got hold of the Tiger, but neither have the police. According to Lindström, he isn't under suspicion, but that's bullshit. They may well put out a national alert for him this evening or later on tonight, you'll have to keep an eye on that. And of course there's the whole Olympics angle, and you're covering that, Ingvar . . .'

The news-editor cleared his throat.

'Yes, yes we are. The security arrangements for the Games, we've got quotes from the President of the International Olympic Committee at the headquarters in Lausanne, he has full confidence in the Swedish

Olympic Committee's abilities to host the Games; he has the greatest possible faith in the Swedish police being able to apprehend those responsible, blah, blah, blah . . . And he goes on to say that the Games aren't under threat, so we'll push hard with that. Then we've got the "what happens now?" stuff, put together by Janet. The stadium will be repaired immediately. They're pretty much going to start work the moment the forensics team moves out. They reckon they'll be finished in seven or eight weeks. Then there's the wounded taxi-driver, we've got the exclusive on him so we'll run hard with that. And we're doing a run-through of previous Olympic attacks, including the Tiger, assuming we don't get hold of him tonight. If we do, then he'll get a piece to himself.'

'His home number's in the database,' Annika put in. 'I've left a message on his machine, so he might get in touch.'

'Okay. Nils Langeby is working on reactions around the world; we can run a side-column on that. And we've got reaction within Sweden, of course – the lines for "Have Your Say" have just opened.'

He fell silent and leafed through his notes.

'Anything else?' the editor-in-chief said.

'Well, we've got the pictures Henriksson took from the torch,' Annika said. 'They were in the later editions yesterday, but they didn't make the national edition. He took several; maybe we could use a different shot for the article about the victim in tomorrow's edition? A bit of recycling?'

Pelle Oscarsson nodded. 'Yes, there are loads of pictures. We'll find something that looks a bit different.'

'Right, the news is starting,' Ingvar Johansson said, turning up the volume on the remote.

They all turned to face the television, to see what the national broadcaster made of the story. They were leading with shots from the press conference in police headquarters, then worked their way back to the early morning when the stadium was still burning. There were interviews with all the obvious candidates: Chief Prosecutor Lindström, Evert Danielsson from the Olympic Committee, one of the detectives, an old lady who lived close to the stadium and had been woken by the blast.

'They haven't got anything new,' Ingvar Johansson said, and turned over to CNN.

They resumed their meeting, with Ingvar Johansson running through everything else they'd got for the paper the next day.

The television was on low volume as CNN went through its Breaking News. A reporter popped up at regular intervals doing a piece to camera in front of one of the roadblocks in the Olympic village. They had another reporter at police headquarters, and a third at the head office of the International Olympic Committee in Lausanne.

The live reports were interrupted every now and then by recorded segments about the Olympics and various violent disturbances over the years. A series of international celebrities gave their opinion, and a White House spokesman gave a statement condemning the terrorist act in Sweden.

Annika realized she was no longer listening to Ingvar Johansson. When he got to the entertainment pages she excused herself and left the meeting. She made her way to the cafeteria again and ordered a pasta dish with prawns, bread and a beer. As the microwave behind the counter whirred, she sat down and stared out at the darkness. If she focused properly, she could see the building opposite. If she relaxed, she could only see her own reflection in the glass.

When she was finished she gathered her own little team, consisting of Patrik and Berit, in her office.

'I'll do the terrorism piece,' Annika said. 'Have you got anything about the victim, Berit?'

'Well, a bit,' the reporter said, looking through her notes. 'The forensics team found a number of items they think belonged to the victim. They're badly damaged, but they've been able to identify a briefcase, a Filofax and a mobile phone.'

She fell silent, and noticed that Annika and Patrik were staring at her, wide-eyed.

'Bloody hell,' Annika said. 'So they know who the victim was?'

'Maybe,' Berit said, 'but they're not letting on. It took me two hours to get this much out of them.'

'But this is brilliant,' Annika said. 'Fantastic! God, you're good! I haven't heard a peep about this anywhere else.'

She leaned back in her chair, laughing and clapping her hands together. Patrik was grinning.

'How are you getting on?' Annika asked him.

'I've done the basic chain of events; you can take a look if you like. It's laid out around the shot of the stadium, like you said. As for the hunt for the Bomber – well, I'm afraid I haven't got much on that. The police have been knocking on doors around the harbour all day, but the new-builds around the Olympic village are still mostly empty, so there aren't many people to talk to.'

'So who was that shadowy figure? And who's the witness?'

'I haven't made much headway on that,' Patrik said.

Suddenly Annika remembered something her taxi-driver had said on the way out to the stadium early that morning.

'There's an underground club out there,' she said, sitting up. 'The injured taxi-driver was on a job out there when the bomb went off. There must have been people there, guests as well as staff. That's where we'll find the witness. Have we spoken to anyone there?'

Patrik and Berit looked at each other.

'We have to get out there and talk to them!' Annika said.

'An underground club?' Berit said sceptically. 'How keen do you reckon they're going to be to talk to us?'

'Fuck knows,' Annika said. 'You can never tell. They can talk anonymously, or even off the record, if they like, as long as they tell us what they saw.'

'That's not a bad idea,' Patrik said. 'It might shed some light.'

'Have the police spoken to them?'

'I don't actually know; I haven't asked,' Patrik said.

'Okay,' Annika said. 'I'll call the police while you get over there and try to get hold of people at the club. Call the injured taxi-driver to find out exactly where the club is – we've got him hidden in the Royal Viking. The club's not likely to be open tonight; it's probably inside the cordon. But check with the driver anyway; see if he knows the name of the customer he took out there. He may even have recommended the club because he knows someone there, you never know.'

'Right, I'm on my way.' Patrik grabbed his jacket and rushed out.

Annika and Berit sat in silence when Patrik had left.

'What do you really think about all this?' Annika eventually asked.

Berit sighed. 'I can't really believe it was terrorism,' she said. 'Who would it have been aimed at, and why?

To stop the Olympics? If so, why start now? Isn't it a bit late for that?'

Annika doodled on her notepad.

'Well, there's one thing I do know,' she said. 'It's absolutely vital that the police catch this bomber, or else the whole country will end up in the sort of trauma we haven't had since Olof Palme was shot.'

Berit nodded, gathered up her things and went back to her desk.

13

Annika called her source but couldn't get hold of him. She emailed an official statement from the police about the underground club to Patrik. Then she pulled out the official government directory and looked up the head of the tax office in Tyresö. She found out his name and year of birth. Because his name was such a common one she couldn't find him in the phonebook, so she had to look on the national database instead. She managed to get a home address, which meant she could get his phone number through Directory Inquiries.

He answered on the fourth ring, and sounded pretty drunk. It was Saturday night, after all. Annika switched on the tape-recorder.

'I can't tell you anything about why Christina Furhage's details are protected,' he said, and it sounded like he was about to slam the phone down.

'Of course not,' Annika said calmly. 'I'd just like to ask a couple of general questions about data protection, threat levels, that sort of thing.'

In the background she could hear a large group of people laughing. She must have called in the middle of a dinner party or something.

'You'll have to call the office on Monday,' the tax official said.

'But the paper will have gone to press long before that,' Annika said smoothly. 'Our readers have a right to a comment tomorrow. What reason should I give for you not wanting to answer?'

Annika could hear the man's breathing down the line. She could sense him considering the matter. He knew that she was referring to the fact that he'd been drinking. Obviously she would never write something like that in the paper, you just didn't do that sort of thing. But if people in public positions of power were playing hard to get, she wasn't afraid to manipulate the situation to get her own way.

'What do you want to know?' he asked coldly.

Annika smiled.

'What does it take for someone's details to be protected?' she asked.

She already knew, but the way he described the process would be a description of Christina Furhage's case.

The man sighed and thought for a moment. It wasn't exactly at the forefront of his mind.

'Well, there needs to be some sort of threat. A serious threat,' he said. 'Not just a threatening phone-call but something worse, something more serious.'

'A death threat?' Annika said.

'For instance, yes. But it usually takes something more than that, even: the sort of thing that would convince a judge to issue a contact prohibition.'

'An actual incident? Some sort of violence?' Annika asked.

'Yes, that sort of thing.'

'Could you impose data protection for anything less than what you've just described?'

'No, I couldn't,' the man said firmly. 'If the threat is of a less serious nature, the details would stay on the database but would just be hidden from general view.'

'How many people have had the higher level of data protection during your time in Tyresö?'

He thought for a few moments, then said, 'Well, three.'

'Christina Furhage, her husband and their daughter,' Annika reasoned.

'I didn't say that,' the man said.

'Would you like to make any comment on the protection of Christina Furhage's details?'

'No, I wouldn't,' he replied abruptly.

'What sort of death threat did Christina Furhage receive?'

'I can't comment on that.'

'What sort of violence led to this level of protection in her case?'

'I can't tell you any more about this. Right, that's enough,' he said, and hung up.

Annika grinned. That was all she needed. Without saying a word about Christina, the man had confirmed everything.

After a few more phone-calls to check the details, she put together her article about the potential threat, keeping the terrorism angle at a relatively low level. She was finished shortly after eleven, but Patrik still hadn't got back. That was a good sign.

She left her text with Jansson, who was now in full flow out at the news desk. His hair was a mess and he was talking non-stop on the phone.

She decided to walk home, in spite of the cold and the darkness and the emptiness in her head. Her legs ached, which always happened when she was too tired. A quick walk was the best medicine, so that she wouldn't have to take painkillers when she got home. She tugged on her coat and pulled her hat firmly onto her head before she had time to change her mind.

'You can get me on my mobile,' she said quickly to Jansson on her way out. He waved in reply without looking up from the phone.

The temperature had been up and down all day, and now it was below freezing again and great flakes of snow were starting to fall. They were almost hanging in the air, swaying one way and then the other on their way to the ground. They muffled all sound in cotton-wool – Annika didn't hear the number 57 bus before it sailed past her.

She went down the steps to Rålambshov Park. The path over the grass was muddy and rutted from push-chairs and mountain bikes; she slid and almost fell, swearing out loud. A startled hare dashed away from her into the shadows. Once again, she wondered at the amount of wildlife in the city. Once, when Thomas was on his way home from the pub, he had been chased down Agnegatan by a badger. She laughed out loud in the darkness at the memory.

The wind was sharper here than up between the buildings, and she pulled her scarf tighter. The snow-flakes were wilder, settling wetly on her hair. She hadn't seen the children all day. She hadn't phoned home since morning – that just made things messy.

Working on weekdays didn't usually feel too bad, when every Swedish child was at nursery and her conscience was clear. But on a Saturday like this, the last before Christmas, you were supposed to be at home, preparing for the holiday and baking special treats.

Annika sighed so hard that the snowflakes swirled away from her. The problem was that things always went wrong whenever she tried to get the kids involved in Christmas baking or some other big joint activity. They always thought it was great to start with, arguing and fighting about who got to stand closest to her. By the time they had argued about the dough and made a mess of the whole kitchen, her patience started to wear thin. It only got worse if she had been under stress at work, and sometimes she couldn't help exploding. In fact, that had happened more often than she cared to remember. The children would go and sulk in front of the television while she finished off in the kitchen as fast as she could. Then Thomas would have to put them to bed while she scrubbed the kitchen clean.

She sighed again. Maybe it would have been different this time. No one would have burned themselves on the cooker, and they would all have settled down in front of the fire to eat freshly baked saffron buns.

She speeded up as she emerged from the park onto the pavement of Norr Mälarstrand beside the water. The ache in her legs was easing already, and she forced them to keep up a steady, even pace. Her breathing quickened and her heart found a new, more intense rhythm.

Once, it had almost been more fun going to work than being at home. As a reporter she saw instant results, everyone appreciated what she did and she managed to get a picture byline several times a week. She was in charge of her own domain, she knew exactly what was required of her in different situations, and she could push her own agenda and make demands of the world around her. At home there were more demands on her, they were louder, more insistent. She never felt sufficiently happy, horny, calm, effective, authoritative or relaxed.

The apartment was always in a mess, the washing basket always seemed to be overflowing. Thomas was good at looking after the children, pretty much better than she was, but he never cleaned the cooker or the worktops, he hardly ever filled the dishwasher, he let clothes and unopened post gather in piles in the bedroom. It was as if he imagined that the dirty plates found their own way into the machine, that the money in their account paid the bills automatically.

These days it wasn't as much fun going to work, not since her promotion eight weeks ago. She hadn't realized that her promotion would arouse such strong reactions. The decision wasn't even particularly controversial. In practice she had actually been running the crime desk alongside her work as a reporter for the past year. The only difference now, as far as she could see, was that she was finally getting paid for it.

But Nils Langeby had gone mad, of course. He believed that the post was his by right. After all, he was fifty-three, and Annika was only thirty-two.

She had also been surprised by the way people felt they had the right to discuss and criticize her, for what seemed the oddest reasons. Suddenly they had started commenting on her clothes in a way that had never happened before. And they had begun to say the most outrageous things about her personality and character. She hadn't foreseen that she would become public property the moment she got the promotion. Now she was only too aware of that fact.

She speeded up her pace once more. She just wanted to get home now. She looked up at the buildings sliding past on the other side of the street, their windows radiating warmth towards the water. Practically every one of them had an Advent candle, giving a wonderful sense of security. She left the water and turned up John Ericssongatan, up towards Hantverkargatan.

14

The apartment was silent and dark. Carefully she pulled off her boots and outdoor clothing and crept into the children's room. They were asleep in their little pyjamas, Ellen's with Barbie on, Kalle's with Batman. She breathed in their scent for a moment, and Ellen shuffled in her sleep.

Thomas had gone to bed, but he was still awake. A bedside lamp spread a gentle light over his side of the bed. He was reading *The Economist*.

'Knackered?' he asked as she pulled off her clothes and kissed his hair.

'More or less,' she said, walking into the dressing room and stuffing her clothes into the washing basket. 'That bombing is a bloody complicated story.'

She came out into the bedroom naked and climbed in beside him.

'God, you're cold!' he said.

Annika was suddenly aware of how frozen her legs were.

'I walked home,' she said.

'Do you mean to say that the paper couldn't afford a taxi on a night like this? When you've been at work for over *twenty* hours on a Saturday?'

A wave of irritation hit her.

'Of course the paper would have paid for a taxi. I wanted to walk,' she almost yelled. 'Don't be so bloody critical.'

He put the magazine on the floor and turned off the light, turning his back to her demonstratively.

Annika sighed. 'Oh, come on, Thomas. Don't sulk.'

'You're out all Saturday and then you come home and shout at me,' he said tiredly. 'Why do we have to take all the crap?'

She felt her eyes welling up with tears, tears of exhaustion and inadequacy.

'Sorry,' she whispered. 'I didn't mean to get cross. But they're on my case the whole time at work; it's really getting to me. And I feel bad about not being here with you and the kids. I'm worried you think I'm letting you down, but the paper won't give me any slack, and I'm sort of stuck in between, in the crossfire—'

She started to cry properly. She heard him sigh from the other side of the bed. After a few moments he turned over and took her in his arms.

'Come on, Anki, you can do this – you're better than the whole lot of them . . . Bloody hell, you really are frozen! You'd better not be getting a cold this close to Christmas.'

She laughed through her tears and snuggled into his arms. Silence descended on them in warm, comforting companionship. She leaned her head back on the pillow and blinked. Somewhere up there in the gloom was the ceiling; and she suddenly remembered seeing the same thing that morning, and the dream she had been having when the phone woke her.

'I was dreaming about you this morning,' she whispered.

'A rude dream, I hope,' he muttered, half asleep.

She laughed quietly.

'You bet! And in a spaceship, too. And the old sods from *Studio Six* were standing there watching.'

'They're just jealous,' Thomas said, as he fell asleep.

Love

I was already grown up, and had reached a certain status in life the first time it hit me. For a few brief moments it shattered my universal isolation, our souls really did merge in a way I'd never known before. It's an interesting thing to have experienced, I can't deny that, and since then the same thing has happened a few more times. Now, in retrospect, most of my reactions seem fairly ambivalent, nothing to cling on to. I say that without bitterness or disappointment, merely as a statement of fact. But now, over the past year, I've started to doubt what I think. Maybe the woman I've found and fallen in love with really could change things.

But deep down I know that isn't the case. Love is so banal.

It fills you with the same chemical rush as a hard-won victory, or the experience of great speed. Your consciousness is blind to everything but your own pleasure; it warps reality and creates an irrational state of possibility and happiness. The object of love may change, but the magic never lasts. In the long run it only leads to weariness and distaste.

The most beautiful love is always the impossible kind. It has to die even as it lives: like a rose, it has to be cut off while at its finest. A dried flower can spread happiness for years. A love that is quickly crushed at the height of passion can continue to enchant people for centuries.

The myth of love is like a fairy tale, as unreal and unrealistic as an endless orgasm.

You mustn't confuse love with genuine affection. That's something entirely different. Love doesn't 'mature', it just withers and is replaced, at best, by warmth and tolerance, but usually by unspoken demands and bitterness. This applies to all forms of love, between the sexes and generations, even at work. How many times have I met bitter wives, their fingers raw from housework, or sexually frustrated husbands? Emotionally inadequate parents and neglected children? Misunderstood bosses and employees who have long since stopped caring about their work and now merely make demands?

But it is possible to love your work. That sort of love has always seemed to me to be more genuine than love for other people. The honest pleasure of achieving a goal I have set myself is better than anything else I know. It seems obvious to me that devotion to a task can be just as strong as devotion to a person who doesn't deserve it.

The idea that my beloved might actually deserve it fills me with horror and anxiety.

Sunday 19 December

15

Sunday has always been the biggest sales day for the evening papers. People have both the time and the inclination to read something straightforward, they're relaxed enough to do the crossword and the quizzes together. For years, most of the papers that publish on Sundays have printed an extra supplement. The national sales statistics regard the supplements as a special case, and therefore count Sundays separately from the rest of the week.

But nothing sells as well as a really good news story. And if it happens on a Saturday there's always the chance of reaching a record high. This Sunday had great potential in that respect. Anders Schyman understood this the moment the courier delivered the first editions of the evening papers direct to his home out in Saltsjöbaden. He took the papers to the breakfast room where his wife was pouring coffee.

'How does it look?' she asked, but the editor-in-chief merely grunted in reply. This moment was the most magical of the day. His nerves tensed and he focused intently on the papers, laying them both out in front of him on the table and comparing the front pages. Jansson had done it again, he concluded with a smile. Both papers were running with the terrorism angle, but the *Evening Post* was the only one with the story of the death threat against the Olympics boss, Christina Furhage. The *Post*'s front page was more striking; it had better celebrities above the title, and a more dramatic picture of the stadium. His smile grew even broader and he relaxed.

'It's good,' he said to his wife, reaching for his mug. 'In fact, it's really good.'

The cartoon voices on morning television were the first thing Annika heard. The hyperactive chatter and sound effects slid under the bedroom door like a torrent of hysteria. She covered her head with the pillow to shut out the noise. That was one of the drawbacks of having children; she had real trouble dealing with the Z-list Swedish actors who did the voiceovers to foreign cartoons. As usual, Thomas was oblivious. He went on sleeping, the covers bundled round his knees.

She lay there for a moment, trying to work out how she felt. She was tired, and the ache in her legs hadn't quite gone away. She immediately started thinking about the Bomber, and realized that she must have been dreaming about the attack. That always happened when there was a big story – she went into a long tunnel and didn't emerge until the story was over. Sometimes she had to force herself to pause for breath, both for her own sake, and for the children's. Thomas didn't like it when she focused so intently on her work.

'It's only a job,' he would say. 'You always write as if it's a matter of life and death.'

Well, most of the time it was, Annika thought, at least in her area of expertise.

She sighed, pushed the pillow and duvet aside and got out of bed. She stood there swaying for a moment, more tired than she had thought. The woman reflected in the hand-blown windowpanes looked a hundred years old. She sighed again and went out into the kitchen.

The children had already eaten. Their dishes were still on the table, swimming in little puddles of spilt milk and yogurt. Kalle could help himself to yogurt and cornflakes these days. He had given up serving Ellen her favourite, toast with peanut butter and jam, since he burned himself on the toaster.

She put water on to boil for coffee and went in to the children. Their cries reached her before she had even entered the room.

'Mummy!'

Four arms and hungry eyes rushed towards her, wet lips kissing and bubbling and hugging and assuring her that Mummy, Mummy, we missed you, Mummy, where were you yesterday, were you at work all day, Mummy, you didn't come home yesterday, Mummy, we went to bed . . .

She rocked them in her arms, crouching down in the doorway of the television room.

'We got a new film yesterday, Mummy. *You're Out of Your Mind, Maggie*, and it's a bit horrid, the man hits Mia, do you want to see my picture, Mummy? It's for you!'

They both struggled out of her arms at the same time, rushing off in different directions. Kalle came back first, with the cover of the film about Astrid Lindgren's childhood friend.

'The headmaster was really stupid, he hit Mia for taking his wallet,' Kalle said seriously.

'I know, that was wrong,' Annika said, stroking the boy's hair. 'That's what schools used to be like. Isn't that horrid?'

'Is school like that now?' he asked anxiously.

'No, not any more,' Annika said, kissing him on the

cheek. 'No one's ever going to hurt my little boy.'

There was a howl from the children's room.

'My picture's gone! Kalle's taken it!'

The boy stiffened.

'No I haven't!' he shouted back. 'You must have lost it yourself. You did it, you did it!'

The cry from the bedroom turned into sobbing.

'Nasty Kalle! You took my picture!'

'You're a stupid idiot! I didn't take it.'

Annika put the boy on the floor, stood up and took him by the hand.

'Right, that's enough,' she said sternly. 'Come on, we're going to look for the picture. It's probably on the table. And don't call your sister an idiot, I don't want to hear that again.'

'Stupid idiot, stupid idiot!' Kalle shouted.

The crying turned back into howling.

'Mummy, he's stupid! He's calling me an idiot.'

'Quiet, both of you!' Annika said, raising her voice. 'You'll wake Daddy.'

As she walked into the room with Kalle, Ellen raised her fist to hit her brother. Annika caught it before she could strike, and felt her patience wearing thin.

'That's enough!' she shouted. 'Stop it, both of you, do you hear?'

'What's that bloody racket?' she heard Thomas say from the bedroom door. 'Can't I have a lie-in just this once?'

'There, now you've woken Daddy up,' Annika shouted.

'You're making more noise than the two of them put together,' Thomas said, and slammed the door shut.

Annika could feel tears welling up again. Damn it, why didn't she ever learn? She slumped to the floor, her limbs suddenly heavy as lead.

100

'Mummy, are you sad, Mummy?'

Soft hands stroked her cheeks and patted her head comfortingly.

'No, I'm not sad; I'm just a bit tired. I did a lot of work yesterday.'

She forced herself to smile and opened her arms to them once more. Kalle looked at her with a serious expression on his face.

'You shouldn't work so much,' he said. 'It makes you too tired.'

She hugged him.

'That's very good advice,' she said. 'Shall we look for the picture now?'

It had slid down behind the radiator. Annika blew the dust off and said how beautiful it was. Ellen lit up like a sun with the praise.

'I'm going to put it up on the wall in the bedroom. When Daddy's got up.'

The water was boiling like mad in the kitchen, half of it had evaporated and the windows were steamed up. She filled the pan again and opened the window a crack to let out the steam.

'Do you want some more breakfast?'

They did: toast this time. Their chatter rose and fell as Annika worked her way through the morning papers and listened to the news. The papers had nothing new, but the radio was quoting both evening papers: her own article about the death threat to Christina Furhage, and the other paper's interview with the Chairman of the Olympic movement. Okay, she thought, they beat us to the Olympic headquarters. A shame, but that wasn't her problem.

She took another piece of toast.

16

Helena Starke pushed the door open and switched off the alarm. Sometimes when she arrived at the office she discovered that the alarm hadn't been set by the last person to leave the night before. This time she knew it had been, because she had been the last to leave last night. Or rather, early this morning.

She went straight to Christina Furhage's office and unlocked it. The answer machine was flashing and Helena felt her pulse race. Someone had called, at four o'clock that morning. She hurried to pick up the receiver and entered Christina's personal code. There were two messages, one from each of the evening papers. She swore and slammed the phone down. Bloody hyenas. They'd both managed to work out Christina's direct number. She sank down onto the director's leather chair with a sigh, spinning it gently to and fro. Her hangover was still rough – there was a sour taste in her mouth and her head felt foggy. If only she could remember what Christina had said to her the night before last. Her memory had cleared to the extent that she could remember that Christina had come back to her apartment with her. Christina had been quite angry, hadn't she? Helena shook herself and stood up.

Someone was coming through the main door.

Helena hurriedly tucked the chair in and walked round the desk.

Evert Danielsson stood in the doorway. There were dark rings under his eyes and his jaw looked clenched.

'Have you heard anything?' he asked.

Helena shrugged. 'About what? The Bomber is still on the loose, Christina hasn't been in touch and you've managed to unleash a whole load of theories about terrorism in the media. I take it you've seen the morning papers?'

Danielsson's jaw clenched tighter. Aha, Helena thought, he's worried about his own mistakes. She felt her distaste for the man grow still further. He wasn't worried about the attack or about the consequences for the Games. No, he was worried about saving his own skin. How egotistical. How pathetic.

'The committee is meeting at four o'clock this afternoon,' Helena said, and left the room. 'You'd better put together some proper information about what's going on before we decide what action to take next . . .'

Evert Danielsson followed her out. 'When did you get to be on the committee?' he said in an ice-cold voice.

Helena Starke froze and stopped for a moment, then pretended she hadn't heard.

'It's probably time to call in the Honorary Board as well. They have to be kept informed, at the very least. They get very grouchy otherwise, and we need them more than ever right now.'

Evert Danielsson watched her lock the door to Christina's office. She was right about the Honorary Board. The business leaders, members of the royal family and the Church, and all the others who made up the high-profile Honorary Board would have to be called in as soon as possible. They needed a good deal of lubrication and polishing to make them shine to the outside world. And they really did need them more than ever right now.

'Can you arrange that?' Evert Danielsson said.

Helena Starke nodded curtly as she disappeared down the corridor.

Ingvar Johansson was at his desk, talking on the phone, when Annika arrived at work. She was the first reporter to get there; the others would be in at ten o'clock. Ingvar Johansson pointed first at the freshly printed bundles of papers along the wall, then at the sofa by the news desk. Annika dropped her coat over the back of the sofa and sat down to read until Johansson had finished his call. His voice rose and fell like background music as Annika checked what they had put together after she went home. Her own piece about the terrorism angle and the threat against Christina Furhage covered pages six and seven – where the most serious news always ended up. The picture desk had come up with an image of Furhage from the archive where she was leading a group of men dressed in dark suits and coats. She was wearing a white suit and a short pale coat, which made her stand out like a beacon of light against the dark figures of the men. She looked determined, slightly stressed – an excellent picture of an innocent, threatened person. On page seven there was a picture of Evert Danielsson leaving the press conference. A good shot of the chairman under pressure.

The next spread was Berit's article on the victim and what the police had found at the crime scene. Jansson had picked another of Henriksson's pictures of the fire to illustrate it. It worked almost as well today as it would have the day before. Then there was the taxi-driver, Arne Brattström, talking about the explosion.

On pages ten and eleven Annika found the most

surprising story so far. Patrik must have worked like a demon overnight to pull together two separate stories: SECRET POLICE WITNESS – I SAW THE MYSTERIOUS MAN OUTSIDE THE STADIUM, and NATIONAL ALERT FOR THE TIGER.

Brilliant! Annika thought. He had got hold of someone working at the club: a bartender, who explained how he had arrived at work and had seen someone hurrying across the plaza towards the entrance to the stadium. That was at one o'clock, though, and not immediately before the explosion, as the police had said.

'It was someone in a dark anorak with the hood up, dark trousers and heavy shoes,' the bartender said in the article.

So now we have an image of the Bomber, at least until we come up with anything better, Annika thought contentedly.

As expected, the police had pulled out all the stops in their search for the Tiger. The same pages also covered the police's rather sketchy theories about the murder and the attack so far.

Thirteen and fourteen covered the Olympics, the consequences for the Games and security measures from now on. And this was where they had put the sequence of previous Olympic attacks. The next spread was a big advert for the final days of Christmas shopping; sixteen and seventeen were readers' reactions to the attack, plus Nils Langeby's overview of the international response.

After that the pages flew by in a flurry of celebrities talking about their ailments, a child we should all feel sorry for, an unknown rock musician who had been caught drink-driving, and a group of homosexual drag-artists complaining about cuts in the health service.

The centrefold was filled with Patrik's overview of events, with the facts about the actual attack. Times, places, arrows, concisely and neatly arranged around the shot from the helicopter.

She looked up when she noticed that Ingvar Johansson had stopped talking. He had evidently been watching her for some time.

'This is bloody good, don't you think?' Annika said, waving the paper, then putting it down on the sofa.

'Yeah, not bad,' Johansson said, turning round. 'That's all history now, though. The main thing now is tomorrow's paper.'

Ruddy pedant, Annika thought. She had always thought that every editor of the evening papers spent too much time thinking about the future, and too little considering the past. If anything ever went wrong no one cared, because it was already yesterday's news. And if anything ever went well, they never took time to enjoy the success. It was a shame, because in her opinion careful consideration of successes and failures was vital, for the sake of routine and to give you a chance to reflect on things generally, as well as providing stability and better quality.

'What have you got for tomorrow?' he asked with his back to her.

What the hell's the matter with him? she wondered tiredly. Why's he being like this? I've done something to annoy him. But what? I haven't done anything to him, have I? Is he annoyed that I took charge of the run-through yesterday?

'How the hell should I know what's going on? I've only just got here,' she said, surprising herself with how angry she sounded. She stood up quickly and grabbed her coat and bag. With her arms full she headed off towards her room.

'The police are holding a press conference at half ten,' Ingvar Johansson called after her.

She looked at her watch as she pulled open her door, fifty minutes until then. She had time to make a few calls first.

She started with the mobile number that was supposed to be Christina Furhage's. The Olympic boss hadn't made any kind of statement anywhere, so presumably the people in her office hadn't managed to get hold of her yet. There was something really weird about the woman's continuing silence, Annika was sure something was wrong.

To her great surprise she got a ringing tone rather than the recorded message. The phone was switched on. She hurriedly cleared her throat as the phone rang. After the fifth ring Telia's automatic answering service clicked in, but at least she knew that the phone was in use and was switched on. She was careful to store the number for future use.

Patrik and Berit appeared in her doorway together.

'Are you busy . . . ?'

'God, no, come in, let's have a quick run-through.' She stood up and went round the desk to sit on the old sofa.

'Brilliant work, both of you,' she said. 'We're the only ones with the details of what was found at the crime scene, and the only ones who tracked down the bartender in the club.'

'The other paper had a great interview with the President of the Olympic Committee, though,' Berit said. 'Have you seen it? He's evidently furious, and has threatened to cancel the Games unless the Bomber's caught.'

'Yes, so I heard,' Annika said. 'It's a shame we didn't have that as well. Mind you, I wonder if that's what he really said. If he really wants to cancel the Games, why hasn't he said so publicly? In everything he's said to the rest of the media and in the press release, he says the Games have to go ahead, no matter what.'

'Maybe all the others swallowed the official line, while our esteemed rivals got him to say what he really meant?' Berit said.

Annika had opened the other paper to look at the interview.

'It was written by their Rome correspondent – he's bloody good,' Annika said. 'I think it's genuine, but the President is still bound to deny it this afternoon.'

'Why this afternoon?' Patrik said.

'CNN have picked it up and are running a short piece about it,' Annika said with a smile. '"The Olympics in Danger", that sort of thing, with lots of suitably sombre, bombastic music.'

Berit smiled.

'So they're having another press conference this morning?' she said.

'Yes,' Annika said, 'probably to give us the name of the victim. I'm starting to wonder if it isn't the Olympic boss herself.'

'Furhage?' Patrik said, eyes wide.

'Well, think about it,' Annika said. 'Either she's in hiding or there's something seriously wrong here. No one can get hold of her, not even her closest colleagues. There's nowhere on this planet where she could be unaware of what's happened – she can't not know about the attack. So either she doesn't want to say anything, which means she's in hiding, or else she can't, which means she's ill, dead or has been kidnapped.'

'That's what I've been thinking,' Berit said. 'I actually asked the police about it yesterday when I was talking to them about what they found at the crime scene, but they categorically denied it.'

'That doesn't mean anything,' Annika said thoughtfully. 'Furhage is a story today, no matter what's happened. We'll have to push further on the death threat – what was that really about? And if she is the victim we'll have to run her whole life-story. Have we got any sort of obit prepared?'

'Not for her,' Berit said. 'Christina Furhage wasn't exactly expected to kick the bucket just yet.'

'We can get them to start looking out pictures and cuttings before we head off to the press conference. Did either of you talk to Eva-Britt yesterday?'

Patrik and Berit both shook their heads. Annika went over to the desk and dialled the secretary's home number. When Eva-Britt Qvist answered Annika gave her a quick outline of the situation.

'I know it's the last Sunday before Christmas, but it would be really great if you could come in,' she said. 'The rest of us are heading off to a press conference in police headquarters, and it would be brilliant if you could look out everything we've got on Christina Furhage by then, pictures and articles—'

'I'm in the middle of baking buns,' Eva-Britt Qvist said.

'Ah,' Annika said. 'That's a shame. But some really big things might be happening here today, and the rest of us are shattered. Patrik was here till half four this morning, I worked from quarter past three yesterday morning till eleven at night, and Berit pretty much the same. And what we really need help with is your area: checking databases and pulling together material and—'

'Look, I told you I can't,' Eva-Britt Qvist said. 'I've got a family.'

Annika suppressed the first reply that came into her head, and said instead, 'Yes, I know what it's like to have to change your plans. It's awful to have to let your children and husband down. Obviously you'll get overtime and time in lieu whenever you want it, either before the New Year or during next half term, if you like. But it would be brilliant if you could pull the material together before we get back from the press conference—'

'I told you, I'm in the middle of baking! I can't do it! Aren't you listening?'

Annika paused and took a deep breath.

'Okay,' she said. 'We'll do it this way, if that's what you want. I'm ordering you to put in the extra hours, starting right now. I expect you to be here in fifteen minutes.'

'But my baking!'

'Your family can finish that,' Annika said, and hung up. Much to her annoyance, she noticed her hand was shaking.

She hated this sort of thing. She would never dream of behaving like Eva-Britt if her boss called and asked her to work extra hours. If you worked at a paper and something big happened, you had to be prepared to do your bit; that was just the way things were. If you wanted a nine-to-five job, Monday to Friday, there were plenty of other places you could work. Of course there were others who could check the databases, she herself, or Berit, or one of the reporters out in the newsroom. But in a situation like this everyone was under a lot of pressure. Everyone was stressed about Christmas. So it seemed fairest to divide the work as evenly as possible, with each person doing what they were best at, even if it was Sunday. She could hardly give Eva-Britt special treatment this time, because she'd end up with a nightmare next time something happened, that much she was sure of. Showing the lack of respect that the secretary had just demonstrated couldn't be rewarded with days off.

'Eva-Britt's on her way,' she said to the others, and thought she caught a hint of a smile on Berit's face.

17

They took two cars to the press conference. Annika and Berit went with Johan Henriksson, the photographer, while Patrik went with Ulf Olsson.

The media scrum was, if anything, even more hysterical today. Henriksson had to park way down by Kungsholmstorg, because the streets around police headquarters were blocked by outside-broadcast trucks and Volvos plastered with media logos.

Annika enjoyed the short walk. The air was bright and clear after the previous day's snow, and sun was lighting up the top floors of the buildings. The snow crunched under their feet.

'That's where I live,' she said, pointing to the newly renovated block from the 1880s a little further up Hantverkargatan.

'Bought or rented?' Berit asked.

'Rented,' Annika said.

'How the hell did you get a flat there?' Henriksson said, thinking of his own sub-let single-room flat out in Brandbergen.

'Stubbornness,' Annika said. 'I got a short-term demolition contract in the block eight years ago. A little three-room flat in the courtyard with no hot water. The bathroom was in the basement of the next building.

It was due for complete renovation and I was only supposed to be there six months. Then the property crash came and the owner went bankrupt. No one was interested in buying a wreck like that, and once I'd been there five years the contract became permanent. By then there were very nearly four of us in there, me and Thomas and Kalle, and I was pregnant with Ellen. So when the building was finally renovated, we got a five-room flat facing the street. Not bad, eh?'

'Jackpot,' Berit said.

'What's the rent?' Henriksson asked.

'That's the only thing wrong with the story,' Annika said. 'Ask me something else, like how much wood-panelling there is, or what height the ceilings are!'

'Capitalist, upper-class snob!' Henriksson said, and Annika burst out laughing.

The *Evening Post* team were late and only just made it before the press conference started. Annika got no further than the doorway and could hardly see anything. She stood on tiptoe, and could see how each of the journalists was trying to show all the others how important and focused they were. Henriksson and Olsson elbowed their way through to the podium, and got there just as the participants marched in. There were fewer of them than yesterday. Annika could only see Chief Prosecutor Kjell Lindström and the press spokesman. Evert Danielsson wasn't there, nor anyone from the investigating team. Over the head of a woman from one of the morning papers she watched the press spokesman clear his throat and start talking. He summarized the situation, repeating what was already known, like the fact that the Tiger was the subject of an extensive search, and the forensic investigation was continuing. He spoke for less than ten minutes. Then

Kjell Lindström leaned forward, and everyone else in the room followed suit. They all had an idea of what was coming next.

'The work of identifying the deceased victim at the stadium has largely been concluded,' the Chief Prosecutor said, and the room was tense with expectation.

'The victim's family has been informed, which is why we have chosen to make public the person's identity, even though some of the final work still needs to be concluded . . . The victim is Christina Furhage, managing director for the Olympic Games in Stockholm.'

Annika's reaction was almost physical: Yes! I knew it! Just what I thought! As the tumult of voices in the press conference reached a crescendo, she was already on her way out of police headquarters.

As she walked she pushed in her earpiece and dialled the mobile number she had memorized earlier. She got the ringing tone.

She sat down on a narrow bench in the lobby of the police station, breathing deeply as she closed her eyes and tried to concentrate on sending a telepathic message: Please, someone answer! Three rings, four, and then a click. Someone was taking the call! Good God, who on earth could it be?

Annika screwed her eyes shut even more tightly and spoke softly and slowly.

'Good afternoon, my name is Annika Bengtzon, from the *Evening Post* newspaper. Who am I talking to, please?'

'My name is Bertil Milander,' a voice replied quietly.

Bertil Milander, Bertil Milander, that was Christina Furhage's husband, wasn't it? Was that his name? Annika decided to play it safe, and asked in the same slow voice as before: 'Am I talking to Bertil Milander, Christina Furhage's husband?'

The man on the mobile sighed.

'Yes, you are,' he said.

Annika could feel her heart in her throat.

This was the most uncomfortable call a reporter could ever make, to a person who has just lost a family member. There was a lot of debate in the journalists' association about whether it was ever right to make calls like this, but Annika believed that it was better to call than not to, if only to explain what the newspapers were doing.

'I'd like to start by saying that I'm very sorry for the tragedy that's hit your family. The police have just announced that it was your wife, Christina, who died in the explosion at the Victoria Stadium,' she explained.

The man didn't reply.

'By the way, is this Christina's mobile phone?' she heard herself ask.

'No, it's the family's,' the man said, surprised.

'I'm calling to tell you that we'll be writing about your wife's death in tomorrow's paper . . .'

'But you've already done that,' the man said.

'Well, we've covered the explosion itself, the actual events.'

'The *Evening Post* . . . Weren't you the ones who had that picture? The one where—' His voice broke up into sobs.

Annika clamped her hand over her mouth and stared up at the ceiling. Of course, he had seen Henriksson's picture of the stand where the medics were picking up the remnants of his wife. Oh shit, oh shit . . . She took a few deep, silent breaths.

'Yes, that was us,' she said calmly. 'I'm sorry I couldn't warn you about that picture, but your wife has only just been identified. I had no way of calling you beforehand. I'm very sorry if the picture came as a shock. That's one reason why I'd really like to talk to you now. We'll be covering the story again tomorrow.'

The man was crying at the other end.

'If there's anything you'd like to say, I'd be happy to listen,' Annika said. 'If you want to express any criticism or ask us to write anything particular, or not to write about something, please, just tell me. Mr Milander?'

He snorted.

'Yes, I'm here,' he said.

Annika looked up and saw through the glass of the main doors that the horde of journalists was heading out of the building towards her. Quickly she opened the door and stood at the side of the steps. There were two insistent bleeps in her ear that told her that someone else was trying to get through on her mobile.

'I understand that this is absolutely awful for you,' she said. 'I can't begin to imagine what it must be like. But this is a global event, one of the worst crimes ever seen in this country. Your wife was a leading figure, a role model for women around the world. That's why we have a duty to report this event. And that's why I'm begging you to talk to us, to give us the chance to show respect, to say what you want us to. It's a terrible thing to admit, but we might make things even worse by writing the wrong thing and unintentionally causing you more pain.'

The 'call waiting' signal came again. The man hesitated.

'I'll give you my direct line, and the editor-in-chief's, so you can call whenever you like—'

'Come over here,' he interrupted. 'I want to tell you.'

Annika closed her eyes, ashamed that she felt so jubilant. She was going to get an interview with the victim's husband! He told her the family's secret address, and she wrote it on the back of a supermarket receipt she

116

had in her pocket. Before she even th‸
it was unethical, she quickly said, 'Y
to be ringing non-stop from now on. I‸
it, you'd be entirely justified in switchin‸

She'd got through now, after all. It wou‸
other journalist did. She pushed her way
police station to find her colleagues. The fir‸
found was Berit.

'I've got hold of the family,' she said quietly.
ing out there with Henriksson. If you could ge‸
on Furhage's final hours, Patrik can take the h
the killer. Does that sound okay?'

'Fine,' Berit said. 'Henriksson is round the
somewhere, he dragged Kjell Lindström out for s‸
pictures. It's probably quicker if you go round . . .'

Annika rushed out and sure enough found Henriksso‸
on Bergsgatan, standing on a container for recycled
paper with Lindström below him and the tunnel leading
below police headquarters in the background. She said
hello to Lindström as she pulled the young photographer
aside.

'Come on, Henriksson, you can have the centrefold
again tomorrow,' she said.

18

Helena Starke wiped her mouth with the back of her hand. She realized it was sticky, but couldn't smell any vomit. Her whole perceptual apparatus had shut down, been disconnected, blown away. Smell, sight, hearing, taste – there was nothing left. She groaned and leaned further over the toilet. Was it really dark in here, or had she gone blind? Her brain didn't work, she couldn't think, there were no thoughts left, everything she had once been had gone up in smoke. She felt salt water trickling down her face, hadn't realized she was crying. All that remained was an echo in her body; her body was an empty space filled with one single roaring phrase: *Christina's dead, Christina's dead, Christina's dead . . .*

Someone was hammering on the door.

'Helena! Are you all right? Do you need help?'

She groaned and sank to the floor, curling up under the basin. *Christina's dead, Christina's dead, Christina's—*

'Open the door, Helena! Are you ill?'

Christina's dead, Christina's dead—

'Break the door in!'

Something hit her, something that hurt. Suddenly there was light from the corridor.

'Good God, help her up. What happened?'

They would never understand, she thought, then realized that she could still think. They would never understand. Never ever.

She felt someone pick her up. She heard the sound of someone screaming, then realized it was her.

The art nouveau building was plastered a bright ochre colour. It lay in the upper reaches of Östermalm, on one of those sober streets where all the cars gleamed and all the old ladies had little white dogs on leads. The entrance hall was magnificent, of course: marble floor, engraved mirrors on the doors, lifts all beechwood and brass, warm yellow marbled walls, a large stained-glass window of flowers and leaves facing the courtyard. There was a thick green carpet running from the door to the staircase, reminding Annika of the Grand Hotel.

The Furhage/Milander family apartment was at the top of the building.

'Okay, we're going to take this really carefully,' Annika whispered to Henriksson before she rang the doorbell. A series of chimes echoed behind the door.

It was opened immediately, as if the man had been standing waiting for them. Annika didn't recognize him; she'd never even seen a picture of him. Christina didn't usually drag her husband around with her. Bertil Milander's face was grey and he had dark rings under his eyes. He hadn't shaved.

'Come in,' he said simply.

He turned and walked into what seemed to be an enormous drawing room. His back was bowed, and Annika was struck by how old he looked as he walked ahead of them in his brown jacket. They took off their coats and boots; the photographer hung a Leica over his shoulder and left the rest of his equipment by the shoe-rack. Annika's stockinged feet sank into the thick rugs. This sort of home must cost a fortune to insure.

The man had sat down on a sofa, and Annika and the photographer ended up sitting opposite him. Annika had her notepad and pen ready.

'We're really here to listen,' Annika began gently. 'If there's anything you want to tell us, anything you'd like us to write, we're happy to consider it.'

Bertil Milander looked down at his clasped hands. Then he started to cry silently. Henriksson ran his tongue over his lips.

'Tell me about Christina,' Annika said encouragingly.

The man pulled an embroidered handkerchief from his trouser pocket and blew his nose. He carefully polished his nose before putting the handkerchief away again. He gave a deep sigh.

'Christina was the most amazing person I've ever met. She was just astonishing. There was nothing she couldn't do. Living with a woman like that was . . .'

He took out the handkerchief and blew his nose again.

'. . . an adventure, every single day. She did everything at home. Food, cleaning, parties, washing, bills, looked after our daughter – she did everything . . .'

He stopped, thinking about what he had said. It looked like he suddenly realized the meaning of his words. From now on, he would have to do all of those things.

He looked down at the handkerchief.

'How did you meet?' Annika asked, mainly for the sake of saying something. The man didn't seem to hear her.

'Stockholm would never have been awarded the Olympics if it hadn't been for her. She had the President of the International Olympic Committee wrapped around her little finger. She built up the whole organization and drove it towards her goal. They wanted to move her out once she'd got the Games and put someone else in as head of the Games, but that was never going to happen. No one but her could hold it all together, and they were forced to recognize that.'

Annika made notes as the man spoke, but could feel herself getting more and more perplexed. She had met plenty of people in shock after traffic accidents and murders, and was well aware that they sometimes reacted oddly, irrationally, but Bertil Milander didn't sound like a husband in mourning. He sounded like an employee.

'How old is your daughter?'

'She was picked as Woman of the Year by that American magazine, whatever it's called . . . ? Woman of the Year. She was the whole of Sweden's Woman of the Year. The whole world's . . .'

Bertil Milander blew his nose again. Annika put down her pen and stared at her notepad. This didn't feel right. Milander didn't know what he was saying or doing. He didn't seem to realize what she and the photographer were doing there.

'When did you find out that Christina was dead?' Annika asked gently.

Bertil Milander looked up.

'She didn't come home,' he said. 'She went to the Christmas party with the rest of her team and didn't come home again.'

'Were you worried when she didn't come home? Had it happened before? She travelled a lot, didn't she?'

The man straightened his back and looked at Annika as though he'd only just noticed her.

'Why do you ask?' he said. 'What do you mean?'

Annika thought for a moment. This really didn't feel right. The man was in too great a state of shock. His reactions were confused and incoherent; he didn't know what he was doing.

There was just one more question that she had to ask.

'Someone had made a threat against your family, hadn't they?' she said. 'What kind of threat?'

The man stared at her open-mouthed. It looked like he hadn't heard her.

'The threat,' Annika repeated. 'Could you say something about the threat against your family?'

The man looked at her reproachfully.

'Christina did all she could,' he said. 'She's not a bad person. It wasn't her fault.'

Annika could feel a shiver go down her spine. This really wasn't going well. She gathered up her pen and notepad.

'Thank you so much for seeing us under such difficult circumstances,' she said, getting ready to stand up. 'We'll—'

A door slammed, making her jump and spin round. A painfully thin young woman with a suspicious look on her face and messy hair was standing behind the sofa.

'Who are you?' the young woman asked.

Christina's daughter, Annika thought, pulling herself together. She explained that they were from the *Evening Post*.

'Vultures,' the young woman said scornfully. 'You got the scent of blood, did you? Ready to fight over the rest of the corpse? Get the best bits for yourselves?'

She walked slowly round the sofa towards Annika. Annika forced herself to remain seated and keep calm.

'I'm sorry about your mother—'

'Well, I'm not,' the daughter yelled. 'I'm glad she's dead!' She burst into tears and ran out of the room. Bertil Milander showed no sign of reaction, just sat there on his sofa, looking down and twisting the handkerchief between his fingers.

'Do you mind if I take a few pictures?' Henriksson asked. Bertil Milander came to life.

'No, of course not,' he said, standing up. 'Is this okay?'

'Maybe closer to the window, so we get better light.'

Bertil Milander posed next to the beautiful high windows. The pictures would be good. The thin daylight seeping through the glass, the blue curtains from Svensk Tenn framing the shot.

As Henriksson took a series of shots, Annika hurried into the next room in search of the young woman. It was a library, tastefully decorated with expensive English furniture and thousands of books.

Christina Furhage's daughter was sitting in a maroon leather armchair.

'I'm sorry you think we're intruding,' Annika said. 'We really don't mean to cause you any pain. Quite the opposite. We just wanted to explain what we're doing.'

The young woman didn't answer; it was as if she hadn't registered Annika's presence.

'You and your dad are welcome to phone if there's anything you want to tell us, if you think we've got something wrong, or if there's anything you want to add.'

No reaction.

'I'll leave my phone number with your dad,' Annika said, and left the room. She closed the ornate double doors carefully behind her.

Henriksson and Bertil Milander had gone out into the hall. Annika followed them, pulling a business card from her wallet and adding the editor-in-chief's direct number alongside her own.

'Call if there's anything we can do,' she said. 'My mobile's always on. Thank you for letting us take up your time.'

Bertil Milander took the card without looking at it. He put it on a little gilded table next to the front door.

'I miss her so much,' he said, and Annika knew she had her headline for the centrefold.

19

The editor-in-chief sighed as he heard the knock on the door. He had been planning to get through at least one of the piles on his desk, but since he arrived in his office an hour or so ago he hadn't had a moment's peace from phone-calls or people at his door.

'Come in,' he said. He tried to relax – after all, he took pride in the fact that any of his staff could come and see him whenever they wanted.

It was Nils Langeby, and Anders Schyman felt his heart sink even more.

'What's on your mind today, then?' he said without getting up from behind the desk.

Nils Langeby stood in the middle of the floor of the corner room and knotted his hands theatrically.

'I'm very worried about the crime desk,' he began. 'There's no real organization any more.'

Anders Schyman looked up at the reporter and suppressed a sigh.

'How do you mean?'

'We're going to miss important stories. It doesn't feel reliable any more. Everyone's unsettled after the changes, we aren't comfortable with the way we're covering crime.'

The editor-in-chief gestured towards a chair on the

other side of the desk and Nils Langeby sat down.

'All changes, even changes for the better, involve a certain amount of turbulence and anxiety,' Schyman said. 'It's entirely natural that the crime desk feels unsettled, you haven't had anyone in charge for a while, and now you have a new boss.'

'That's just it, I think that's where the problem lies,' Nils Langeby said. 'I don't think Annika Bengtzon is up to the job.'

Anders Schyman thought for a moment.

'Really? I have to say I think the exact opposite. I think she's a formidable reporter with good organizational skills. She can prioritize and delegate. And she never hesitates to tackle unpleasant jobs. She's smart and knowledgeable; today's paper is proof of that if proof were needed. What makes you doubt her?'

Nils Langeby leaned forward conspiratorially.

'People don't trust her. She thinks she's something special. She treads on people's toes and doesn't know how to handle people.'

'How has this affected you?'

The reporter held out his hands.

'Well, I'm not sure I've been affected, but I've heard . . .'

'So you're here out of a sort of general anxiety on behalf of your colleagues?'

'Yes, and we're losing sight of our coverage of crime in schools, and environmental crime.'

'But aren't those your areas of responsibility?'

'Yes, but—'

'Has Annika tried to take those areas away from you?'

'No, not at all.'

'So if we're failing to develop our stories within those specific areas, that would be down to you, wouldn't it?

126

Surely that doesn't have anything to do with Annika Bengtzon?'

Nils Langeby suddenly looked confused.

'I think you're a good reporter, Nils,' the editor-in-chief went on calmly. 'Men like you, with weight and experience, are just what this paper needs. I hope you can continue to come up with exclusives and exposés for a long time yet. I have every confidence in you, just as I have every confidence in Annika Bengtzon as head of the crime section. That's what makes my job better and better with each passing day, the fact that people grow and learn to work together for the good of the paper.'

Nils Langeby was listening carefully. He seemed to grow with every word. This was the sort of thing he wanted to hear. The editor-in-chief had faith in him, he could continue to come up with exclusives, he was a force to be reckoned with. When he left the room he had a spring in his step. He was even whistling by the time he got back to the newsroom.

'Hello, Nils, what have you got on the go today?' he heard someone call behind him.

It was Ingvar Johansson, the news-chief. Nils Langeby stopped and thought for a moment. He hadn't actually planned to do any work today, and no one had called him into the office. But the editor-in-chief's words ringing in his ears made him aware of his responsibilities. So he said, 'Well, a few different leads. The terrorist attack, the whole terrorism angle. That's what I'm up to today . . .'

'Great, it would be good if you could put it together as soon as possible so we've got it ready when the layout guys get in. The rest of the gang are going to be up to their necks with Furhage.'

'Furhage?' Nils Langeby said. 'What about her?'

Ingvar Johansson looked up at the reporter.

127

'You haven't heard? The bits and pieces they found at the stadium – that was the head of the Olympics.'

'Oh that, yes, of course. Well, I've got sources saying it was a terrorist act, pure and simple.'

'Police sources?'

'Cast-iron police sources,' Nils Langeby said, puffing out his chest. He pulled off his leather jacket and started rolling up his shirtsleeves as he headed off down the corridor towards his office with its view of the car park.

'Right, you bitch, now I'm really going to show you!'

20

Anders Schyman hardly had time to take the first piece of paper off the biggest pile when there was another knock on the door. This time it was the new photographer, Ulf Olsson, who wanted a word. He had just arrived from the press conference in police headquarters, and wanted to talk in confidence to the editor-in-chief about the way the head of crime, Annika Bengtzon, had treated him the day before.

'I'm not used to being shouted at because of the way I dress,' the photographer said, explaining that he had been wearing an Armani suit the previous day.

'Is that what happened, then?' Anders Schyman wondered.

'Yes, Annika Bengtzon expressed her disapproval of the fact that I was wearing a designer label. I don't think I should have to put up with that. I certainly didn't have to in any of my previous positions.'

Anders Schyman looked at the man for several seconds before replying.

'I don't know what was said between you and Annika Bengtzon,' he said. 'And I don't know where you worked before and what the dress-code was like there. As far as I'm concerned, and I know the same goes for Annika, you're more than welcome to wear

Armani everywhere, down coal-mines, at crime scenes, wherever. But don't blame anyone but yourself if you're not dressed appropriately for a job. I, and the rest of the senior staff here, expect you and every other journalist working here to be at least moderately well-informed about what's going on before you come to work. If there has been some spectacular murder, or a serious bomb attack, you have to presume that you will be covering it. I suggest that you get hold of a large bag and keep a pair of long-johns and maybe a tracksuit handy in your car . . .'

'I've already got a bag,' the photographer said sourly. 'From Annika Bengtzon.'

Anders Schyman looked blankly at the young man.

'Is there anything else I can help you with?' he said, and the photographer got up and left.

The editor-in-chief gave a deep sigh as the door closed. Sometimes the playground politics went way beyond his tolerance levels. He just wanted to get home to his wife, and a large glass of Scotch.

Annika and Johan Henriksson stopped at the McDonald's on Sveavägen for a couple of Big Mac meals. They ate them in the car on the way back to the office.

'That sort of thing's terrible,' Henriksson said, chewing on the last fry.

'Visiting relatives? Yes, it's probably the worst part of the job.' Annika wiped the ketchup from her fingers.

'I can't help it, but I always feel like a real low-life sitting there like that,' Henriksson said. 'As if we're sniffing about in their tragedy, making the most of their own little hell, just because it looks good in the paper.'

Annika wiped her mouth and thought for a moment.

'Yes,' she said, 'it's easy to think that. But sometimes

130

people actually want to talk. We mustn't make the mistake of thinking people are stupid just because they're in shock. Obviously you have to be careful. And we don't always write about the relatives just because we've listened to them and talked to them.'

'But people who've just lost a loved one don't always know what they're doing,' Henriksson said.

'How can you be sure?' Annika said. 'Who are you or I to decide if someone should be allowed to talk or not? Who should judge what's best for anyone in a particular situation? You, me, or the person themselves? There's been a huge debate about this in the media in recent years, and sometimes the debate has hurt people more than the interviews with them have.'

'I still think it's crap,' Henriksson said lamely.

Annika smiled.

'Well, yes. Talking to someone who's just had the very worst thing imaginable happen to them is terrible, of course it is. You can't handle too many of them in a month. But you do get used to it, after a while. After all, people working in hospitals, or the Church, have to deal with tragedies every single day.'

'Yeah, but they don't splash them all over a newspaper,' Henriksson said.

'God, you're really milking this!' Annika said, suddenly annoyed. 'Ending up in the paper doesn't have to be a punishment, you know! It proves that you're important, that you matter. Or should we ignore the victims of crime, all the relatives? Think about what happened with the relatives of the people who died when the *Estonia* sank. They thought they got far too little attention in the media. They said the papers were only interested in bow doors failing, and they were right. For a while it was practically taboo to talk to any of the *Estonia* families – if you did, all the self-righteous media and consumer rights programmes came down on you like a ton of bricks.'

'No need to get so angry,' Henriksson said.

'I'll get as fucking angry as I like, thank you,' Annika snapped.

They sat in silence the rest of the way back to the office. As they stood in the lift on the way up to the newsroom Henriksson gave Annika a disarming smile and said, 'I reckon that shot of Milander by the window is going to be pretty good.'

'That's good,' Annika said. 'We'll have to see if we can publish it.'

She pushed open the lift door and hurried away without bothering to wait for a reply.

21

Eva-Britt Qvist was busy pulling out background material on Christina Furhage when Annika passed her on her way to her room. The secretary was surrounded by files of old cuttings and reams of computer printouts.

'There's an incredible amount of stuff about this woman,' she said, trying to sound annoyed. 'But I think I've dug out most of it now.'

'Can you do a preliminary sort-through so that someone else can take over later?' Annika said.

'You have such a lovely way of making orders sound like questions,' Eva-Britt said.

Annika couldn't be bothered to reply, so just went into her office and hung up her coat. She picked up a mug of coffee, then headed over to Pelle Oscarsson, the picture editor, and pulled up a chair so that she could look at his computer screen. It was covered in thumbnail pictures from the paper's archive, all of them representing Christina Furhage.

'We've printed over six hundred of our own pictures of that woman,' Pelle Oscarsson said. 'We must have taken an average of one shot a week for the last eight years. More than the King.'

Annika gave a wry smile. Yes, that could well be true. Everything Christina Furhage had done in recent years had got a lot of attention. Annika studied the screen: Christina Furhage opens the Victoria Stadium, Christina Furhage meeting the Prime Minister, Christina Furhage meets famous singers, Christina Furhage hugging the President of the International Olympic Committee, Christina Furhage showing off her new autumn wardrobe in the Sunday supplement . . .

Pelle Oscarsson clicked on to a new screen of thumbnails: Christina Furhage at the White House, at the premiere of some play at the National Theatre, drinking tea with the Queen, speaking at a conference on female leadership . . .

'Have we got a single picture of her home, or of her family?' Annika asked.

The picture editor thought for a moment.

'I don't think we have,' he said in surprise. 'Now that you come to mention it, I don't think we've got any shots of her in any sort of private context.'

'Oh well, I dare say we'll manage,' Annika said, as the pictures flew past.

'I think we'll have this one on the front,' Pelle said, clicking on a picture taken in the paper's own studio.

After a second or so the picture covered the whole of the screen, and Annika knew the picture editor was right. It was an excellent portrait of Christina Furhage.

The woman was professionally made up, her hair styled and glossy, the lighting warm and subdued, softening the wrinkles on her face; she was wearing an expensive, close-fitting dress and was seated in a relaxed pose on an antique chair.

'How old was she, anyway?' Annika said.

'Sixty-two,' Pelle said. 'We did a feature on her last birthday.'

'Wow,' Annika said. 'She looks at least fifteen years younger.'

'Surgery, healthy living or good genes?' Pelle said.

'Or all of them,' Annika said.

Anders Schyman was on his way to the canteen, holding an empty and very dirty coffee mug. He looked tired, his hair was a mess and he had loosened his tie. He stopped beside them.

'How's it going?'

'We've been to see Furhage's family.'

'Anything we can use?'

Annika hesitated. 'Well, I think so. Something, anyway. Henriksson took some pictures of her husband, but he was pretty confused.'

'We'll have to go through it carefully before we decide,' Schyman said, heading off to the canteen.

'What pictures have we got for the news?' Pelle Oscarsson asked, closing the file of photographs.

Annika swallowed the last of her coffee.

'We'll have a run-through as soon as the others get in,' she said.

She threw the plastic cup in Eva-Britt Qvist's bin, went into her room and closed the door firmly behind her.

It was time for some phone-calls. She started with her source: he was on the day shift today. She dialled a direct number inside police headquarters and struck lucky: he was in his room and answered straight away.

'How did you find out about her personal details being withheld?' he wondered.

'When did you realize it was Furhage?' she countered.

The man sighed.

'Almost at once. We found her things in the stadium. Although the actual process of identification took a bit longer. You don't want to make a mistake in a case like this . . .'

Annika waited without saying anything, but he didn't go on. So she said, 'What are you doing now?'

'Checking, checking, checking. It wasn't the Tiger, we know that much at least.'

'Why not?' Annika said in surprise.

'I can't tell you, but it wasn't him. It was an inside job, just as you guessed yesterday.'

'I have to write about the story today. You appreciate that, don't you?'

He sighed again.

'Yes, I guessed as much,' he said. 'Thanks for keeping quiet for twenty-four hours, anyway.'

'Give and take,' Annika said.

'So what do you want?' he said.

'Why were her personal details protected?'

'There was a threat, a written threat, two or three years ago. A bit of violence, too, but that wasn't so serious.'

'What sort of violence?'

'I don't want to go into details. The person in question was never charged. Christina didn't want to cause that person any trouble, as she apparently put it. The file says that she also said everyone deserves a second chance. She moved house instead, and asked to have her personal details, and those of her family, hidden.'

'Very magnanimous of her,' Annika said.

'Yes, wasn't it?'

'Were the threats anything to do with the Olympics?'

'Not a thing.'

'Was it someone she knew, a relative, maybe?'

The policeman hesitated.

'You could say that. The motive was purely private. Which is why we can't make it public, it was too close to her. But there's absolutely nothing to suggest that the bomb at the stadium was an act of terrorism. We believe it was aimed at Christina personally, not that that necessarily means that the culprit was particularly close to her.'

'Are you questioning the person who made those threats against her?'

'We already have.'

Annika blinked.

'Wow, quick work,' she said. 'Any results?'

'We can't comment on that. But I can say that at the moment no single person is under any more suspicion than anyone else.'

'And who might this "anyone else" be?'

'You can work that out for yourself. Anyone who ever had any contact with her. So four, maybe five thousand people. We can rule some of them out, but I don't intend to tell you which ones.'

'There must be a hell of a lot of people with entry-cards to the stadium,' Annika teased.

'Like who?'

'The Olympic office here, the members of the IOC, caretakers, the people building the facilities, electricians, builders, welders, transport companies, architects, advertising agencies, the security company, television sport . . .'

He didn't reply.

'Am I wrong?' she said.

'No, not really. All the people you mention have had, currently have or will have entry-cards – that much is true.'

'But?'

'You can't get in in the middle of the night with just an entry-card.'

Annika's brain was whirring.

'The alarm codes! That's a much smaller group!'

'Yep, but you have to keep quiet about that for the time being.'

'Okay. How long? Who had access to the codes?'

The man laughed.

'You're incorrigible,' he said. 'We're going through that right now.'

'But couldn't the alarms have been switched off?'

'And the doors unlocked? Really, Bengtzon!'

She heard two new voices in the background, and the man on the other end put his hand over the receiver to say something to them. Then he took his hand away and said, 'Look, I've got to go now.'

'One more thing!' Annika said.

'Make it short . . .'

'What was Christina Furhage doing at the Victoria Stadium in the middle of the night?'

'That, my dear, is a fucking good question. We'll speak soon.'

They hung up and Annika tried to phone home. No answer. She dialled Anne Snapphane's number, but only got the fax instead. She called Berit's mobile and got voicemail. Patrik the mobile-geek answered, though, he always did. It was a weakness of his. Once when Annika had called he was in the shower.

'I'm at Olympics headquarters,' he yelled down the phone, another little peculiarity of his. In spite of his affection for his mobile, he didn't really trust it, so always shouted to make sure he would be heard.

'Where's Berit?' Annika asked, noticing that she too was talking louder.

'She's here with me, she's doing Furhage's last evening,' Patrik roared. 'I'm doing the Olympic headquarters in shock.'

'Where are you right now?' Annika said, forcing herself to lower her voice.

'In some corridor. People are really upset,' he bellowed.

Annika practically blushed on his behalf, imagining all the office-workers listening to the reporter shouting in the corridor outside their doors.

'Okay,' Annika said. 'We'll have to cook something up about the police hunt for the Bomber. When will you be back?'

'An hour or so?' he roared.

'Good, see you then,' Annika said, and hung up. She couldn't help smiling.

22

Evert Danielsson closed the door to shut out the noise of a journalist bellowing into his mobile out in the corridor. In an hour the committee was due to meet, the operational, active, expert committee that Christina called her 'orchestra'. The committee was made up of doers, unlike the Honorary Board, which was mostly for show. Officially, all important decisions were supposed to be taken by the Board, but that was really only a formality. The people on the Honorary Board were like members of parliament, whereas the committee consisted of the people who actually came up with policy in the governing party.

The chair of the committee was nervous. He was aware that he had made a number of mistakes since the explosion went off. He should have called the committee together yesterday, for instance. But now someone else had called the meeting, one day late, which was a serious slip-up. Instead of gathering the committee, he had appeared in public, telling the world's media a lot of things that it wasn't his job to tell them – mainly the unfortunate speculation about terrorism, but also those details about rebuilding the stand. He knew perfectly well that it should have been discussed by the committee first. But the informal, core management group had met yesterday morning – a meeting that seemed more and more panicky with the benefit of hindsight – and decided to take the initiative in the debate, and not attempt any sort of cover-up. The idea was to show they were meeting the problem head on. In Christina's absence, he had been chosen to act as their representative, as chairman of the committee, rather than the usual press experts, in an effort to add more weight to their response.

In actual fact, though, the informal management group had no real authority. The committee itself took the actual decisions. Its members were real heavyweights: political representatives like the Minister for Business and the Commissioner of Stockholm City Council, an expert from the IOC, two representatives from the sponsors, and a leading international lawyer. The head of the committee was another politician, the Governor of the Stockholm region, Hans Bjällra. The core management group may have been quick and effective, but it was lightweight in comparison to the committee. The core group was made up of the people responsible for the day-to-day running of the project: the financial director, Christina, him, Helena Starke and the press officer, together with a couple of deputy directors and Doris from accounts.

This core group had managed to push through practical decisions quickly and efficiently. Then Christina would guide the decisions past the committee afterwards. This applied mainly to financial decisions, but also to matters regarding the environment, infrastructure, construction, legal issues and all manner of publicity campaigns.

But now there was no Christina to tidy up after them. He realized there was no escape this time.

He leaned his elbows on the desk and rested his head in his hands. A shiver ran through his whole body.

Damn, damn! After all these years of hard work! He really didn't deserve this.

Tears started to well up and trickle through his fingers, dripping onto the papers on his desk, forming little transparent blisters and blurring letters and graphs. He didn't care.

Annika turned on her computer and sat down to write. She started with the information she had got from the conversation with her police source. She didn't mention a word about anything she had learned from her unofficial channels. She never recorded conversations of that sort – there was always a risk of the tapes getting left in the machine and someone else hearing them. Instead she made notes, then filled in the gaps as soon as possible to make a complete text on her computer. She saved the files onto USB sticks, which she kept locked in a drawer of her desk, and destroyed the notes. She never mentioned the information gleaned from such sources in handovers or editorial meetings. The only person who ever got to hear any of the confidential material, and only if it was strictly necessary, was the editor-in-chief, Anders Schyman, because he was legally responsible for everything published in the paper.

She had no illusions about why the information was being shared with her. It wasn't that she was better or in any way more remarkable than any other journalist. But she was reliable, and this, combined with the influence she had as a member of the *Evening Post*'s editorial team, made her an ideal channel for the police to spread any information they wanted to make public. Of course, there were any number of reasons why the police might want such information spread, and the police were no different to any other organization: they wanted to present their own version of events in the media. And with particularly dramatic events, both television and the papers had a tendency to rush to conclusions and make mistakes. Leaking just enough accurate information allowed the police to prevent the most misleading reports.

Some journalists thought it was unethical not to make use of everything you knew at all times. If you were a journalist, then that was what you were, and you were nothing but a journalist. Which meant that you had a duty to reveal anything you knew about your neighbours, your friends' children, your mother-in-law, and Father Christmas if you found out anything. There was no question of any off-the-record conversations with the police or politicians. Annika, on the other hand, thought this was a ridiculous attitude. She regarded herself first and foremost as a human being, then as a mother, then as a wife, and then, and only then, as an employee of the *Evening Post*. She didn't even think of herself as a journalist, at least not in the sense of it being some sort of God-given vocation. Bitter experience had taught her that the journalists with the noblest and loftiest principles were often real bastards. So she was perfectly happy if people wanted to speculate about her sources or laugh at the way she worked. But that didn't mean that she took her job any less seriously.

Once the files were locked away in her desk-drawer she wrote a short article about her visit to see Bertil Milander. She kept it fairly concise and straight-forward, pointing out that he had personally invited the paper's attention, and presenting the positive image of his wife that he had been keen to promote. She didn't mention the daughter at all. She left the article in the shared editorial filestore, commonly known as 'the can'.

Then she stood up, restless, stretching her legs in her

glass-walled office. The room was between two editorial sections, news and sport, with glass walls facing out onto each of them. There was no natural light, except indirectly from beyond the two expanses of desks. To counteract the feeling of being in a goldfish bowl, one of her predecessors had hung up a set of thick blue curtains. But it had to be at least five years since anyone had paid them any attention at all, let alone washed or shaken them. Maybe they had looked fresh and modern once upon a time, but now they just seemed sad and hopeless. Annika kept hoping that someone would do something about them. But she knew full well that that person wasn't going to be her.

She went out to Eva-Britt Qvist's desk, just outside her office. The secretary had gone home without telling anyone. The research material was arranged in piles on the desk, marked with yellow Post-it notes. Annika sat down and started to look through them, curious, but without knowing exactly what she was hoping to find. Bloody hell, the amount of stuff that had been written about that woman! She picked up a printout from the top of the pile marked 'overviews' and started to read. It was a long article from one of the Sunday papers, a positive, intelligent piece that actually managed to give an idea of what sort of person Christina Furhage was. The questions were incisive and concrete, Furhage's replies smart and focused. The subject-matter wasn't exactly personal – things like the funding of the Olympics, organization theory, gender-equality in the jobs market, the importance of sport in national consciousness. Annika skimmed the text and realized to her surprise that Christina Furhage had managed to avoid giving away anything that could be considered remotely personal.

Mind you, the article was from one of the morning

papers, and they really weren't interested in anything private or personal. Their policy could be summed up fairly simply: deal only with masculine, politically correct and respectable subjects; avoid anything emotional, interesting and feminine. She put the printout down and rifled through the piles to find something from one of the evening papers' supplements. There were several of them, each with its obligatory little box of facts about Furhage. Name: Ingrid Christina Furhage. Family: husband and one child. Home: a detached house in Tyresö. Income: high. Smoke: no. Drink: yes, water, wine and coffee. Best characteristic: that's for others to decide. Worst characteristic: that's for others to decide ... Annika carried on through the articles: the answers had been the same for the past few years, since her details became confidential. Husband and child not named, home given as a detached house in Tyresö. She found one article from six years ago from the Sunday supplement where her family was named as Bertil and Lena. So that was the daughter's name. Presumably her surname was Milander.

She abandoned the pile of general articles and moved on to the smallest pile, marked 'disputes'. Evidently there hadn't been many of those. The first piece was about the fuss when one of the sponsors pulled out. It had nothing to do with Christina Furhage; she was only mentioned once at the end of the article, which was why the article had come up in the search of the database. The next article was about a protest against the environmental impact of the Victoria Stadium. Annika could feel herself starting to get irritated. This sort of dispute had nothing to do with Christina Furhage! Eva-Britt had done a useless job. She should have weeded out stuff like this. That was the whole point of having a researcher on the crime desk. Eva-Britt was supposed to compile background information that saved time for journalists working to deadlines.

Annika picked up the whole pile marked 'disputes' and leafed through the articles: demonstrations, protests, one op-ed piece . . . Annika stopped. What was this? She put the rest of the pile down, holding on to one small cutting from near the bottom of the pile. OLYMPICS SECRETARY SACKED AFTER AFFAIR. Annika didn't need to check which paper it had appeared in, it was obviously from the *Evening Post*. Dated seven years ago. A young woman had been forced to leave the newly established Olympic headquarters because of a relationship with one of her superiors.

'It feels degrading and ridiculously old-fashioned,' the woman had told the paper's reporter.

Christina Furhage had explained that the woman hadn't been fired, but had left because her temporary contract had expired. It had nothing to do with the affair. End of story. There was no indication of who the woman or her superior were. No one else had picked up the story, but that wasn't in itself remarkable. It was extremely thin – and this was the only conflict involving Christina Furhage that had appeared in the media. Annika could only conclude that she must have been a bloody good manager.

Her thoughts drifted to the vast number of articles covering conflict in her own workplace over the years, and even so, this wasn't a particularly bad set-up.

'Anything interesting?' Berit said behind her.

Annika got up from the edge of the desk.

'You're back, great! No, nothing much, just one possibility. Furhage got rid of a young woman for having an affair with a superior. Might be worth bearing in mind . . . What have you got?'

'Quite a lot. Do you want a quick run-through?'

'We'd better wait for Patrik,' Annika said.

'I'm here!' came a shout from the other side of the picture desk. 'I'm just—'

'My office!' Annika said.

23

Berit hung her outdoor clothes at her desk, then went into Annika's office and settled into the old sofa with her notes and a styrofoam cup of coffee from the machine.

'I've been trying to piece together Christina Furhage's final hours. The Olympics headquarters had an office Christmas party at a bar on Kungsholmen on Friday night. Christina was there until midnight. I've been out there and spoken to the staff, and I also had a private chat with Evert Danielsson, the chairman.'

'Great!' Annika said. 'So what did she do after that?'

Berit picked up her pad.

'She arrived at the bar late, after ten. The others had already eaten. They had a Basque Christmas dinner, apparently. She left with another woman, Helena Starke, just before midnight. And no one's seen her since then.'

'The bomb went off at three seventeen, so we've got a three-hour gap,' Annika said. 'What does this Helena Starke say?'

'Don't know. Her number's ex-directory. She's registered on Södermalm, but I haven't had time to get out to see her yet.'

'Starke sounds promising; we need to get hold of her,'

Annika said. 'Anything else? What was Furhage doing before she got to the bar?'

'Danielsson thinks she was working late in the office, but he's not sure. Apparently she used to work really long days – fourteen, fifteen hours was nothing unusual.'

'Superwoman,' Annika muttered, thinking about Christina's husband's tribute to her work back in the apartment.

'Who's doing The Furhage Story?' Berit wondered.

'One of the writers out in general news. I met the family, but that didn't really give anything useful. They're a bit tricky . . .'

'How do you mean?'

Annika thought for a moment.

'The husband, Bertil, was old and grey. Pretty bewildered. It was like he admired his wife more than he actually loved her. The daughter came in screaming and crying, said she was glad her mother was dead.'

'Happy families,' Berit said.

'How's it going?' Patrik said as he came in.

'Fine. How about you?' Annika said.

'This is going to be bloody good,' he said, sitting down next to Berit. 'So far the police have found one hundred and twenty-seven pieces of Christina Furhage.'

Berit and Annika both recoiled in revulsion.

'That's disgusting! You can't use that!' Annika said.

The young reporter smiled nonchalantly.

'They've found blood and teeth as far away as the main entrance. That's several hundred metres away.'

'You're terrible. Surely even you can't come up with anything worse than that?' Annika said.

'They still don't know what the Bomber used to shred her. Or else they're not saying.'

'So what's your story going to be?'

149

'I spoke to a good source in the police about the hunt for the killer. I can do that one.'

'Okay,' Annika said. 'I can fill in what I know. So what have you got?'

Patrik leaned forward, his eyes twinkling.

'The police are looking for Christina Furhage's powerbook. They know she had a laptop with her on Friday evening, a girl from the office saw it. But the computer's gone; it wasn't among the stuff they found in the stadium. They think the killer took it.'

'Surely it could have been blown to smithereens in the explosion?' Berit said.

'No, they've ruled that out, at least according to my source,' Patrik said. 'The computer's missing, and that's their best lead right now.'

'Anything else?' Annika said.

'They're thinking about getting Interpol involved in tracing the Tiger.'

'It wasn't the Tiger,' Annika said. 'It was an inside job, the police are sure of it.'

'How can they be sure?' Patrik said, surprised.

Annika remembered her promise not to say anything about the alarm codes.

'Believe me, my source is reliable. Anything else?'

'I've spoken to the staff at Olympic headquarters. Christina Furhage seems to have been some sort of messiah for them. They're all in tears, even Evert Danielsson. I heard him through a door. They have no idea how to cope without her. She seems to have embodied every good quality a person could possibly have.'

'Why do you sound so surprised?' Berit said. 'Why shouldn't a middle-aged woman be liked and respected?'

'That's not what I mean. It's just that they're pretty extreme . . .'

'Christina Furhage had a remarkable career, and she was doing a damn good job with these Olympics. If a woman can manage to steer a huge project like this from start to finish, you can put money on the fact that she's pretty extraordinary. The Olympic Games is like organizing twenty-eight World Cups simultaneously,' Berit said.

'Okay, but does the fact that she was a woman make her achievements any more remarkable?' Patrik countered, making Berit properly cross.

'Oh grow up!'

Patrik stretched to his full height, one metre ninety in his socks.

'And what the hell do you mean by that?'

'Okay, okay, that's enough now,' Annika said, trying to sound calm and collected. 'Sit down, Patrik. We'll forgive you for not knowing about the oppression of women, seeing as you're a man. Obviously it's harder for a woman to do a job like head of the Olympics than a man, just as it would be harder for a deaf-mute than an able-bodied person. Being a woman is like being a walking bundle of disabilities. Have you got anything else?'

Patrik had sat down, but was clearly still upset.

'*Walking bundle of disabilities*, what sort of feminist crap is that?'

'Have you got anything else?'

He looked through his notes.

'The hunt for the Bomber, Olympic headquarters in shock . . . that's it from me.'

'Right, Berit, you do Christina Furhage's last day, I'll do the family and fill in any gaps on the hunt for the killer. Okay?'

The meeting broke up without any more talk. We're starting to run out of steam, Annika thought as she

151

switched on the radio to hear the 5.45 news. The lead story was of course the fact that one of the most powerful and well-known women in Sweden, Christina Furhage, was dead. They began with a short run-through of her life and achievements, before looking at the impact her death would have on the Olympics and sport generally. The President of the International Olympic Committee, as expected, had withdrawn his statement to the other evening paper.

Only after eleven minutes came the fact that Furhage had been murdered. That was the way the radio news handled things: first you got the impersonal, general information, and only then – in so far as you got it at all – anything uncomfortable and unsettling. Any time radio news covered a murder, they almost always focused on judicial process and never on the victim, the victim's family or the perpetrator. But they were perfectly happy to include umpteen different items on the equipment used to scan the murderer's brain, because that was regarded as research, and therefore an appropriate subject.

Annika sighed. They also mentioned her own piece in today's paper, about the threat that led to Furhage's personal details being withheld from public view, but only in passing. She switched off the radio and gathered the material she needed for the editorial meeting in the editor-in-chief's room. On her way there she had felt strangely ill at ease. Ingvar Johansson had been behaving very oddly all day, touchy and short with her. She knew that she must have done something wrong, but had no idea what. And now there was no sign of him.

Anders Schyman was on the phone, it sounded like he was talking to a child. Pelle from the picture desk was already seated at the conference table with his long lists. Annika stood by the window and stared at her own reflection. If she held up her hand to block the light from the ceiling and put her head close to the glass, she could see through it. The darkness outside was dense, heavy. The yellow lamps of the Russian Embassy hung like small golden islands in a sea of darkness. Even this little piece of Russia was gloomy and oppressive. The cold of the window made her shiver.

24

'*Alles gut?*' Jansson said behind her, his voice fresh from sleep, as he spilled a bit more coffee on the editor-in-chief's carpet. 'My last night with the gang, then I'm off for three days. Where the hell's Ingvar Johansson?'

'Here! Shall we start?'

Annika sat down at the table and noted that Ingvar seemed intent on taking control today. That suited her fine; she had done all her talking the day before.

'Yes, let's get going,' Anders Schyman said as he hung up. 'What have we got and where are we going with it?'

Ingvar Johansson began to speak as he passed round copies of his outline.

'I think we should run with Nils Langeby's piece: the police are confident it was a terrorist attack. They're hunting a foreign group of terrorists.'

Annika was struck dumb.

'What?' she spluttered. 'I didn't even know that Nils was here today. Who called him in?'

'I don't know,' Johansson said, irritated. 'I presumed that you must have done, seeing as you're his boss.'

'Where the hell has he got that stuff about terrorism from?' Annika said, aware that she was on the brink of losing control of her voice.

'What makes you think you can ask him to give up his sources, when you never do?' Ingvar Johansson countered.

Annika felt the blood rise to her face. Everyone round the table was watching her reaction. It suddenly struck her that they were all men apart from her.

'We have to synchronize our work,' she said in a muffled voice. 'I've been told the exact opposite by my source, that the attack was definitely not an act of terrorism, but aimed at Christina personally.'

'How do you mean?' Ingvar Johansson said, and Annika knew she had no way out of this.

If she told them what she knew, Jansson and Ingvar Johansson would demand that she wrote an article about the alarm codes. There wasn't an editor in the world who would let an opportunity like that slip by. If she kept quiet . . . But she couldn't do that – they'd take her apart if she tried. She quickly came up with a third option.

'I'll call my source again,' she said.

Anders Schyman was looking at her thoughtfully.

'We'll wait before deciding if we're going to go with the terrorism angle,' he said. 'Let's move on.'

Annika sat in silence, waiting for Ingvar Johansson to go on. Which of course he was happy to do.

'We're doing a supplement: *Our Christina. Her Life in Words and Pictures.* We've got loads of good quotes, from the King, the White House, the government, the President of the Olympic Committee, loads of sports stars, TV celebs, and so on. They all want to have their say. It's going to be pretty impressive, powerful stuff . . .'

'So what about the sport supplement?' Anders Schyman asked quietly.

Ingvar Johansson was nonplussed.

'Well, yes, we're using those pages for the memorial supplement, sixteen pages of full colour, so we'll add extra pages to the main paper for sport.'

'Full colour?' Anders Schyman said thoughtfully. 'Doesn't that mean that we're taking a load of colour pages from the main paper for this supplement? Which means that the main paper will be almost entirely without colour?'

Ingvar Johansson was practically blushing.

'Well, yes, when you put it like that . . .'

'Why wasn't I told about this idea?' Anders Schyman said calmly. 'I've been here pretty much all day. You could have come and discussed this with me at any time.'

The news-editor looked like he wanted the floor to swallow him up.

'I can't really explain. Everything happened so quickly.'

'That's a shame,' Schyman said, 'because we aren't going to publish a full-colour supplement on Christina Furhage. She wasn't some sort of national heroine. She was an elitist business leader, admittedly one who was greatly admired by people in certain circles, but she wasn't royalty, no one elected her, and she wasn't a TV star. We'll do the memorial stuff on some extra pages inside the main paper instead and give up any idea of a supplement. I take it that sport haven't got anything for their own supplement now?'

Ingvar Johansson was staring down at the table.

'What else have we got?'

No one spoke. Annika waited in silence. The atmosphere was incredibly uncomfortable.

'Bengtzon?'

She straightened her back and looked at her notes.

'We can put together a good piece on the hunt for the

killer. Patrik's found out that Furhage's laptop is missing, and I have a good source for the theory that it was an inside job . . .'

She fell quiet, but when no one else said anything she went on: 'Berit is doing Furhage's last day, and I've been to see her family.'

'Ah, yes. What have you got from that?' Schyman said.

Annika thought for a moment.

'The husband was pretty confused. The daughter was completely unhinged; I didn't even try with her. The question is whether we should publish any of it. We could get attacked for approaching the husband at all.'

'Did you trick him into talking?' Anders Schyman asked.

'No, absolutely not.'

'Was he at all reluctant?'

'Not at all. He invited us over so he could talk about Christina. I've written up what he had to say, but it doesn't amount to much. It's on the filestore.'

'Have we got pictures?' Schyman said.

'Henriksson got some great shots,' Pelle Oscarsson said. 'The old boy standing at the window, eyes moist with tears, really lovely.'

Schyman regarded the picture editor expressionlessly.

'I see. Well, I want to see the pictures before we decide to use one.'

'Of course,' Oscarsson said.

'Good,' Schyman said. 'There's one other subject I'd like to get out of the way, now that we're all here.'

He ran his fingers through his hair and stood up straight, reaching for his coffee but changing his mind. Annika felt the hairs on the back of her neck prickling. Had she done something else wrong?

'We've got a killer on the loose,' the editor-in-chief

said. He clearly had a sense for the dramatic gesture. 'I want us to bear this in mind when we publish pictures and interviews with people who knew Christina Furhage. Most murders are committed by people close to the victim. And that seems to be the case this time – the Bomber might well be someone who wanted to take some sort of personal revenge on Christina.'

He fell silent and looked round the table. No one else spoke.

'Well, you understand what I'm saying, don't you?' he said. 'I'm thinking in particular of the Bergsjö murder, which I'm sure you all remember? The little girl found murdered in the cellar, and the mother crying all over the papers while the father was under suspicion. And then she turns out to be guilty after all.'

He raised his hand against the protests.

'Yes, yes, I know, we aren't the police and it isn't our place to judge, but I just think we ought to bear that in mind in this case, that's all.'

'Statistically, it ought to be her husband,' Annika said drily. 'Almost all murdered women are killed by their husbands and partners.'

'Is that a possibility in this case?'

Annika thought for a moment.

'Bertil Milander was old, tired. I can't see him running around a stadium with his arms full of explosives. Mind you, he needn't necessarily have done it himself. He could have hired someone.'

'Are there any other suspects we can think of? Anyone in the Olympic office?'

'Evert Danielsson, chairman of the committee,' Annika said. 'The people in charge of the various divisions there: accreditation, transport, the stadiums, the sports themselves, the Olympic village. There are quite a few of them. The chairman of the Board, Hans

158

Bjällra. The members of the Board – including politicians and ministers . . .'

Schyman sighed. 'Well, there's no point thinking about that right now. What have we got for the rest of the paper?'

Ingvar Johansson ran through the rest of his list: a pop star who had got planning permission for a conservatory in spite of his neighbours' protests, a cat that survived a full cycle in a tumble-drier, a thrilling indoor hockey derby, and record viewing figures for Saturday-night television.

The meeting broke up soon after that, and Annika hurried back to her office. She shut the door behind her, and realized that she felt quite giddy. She had forgotten to have any dinner, but she was also aware that the power struggles of editorial meetings got her down. She clung to the desk as she made her way round to her chair. She had only just sat down when there was a knock on the door and the editor-in-chief came in.

'What does your source say?' Anders Schyman asked.

'That the motive was personal,' Annika said, opening the bottom drawer of her desk. If she remembered rightly, there was a cinnamon bun down there.

'Against Furhage herself?'

The bun was mouldy.

'Yes, not aimed at the Games. The alarm codes were only known to a fairly small group. The threat against her had nothing to do with the Olympics. It came from someone close to her.'

The editor-in-chief let out a whistle.

'How much of that are you allowed to write?'

She pulled a face. 'Nothing, really. It's difficult to say anything about the serious threats to her and her family without the family commenting, and they don't want to say anything. I asked them today. And I promised not to say anything about the alarm codes. Those codes, together with the missing laptop that Patrik found out about, are pretty much all the police have to go on.'

'As far as the police are telling you, anyway,' Schyman said. 'We can't be sure they're telling you everything.'

Annika looked down at her desk.

'Well, I'm going to find Langeby and ask what the hell he thinks he's playing at. Don't move; I'll be right back.'

He stood up and closed the door quietly behind him. Annika sat still, her head empty, her stomach even more so. She had to eat something before she fainted.

25

Thomas didn't get home with the children until almost half past six. All three of them were soaking wet and exhausted, but exhilarated. Ellen had almost fallen asleep on the sledge on the way home from the park, but a bit more singing and a few snowballs had soon got her laughing again.

They collapsed in a heap in the hall, helping each other out of their wet clothes in a tangle of arms and legs. The children each took hold of one of Thomas's boots, but weren't strong enough to pull them off, just kept tugging and tugging in different directions until Thomas pretended to split down the middle. He got them into a hot bath, where they splashed about as he prepared some semolina porridge for them all. Good Sunday-night food, with lots of cinnamon and sugar, then ham sandwiches. He took the opportunity to wash Ellen's long hair, using the last of Annika's conditioner – Ellen hated having her hair washed. He let them eat in their dressing gowns, then they all got into the big double bed and read a bedtime story about Bamse the Bear. Ellen fell asleep after two pages, but Kalle listened wide-eyed right to the end.

'Why is Bamse's daddy always so stupid?' he asked afterwards. 'Is it because he hasn't got a job?'

Thomas thought before replying. He ought to be able to answer that – after all, that was what he did at the Association of Local Councils.

'Not having a job doesn't make you stupid or mean,' he said. 'But if someone's stupid and mean enough, they might not be able to get a job. Because no one would want to work with someone like that, would they?'

The boy thought about this.

'Mummy sometimes says I'm mean to Ellen. Do you think I'll get a job?'

Thomas hugged the boy to him and blew on his still damp hair, rocking him slowly back and forth, feeling the warmth of his little body.

'You're a lovely little boy, and you can have whatever job you want when you're grown up. Mummy and I just get a bit sad when you and Ellen fight, and sometimes you do tease her. There's no need for any teasing or fighting. You and Ellen love each other, after all, because you're brother and sister. It would make everything even nicer for the whole family if we could all be friends . . .'

The boy curled into a little ball and put his thumb in his mouth.

'I love you, Daddy,' he said, and Thomas felt a warm, overwhelming happiness spread through him.

'I love you too, champ. Do you want to sleep in the big bed?'

Kalle nodded, and Thomas pulled off the boy's damp dressing gown and put his pyjamas on. He carried Ellen to her own bed and put her nightdress on. He stood and watched her sleeping in her little bed, aware that he would never get tired of looking at her. She was the image of Annika.

Kalle looked just like he himself used to at that age. The pair of them were proper little miracles. It was a cliché, but it was true.

He turned out the light and closed the door quietly. The children had hardly seen Annika all weekend. He had to admit that it annoyed him when she spent this much time at work. She threw herself into her work in a way that wasn't entirely healthy. She got swallowed up by it, and everything else had to take second place. She lost her temper with the children, couldn't think of anything but her articles.

He went into the TV room, picked up the remote and settled into the sofa. This business with the explosion and Christina Furhage's death was undoubtedly a big deal. It was on all the channels, including Sky, the BBC and CNN. One of the Swedish channels was showing a programme about the Olympics boss, with loads of people in a studio discussing the Olympics and Christina's life's work, cut with extracts of an interview with the dead woman from a year or so ago. Christina Furhage really had been pretty smart, and very funny. He watched for a while, fascinated. Then he called Annika to see if she was on her way home.

Berit looked in through the doorway.

'Have you got a minute?'

Annika waved her in as the phone started to ring. She looked at the caller-display, then went back to typing.

'Aren't you going to answer?' Berit wondered.

'It's Thomas,' Annika said. 'He'll want to know when I'm going to be finished. He tries to sound sweet about it, but I still hear the reproach in his voice. He'll be happier if I don't answer, because he'll think I'm on my way home.'

The telephone stopped ringing and her mobile started up instead, playing an electronic tune that Berit vaguely recognized. Annika didn't answer that either, letting it go to voicemail.

'I can't get hold of that Helena Starke woman,' Berit said. 'Her number's ex-directory, and I've asked her neighbours to try her door, and to leave notes for her, asking her to call us, all the usual, but she hasn't got in touch. I haven't got time to go out there now, because I've got to tidy up the Christina Furhage story—'

'Why are you doing that?' Annika said in surprise, looking up from her screen. 'I thought one of the copy-editors was going to do that?'

Berit gave a wry smile.

'He was, but he suddenly got a migraine when he heard the supplement had been scrapped, so I've got three hours of editing ahead of me.'

'Oh, for heaven's sake!' Annika said. 'I'll drop in on Starke on my way home. She lives on Södermalm, doesn't she?'

Berit gave her the address. As the door closed behind her Annika tried calling her police source again, without result. She groaned silently. She had to pull her piece together anyway now; she couldn't sit on this information any longer. She performed various stylistic somersaults to avoid writing the words 'alarm codes', but the meaning was still pretty clear. It turned out better than she expected. Her angle, after all, was that the attack was an inside job. She was allowed to write that the alarms at the stadium were switched off, and that there were no signs of a break-in. She quoted other sources outside the police about access to pass-cards, and ways of getting into the stadium at night. She was also able to say that the police were looking at a fairly limited number of people who, entirely theoretically, might have been able to carry out the attack. What with this and Patrik's piece, they had two really excellent stories.

Once she was finished with that, she moved on to

a separate piece about how the police had already interviewed the person who had made threats against Christina Furhage a couple of years ago. She was almost done when Anders Schyman appeared again.

'Bloody hell,' he said, sitting down on the sofa. 'Who'd be editor-in-chief?'

'So which way are we going?' Annika said. 'Is it time to start checking out international terrorist groups, or are we pointing the finger at Olympic headquarters?'

'I think Nils Langeby is slightly deranged,' Schyman said. 'He swears his article is accurate, but refuses to reveal a single source or be specific about what they told him.'

'So what do we do?' Annika said.

'We're going with the insider theory, of course. I just want to read it first.'

'Fine, here it is.'

Annika clicked open the file. The editor-in-chief pulled himself up and went over to her desk.

'Do you want to sit down?'

'No, no, I'm fine . . .'

He looked through the text.

'Crystal clear,' he said, getting ready to leave. 'I'll tell Jansson.'

'What else did Langeby say?' Annika wondered in a low voice.

He stopped and looked solemnly at her.

'I think Nils Langeby is about to turn into a really serious problem for the two of us,' he said, and walked out.

26

Helena Starke lived in a brown 1920s building at the eastern end of Ringvägen. The door had a coded lock, of course, and Annika didn't have the code, so she pulled out her mobile and asked Directory Inquiries for a couple of numbers of people living at 139 Ringvägen.

'We can't give out numbers like that,' the woman on the other end said curtly.

Annika sighed. Occasionally that approach worked, but not this time.

'Okay,' she said. 'I'm looking for an Andersson at 139 Ringvägen.'

'Arne Andersson or Petra Andersson?'

'Both,' Annika said quickly, and jotted the numbers in her notebook. 'Thanks very much.'

She dialled the first number, for Arne. No answer, maybe he had already gone to bed. It was almost half past ten. Petra was home, though, and she sounded rather cross.

'I'm terribly sorry,' Annika said, 'but I'm on my way up to a friend of mine who lives in the same block as you and she forgot to give me the code for the door . . .'

'Who's that then?'

'Helena Starke,' Annika said, and Petra Andersson laughed. It wasn't a normal laugh.

'So you're on your way to see Starke at half ten in the evening? Right, well, good luck with that,' she said, and gave Annika the code.

People say some weird things, Annika thought, as she let herself in and climbed up until she found Helena Starke's apartment on the fourth floor. She rang the bell, but there was no answer. She looked around the stairwell, trying to get an idea of which way Helena Starke's apartment faced, and how big it might be. Then she went downstairs and out into the street again, and counted the windows. Starke ought to have at least three windows facing the street, and there was light coming from two of them. So she was probably home. Annika went inside again, took the lift up and rang the bell insistently. Then she opened the letterbox and said, 'Helena Starke? My name's Annika Bengtzon, I'm from the *Evening Post*. I know you're in there. Can you just open the door?'

She waited in silence for a while, then heard a security chain on the other side. The door opened slightly and a woman's face, puffy from crying, appeared in the gap.

'What do you want?' Helena Starke said quietly.

'Sorry to disturb you, but we've been trying to reach you all day.'

'I know. I've had fifteen notes through my letterbox from you and all the others.'

'Can I come in for a minute?'

'Why?'

'We're writing about Christina Furhage's death in tomorrow's paper and I just wondered if I could ask a few questions.'

'About what?'

Annika sighed. 'I'd be happy to tell you, but I'd rather not do it out here.'

Starke opened the door and let her into the apartment.

It was a real mess, and Annika thought she could smell vomit. They went into the kitchen, where the sink was overflowing with dishes, and on top of the stove was an empty cognac bottle. Helena Starke herself was wearing nothing but a T-shirt and pants. Her hair was all over the place and her face was a mess.

'Christina's death is a terrible loss,' she said. 'We'd never have got the Olympics in Stockholm if it hadn't been for her.'

Annika took out her pen and notepad and started writing. How was it that everyone kept saying the same things about Christina Furhage?

'What was she like as a person?' Annika asked.

'Wonderful,' Helena Starke said, staring at the floor. 'She was an example to us all: hard-working, intelligent, resilient, funny . . . everything, really. She could do anything.'

'If I've got this right, you were the last person to see her alive?'

'Apart from the killer, yes. We left the Christmas party together. Christina was tired, and I was pretty drunk.'

'Where did you go?'

Helena Starke gave a start.

'What do you mean? We went our separate ways at the underground station, I came home and Christina got a taxi.'

Annika raised her eyebrows. This was new; she hadn't heard that Christina Furhage had taken a taxi after midnight. So there was someone else who had seen her alive after Helena Starke: the taxi-driver.

'Did Christina have any enemies inside the Olympic organization?'

Helena Starke sniffed.

'Like who?'

'Well, that's what I'm asking. You work in the office too, don't you?'

'I was Christina's personal assistant,' the woman said.

'Does that mean you were her secretary?'

'No, she had three secretaries. I did everything else, I suppose. But I think you should go now.'

Annika gathered her things together silently. Before she left she turned and asked, 'Christina fired a young girl from the Olympic headquarters for having an affair with a superior. How did the rest of the staff react?'

Helena Starke stared at her.

'Just go.'

'Here's my card. Ring me if there's anything you want to add, or to say we've got something wrong,' she muttered, and put the card down on the table in the hall. She noted that there was a scrap of paper with a telephone number next to the phone, and quickly wrote it down. Helena Starke didn't accompany her to the door, so Annika closed it quietly behind her.

Humanity

I've always done a lot of walking. I love light, wind, gales, stars and sea. I've spent so long walking that my body has started walking of its own accord, hardly touching the ground, dissolving into the elements around me and becoming an invisible roar of joy. But sometimes my legs help focus my attention on my surroundings. Instead of opening up the world around me, they shrink it down to a single, diminishing point. I've walked along pavements, concentrating on my body, letting the tread of my heels reverberate up through my limbs. With every step, the same questions: What am I? Where am I? What is it that makes me, me?

In the days when those questions were important to me, I lived in a town where it was always windy. Whichever way I walked, I always had the wind against me. The squally gale was so strong that it sometimes took my breath away. As damp crept into my very marrow, I would work my way through my flesh and blood, trying to discover where inside me I could find my core. Not in my heels, nor in my fingertips, and not in my knees, or genitals, or stomach. The conclusion I reached after all those long walks was hardly controversial. I was to be found somewhere behind my eyes, above my neck but *under my scalp, just above my mouth and ears. That's where I live. That's my home.*

In those days, that place where I lived was cramped and dark, but I remember it as being infinite, impossible to possess and conquer. I was completely obsessed with understanding what I was. In my bed each evening I would close my eyes and try to work out if I was a man or a woman. How was I supposed to know? My genitals throbbed with something I can only attribute to lust. If I didn't know what they looked like, I couldn't have described them as anything other than weighty, bottomless, and pulsating. Man or woman, black or white? My consciousness was incapable of finding any explanation for me, other than deciding that I was human.

When I opened my eyes they would encounter the electromagnetic rays we call light. They interpreted colour in a way I was never sure was shared by other people. What I called red, and regarded as warm and pulsating, maybe looked different to other people. We might agree on and learn common names, but our understanding of them might well be extremely subjective.

You can never know for sure.

Monday 20 December

27

Thomas left the flat before Annika and the children had woken up. He had loads of work to get done by Christmas, and he was supposed to be picking up the children early today. They had agreed to take turns this week, getting them at three o'clock, ideally. Partly because the children were tired and seemed to be suffering with the winter, and partly to get things organized at home for Christmas. Annika had hung up their copper Advent star and got out the candlesticks, but that was as far as they had got. They hadn't started buying food or presents yet, let alone preparing the salmon and Christmas ham, and they hadn't ordered a tree. Then there was the cleaning, which was something like six months behind. Annika wanted them to start paying for a Polish cleaner, the same one Anne Snapphane had, but he refused. He could hardly work for the Swedish Association of Local Councils and then go and employ an illegal cleaner. She saw the sense in this, but she still did no cleaning.

He gave a deep sigh and headed out into the slushy snow. The timing of Christmas this year was hopeless, from an employee's point of view: Christmas Eve was a Friday, so there was a normal working week between Christmas and New Year. He ought to have appreciated that, seeing as he was theoretically on the employers' side of the argument. But he sighed again, thinking of the personal implications, as he crossed Hantverkargatan, heading for the number 48 bus-stop on the far side of Kungsholmstorg. His lower back ached as he strode along; it often did if he had slept in a strange position. Kalle had spent the night in their bed, with his feet against Thomas's back. He twisted from side to side, like a boxer, trying to get his stiff muscles to loosen up.

It was ages before the bus came. He was wet and cold by the time it finally drew to a halt outside the bank. He hated having to use the bus, but the alternatives were worse. There was an underground station round the corner, but it was the blue line, which was so deep it was halfway to hell. It took longer to weave through all the passageways down to the platform than it did to walk through the streets to get to the Central Station. And you had to change lines after just one stop anyway. Then a new set of tunnels and escalators, moving walkways and urine-splashed lifts. And then the train to Slussen, with steamed-up windows and the elbows of countless *Metro*-reading commuters. And there was no point even thinking of going by car. He'd had his Toyota Corolla in town when they first moved in together, but when the monthly accumulation of parking fines finally exceeded their childcare costs Annika got her way and he got rid of it. Now it was parked under a tarpaulin in his parents' garden out in Vaxholm, slowly rusting away. He wanted them to move out of the centre and buy somewhere, but Annika refused. She loved their flat, even if the rent was extortionate.

The bus was packed and he had to stand next to the pushchairs by the doors in the middle, but it started to empty when they reached the City Hall. By Tegelbacken he was able to sit down – right at the back on top of the wheel, but it was still a seat. He pulled his legs up and peered out at the government offices as they drove past Rosenbad, and couldn't help wondering what it would be like to work there. And why not? His progress from the council in Vaxholm to his current post in the Association of Local Councils had been remarkably swift. He preferred to ignore the help he had got from Annika and her career. If it carried on like this, there was every chance he might be working in parliament or for a government department by the time he was forty.

The bus rumbled past Strömsborg and Riddarhuset. He felt impatient and restless, but was unwilling to admit to himself that it was Annika's fault. He had hardly spoken to her all weekend. Yesterday evening he had thought she was on her way home when she didn't answer her phone at the paper. He had got tea and sandwiches ready for when she got back, but it was several more hours before she finally appeared. He had eaten the sandwiches, the tea was stewed, and he had finished reading *Time* and *Newsweek* before he heard her banging about outside. And when she'd finally stumbled through the double doors, she was talking to someone at the paper on her mobile.

'Hello, you. God, you've had a long day,' he said, walking over to her.

'I'll call you on another line,' she said, ending the call and walking past him with just a pat on the cheek. She had gone straight to her desk, dumping her outdoor clothes in a heap at her feet as she called the paper again. She was talking about some taxi ride that needed to be checked with the police, and he could feel his anger growing by the moment. When she hung up she stood there, holding on to the desk, for a while, as if she was feeling giddy.

'Sorry I'm late,' she had said quietly, without looking

up. 'I had to go out to Södermalm for an interview on my way home.'

He had said nothing, just stood there, arms by his sides, staring at her back. She was swaying slightly, and seemed utterly exhausted.

'You mustn't work yourself to death,' he had said, more tersely than he intended.

'No, I know,' she said, putting her clothes on the desk and going out into the bathroom. He had gone back to the bedroom and lay there listening to the sound of water splashing and her brushing her teeth. When she came to bed he pretended to be asleep, and she didn't notice that he was faking. She kissed him on the neck and ran her hand over his hair, then fell asleep. He had lain awake for a long time listening to the cars in the street and the sound of her gentle breathing.

He got off the bus at Slussen and set off to walk the last few blocks to his office on Hornsgatan. A damp wind was blowing from the Baltic and an eager stall-holder had already set up his stall outside the entrance to the underground station.

'An early-morning cup of mulled wine, sir?' the stall-holder said, holding out a steaming cup of mass-produced punch as Thomas approached.

'Yes, why not?' Thomas said, fishing a note from his pocket. 'And a cookie as well, a heart-shaped one, the biggest one you've got!'

28

'Mummy, can I have a ride too?' Kalle said, climbing up on the back of the pushchair so that it started to topple backwards. Annika only caught it at the last moment.

'You know what, let's not bother with the pushchair today; it's so slushy.'

'But I don't want to walk, Mummy,' Ellen said.

Annika went back to the lift and guided the girl out, pulling the gate shut and closing the door behind them. She crouched on the hall carpet and gave Ellen a hug. The shiny nylon snowsuit was cold against her cheek.

'We're getting the bus today, so I'll carry you. Will that be all right?'

The girl nodded and wrapped her arms around Annika's neck, hugging her tight.

'But I want to stay with you today, Mummy.'

'I know, but I'm afraid I have to go to work. But I've got the day off on Friday, because do you know what day that is?'

'Christmas Eve, Christmas Eve!' Kalle yelled.

Annika laughed. 'That's right, it's Christmas Eve. Do you know how many days it is until then?'

'Three weeks?' Ellen said, holding up three fingers.

'Stupid,' Kalle said. 'It's four days.'

'We don't say stupid, do we? But you're quite right,

179

it's four days. Now, where are your gloves, Ellen? Did we leave them upstairs? No, here they are . . .'

Out on the pavement the slush was turning to water. It was raining and the world was completely and uniformly grey. She carried her daughter in her left arm and held on to Kalle with her right hand. Her bag slapped against her back with every step.

'You smell nice, Mummy,' Ellen said.

They turned into Scheelegatan and caught the number 40 bus outside the Indian curry house, and got off just two stops later by the white 1980s building where Radio Stockholm was based. The children's nursery was on the third floor. Kalle had been going there since he was fifteen months old, Ellen since she was about a year. When she talked to other parents she realized they had been lucky – the staff were experienced and competent, the manager engaged, and half of the pre-school teachers were men – male role models seemed to be lacking in society.

The entrance-hall was crowded and noisy, and the grit and snow had formed a little dam by the door. The children were shouting, and the adults were trying to calm them down.

'Is it okay if I stay for a bit?' Annika asked, and one of the staff nodded.

The children sat at the same table for breakfast and lunch. Even though they argued a lot at home, they got on well together at nursery, where Kalle looked out for his little sister. Annika sat with Ellen in her lap as they ate breakfast, taking a sandwich and a cup of coffee so they could see she was joining in.

'We're going on an outing on Wednesday, so they'll need a packed lunch,' one of the teachers said, and Annika nodded.

After breakfast the children gathered in one corner

180

of the room for the register, and then there was singing. Some of the children had already disappeared for Christmas. But the remaining ones sang Christmas carols with great enthusiasm. Then they talked about Christmas, before finishing off with a burst of 'Jingle Bells'.

'I've got to go now,' Annika said. Ellen started to cry and Kalle clung to her arm.

'I want to go with you, Mummy,' Ellen sobbed.

'Daddy's going to pick you up early today, after the afternoon break,' Annika said briskly, trying to extricate herself. 'That'll be fun. Then you can go home and start getting ready for Christmas. Maybe get a Christmas tree, too? You'd like that, wouldn't you?'

'Yeah!' Kalle cried, with Ellen joining in as a small echo.

'See you later!' she said, and quickly shut the door on their little faces. She stood outside for a moment, listening to see if there was any reaction inside. Nothing. With a sigh, she pushed open the door to the stairs.

She took the 56 bus from the Trygg Hansa building and got to the office at half past ten. The newsroom was packed with people chatting and bustling about. For some reason she never got used to that. She always thought that the normal state of the newsroom was when it was a large empty room with just a few people concentrating on shimmering computer screens, with the sound of phones persistently ringing in the background. It was like that at weekends and at night, but right now there had to be ninety people in there. She took a bundle of newspapers and headed towards her office.

'Good work, Annika!' someone called, she couldn't tell who. She waved a hand above her head in thanks.

Eva-Britt Qvist was typing at her computer.

'Nils Langeby has taken the day off,' she said without looking up.

Still cross, then. Annika hung up her coat and went to get a mug of coffee from the machine, then made her way to her pigeon-hole in the postroom. It was full to bursting. She groaned out loud and looked round for a rubbish bin where she could get rid of the coffee. She'd never make it back to her office with all that post and a full mug of coffee.

'Why the groan?' Anders Schyman said behind her, and she smiled awkwardly.

'Oh, all this post just gets to me. We get over a hundred press releases and letters every day. It takes for ever to go through it all.'

'But there's no reason why you should be sitting there opening envelopes,' Schyman said in surprise. 'I thought Eva-Britt did that?'

'No, I started doing it when the last head of crime went to New York, and I suppose I've just carried on doing it.'

'Eva-Britt used to do it before he went to the States. It would make much more sense for her to do it again, unless you want to keep it under your own control? What do you think? Shall I have a word with her?'

Annika smiled and took a sip of coffee.

'If you wouldn't mind, that would be a great help.'

Anders Schyman took the bundle of post and stuffed it in Eva-Britt's pigeon-hole.

'I'll have a word with her at once.'

Back in the newsroom, Annika went over to Ingvar Johansson, who was sitting there with his phone glued to his ear, as usual. He was in the same clothes as yesterday, and the day before that. Annika wondered if he got undressed before going to bed.

'The police are bloody unhappy about your article on

the alarm codes,' he said when he'd hung up.

Annika stiffened, feeling anxiety hit her like a blow to the stomach. Her head was reeling.

'What? Why? Did I get something wrong?'

'No, but you blew their best lead. They say you promised not to write about the alarm codes.'

She felt panic rising in her veins like a bubbling poison.

'But I didn't write about the alarm codes! I didn't even mention the words!'

She threw down her coffee and grabbed a copy of the paper. BOMBER CLOSE TO CHRISTINA – SUSPECT BEING QUESTIONED was the front-page headline. The big headline inside stood out, heavy and black: ALARM CODES HOLD THE KEY.

'What the fuck?' she yelled. 'Who the hell came up with that headline?'

'Calm down, you sound completely hysterical,' Ingvar Johansson said.

She felt her field of vision grow red and hot, as her eyes hit the self-important man slouched in his office chair. Behind his nonchalant façade she could tell how pleased he was.

'Who authorized this?' she said. 'Was it you?'

'I have nothing to do with the headlines inside the paper; surely you know that?' he said. He turned away to carry on working, but she wasn't going to let him get away that easily. She spun his chair round, knocking his legs against the desk.

'Stop behaving like an idiot who likes watching things go wrong for other people,' she said, and it came out like a snarl. 'It doesn't matter if it's me this time, don't you get it? It hurts the paper. It hurts you, Ingvar Johansson, it hurts Anders Schyman, and it hurts your daughter's summer cleaning job. I'm going to find out who wrote that headline, and who authorized it. Don't think I won't. Who was it who called?'

The smug look had vanished, to be replaced by a look of distaste.

'Don't get things out of proportion,' he said. 'It was the police press officer.'

She stood up, surprised. The man had been lying. The police press officer didn't have a clue about anything she might have promised. He was probably just annoyed that the story had got out, and that headline was completely unnecessary. But Ingvar Johansson would never get the satisfaction of seeing her dragged down for breaking a confidence.

She turned on her heel and walked away, not noticing that people were staring at her. Scenes like that were fairly common at the paper, and people seemed to find it interesting to listen in to them. So now they were all wondering what the head of the crime section was so angry about. It was always fun when heads of sections argued. They grabbed for copies of the paper to look at Annika's article on pages six and seven, but couldn't see anything odd, and the spat was quickly forgotten.

But Annika didn't forget. She added Ingvar Johansson's vindictive attack to the pile of crap that was getting bigger by the day. She was worried that the shit would actually reach the fan one day, and then no one in the office would escape without a splattering.

'Do you want your personal mail, or do you want me to deal with that, too?'

Eva-Britt Qvist was standing in the doorway holding a couple of letters.

'What? No, leave them here, thanks . . .'

The secretary came over to Annika's desk on noisy stilettos and threw the letters down.

'There you are. And if you want me to start getting coffee for you, you can tell me to my face instead of running to the editor-in-chief!'

Annika looked up in surprise. The other woman's face was dark with anger. Before Annika had time to reply she had stormed out.

Oh, good grief, Annika thought, this can't be happening! Now she's furious because she thinks I complained about her behind her back just to get her to open the post. God, give me strength!

And the pile of crap got a tiny bit higher.

Evert Danielsson was staring at his bookcase, his head empty of thought, his heart echoing. He had a peculiar feeling that he was hollow. He was holding tight to the top of his desk with both hands. Trying to hold on to it. Trying to attach himself more firmly to it. It wasn't going to work, he was sure of that. It was just a matter of time before the Board published the press release. They weren't going to wait until his new responsibilities were sorted out, they just wanted to make a show of strength, and prove that they could take tough decisions without Christina. If he was honest with himself, he had to admit that he hadn't always handled every aspect of his job well, but with Christina in charge he had had a measure of protection. But she was no longer there to shield him, and there was nothing he could cling on to. He was finished, and he knew it.

He had learned a fair amount over the years, about what happened to people who were no longer wanted, for instance. Often there was no need for any formal decision to move people, they left voluntarily.

There were any number of ways of freezing a person out, and he was familiar with most of them, even if he personally hadn't used them much. Once the decision was taken, by whoever it might be, human resources were informed. The internal reaction was generally positive: people who were forced to leave had usually lost any popularity they may once have had.

Then the rest of the office was told, and if the person in question was even remotely a public figure, the media were set loose. At which point things developed in one of two ways. The media either paraded the expelled individual in tears or wallowed in the tragedy and shrieked, 'Serves you right!' The first category consisted largely of women, as long as they weren't in very senior positions. The second was mainly made up of businessmen with large parachute payments.

He guessed he would be in the second category. One thing in his favour was that he had got the sack, and had been made the scapegoat for the fallout from Christina Furhage's death. There would be ways of spinning that, he knew that much, without actually formulating the thought in his echoing head.

There was a knock at the door and his secretary popped her head in. She looked like she had been crying, and her hair was a mess.

'I've prepared the press release, and Hans Bjällra is here to go through it with you. Can he come in?'

Evert Danielsson looked at his faithful assistant of many years. She was close to sixty and would never get another job. That was what happened when someone left: the people who had worked most closely with them had to go as well. No one wanted to inherit someone else's staff.

It would never work. There'd never be any real loyalty that way.

'Of course, yes. Show him in.'

The head of the committee came in, a towering figure in a dark suit. He was in mourning for Christina, the hypocrite, even though everyone knew he couldn't stand her.

'Let's make this process as quick and as bearable as possible,' he said, sitting down on the sofa without being invited.

Evert Danielsson nodded eagerly.

'Yes, I'm also keen that this should be done in a neat and tidy way . . .'

'I'm glad we agree. The press release will say that you are leaving your post as chair of SOCOG, the Stockholm Organizing Committee of the Olympic Games. The reason is that after Christina Furhage's tragic death you will have other responsibilities. What these are is as yet unclear, but we will be working this out with you. Nothing about dismissal, nothing about scapegoating, nothing about your parachute. The entire Board agrees that that should remain confidential. What do you think?'

Evert Danielsson let the words sink in. This was much better than he had dared hope. It was almost a promotion. His hands let go of the desk.

'Yes, I think that sounds good,' he said.

29

'I want to talk to you about a couple of things,' Annika said to Eva-Britt. 'Can you come into my office for a moment?'

'Why? We can talk here. I've got a lot to do.'

'No, right now,' Annika said, and walked into her office, leaving the door open. She heard Eva-Britt typing demonstratively for a few seconds, then she appeared in the doorway with her arms folded. Annika sat down behind her desk and gestured at the chair opposite her.

'Sit down and close the door.'

Eva-Britt sat down without closing the door. Annika sighed, got up and went over to close the door. She noticed that she was trembling slightly: confrontations were always unpleasant.

'Eva-Britt, what's the matter?'

'What? What do you mean?'

'You seem so . . . angry and sad. Has anything happened?'

Annika was forcing herself to sound calm and gentle, as the woman twisted on her chair.

'I don't know what you mean.'

Annika leaned forward, noting that Eva-Britt had

crossed both her arms and legs in an unconsciously defensive posture.

'You've been a bit off with me over the past week or so. And yesterday we had a proper argument . . .'

'So this is some sort of telling-off because I'm not being nice enough to you?'

Annika felt her anger bubble over.

'No, this is about you not doing what you're supposed to. You didn't arrange the material yesterday in any order of significance, you left no notes, and you went home without telling anyone. I wasn't aware that opening the post was one of your duties, and it was Schyman, not me, who suggested that you start doing it again. You have to learn to work together with us, otherwise this office won't work properly.'

The woman looked at her coldly.

'This office worked perfectly well long before you arrived.'

The conversation was going nowhere. Annika stood up.

'Okay, there's no point in carrying on with this now. I've got a call to make. Are you sure you've been through everything we've got on Christina Furhage? Archive, books, pictures, articles, databases . . . ?'

'Absolutely everything,' Eva-Britt said, and walked out.

Annika was left with the bitter taste of failure in her mouth. She was no good as a boss; she was a hopeless team-leader who couldn't get her staff to follow her lead. She sat down and hit her head against the keyboard. What to do next? Well, she could start with the police press officer. She raised her head, picked up the phone and dialled his direct line.

'You have to see that if you write about pretty much

189

everything we know, then that makes our work that much harder?' the press officer said. 'There are certain things we can't put into the public domain, because they spoil our investigation.'

'So why tell us everything then?' Annika said innocently.

The press officer sighed. 'Well, it's a question of balance. There are some things we have to get out, but they don't necessarily have to make it into the paper.'

'Oh, please!' Annika said, putting her feet up on her desk. 'Who could possibly know what you want to get out, and what you want kept quiet? Surely you don't expect me or my colleagues to work out what's best for your investigation? We'd be guilty of a dereliction of duty if we even tried.'

'Of course, but that wasn't what I meant. This business with the alarm codes – it's a great shame that that got out.'

'Yes, and I'm sorry. You probably noticed that there's no mention of the codes anywhere in the text. The wrong wording just got used in the headline. I really am sorry if it's damaged your work in any way. That's one reason why I think we need to have an even closer dialogue from now on.'

The press officer started to laugh.

'Brilliant, Bengtzon, that's a magnificent way of turning it round. If we got any closer to you, you'd end up in the office next to the chief of police!'

'That's not such a bad idea,' Annika said, smiling. 'What's happening today?'

The policeman grew serious.

'I can't tell you anything at the moment.'

'Come on, there are still seventeen hours to our deadline, nothing will get out until tomorrow morning. There must be something you want to get out?'

'Well, seeing as it's already out, I may as well tell you that we're working on the list of people who had access to the alarm codes. We're pretty sure the killer is on that list.'

'So the alarms at the stadium were active that night?'

'Yes.'

'How many people are on the list?'

'Enough to give us a whole lot of work. I have to take another call—'

'Just one more thing,' Annika said quickly. 'Did Christina Furhage go anywhere by taxi after midnight the night she died?'

She could hear the police press officer breathing down the line, and another phone ringing in the background.

'Why do you ask?' he said.

'Just something I've been told. Is it true?'

'Christina Furhage had her own chauffeur. The chauffeur drove her to the bar for the Christmas party. After that he had the night off, he was actually at the party. Christina Furhage had a business account with Taxi Stockholm, but as far as we are aware, it wasn't used that night.'

'So where did she go after the Christmas party, then?'

The press officer was quiet for a moment, then he said, 'That's the sort of thing that shouldn't get out, both for the sake of the investigation and for Christina Furhage herself.'

They hung up and Annika felt more confused than ever. There were several things that didn't make sense. First the alarm codes. If there really were so many people who had access to them, then why was it such a big deal if the information got out? And what sort of murky secret was lurking behind perfect Christina Furhage's private life? Why was Helena Starke lying? She phoned her source, but got no answer. If anyone had a right to be angry with her, it was him.

She called reception and asked if Berit or Patrik had said when they would be coming in today. Two o'clock, they had both said as they left last night.

She put her feet up on the desk and started to go through the bundle of newspapers. One of the morning papers had uncovered an interesting passage in the legal protocols regulating the franchise agreement between SOCOG – the Stockholm Olympic Committee – and the IOC, the International Olympic Committee. There had been a mass of legal agreements between SOCOG and the IOC, not only governing the right to hold the Games themselves, but also things like the definition of international, national and local sponsorship. The morning paper had dug out a clause that gave the main sponsor the right to pull out of the Games if the Victoria Stadium wasn't ready for use by 1 January of the year the Games were to be held. Annika didn't bother to read the whole article. If she remembered rightly, there were several thousand different clauses, and in her opinion their contents were fairly uninteresting as long as none of the parties decided to invoke them. And the author of the article hadn't managed to get any comment from the main sponsors. End of story.

The other evening paper had spoken to a lot of people who worked with Christina, including the chauffeur, but not Helena Starke. The chauffeur told the paper that he had driven Christina to the bar, that she had been her usual cheerful self, not at all anxious or worried, just focused, as usual. He missed her hugely, because she had been a wonderful boss and a really friendly person.

'Soon she'll have wings,' Annika muttered.

But mostly the papers had nothing new. It took ages to go through them, they were all padded with loads of adverts. November and December were the most important months financially for the Swedish press, with January and July the worst.

She went out to the women's toilet to get rid of the coffee and wash the print from her fingers. She encountered her own reflection in the mirror, and it wasn't a pretty sight. She hadn't bothered to wash her hair that morning, just tied it up with a clip. Now it was hanging greasily over her scalp in brown clumps. There were dark rings under her eyes and a red blush from stress on her cheeks. She searched her pockets for some foundation to hide the worst of it, but couldn't find any.

Eva-Britt Qvist had gone to lunch, and her computer was switched off. Eva-Britt logged off whenever she left her desk; she was terrified that someone might send false emails from her account. Annika went into her office and smeared some face-cream over the blotches, then went out into the newsroom again. What was it she needed to know? What was she going to check next? She went out into the corridor where they kept their reference library, and idly looked up the Olympics boss in the *Dictionary of National Biography*: Christina Furhage, née Faltin, only child of a poor but respectable family, partly raised by relatives in upper Norrland, career in banking, the driving force behind Stockholm's Olympic bid, managing director of SOCOG. Married to businessman Bertil Milander. Nothing more than that.

Annika looked up. The fact that Christina had been born Faltin was news to her. So where did the name Furhage come from?

She read the entry that followed: Carl Furhage, born in the late nineteenth century into a family of foresters in Härnösand, and a manager within the forestry industry. Third marriage to Dorotea Adelcrona. Left his mark on the world and guaranteed his place in the dictionary by establishing a foundation for young men who wanted to study forestry. Died in the 1960s.

Annika closed the book with a snap. She hurried over to the nearest computer terminal and typed in Carl Furhage. Seven hits. So he had been written about seven times since the archive was computerized in the early 1990s. Annika clicked up the results and let out a whistle. The foundation was pretty wealthy: a quarter of a million kronor was handed out each year. But there was nothing else about Carl Furhage.

She logged off the system, collected her pass-card, and went out of the fire-door behind the sports desk. A steep staircase led her down two floors, and she passed through another door that required both pass-card and code. She emerged into a long corridor with a worn, grey linoleum floor and buzzing fluorescent lights in the ceiling. At the end of the corridor lay the paper's text and picture archive, protected behind double fire-doors. She went in, saying hello to the staff hunched over their computers. The grey filing cabinets containing the archive of everything published in the *Evening Post* and its sister morning paper since the 1800s filled the whole of the vast room. She wandered slowly through the aisles. She reached the archive for individuals, and read A–Ac, Ad–Af, Ag–Ak. She skipped a few rows until she reached Fu. She pulled open a large drawer with unexpected ease. She soon found Furhage, Christina, but there was nothing for Furhage, Carl. She sighed. A dead end.

'If you're after cuttings about Christina Furhage, they're already booked out,' a voice said behind her.

It was the archivist, a severely competent little man with very definite opinions about what should be archived, and under what search words.

194

Annika smiled.

'No, I'm actually looking for another Furhage, a Director Carl Furhage.'

'Have we written anything about him?'

'Well, he set up a wealthy foundation. He must have been as rich as Croesus.'

'Dead?'

'Yes, he died in the sixties.'

'Then he may no longer be archived under his own name. The cuttings will still be here, of course, but they might be sorted under another category. Do you have any idea what we could look under?'

'No idea. Scholarships, maybe?'

The archivist looked thoughtful.

'There'll be a lot there. Do you need it today?'

Annika sighed and made to leave.

'No, not really. It was just a thought. Thanks anyway—'

'Hang on – is there a chance we might have printed his picture?'

Annika stopped.

'Maybe, I suppose so, at some awards ceremony or other. Why do you ask?'

'Because he'll be in the picture archive in that case.'

Annika went over to the far side of the room, past the sport archive and reference section. She found the right drawer and leafed through until she reached Furhage. Christina's file filled almost the whole drawer, but right at the back was a small brown envelope. It was fairly tatty, but the faded text on the front read: *Furhage, Carl. Director.* Annika got covered in dust as she pulled it out. She sat on the floor and tipped out the contents. There were four pictures. Two small black-and-white portraits of a stern-looking man with receding hair and a heavy jaw, Carl Furhage at fifty, and Carl Furhage at seventy. The third picture was a wedding photograph of the ageing director and an elderly woman, Dorotea Adelcrona.

The fourth picture was the biggest. It had landed upside down, and as Annika turned it over she felt her heart skip a beat. The caption was taped to the bottom of the picture: *Director Carl Furhage, 60 years old today, with his wife Christina and son Olof.* Annika read the words twice before she believed her own eyes. It was definitely Christina Furhage, an incredibly young Christina. She couldn't be more than twenty. She was very thin, and her hair was cut in an unflattering old-lady style. She was wearing a dark outfit, the skirt reaching her calves. She was looking shyly into the camera and trying to smile. In her lap sat an enchanting fair-haired boy, about two years old. He was wearing a white top with shorts and braces, and was holding an apple in his hands. The director himself was standing behind the sofa, looking authoritative and with a protective hand on his young wife's shoulder.

The whole picture was extremely rigid and arranged, and looked much older than the 1950s, which was the earliest it could have been. She hadn't read anything about Christina having been married to Furhage, still less about her having a young son. So she had two children!

Annika lowered the picture to her knees. She didn't know how or why, but this fact suddenly felt very important, she just knew it. A child didn't just disappear. This child was out there somewhere, and would surely have one or two things to say about his mother Christina.

She put the pictures back in the envelope, got up and went over to the archivist.

'I'd like to take this up with me,' she said.

196

'Okay, just sign it out,' he said, without looking up.

Annika scribbled her signature and went back through the corridor and up to her office. She had a feeling it was going to be a long afternoon.

30

The press release about Evert Danielsson's departure was sent to the news agencies at 11.30. Then it was faxed to all the other news organizations by the Olympic office's press department – first to the morning papers and television, then radio, the evening papers and the larger local papers, in a gradually diminishing order of importance. Danielsson hadn't been a prominent figure within the Olympics, so editors up and down the country didn't exactly throw themselves at the news. Roughly forty minutes after the press release reached the main news agency in Kungsholmstorg, a short telegram was sent out, saying that the chair of the Olympic committee was moving from his current responsibilities to work instead with the direct consequences of Christina Furhage's death.

Evert Danielsson sat in his room as the fax machines whirred. He had the use of the office until his new responsibilities had been worked out. Anxiety was thumping just below his temples. He couldn't concentrate long enough to read a whole sentence in a report or paper. He was waiting for the wolves to attack, for the hunt to begin. He would be fair game now, and the mob would soon pick up his scent. But to his surprise his phone hadn't yet rung.

To some extent he had convinced himself that it would be the same as after Christina's death; that all the telephones in the office would start ringing at once, and would go on ringing. But they didn't. An hour after the press release had gone out one of the morning papers got in touch for a comment. He was surprised that his voice sounded quite normal as he said that he preferred to see this as promotion, and that someone had to sort out the chaos caused by Christina Furhage's death. And the journalist seemed to be satisfied with that. His secretary came in and wept for a few minutes, then asked if there was anything she could get for him. Coffee? Some cake? A salad, perhaps? He thanked her, but said no, he couldn't eat anything. His fingers gripped the edge of his desk as he waited for the next call.

Annika was on her way down to the canteen to get something to eat when Ingvar Johansson approached, holding a sheet of paper.

'Isn't this one of your boys?' he said, holding out a press release from the Olympic office to her. She took it and read the start.

'Well, *my boys* is pushing it a bit,' she said. 'I've spoken to him on the phone. Why, do you think we should do something with this?'

'I don't know. I just thought you might like to know.'

Annika folded the sheet of paper.

'Thanks. Is anything else going on?'

'Not in your area,' he said, and walked away.

Bastard, Annika thought, as she made her way to the canteen instead. She didn't feel particularly hungry. She bought a pasta salad and a bottle of Christmas cola and took them back to her room, where she ate the salad in four minutes flat. Then she went back to the cafeteria and bought three more bottles of Christmas cola. She was on her second bottle by the time she dialled the Olympic office and asked to speak to Evert Danielsson. He sounded strangely distant. He said he preferred to think of this change of role as a promotion.

'What are you going to be doing?' Annika asked.

'The details aren't quite sorted out yet,' Evert Danielsson replied.

'So how can you regard it as a promotion?'

The man on the other end was silent.

'Er, well, I certainly don't think of it as being dismissed.'

'So have you been?' Annika said.

Evert Danielsson thought for a moment.

'That depends on how you look at it,' he said.

'I see. So did you resign?'

'No, I didn't.'

'So who decided about the change of job? The Board?'

'Well, they need someone to sort out the muddle after—'

'But surely you could have done that in your role as head of the committee?'

'Well, that's true.'

'By the way, did you know that Christina Furhage has a son?'

'A son?' he said, confused. 'No, she's got a daughter, Lena.'

'No, she's got a son as well. Do you know where he is?'

'Haven't the faintest idea. A son? I've never heard of him.'

Annika thought for a moment.

'Okay,' she said. 'Do you know which Olympic official had an affair that led to a woman being dismissed from the office seven years ago?'

Evert Danielsson felt his jaw drop.

'How do you know about that?' he said when he had composed himself.

'A note in the paper. Do you know who it was?'

'Yes, I do. Why?'

'What happened?'

He thought for a moment, then said, 'What exactly do you want?'

'I don't know,' Annika said, and Evert Danielsson believed her. 'I just want to know how it all hangs together.'

To say that Annika was surprised when Evert Danielsson invited her up to the office for a chat would be an understatement.

31

Berit and Patrik still hadn't shown up in the office by the time Annika set off for Hammarby Harbour.

'I'll have my mobile,' she said to Ingvar Johansson, who nodded in acknowledgement.

She took a taxi and paid by card. The weather was still atrocious. All the snow had vanished in the rain, leaving the ground heavy and muddy. South Hammarby Harbour was a desolate part of town now, with its empty and half-built Olympic village, dull Olympic offices and now the ruined stadium. There was mud everywhere, because the beds planted up the previous summer hadn't had time to anchor the soil yet. She jumped across the worst of the puddles, but still got mud all over her trousers.

The SOCOG reception was spacious, but the offices within seemed surprisingly small and basic. Annika compared them with the only other official building she knew well: the Association of Local Councils where Thomas worked. Those offices were both more attractive and better suited to their purpose. The Olympic offices were fairly spartan: white walls, plastic flooring, fluorescent lighting, plain white bookcases, desks that looked like they came from IKEA.

Evert Danielsson's office was halfway along a long

corridor. His room wasn't much bigger than the secretaries', which struck Annika as a bit unusual. A tired sofa, desk, and bookcase, that was all. She thought chairmen had mahogany furniture and lovely views.

'So what makes you think Christina had a son?' Evert Danielsson said, gesturing to the sofa.

'Thanks,' Annika said, sitting down. 'I've got a picture of him.'

She took off her coat but decided against taking out her notepad and pen. Instead, she studied the man before her. He had sat down behind his desk, gripping onto the desk with one hand. It looked a bit odd. He was about fifty, with thick, steel-grey hair and a friendly face. But his eyes were tired, and his mouth looked sad.

'I have to say that I'm fairly sceptical about this,' he said.

Annika pulled a photocopy of the Furhage family portrait from her bag. She had returned the original to the archive, no one was allowed to take archive pictures out of the building, but it was easy enough to scan and copy them these days. She passed the picture to Evert Danielsson, who looked at it with growing surprise.

'Well, I never,' he said. 'I had no idea.'

'About what? Husband or child?'

'Both of them, actually. Christina never really spoke about her personal life.'

Annika waited in silence, hoping he would go on. She didn't really understand why he'd asked her to come out here. He shuffled in his chair, then said, 'You were asking about the secretary who lost her job.'

'Yes, I found a short piece about it in the archive. But there was no indication that she was a secretary, or that she had been dismissed, just that she worked here, then had to leave.'

Evert Danielsson nodded.

'That was the way Christina wanted it. To keep up appearances. But Sara was an excellent secretary, and would undoubtedly have been allowed to stay if . . .' He fell silent.

'There's a rule forbidding romantic relationships between any two people working within the Olympic organization,' he continued. 'Christina was very strict about that. She said it got in the way of work, made people lose their focus, led to a loss of loyalty, and caused other colleagues extra stress and forced them to make allowances.'

'Who was the man?' Annika asked.

Evert Danielsson hesitated.

'Me.'

Annika raised her eyebrows.

'Who set the rule?'

'Christina. It was applied without discrimination.'

'And still is?'

Evert Danielsson let go of the desk.

'I don't actually know. But as far as I'm concerned, it doesn't really matter.'

He covered his face with his hands, and a sob racked his body. Annika waited in silence for a moment as he composed himself.

'I really loved Sara, but I was married at the time,' he said eventually, and dropped one hand to his lap, as the other took hold of the desk again. His eyes were dry but red.

'You're no longer married?'

He laughed. 'No. Someone told my wife about Sara, and Sara kept her distance once she realized I couldn't arrange for her to keep her job. So there I was – no wife, no children, and without the love of my life.'

He fell silent for a moment, then went on, almost to himself: 'Sometimes I wonder if she seduced me because

204

she thought I could help her career. Certainly, when the opposite happened she dumped me at once.' He laughed again: a short, bitter laugh.

'Then maybe she wasn't much of a loss after all,' Annika said.

He looked up.

'No, you're right there. But what are you going to do with this? Are you going to write about it?'

'Not now, at least,' Annika said. 'Maybe never. Would it matter to you if I did?'

'Well, I don't know, do I? It depends what you write. What exactly are you after?'

'Why did you ask me to come out here?'

He sighed. 'A day like this stirs up a lot of things, a lot of thoughts and feelings, it all feels very muddled. I've worked here since the start, there's a lot I could tell you . . .'

Annika waited. The man was staring at the floor, lost in his own silence.

'Was Christina a good boss?' Annika said eventually.

'She was the reason I got this job,' Evert Danielsson said, letting go of the desk. 'And now she's not here, and I'm on my way out. Well, I think I shall go home now.'

He stood up, and Annika followed his lead.

She pulled her coat on again, hoisted her bag onto her shoulder, then shook his hand and thanked him for seeing her.

'Just out of interest, where was Christina's office?'

'Didn't you see it? Just by the entrance, I'll show you on the way out.'

He pulled on a coat, wrapped a scarf round his neck, picked up his briefcase and gazed thoughtfully at his desk.

'Well, I don't have to take a single document home with me today.'

He turned off the light and left the room with his empty briefcase, locking the door carefully behind him. He put his head into the office next door and said, 'I'm going now. If anyone calls, refer them to the press release.'

They walked together down the white corridor.

'Christina had several offices,' he said. 'This was her day-to-day office, you could say. She had two secretaries here.'

'And Helena Starke?' Annika said.

'Christina's Rottweiler? Her office was next to Christina's,' Evert Danielsson said, turning a corner. 'Here it is.'

The door was locked. The man sighed.

'I haven't got the key,' he said. 'Well, it's nothing special, a corner room with windows facing both ways, a large desk, two computers, a corner sofa and coffee table . . .'

'I would have expected something a bit more flash,' Annika said, recalling an old picture of a magnificent office in a palace somewhere, with an English desk, dark wood panelling and crystal chandeliers.

'Well, this was where she did the nuts-and-bolts stuff. She had a smarter office for receiving people in the centre of the city, just behind Rosenbad. She had a third secretary there, and that was where she conducted all her meetings and negotiations, dealt with the press and all manner of guests . . . Can I give you a lift anywhere?'

'No thanks, I thought I might visit a friend over in the old Luma Building,' Annika said.

'You can't walk there through this quagmire,' Evert Danielsson said. 'I'll give you a lift.'

He had a brand-new company Volvo – of course: Volvo were one of the big sponsors. He unlocked it with the remote key, and stroked the roof as he opened the door. Annika got in the passenger seat, did up the seatbelt, and asked, 'Who do you think blew her up?'

Evert Danielsson started the car, testing the throttle a couple of times before putting it in reverse and slowly pulling out.

'Well,' he said, 'one thing's for sure: there's no shortage of people with a motive.'

Annika started.

'What do you mean by that?'

He didn't answer, just drove the half kilometre to the old light-bulb factory in silence. He stopped by the main gates.

'I'd like to know if you do ever write anything about me,' he said.

Annika gave him her card and told him to call if he wanted to talk. She thanked him for the lift and got out.

'One thing's for sure,' she said to herself as the Volvo's rear lights disappeared into the rain, 'this story's getting more and more muddled.'

32

She went up to the television company where Anne
Snapphane worked. Anne was still working in the editing
suite, and seemed almost relieved at the interruption.

'I'm almost done,' she said. 'Do you want some mulled
wine?'

'Only if it's alcohol-free,' Annika said. 'I need to make
some calls.'

'Use my desk. I've just got to . . .'

Annika went over to Anne's chair and tossed her coat
on the desk. She started by phoning Berit.

'I've spoken to the chauffeur,' Berit said. 'The competition got to him yesterday, but he had a few new
things to say. He confirms, for instance, that Christina
had her laptop with her, because she left it at the office
and they had to go back for it. He hadn't been working
for Christina very long, just two months. Looks like her
drivers changed pretty regularly.'

'Really?'

She heard Berit leaf through her notepad.

'He also said she was very worried about being
followed. She never let him take her home the most
direct route from the office. He also had to check her car
thoroughly every day. Christina was scared of bombs.'

'Wow!'

'And . . . what else? . . . Yes, he had specific orders never to let the daughter, Lena something, go anywhere near the car. Weird or what?'

Annika sighed.

'Our Christina seems to have developed serious paranoia. But it'll be a great article: Christina was scared of being blown up. We'll have to leave out that bit about the daughter, of course.'

'Of course. I'm trying to get a comment from the police now.'

'What's Patrik doing?'

'He's not here yet, he was here most of the night. Where are you?'

'With Anne Snapphane. I've just been having a little talk with Evert Danielsson. He's been pushed out in the cold.'

'What, fired?'

'Not quite, but he didn't seem too sure. There's hardly anything I can use, but who cares? He doesn't want to spill his story, and he doesn't want to go on the attack.'

'So what did he say?'

'Not much. He was the one who had the affair in the office, so that was what we talked about most. And he gave the impression that Christina had a lot of enemies.'

'Oh, so it's all coming out now, is it?' Berit said. 'What else are we doing?'

'Christina was married before and had a son. I was thinking of digging away at that for a while.'

'A son? But I wrote her entire life story last night, and there was no son there.'

'She kept him well hidden. I wonder if there are any more secrets in that closet . . .'

They hung up and Annika pulled out her pad. On the back she had scribbled the number she took from

Helena Starke's telephone. She recognized the first three numbers, 702, as belonging to the old Ringvägen exchange, and hoped that was still the case.

Helena Starke had slept badly, waking several times from terrible nightmares. When she finally got up and looked out of the window, she almost went back to bed again.

It was raining, pissy grey bloody rain that killed any trace of colour on the streets outside. The stink from the cupboard was almost unbearable now. She pulled on a pair of jeans and went down to the communal laundry to book a time. No gaps until after New Year, naturally. So she quickly emptied one of the machines of its wet load and rushed to get the rug. She jammed it into the machine, added loads of washing powder, and hurried away. Then she showered to get the smell of vomit out of her hair, and, finally, scrubbed the wardrobe and hall floor.

She wondered about going to get the rug, but thought better of it. It would be wiser to leave it until evening, and let the old women work off their rage at her anti-social behaviour first.

She went into the kitchen for a cigarette. Christina didn't like the fact that she smoked, but that no longer mattered. Nothing mattered any more.

She stood in the darkness beside the kitchen table, and had just taken the second drag from the cigarette when the telephone on the window sill rang.

It was the woman from last night, the one from the *Evening Post*.

'I'm not sure I want to talk to you,' Helena Starke said.

'Well, you don't have to, of course . . . Are you smoking?'

'Yes, I'm smoking; but why the hell is that any of your business?'

'It's not. Why did they call you Christina's Rottweiler?'

The woman was taken aback.

'What the hell do you want from me?'

'Well, nothing really. It's Christina I'm interested in. Why didn't she want anyone to know she had a son? Was she ashamed of him?'

Helena Starke's head started to spin. She sat down and put out the cigarette. How did this woman know about Christina's son?

'He died,' she said. 'The boy died.'

'Died? When?'

'When he was . . . five, I think?'

'Oh dear, that's terrible. Five years old, the same as Kalle.'

'Who?'

'My son, he's five. That's just awful. What did he die of?'

'Malignant melanoma, skin cancer. Christina never got over it. She didn't like to talk about him.'

'Sorry, I . . . sorry. I didn't know . . .'

'Was there anything else?' Helena Starke said, trying to sound as cold as possible.

'Well, yes, there is actually. Have you got a minute?'

'No, I've got a time booked for the laundry.'

'The laundry?'

'What's so strange about that?'

'Nothing, I just . . . I mean, you knew Christina so well, you were so close to her, I didn't think you'd be doing anything like that so soon after—'

'Yes, I knew her well!' Helena Starke yelled, as the tears started to fall. 'I knew her better than anyone!'

'Apart from her family, I suppose.'

'Ha! The bloody family! That senile old man and the idiot daughter. Did you know she's a pyromaniac? Yep, completely fucking mad; spent her teens locked away in a psychiatric hospital. Set fire to anything she could. The children's home in Botkyrka that burned down six years ago, you remember that one? That was her; that was Lena. Talk about crazy – she couldn't even be left at home on her own.'

She was sobbing straight into the receiver, loud and uncontrollably, she was aware of how awful she must sound, like some animal caught in a trap. She put the phone down and let her arms fall to the kitchen table, her head landing among the crumbs on the tabletop, and she cried and cried and cried until it was completely black outside and there was nothing left inside her.

33

Annika could hardly believe her ears. She sat for a long time, the phone a little way from her ear, listening to the silence that followed Helena Starke's unbearable wailing.

'What is it? Why are you sitting like that?' Anne Snapphane said, putting a coffee-cup full of mulled wine and a couple of biscuits in front of Annika.

'Wow,' Annika said, gently putting the receiver down.

Anne Snapphane stopped chewing.

'You look really shaken. What's happened?'

'I've just been talking to a woman who knew Christina Furhage. It got a bit messy.'

'Oh, why?'

'She started howling, really howling. It always feels terrible when you push too hard.'

Anne Snapphane nodded sympathetically, and gestured towards the wine and biscuits.

'Come over to the editing suite with me and I'll show you the start of our New Year's Eve programme. It's called *Things We Remember – and Things They'd Rather Forget*. All about celebrity scandals.'

Annika left her coat on the desk but hoisted her bag onto her shoulder and set off after Anne, balancing the biscuits on the cup. The office was fairly empty, the Christmas programming was all done and the next round of production wasn't due to start until after the holiday.

'Do you know what you've got for next season?' Annika asked as they went down the spiral stairs to the technical department.

Anne Snapphane made a face. 'What do you think? I just hope I don't have to do *Sofa Talk* again. I've been round the block with that one so many times now. He cheated on me with my best friend, my best friend seduced my son, my son slept with my dog . . . Fucking hell!'

'So what would you rather do?'

'Anything. I might be going to Malaysia to report for a new project we've got coming up next spring. Two teams living on a desert island, trying to stay as long as possible before getting voted off. Good, eh?'

'Sounds boring as hell,' Annika said.

Anne Snapphane looked at her sympathetically as they turned into another corridor.

'It's a good job you're not in charge. I reckon it's got a good chance of getting a big audience if there's enough fighting. Here we are.'

They went into a room full of television monitors, recording equipment, control panels and cables. The room was much bigger than the little cupboards used for editing on the television news that Annika had been in. They even had a sofa, two armchairs and a coffee table in one corner. An editor was sitting on an office chair in front of the biggest control desk, a young man who was piecing together the programme, staring at a television screen as images flickered past. Annika said hello and sat down in one of the armchairs.

'Run the clip,' Anne said, lying back in the sofa.

The man reached over and flicked a switch. An image appeared on the largest monitor, a clock counting down. Then the New Year's Eve programme began, and the famous presenter walked onto the set to thunderous applause from the audience. He outlined the highlights of the programme: a politician throwing up in a fashionable restaurant, the most famous divorces of the year, various mistakes on live television, and other equally vital clips.

'Okay, turn the sound down,' Anne said. 'What do you think? Good, isn't it?'

Annika nodded and took a sip from the mug. The mulled wine was pretty strong.

'Do you know a Helena Starke?'

Anne put her biscuit down and thought for a moment.

'Starke . . . the name sounds very familiar. Who is she?'

'Works at Olympic headquarters with Christina Furhage. Lives on Södermalm, around forty, short dark hair . . .'

'Helena Starke. Yes, now I know! She's that macho-lesbian activist.'

Annika looked sceptically at her friend.

'What do you mean, macho-lesbian?'

'She's active in the campaign for gay rights, writes articles, and so on. Doesn't like the cutesy image lesbians have; often writes dismissively about vanilla sex, and so on.'

'How do you know that?'

Now it was Anne Snapphane's turn to look sceptical.

'Come on, what do you think I spend my days doing? There isn't a single freak in this country whose phone number I haven't got. How do you think we put our programmes together?'

Annika raised her eyebrows apologetically and drank the last of the wine.

'Did you get Starke on the *Sofa*?'

'Nope, we never got her to come on. But come to think of it, we did try several times. She was happy to stand up for her sexuality, she said, but she had no intention of being exploited.'

'Wise woman,' Annika said.

Anne Snapphane sighed. 'It's a good job that not everyone thinks like her; otherwise we'd have no *Sofa Talk*. More mulled wine?'

'No, I've got to get back to the snake-pit. They'll all be wondering where their rabbit has got to.'

Anders Schyman had been having an interesting afternoon. He had had a meeting with two men from the marketing department, the sales analyst and a number cruncher. Two economists whose task it was to stick their noses into everything that really shouldn't concern them. They had both attacked his focus on responsible, investigative, socially engaged journalism. The analyst had come armed with graphs showing the sales percentages of the three biggest evening papers, showing the differences day by day.

'Here, for instance, our main competitor sold exactly 43,512 more copies than the *Evening Post*,' he said, pointing at a date in early December. 'That day we ran the sort of front-page headline that doesn't stand a chance in a competitive market.'

The number cruncher joined in.

'The focus on serious stories at the start of December really didn't work. Our like-for-like sales haven't increased much on last year. And you used money that was earmarked for other posts.'

Anders Schyman had been playing with a pen as the

economists talked, and once they had finished he said thoughtfully, 'Well, there's a lot in what you say, of course. As far as that particular date is concerned, the headline probably wasn't that successful, but we have to ask ourselves: what was the alternative? The revelations that defence spending was over budget wasn't likely to be a big draw, but it was our own story and we got a lot of credit for it in other media. And our main competition was running a special supplement about cheap Christmas presents, and had a television celebrity talking about her eating disorder. So it's difficult to draw conclusions from one individual day's sales.'

The editor-in-chief stood up and walked over to the window that overlooked the Russian Embassy. It really was very grey out there.

'Last year the beginning of December was extremely dramatic, if you recall,' he went on. 'A passenger plane crashed on landing at Bromma, one of our top footballers was caught drink-driving and thrown out of his club, and a TV star was found guilty of rape. We put on a lot of extra sales last December. So the fact that we exceeded those sales at all this year is hardly a failure, but the very opposite. In spite of serious, investigative effort on our own stories, we've met and surpassed last year's results. The fact that we lost out against the competition on one particular day doesn't mean that our investigation into the uses and abuses of power is wrong. I think it's far too early to draw that conclusion.'

'Our finances are based on sales of the paper on many individual days,' the number cruncher said drily.

'Superficially, yes, but not in the long term.' Anders Schyman turned to face the two men again. 'What we're in the process of doing at the moment is building up our credibility capital. We've ignored that for far too long. Of course we can sell the paper with busty blondes and car crashes, but we have to continue to focus on long-term quality.'

'Well,' the number cruncher said, 'we have to deal with the available resources.'

'But there are different ways of using them. As far as the budget is concerned, within certain fixed parameters the board has given me the authority to allocate funds as I see fit.'

'That's an issue that would probably be worth putting on the agenda again,' the number cruncher said.

'I think it's a shame that we have to have this discussion yet again. I don't find it very illuminating.'

'You should,' the other man said, waving his folders. 'Our calculations contain the formula for a really successful evening paper.'

Anders Schyman went over to him, put his hand on the armrest and leaned over him. 'No, my friend,' he said, 'I can promise you that they don't. Why do you think I'm here? Why don't we put a big calculator in this room and save on my salary, if it's just a matter of balancing plus and minus? You can't produce an evening paper by looking at sales figures; it has to come from the heart. Instead of the sort of ill-thought-out editorial criticism that you've just presented, I'd much rather you concentrated on purely marketing issues. Where do we sell best? How come? Can we improve our distribution? Should we change our print times? Can we save time if we print in different locations via satellite? You know, all that.'

'All that has already been worked out,' the number cruncher said flatly.

'So do it again, better,' Schyman said.

He had let out a sigh when the door closed behind the two men. Maybe that sort of discussion was worthwhile after all. It wouldn't have happened ten years ago. In those days the bulkheads between the marketing department and the newsroom were watertight.

The crisis a couple of years ago had torn down all those barriers, and he saw it as one of his many tasks to try to rebuild some sort of wall between Numbers and Letters. The marketing team must never get the idea that they could dictate editorial content, but their skills were vital to his chances of success, he was in no doubt about that.

He knew perfectly well that the sales figures for individual days were extremely important; he spent hours each week with the sales analyst. But that didn't mean that the number cruncher should try to teach him his job.

Any analysis of sales of an evening paper is a highly sensitive mechanism based upon an almost infinite number of factors. Every morning, at around four o'clock, an analyst arrived at the paper to present the sales figures from the thousands of outlets around the country. Variables such as seasons, weekends, holidays, were already programmed into the computer.

If it was raining, you shifted distribution from seaside resorts to IKEA stores.

People did most of their shopping on Thursdays, and often bought papers out of habit. So, more papers to supermarkets on Thursdays. And if it was Christmas and a lot of people were travelling round the country, you shifted distribution to the motorways.

A large occurrence in a small place usually generated local billboards, and they lifted sales considerably. The analysts had to take factors like this into consideration, and not just add ten per cent to sales without understanding why. In a small kiosk that usually only sold ten copies, that only meant one extra copy. But local factors could lift sales by four hundred per cent.

The last factor that the sales analyst should be looking at was the strap-line itself. That was of fairly limited importance, unless the King had got married or a plane had crashed.

There were other variables apart from the basic sales analysis. If something big happened in Norrland, the analyst could quickly arrange for an extra flight to take papers up there.

There was naturally a financial balance to be struck: the cost of the extra flight against the value of the extra sales. But you also had to take into account how much a disappointed customer buying the competition was worth. In cases like that, the extra flight often won.

Anders Schyman sat down at his computer and logged on to the main news agency. He scanned all the bulletins from the past twenty-four hours. There were a couple of hundred, covering sport, domestic and international news. Together they constituted the bedrock on which pretty much every paper in Sweden was built. A lot of papers selected their domestic and international stories from this agency. This was the source of a lot of the information that reached their readers.

Anders Schyman reflected on the number cruncher's last presentation. He had described the standardized average reader of the *Evening Post*: a man in his fifties, wears a cap, had been buying the paper since his twenties.

All the evening papers have their own loyal readers, the ones who would go through hell and high water for their paper. They were known as the 'elephant hides', and, as far as Anders Schyman could see, they were a dying breed for the *Evening Post*.

The next category of readers was the 'faithful readers', those who bought the paper several times a week. If these faithful readers bought the paper one day less a week, it would have disastrous consequences for the future. And that was what had happened a couple of years ago. So the hunt was on for new target groups, and Anders Schyman was sure they were succeeding, but the new groups hadn't overtaken man-in-cap yet. It was just a matter of time, but he needed people in charge who could see things in different ways. There was no way they could continue to run the paper just with men over forty-five. Anders Schyman was utterly convinced of this, and he was quite sure what he needed to do to bring it about.

34

Annika was a little befuddled from the mulled wine when she got back to the office, and it wasn't a nice feeling. She concentrated on walking straight and purposefully, not talking to anyone on the way to her room. Eva-Britt's chair was empty. She had gone home already, even though she was supposed to stay until five.

Annika tossed her outdoor clothes on the sofa and fetched two mugs of coffee. Why on earth had she drunk that wretched wine?

She started by phoning her source, but the line was engaged. She hung up and started to type up what she had found out about Christina's children, the son dying and the daughter being a pyromaniac. She emptied the first mug and started on the second as she did a computer search of the archive. True enough, a children's home in Botkyrka had burned down six years ago. A fourteen-year-old girl was responsible, no one had been injured, but the building had been completely destroyed. So Helena Starke's outburst checked out so far.

She tried phoning her source again. This time the phone rang.

'I know you've every right to be annoyed about the alarm codes,' was the first thing she said when he answered.

The man on the other end sighed. 'What do you mean, annoyed? Annoyed? Huh? You ruined our best line of inquiry, but why on earth would I be annoyed? No, I'm pissed off, mostly with myself for telling you.'

Annika shut her eyes, feeling her heart sink. There was no point making excuses about editors adding headlines they shouldn't. No, attack was the only option here.

'Oh, please!' Annika said, as critically as she could. 'Who told who anything? I had the whole story and held on to it for twenty-four hours, for your sake. I think this is bloody unfair.'

'Unfair? This is a murder inquiry, for fuck's sake! Do you think that's fair?'

'Well, I pray to God that it is,' Annika said wryly.

The man sighed again. 'Okay, get the excuses out of the way and we can move on.'

Annika took a deep breath.

'I'm really sorry the headline mentioned alarm codes. You might have noticed that those words didn't appear anywhere in the actual article. The editor added the headline sometime early in the morning, he was just trying to make it look as good as possible.'

'These editors,' the policeman said. 'They seem to creep out at night like the shoemaker's elves. Okay, what do you want?'

Annika smiled.

'Have you spoken to Christina's daughter, Lena Milander?'

'About what?'

'About what she was doing on Friday night?'

'Why are you wondering about that?'

'I found out about her pyromania.'

'Pyrophilia,' he corrected. 'Pyromania is a very unusual condition. A pyromaniac has to fulfil at least five

223

special criteria, which basically show that the individual has an unhealthy fascination with and response to fires and anything connected to fires: firemen, extinguishers, and so on . . .'

'Okay, pyrophilia, then. Well?'

'We've checked her out, yes.'

'And?'

'I can't say more than that.'

Annika fell silent. She was wondering if she should say anything about the son, but decided against it. A dead five-year-old was nothing to do with this.

'So what's happened with the alarm codes?'

'Am I safe to talk about those, then?'

'Stop it,' Annika said.

'We're still looking into that,' the man said simply.

'Any suspect yet?'

'No, not so far.'

'Any lines of inquiry?'

'Of course there are! What the hell do you think we do up here?'

'Okay.' Annika looked down at her notes. 'So is it safe to say that you're still working on the alarm codes – that's okay now, seeing as the information's out there? – and that you've questioned a number of people but don't yet have a definite suspect, and that you're following various lines of inquiry?'

'That sounds about right,' her source said.

Annika hung up, the bitter taste of disappointment in her mouth. The idiot who came up with the headline about the alarm codes had ruined several years of hard work for her. The trust was gone, so the *Evening Post* would no longer get information first. What she had just got was nothing, nada, *rien*, the usual bullshit. She would have to rely on her colleagues and their contacts.

At that moment Berit and Patrik both appeared in the doorway.

'Are you busy?'

'No, come in. Sit down. Chuck my clothes on the floor – they're already filthy.'

'Where have you been?' Berit said, hanging Annika's dirty coat up on a hook.

'Playing in the mud outside Olympic headquarters. Hope you've had a better day than I have,' she said morosely.

She gave a quick summary of the conversation with her source.

'It's one of the pitfalls of the job,' Berit said. 'Things like that happen.'

Annika sighed. 'Okay, what have we got? What are you working on, Berit?'

'Well, I've spoken to Christina's driver – he's actually pretty good. And I checked out the lead about the taxi, but that one's a bit odd. No one wants to say where Christina went after the Christmas party. That gap between midnight and three seventeen is getting more and more mysterious.'

'Okay, so you've got two articles: "Christina Scared of Being Blown Up – Her Driver Speaks" and "Her Missing Hours – the Mystery Grows". Patrik?'

'Well, I've only just got here, but I've made a few calls. Interpol are putting out an alert for the Tiger this evening.'

'Wow,' Annika said. 'Worldwide?'

'I think so. Zone two, they said.'

'That's Europe,' Berit and Annika said at the same time, and burst out laughing.

'Any country in particular?'

'Don't know,' Patrik said.

'Good. Well, you can pick up anything that happens

this evening,' Annika said. 'I'm afraid I haven't got much we can use, but I've found out a few peculiar things. See what you make of this!'

She told them about Christina Furhage's first husband, the rich old director, her dead son and pyromaniac daughter; about Evert Danielsson's fateful affair at work and his uncertain future, and about Helena Starke's unexpected outburst and the fact that she was a militant lesbian.

'Why are you digging about in stuff like that?' Patrik said sceptically.

Annika looked at him with gentle condescension.

'Because, my dear, this sort of background research eventually leads you to the holy grail of journalism: cause and effect. An understanding of individuals and their impact on society. You'll learn that when you get a bit older.'

Patrik looked like he didn't quite believe her.

'I just want to do headline articles,' he said.

Annika smiled.

'Good. Shall we get going?'

Berit and Patrik left. She listened to the news on the radio before she went off to the six o'clock handover. Radio news were running with that morning's story about the legal technicality, and then moved on to parliamentary elections in Pakistan. Annika switched it off.

She went past the kitchen and drank a large glass of water on her way to the meeting. The effects of the wine had faded, thank goodness.

35

The editor-in-chief was alone in his room when she arrived. He seemed to be in a good mood.

'Good news?' Annika said.

'Bloody hell, no. We're not selling enough. I've just had a run-in with the marketing department, and that always livens me up. How are things going for you?'

'The headline about the alarm codes was uncalled for; I was going to raise that at the meeting. It's caused huge problems. But I've found a number of skeletons in Christina Furhage's closet, maybe I could tell you later if you've got time . . . ?'

Ingvar Johansson, Pelle Oscarsson, and Spike, the other night-editor, came in together. They were talking loudly, laughing the way men do with their peers. Annika sat in silence and waited for them to sit down.

'There's one thing I just want to start with,' Anders Schyman said, pulling out a chair and sitting down. 'I know no one in this room has anything to do with this, but I want to talk about it as a basic principle. It's about the headline on pages six and seven today, the one that reads "Alarm Codes Hold the Key". The phrase alarm codes should never have been used, and no one could have been in any doubt about that after yesterday's discussions. But the headline still appeared in the paper, and that was a serious fuck-up. I'm going to call Jansson as soon as we're finished here to find out how the hell it happened.'

Annika could feel herself blushing as he spoke. She tried to look unconcerned, but wasn't very successful. It was obvious to everyone in the room who was involved in the conflict, and whose side he was on.

'I think it's pretty remarkable that I should have to explain things like this. I thought it was obvious that the decisions taken in these meetings and the directives that I give are to be followed. There are certain occasions when we know things that we don't print, and it is up to me when that happens. Annika's deal with her source was not to mention the alarm codes, and she didn't. Yet this still happened. So how the fuck did it happen?'

Silence. Annika stared at the table. To her annoyance, she could feel tears rising, but she swallowed and forced them down again.

'Okay,' Anders Schyman said. 'Seeing as no one has anything to say, we'll learn from this and never let it happen again, ever. Is that understood?'

The men muttered inarticulately, and Annika swallowed again.

'Right, let's move on,' the editor-in-chief said. 'Annika, what have we got from crime?'

Ingvar Johansson's lips narrowed as Annika straightened up and cleared her throat.

'Berit's writing two pieces: she met the driver, who told her that Christina was afraid of being blown up, and she's been looking into Christina's final hours. Patrik has found out that Interpol are putting out an alert for the Tiger this evening. And he'll be writing about police progress tonight. My source has gone quiet. I've spoken to Evert Danielsson, Furhage's number two, who got the push today . . .' She fell silent and looked down at the table.

'That sounds promising, but I don't think we'll lead with the bombing tomorrow,' Schyman said, thinking of the number cruncher. Their calculations said that no story sold for more than two days – three at most – no matter how big it was. 'We're into the fourth day and we have to have a change. What have we got instead?'

'Are we really dropping the terrorism angle already?' Spike said. 'It strikes me that we've dropped that thread completely.'

'How do you mean?' the editor-in-chief said.

'Everyone else has run overviews of various terrorist attacks on the Olympics over the years, and looked at the terrorist groups that might be responsible for this attack. We never even got onto the track with that.'

'I know you've been off the past few days, but surely you can get a copy of the paper from the kiosk out in Järfälla?' Anders Schyman said sweetly.

Spike stopped abruptly.

'We ran the list of previous attacks on the Olympics on both Saturday and Sunday, but we have consciously resisted indulging in unethical speculation about various bomb-throwing terrorist groups. We have our own information, which has been considerably better than that, and we can only hope that today's idiotic headline hasn't ruined our chances of getting more of the same in the future. Instead of barking about terrorists, we have been leading the news, and we should be proud of that. Our sources say this wasn't aimed at the Olympics, neither the organization nor the stadium. Our sources indicate that it was a personal attack against Christina Furhage, and that is what we happen to believe as well. So we won't be listing any terrorist groups tomorrow either. But what are we going to lead with?'

Ingvar Johansson puffed himself up and started to run through his long list. Annika had to admit that he was effective, and usually showed good judgement. But as he was talking she could feel Spike looking daggers at her. It came as a relief when the meeting broke up and the men left the room.

'So what have you found out today?' Schyman said.

Annika told him what she knew, and showed him the photograph of the young Christina and her son.

'The more I dig into her background, the murkier it gets,' she said.

'Where do you think it's taking us?' the editor-in-chief said.

She hesitated.

'What we've got so far is unpublishable. But somewhere in her closet lies the explanation to all of this, I'm sure of it.'

'What makes you think that the truth is publishable?'

She blushed.

'I don't know. I just want to know how it all fits together . . . I want to be one step ahead. Then I can ask the police the right questions, which means that we get the answers first.'

The editor-in-chief smiled.

'Good,' he said. 'I'm very happy with your work these past few days. You don't give up, it's a good characteristic, and you're not afraid to fight if you have to. That's even better.'

Annika looked down and blushed even more.

'Thanks.'

'Right, now I'm going to call Jansson and find out what happened last night with that bloody headline.'

She headed back to her office, suddenly aware of how hungry she was. She went over to Berit and asked if she wanted to go to the canteen. Berit agreed willingly, so they dug out their luncheon vouchers and set off. The canteen was serving Christmas ham with potatoes and apple sauce.

'Good grief,' Berit said. 'It's starting already. They won't change the menu until New Year now.'

They skipped the ham and went to the salad bar instead. The large room was almost empty. They settled down in one corner.

'So what do you think Christina was doing after midnight?' said Berit, biting a piece of carrot.

Annika thought for a moment as she chewed a forkful of sweetcorn.

'She left the bar, in the middle of the night, with a well-known macho-lesbian. Maybe they went somewhere together?'

'Helena Starke was really drunk. Maybe Christina helped her home?'

'How? Night-bus?'

Annika shook her head, thinking through the scenario.

'She had a charge-card for a taxi, money, and maybe two and a half thousand employees who could help a colleague get home by car. So why would she, the head of the Olympic Games, Woman of the Year, help a drunk lesbian down into the underground? It doesn't make sense.'

The thought struck them both at the same time.

'Unless . . .'

'Do you think . . . ?'

They started to laugh. The idea of Christina Furhage as a closet lesbian was too absurd.

'Maybe they snuck away to register their partnership,' Berit said, making Annika laugh so much that she was squirming on her chair.

Then they suddenly settled down again.

'But what if it's true? Could they have been having a relationship?'

They carried on eating their salad as they mulled over the possibility.

'Why not?' Annika said. 'Helena Starke was yelling that she knew Christina better than anyone.'

'That doesn't necessarily mean they were sleeping together.'

'No, of course not,' Annika said. 'But it just might.'

One of the waitresses came over to their table.

'Excuse me, but is one of you Annika Bengtzon?'

'Yes, I am,' Annika said.

'They want you back upstairs. They're saying the Bomber has struck again.'

36

The others were already gathered in the editor-in-chief's office when Annika got back. No one looked up as she walked through the door, with pieces of sweetcorn stuck in her teeth, and her bag slung over her shoulder. The men were busy planning their strategy of how to squeeze everything they could out of the terrorism angle.

'We're way behind everyone else,' Spike said, just a little too loudly. Annika got his point. She had found out the basics on her way up from the canteen. She sat at the far corner of the table, scraping the chair and getting her legs tangled, almost tumbling onto the floor. They all fell silent and waited.

'Sorry,' she said, and the word hung ambiguously in the air, taunting her.

Oh hell, now they were going to make her pay! Only an hour ago she had sat here and forced through her line about the Bomber being out after Christina Furhage personally, and that there was no link whatsoever to the Olympics, then bang! Another explosion, at another Olympic venue.

'Have we got anyone there?' Schyman asked.

'Patrik Nilsson's on his way,' Spike said, sounding very important. 'He should get to Sätra Hall in ten minutes or so.'

'Sätra Hall?' Annika said in surprise. 'I thought the blast was at one of the Olympic venues?'

Spike looked condescendingly at her.

'The Sätra Hall is actually an Olympic venue.'

'What sport? A training camp for shot-putters?'

Spike looked away.

'No, the pole-vault.'

'So where do we go with this?' Anders Schyman interrupted. 'We'll have to try to recapitulate what the other media have done on terrorism over recent days, and make it sound as though we've been with them all along. Who wants to do that?'

'Janet Ullman is on tonight, we can ask her to come in early,' Ingvar Johansson said.

Annika felt suddenly giddy, a feeling that threatened to pull her away from the table and drag her halfway up the wall. What a nightmare. How could she have been so wrong? Had the police been lying to her all along? She had staked her standing at the paper on her approach to this story. Was there any way she could stay on as head of the crime section after this?

'We have to go out and check security in the other venues,' Spike went on. 'We'll have to get extra people in, the other night crew . . .'

The men were facing each other, their backs to Annika as she sat off in the corner. Their voices merged into a single cacophony, and she leaned back, trying to get some air. She was finished, she knew she was finished. How the hell could she even stay on at the paper after this?

The meeting was short and to the point, and the others were unanimous. They all wanted to get back to their desks and run with the terrorism angle. Only Annika was left, sitting in her corner. She didn't know how she was going to be able to leave without falling apart. She was on the verge of tears.

Anders Schyman went and made a couple of calls from his desk; Annika heard his voice rise and fall. Then he came back and sat on the chair next to hers.

'Annika,' he said, trying to catch her eye. 'Don't worry, do you hear me? There's no need to worry!'

She turned away and blinked back the tears.

'Everyone makes mistakes,' the editor-in-chief continued quietly. 'That's the oldest truth in the world. I was wrong as well; I thought exactly the same as you. Now things have happened that mean we have to think again. We have to make the best of the situation now, don't we? We're going to need you on this, Annika . . .'

She took a deep breath and looked down at her lap.

'Yes, you're right, of course you are. But it feels terrible. I was so sure my theory was right . . .'

'It may yet turn out to be right,' Schyman said thoughtfully. 'It's unlikely, I suppose, but Christina Furhage may have had some personal connection to Sätra Hall.'

Annika couldn't help laughing.

'Not very likely!' she said, smiling.

The editor-in-chief put his hand on her shoulder and stood up.

'Don't let this break you,' he said. 'You've been right about everything else in this story.'

She pulled a face and stood up as well.

'How did we hear that there'd been another explosion? Did Leif ring?'

'Yes, either him or Smoothy in Norrköping; it was one of them.'

Schyman sank onto the chair behind his desk with a deep sigh.

'Are you going out there tonight?' he asked.

Annika tucked her chair under the table and shook her head.

'No, there's no point. Patrik and Janet have it covered. I'll get going early tomorrow morning instead.'

'Okay. I think you should take some time off when this calms down. You earned practically a whole week off over this past weekend alone.'

Annika smiled weakly.

'Yes, I think perhaps I will.'

'Go home and get some sleep now, and let the boys out there deal with this tonight. They're on a roll now.'

The editor-in-chief picked up his phone, indicating that their conversation was over. She picked up her bag and left.

37

The newsroom was bubbling in that intense way it did when something big had happened. On the surface everything seemed calm, but the tension was clearly visible in the section heads' alert eyes and the editors' ramrod-straight backs. Words flew, short and concise, reporters and photographers marched purposefully towards the exit. Even the receptionists were caught up in it, their voices deeper and their fingers more focused as they flew over the keyboards. Usually Annika enjoyed the feeling, but today even crossing the floor felt difficult.

Berit came to her rescue.

'Annika! Come here, I've got something to tell you!'

Berit had brought her salad with her, and was sitting in the radio room, the cubicle next to the crime desk that had access to every police channel in the Stockholm district, as well as one national channel. One wall was covered with built-in speakers, with individual circuit-breakers and volume controls. Berit had turned up the ones covering the southern suburbs and the central police district, the ones that could be expected to be involved in the explosion at Sätra Hall. Annika could only hear static and bleeping.

'What is it?' she said. 'What's happened?'

'I don't really know,' Berit said. 'The police got there a minute or so ago. They started calling for a scrambled channel—'

At that moment the chatter started again. The Stockholm police had two protected channels, usually known as 'scrambled'. You could hear someone talking, but what they said was completely incomprehensible. It sounded like Donald Duck talking backwards. The scrambled channels were used very rarely, usually for drugs cases. The security services could also use them when they suspected that criminals had access to police radio. There was a third possibility: that the information was so sensitive that it had to be kept secret for other reasons.

'We have to get hold of scrambling equipment,' Annika said. 'We could be missing really important stuff like this.'

The chatter died away and static took over on the other channels. Annika looked at the speakers. The eight police districts in Stockholm used two different radio systems, System 70 and System 80.

The 70 contained all the channels from 79 megahertz and upwards, and the 80 started at 410 megahertz and took its name from the simple fact that it came into use in the 1980s. The idea was that everyone should have switched to the System 80 ten years ago, but the complete reorganization of police services in that time meant that the old system was still in use.

Annika and Berit listened to the crackling and the electronic bleeps for another minute or so, until a male voice broke through the static on the southern suburban channel, 02.

'Twenty-one ten here.'

The numbers indicated that the call was from a radio car from Skärholmen.

The response from central command on Kungsholmen came a second or so later.

'Yes, twenty-one ten, over.'

'We need an ambulance to the address, well, actually a police wagon—'

The crackling took over again, as Annika and Berit looked at each other in silence. 'Police wagon' was a euphemism for a hearse. 'The address' was undoubtedly Sätra Hall, because there was nothing else going on in the southern district right now. The police often used phrases like that when they didn't want to be too obvious over the radio, talking about 'the address' or 'the location', and suspects were referred to as 'the object'.

Central command responded: 'Twenty-one ten, ambulance or police wagon, over?'

Both Annika and Berit leaned forward together, the answer was crucial.

'Ambulance, over.'

'One dead, but not as bad as Furhage,' Annika said.

Berit nodded.

'The head's still on, even if the rest is badly messed up,' she said.

A policeman was only able to confirm death if the head had been severed from the body. So that was clearly not the case here, even if it was obvious that the person was dead. Otherwise the police wouldn't have spoken of a police wagon – a hearse.

Annika went out into the newsroom.

'There's evidently one fatality,' she said.

Everyone round the large nest of tables where the night-editors worked stopped and looked up.

'Why do you think that?' Spike said expressionlessly.

'Police radio,' Annika said. 'I'll call Patrik.'

She turned on her heel and went into her office. Patrik

239

answered immediately, he must have been holding his phone, as usual.

'How does it look?' Annika asked.

'Bloody hell, there's flashing lights everywhere,' the reporter yelled.

'Can you get in?' Annika said, forcing herself not to shout.

'No, not a chance,' Patrik roared. 'They've cordoned off the whole of Sätra sports centre.'

'Any indication of fatalities?'

'What?'

'Any indication of fatalities?'

'Why are you shouting? No, no fatalities, there's no ambulance, and no hearse.'

'There's one on its way, we heard it over the radio. Stay there, and give your report to Spike, I'm going home.'

'What?' he yelled through the receiver.

'I'm going home now. Talk to Spike!' Annika shouted back.

'Okay!'

Annika hung up. Berit was doubled up with laughter in the doorway.

'No need to tell me who you were talking to,' she said.

38

It was just after eight o'clock when she got home to the flat on Hantverkargatan. She had taken a taxi, and was struck by a strange sense of giddiness on the back seat.

The taxi-driver was angry about something the paper had printed, and was going on about journalistic responsibility and political autocracy.

'Talk to one of the editors; I just clean the stairs,' Annika said, leaning her head back and shutting her eyes. The giddiness was growing into a real sense of illness as the car wove through the traffic on Norr Mälarstrand.

'Are you okay?' Thomas asked as he came into the hall with a tea-towel in one hand.

She gave a deep sigh.

'I just feel a bit dizzy,' she said, brushing the hair from her face with both hands. Her hair felt really greasy, she would have to wash it tomorrow morning. 'Is there any food left?'

'Didn't you eat at work?'

'Half a salad, then stuff happened . . .'

'There's some left – pork chop and roast potatoes.'

Thomas threw the towel across his shoulder and went back into the kitchen.

'Are the children asleep?'

'They went off an hour ago. They were worn out. I'm worried Ellen might be coming down with something. Did she seem tired this morning?'

Annika thought back.

'No, not really. A bit clingy, maybe, so I carried her to the bus.'

'I can't take time off now,' Thomas said. 'If she gets ill you'll have to look after her.'

Annika felt her anger welling up.

'I can't be away from work at the moment, surely you can see that? There was another Olympic killing tonight, haven't you heard the news?'

Thomas turned round.

'Oh shit,' he said. 'No, I heard the news on the radio this afternoon, but they didn't say anything about a new murder.'

Annika went into the kitchen. It looked like a bomb had hit it. Her plate of dinner was waiting for her on the table. Thomas had dished up potatoes, pork chop, cream sauce, fried mushrooms and lettuce salad for her. Beside her glass stood a bottle of weak beer that would have been ice-cold a couple of hours ago. She put the plate in the microwave and set it for three minutes.

'The lettuce will be disgusting,' Thomas said.

'I've been wrong all along,' Annika said. 'I forced the paper to drop the terrorism angle because I had other information from the police. It looks like I fell for an almighty red herring, because there was an explosion at Sätra Hall tonight.'

Thomas sat down at the table and tossed the tea-towel onto the draining-board.

'The sports hall? There's hardly any room for spectators there. They can't use that as an Olympic venue, can they?'

Annika poured herself a glass of water and hung up the tea-towel.

'Don't leave this here, it's soaking wet. Every damn sports hall in the city seems to have something to do with the Olympics. There are evidently more than a hundred venues that are involved one way or another, either as actual competition venues or as training centres and warm-up tracks.'

The microwave let out three little bleeps to indicate it was finished. Annika took the plate out and sat down opposite her husband. She ate greedily, without saying a word.

'So how was your day?' she asked, opening the luke-warm bottle of beer.

Thomas sighed and stretched.

'Well, I hope I'll be ready for the planning meeting on the twenty-seventh, but it didn't go well today. The phone never stops ringing. This regional issue keeps getting bigger, which is no bad thing, but sometimes there's no time for anything but meetings and phone-calls.'

'I can pick the kids up early tomorrow, so you might get a bit more done,' Annika said, suddenly feeling guilty. She chewed a piece of pork: the microwave had made it really tough.

'I thought I might sit down and go through one of the preliminary reports now. One of the young guys has put it together; he's been working on it for months. It's probably unreadable – things usually are when trainees have spent too long working on a text. Official Swedish can be completely impossible to read.'

Annika smiled weakly. Sometimes her conscience gave her such a bad time. Not only was she an unbalanced head of section and a useless reporter, but she was a rotten wife and a hopeless mother, too.

'You sit and read. I'll clear up.'

He leaned over and kissed her on the mouth.

'I love you,' he said. 'The Christmas ham is in the oven. Take it out when it gets to seventy-five degrees.'

Annika opened her eyes wide in surprise.

'You found the meat thermometer?' she said. 'Where was it?'

'In the bathroom, next to the kids' thermometer. I took Ellen's temperature when we got home, and there it was. I think Kalle must have put it there. It's the logical place for it, really. He swears blind he didn't put it there, of course.'

Annika pulled Thomas to her and kissed him properly.

'I love you too,' she said.

Happiness

Deep in the forest, past the barn and the swamp, lay a lake, Långtjärn. In early childhood it came to represent the end of the world, probably because that was where the grown-ups' land stopped. I often heard it mentioned as a symbolic end point, and I imagined the lake as a bottomless hole full of darkness and terror.

The day when I finally got permission to go up there alone, any thoughts of that sort vanished. Långtjärn was a wonderful place. The little lake was nestled in ancient forest, scarcely a kilometre long, just a couple of hundred metres wide, with glittering water and pine-strewn shores. It gave me a sense of innocence, of a new beginning. This was what the world looked like before human beings arrived.

Evidently there had once been fish in the lake, because just beside the little stream running out from it a ramshackle little wooden shack lay among the trees. It had once been a fishing and hunting cabin, and it was a surprisingly ambitious building for what it was. It consisted of one single room, with an open fireplace in the far gable, a planed floor and a little window facing the water. The furniture consisted of two bunks, fixed to the walls, two rough stools, and a small table.

Now, looking back, I can see that the happiest

moments in my life were spent in that little shack. Every now and then I return to the peace of the lake. Its surface, its reflection, change with the seasons, and human progress has left its marks. The trees along the track leading to the lake have been cut, but the ones by the water have been left. I light a fire in the stove and look out over the water, and feel a sense of perfect harmony.

Maybe this way of thinking seems provocative, and could be interpreted as ingratitude or nonchalance, but nothing could be further from the truth. I'm very happy with the success I have enjoyed, and the things I've achieved, but you mustn't confuse that with happiness. Society's fixation with success and ecstatic joy are the polar opposite of real happiness. We have all become happiness junkies. Constantly striving for more – aiming higher – will never make us happy with our lives.

Success and well-being are actually far less interesting than failure and misery. Real success gives you a feeling that borders on the erotic, an obvious, well-trodden path to the stars. But real failure has many more nuances and depth. It forces you to analyse and reflect, to focus inwards instead of upwards, and eventually leads to a more worthy life. At best, well-being breeds tolerance and generosity, but more often just jealousy and a lack of engagement.

The secret of a happy life is being content with what you have. To stop scrambling higher, and find peace instead.

Sadly I have seldom managed this myself. Apart from in that cabin by the lake.

Tuesday 21 December

39

The smell of newly baked ham was still hanging in the air when she woke up, one of the few advantages of having an extractor fan that didn't work properly. She loved freshly baked Christmas ham, but it had to be properly hot, just out of the oven, still running with salty juices. She took a deep breath and threw the duvet aside. Ellen moved in her sleep beside her. Annika kissed her daughter on the forehead and stroked her chubby little legs. She would have to make an effort to get to work on time, so she could get everything done and be back to pick the children up at three.

She got into the shower, and let go of her morning urine down the plughole. The strong smell mixed with the steam hit her in the face, making her turn away instinctively. She washed her hair with dandruff shampoo, and swore when she discovered the bottle of conditioner was empty. Now her hair would look like straw until she next washed it.

She got out of the shower, dried herself and wiped the floor where the water had leaked out. She sprayed a hefty dose of deodorant under her arms, and smeared skin-cream on her cheeks. The blotches were still there, so she added some cortisone cream just to be sure. Mascara, eye-shadow; finished.

She crept into the bedroom and opened the door to her wardrobe. The noise made Thomas shift in his sleep. He had sat up reading work reports long after she had gone to bed. The main report into the regional issue, which Thomas had overall responsibility for, was supposed to be finished in January. But Thomas's assistants hadn't yet finished the smaller reports upon which the main one would be based, and Thomas was getting more and more stressed. She realized that he could get at least as stressed as her, even if his deadlines tended to be longer than hers.

She was feeling festive, and put on a red top, red jacket and black trousers. She had just finished getting dressed when the first television news of the day started.

The pictures from Sätra Hall weren't very dramatic: the camera crew evidently hadn't got through the cordon; they only had pictures of the usual blue and white tape fluttering in the night wind. The voiceover said that the explosion had taken place in one of the changing-rooms in the older part of the building. The fire brigade had found the remains of a dead man inside.

There was currently a dispute between the police and the fire brigade about whose responsibility it was to deal with dead bodies. The fire service had said that it wasn't their responsibility. The police said the same. The news spent some time on this point of procedure, and announced that it would be a subject for discussion in the following programme.

Then there were shots of a reporter wandering about in an empty stadium in one of the suburbs, shouting 'Hello?' No answer, which the reporter thought was scandalous.

'What exactly are the police doing about security?' was the final rhetorical question. The police spokesman, looking ridiculously tired, appeared, and explained that it was completely impossible to guard every single part of every single venue all of the time.

'So how will you manage it during the Olympics?' the reporter asked in an insinuating tone of voice.

The spokesman sighed and Annika realized that the police had been lumbered with the very debate they'd been trying to avoid. The debate about security during the Olympic Games would get louder and louder until the Bomber was caught. The President of the International Olympic Committee appeared on screen, telling Reuters that the Games were not under threat.

The bulletin concluded with a long item about the National Bank meeting later that day, and the likelihood of a change in the interest rate. The reporter seemed to think it would remain the same, which Annika took as a sure sign that it would rise or fall.

She turned off the television and fetched the morning papers from the door. They had nothing beyond what she had already seen on the news. The dead man's name was not being released, a reporter had gone round another venue in another suburb shouting 'Hello?', the President of the International Olympic Committee and the police spokesman said exactly the same things they said on television. None of the papers had put together any graphics to show where the bomb had gone off, so she would have to wait until she got to work to see what the evening papers had come up with.

She ate some strawberry yogurt and cornflakes, dried her hair and piled on her outdoor clothes. The weather had changed during the night, and it was now snowing in squally showers. She had planned to take the 56 bus to the paper, but changed her mind when the first flurry of snow hit her face and messed up her mascara. She took a taxi instead.

The seven o'clock news came on the radio just as

she settled into the back seat. They too had been out to another deserted venue during the night, the police spokesman was still tired and stressed, and the Olympic Committee President was starting to get really repetitive.

She tried not to listen and stared at the buildings along Norr Mälarstrand, one of the most expensive addresses in Sweden. She couldn't understand why. The buildings were in no way remarkable. They were side on to the water, a few had balconies, but that was all. But the heavy traffic below must make it impossible to sit and enjoy the view. She paid with her credit card, hoping she could claim it back on expenses.

Most days Annika picked up a copy of that day's paper from the large pile in reception. She usually managed to leaf through to the middle by the time the lift reached the fourth floor, but not today. The paper was so full of adverts that it was almost impossible to get through at all.

Spike had gone home, which was a relief. Ingvar Johansson had just arrived, and was sitting with his first mug of coffee, deeply immersed in the morning papers. She picked up a copy of the other evening paper and fetched a cup of coffee from the machine, then went into her room without talking to anyone.

Both papers identified the new victim, and had a picture. He was a thirty-nine-year-old builder from Farsta called Stefan Bjurling, married with three children. He had worked for one of the hundreds of small companies employed by SOCOG, the Stockholm Organizing Committee of the Olympic Games, for the past fifteen years. Patrik had spoken to his boss.

'Stefan was the most competent foreman you could ask for,' the boss said. 'He was responsible, he kept to deadlines, and he would work as long as it took to get the job done. There was never any slacking in Stefan's team.'

And of course Stefan Bjurling was incredibly popular and had a great sense of humour and was always in a good mood.

'He was a great colleague, really good to work with, always happy,' another workmate had said.

Annika felt rage bubbling up inside her. What bastard had killed this man and ruined his family's lives? Three small kids had lost their father. She could only imagine how Kalle and Ellen would react if Thomas died suddenly. And how on earth would she react? How did people ever get over tragedies like this?

And what a way to die, she thought, feeling sick as she read the police's preliminary report about what had happened.

They believed that a bomb had been strapped to the man's back, roughly at kidney-height. The man's hands and feet had been tied to a chair before the explosion. It wasn't yet clear what sort of explosive had been used, or how it had been detonated, but the killer had probably used some sort of timer or delayed charge.

'Bloody hell,' Annika said out loud, wondering if it wouldn't have been better to spare the readers some of the detail.

She could see the man sitting there, with the bomb ticking on his back, struggling to get free. What would go through your mind in a situation like that? Would your whole life flash before you? Did you think of your children? Your wife? Or just the rope holding you down? The Bomber wasn't only completely mad; he seemed to be a real sadist as well. She shivered, in spite of the heat of the office.

She went on through the paper, past Janet Ullberg's evocative description of yet another echoing, empty venue in the middle of the night, and started reading the adverts. One thing was certain: there was no shortage of toys in the world.

She went and got another fix of coffee, and took a detour past the picture desk on the way back. Johan Henriksson was on duty, and was sitting there reading one of the morning papers, *Svenska Dagbladet*.

'A pretty disgusting way to kill someone, isn't it?' Annika said, sitting down opposite him.

The photographer shook his head. 'Yep, it's pretty deranged. I've never heard of anything like it.'

'Do you feel like taking a trip out to get a look?' Annika said hopefully.

'It's still too dark,' Henriksson said. 'We wouldn't see anything.'

'Not yet, no, but it might be possible to get inside now. They might have removed the cordon.'

'Not very likely; they're probably still picking up the pieces.'

'The other builders are probably turning up now, his workmates . . .'

'We've already spoken to them.'

Annika stood up, irritated.

'Fine, I'll wait until another photographer turns up who can be bothered to get off his arse.'

'Hey, calm down,' Henriksson said. 'I'm happy to go. I'm not trying to duck out of it.'

Annika stopped and tried to smile.

'Okay, sorry, that was out of order. I'm just trying to show a bit of enthusiasm.'

'No problem,' Henriksson said, and went to get his camera bag.

Annika gulped down her coffee and went over to Ingvar Johansson.

'Do you know if the morning crew need Henriksson,

or can we go and see if we can get into Sätra Hall?'

'The morning crew won't be getting a word in unless World War Three breaks out, the paper's already huge,' Ingvar Johansson said, putting down the other evening paper. 'We've got sixteen more pages than usual for the next edition, adverts all over the place. They've got a team out covering traffic problems caused by the snow, but they can't seriously think we're going to have room for that.'

'You know how to reach us,' Annika said, and went to her room to fetch her outdoor clothes.

They took one of the paper's cars, with Annika driving. The roads really were terrible; the traffic on the Essinge motorway was crawling along.

'It's hardly surprising that you get pile-ups in this sort of weather,' Henriksson said.

It was starting to get brighter, which was something. Annika headed south and the traffic thinned out a bit. She speeded up, turning off at the Segeltorp junction and driving along the Skärholmen road, past Bredäng. To their right were row after row of identical yellow brick blocks of flats, and to their left low warehouses and industrial units.

'I think you've missed the turning,' Henriksson said, just as Sätra Hall sailed past through the snow on their right.

'Shit,' Annika said. 'We'll have to go into the centre of Sätra and turn back.'

She shivered as she saw the enormous blocks of flats, their upper floors hidden in the snow. She had only been out there once, when Thomas was buying Kalle's first bicycle. Thomas said they should get a second-hand one, because it was cheaper, and was also a form of recycling. So they had got hold of a copy of the *Advertiser* and scoured the small ads. When Thomas found a bike that sounded suitable, he started to get nervous that it might have been stolen. He wouldn't hand over any money until he had seen the receipt and the child who had outgrown it. And that family lived in one of these blocks.

The big blocks of social housing disappeared behind them as they headed along the Eksätra road. She turned left into Björksätravägen. The explosion had happened in changing-room number six, the referees' room, which was at the back of the building, between the sports hall and the old skating rink.

'Blocked off,' Henriksson said.

Annika didn't reply, just turned the car round. She drove back and parked between the snowdrifts in a desolate car park on the other side of the Eksätra road.

She got out and looked at the building, which was covered in dark red wooden panelling. From the end it looked like a weird UFO, with a low sloping roof giving way to a fairly steep section in the middle, reaching an oddly crooked peak.

'Have you been out here before?' she asked Henriksson.

'Never,' he said.

'Bring your cameras, we'll see if we can't find another way in,' she said.

They tramped through the snow until they reached the back of the building. If Annika was right, they were now as far away from the entrance as possible, diagonally across from it.

'This looks like the deliveries entrance,' she said, and set off towards it. The door was locked. They went on through the snow, going round the corner and carrying on along the length of the building. At its centre were two small doors: emergency exits, Annika assumed. The first was firmly shut, but the second one was unlocked.

There was no sign of any cordon or barrier. Annika felt almost giddy with joy.

'After you,' she muttered, pulling the door open.

'Do you think we can just go in like this?' Henriksson said.

'Of course we can,' Annika said. 'You put one foot in front of the other, and carry on repeating the process.'

'Yeah, yeah, but aren't we breaking and entering, or something?' Henriksson said.

'We'll find out, but I doubt it. This is a public sports hall, owned by Stockholm City Council. It's open to the public and the door isn't locked. There shouldn't be any problems.'

Henriksson went in, a sceptical look on his face, and Annika pulled the door shut behind them.

40

They were at the top of the hall's small stand. Annika looked round; it was an attractive building. Seven wooden arches held the roof up. The weird top of the building turned out to be a row of skylights up in the roof. The hall was dominated by a banked running track, and off to the right were the long-jump pit and high-jump and pole-vault frames. On the far side of the track was a row of what looked like offices.

'There's a light on over there,' Henriksson said, pointing to the far left of the row of offices.

'So that's where we go,' Annika said.

They followed the wall until they reached what looked like the main entrance to the hall. In a nearby room they could hear the sound of someone crying. Henriksson stopped.

'Oh shit,' he said. 'I don't want to do this.'

Annika took no notice of him, just headed towards the source of the noise. The door was ajar, and she knocked gently and waited for a reply. When none came, she pushed the door open and looked in. The room looked like a building site, electric cables were hanging from the walls, there was a large hole in the floor, and there were planks of wood and a drill on a small bench. A young blonde woman was sitting on a plastic chair in the middle of the mess, crying.

'Excuse me,' Annika said. 'I'm from the *Evening Post*. Can I help you at all?'

The woman carried on crying, as if she hadn't heard.

'Can I go and get someone for you?' Annika asked.

The woman didn't look up, just carried on sobbing with her hands over her face. Annika waited quietly for a while in the doorway, then turned back, and was about to shut the door behind her.

'Can you understand how anyone can be so evil?' the woman said.

Annika stopped and turned to face the woman again.

'No,' she said. 'It's completely unbelievable.'

'My name's Beata Ekesjö,' the woman said, blowing her nose on a piece of toilet paper. She wiped both her hands, then held out her right hand to Annika. Annika took it with no hesitation. Handshakes were important. She remembered the first time she had shaken hands with someone with HIV, a young woman who had been infected when she gave birth to her second child. She had been given a blood transfusion in a Swedish hospital, and had got the virus into the bargain. Her soft, warm handshake had burned in Annika's hand all the way back to the office. Another time she had been introduced to the leader of an offshoot of the Hell's Angels. Annika had held out her hand to him, and he had peered into her eyes as he slowly licked his hand, from wrist to fingertips.

'People are really fucked up,' he had said, holding out his saliva-smeared hand. Annika had taken it without a moment's hesitation. The memory floated past as she held the crying woman's hand, feeling the remnants of her tears and snot between her fingers.

'I'm Annika Bengtzon,' she said.

'You wrote about Christina Furhage,' Beata Ekesjö said. 'You wrote about Christina Furhage in the *Evening Post*.'

'Yes, that's right,' Annika said.

'Christina Furhage was the most wonderful woman in the world,' Beata Ekesjö said. 'It was so awful that it had to happen to her.'

'Yes, it was,' Annika said, and waited.

The woman blew her nose again, and pushed her flax-blonde hair back behind her ears. Natural blonde, Annika noted; no streaky roots like Anne Snapphane. She looked about thirty, the same as Annika.

'I knew Christina,' Beata Ekesjö said, looking down at the roll of toilet paper in her lap. 'I worked with her. She was my idol. That's why I think it's so awful that it had to happen to her.'

Annika was starting to feel restless. This was going nowhere.

'Do you believe in fate?' the woman suddenly asked, looking up at Annika.

Annika noticed that Henriksson had come in and was standing just behind her.

'No,' Annika said. 'Not if you mean that everything is predetermined. I think we make our own fate.'

'Why?' the woman said with interest, straightening up.

'Our future is determined by the choices we make. Every day we make life-changing decisions. Shall I cross the road now or wait until that car has passed? If we make the wrong decision, our life ends. It's up to us.'

'So you don't think there's anyone watching over us?' Beata said, wide-eyed.

'What, like God? I think there's a purpose to our time on earth, if that's what you mean. But I don't think we're supposed to know what it is, because if that were the case we'd know about it, wouldn't we?'

The woman stood up, evidently considering this. She was short, no more than one metre sixty, and skinny as a teenager.

'What are you doing here now, sitting in here?' Annika said eventually.

The woman sighed and stared at one of the holes left by the cables in the wall.

'I work here,' she said, blinking back the tears again.

'Did you work with Stefan?'

She nodded, and the tears started to fall again. 'Evil, evil, evil,' she muttered as she rocked from side to side with her hands in front of her face. Annika picked up the toilet roll from where the woman had put it on the floor, and tore off a long piece.

'Here you are,' she said.

The woman turned round so abruptly that Annika took a step back and trod on Henriksson's foot.

'If there's no such thing as fate, who decided that Christina and Stefan had to die?' she said, her eyes flaming.

'A human being,' Annika said calmly. 'Someone murdered both of them. I wouldn't be surprised if it turned out to be the same person.'

'I was here when the bomb went off,' Beata said, turning away again. 'I was the one who asked him to stay late and check the changing-rooms. So how responsible does that make me?'

Annika didn't answer, just studied the woman more closely. She didn't fit in here. What did she mean, and what was she doing here?

'If it wasn't fate that put Stefan in the way of the explosion, then it must be my fault, mustn't it?' she said.

'Why do you think it was your fault?' Annika said, and at that moment she heard voices behind her.

A uniformed policeman was coming through the main entrance together with eight or nine builders.

'Can I take your picture?' Henriksson said to the woman.

Beata Ekesjö patted her hair.

'Yes,' she said. 'I want you to write about this. It's important that it gets out. Write about what I said to you,' she said.

She stared at the photographer as he took a couple of pictures without a flash.

'Thank you for talking to us,' Annika said quickly, shaking Beata's hand again and then hurrying after the policeman. The police would be able to give her something, unlike this poor, confused woman.

The group of men were on their way into the hall when Annika caught up with them. She introduced herself and Henriksson, and the policeman lost his temper immediately.

'How the hell did you get in here? How did you get past the cordon?'

Annika looked him calmly in the eye.

'You were pretty sloppy last night, officer. You didn't cordon off the south side of the hall, and you didn't check the emergency exits.'

'Never mind, you're leaving now,' the officer said, taking hold of Annika.

At that moment Henriksson took a picture, this time with a flash. The policeman stopped and let go of Annika.

'What's happening now?' Annika said, fishing her notepad and pen out of her bag. 'Questioning and forensics?'

'Yes, and you need to leave.'

Annika sighed, lowering the pad and pen to her thighs.

'Come on. We need each other. Give us five minutes to talk to the men and take a group picture inside the hall and we'll be happy.'

The policeman clenched his teeth, turned and pushed his way through the group of builders out towards the main entrance. He was presumably going to get back-up. Annika realized she would have to move quickly.

'Okay, can we have a group picture?' she said, and the men gathered hesitantly next to the small stand.

'Sorry, you probably think we're being intrusive, but we're just trying to do our job as well as possible. It's vital that Stefan's killer is caught, and hopefully the mass media can help,' Annika said as Henriksson snapped away.

'To start with, we're really sorry you lost your workmate, it must be terrible to lose a colleague like that.'

The men didn't answer.

'Is there anything you'd like to say about Stefan?' she asked.

The photographer had got them all to sit on the stand; they were all facing him, with the hall behind them. It would be an evocative picture.

The men were still hesitant, none of them wanting to talk. They were all focused, serious, dry-eyed. They were probably in a state of shock.

'Stefan was our boss,' said a man in faded overalls. 'He was a really good bloke.'

The others muttered their agreement.

'What sort of work are you doing here?' Annika asked.

'We're going through the whole building and making a few changes for the Olympics. Health and safety,

263

electricity, pipes . . . The same thing's happening at all the Olympic venues.'

'And Stefan was in charge?'

The men started to mutter again, until the same man spoke once more: 'Nah, he's our boss,' he said. 'That one over there, the blonde, she's the project leader.'

Annika raised her eyebrows.

'Beata Ekesjö?' she said in surprise. 'She's in charge?'

The men laughed slightly, glancing at each other conspiratorially: yes, Beata was in charge. The laughter was joyless and sounded more like a series of snorts.

Poor cow, Annika thought. She can't have an easy time with this lot.

Unable to think of anything else to say, Annika asked if they knew Christina Furhage, and they all nodded enthusiastically.

'Now she was a real woman,' the man in blue overalls said. 'Don't suppose anyone else could have got this all going.'

'Why do you think that?' Annika asked.

'She went out to all the sites, talking to the builders. God knows how she found the time, but she always wanted to meet everyone and see how it all worked.'

The man fell silent, and Annika tapped her pen thoughtfully on her notepad.

'Are you going to do any work today, then?'

'We have to talk to the police, then we're probably going home. And we'll have a minute's silence for Stefan,' the man said.

At that moment the policeman came back with two colleagues. They looked pretty cross, and were heading straight towards the little group.

'Thanks very much,' Annika said quietly, and picked up Henriksson's camera case, seeing as she was closest to it. Then she turned on her heel and started to walk along the track, heading for the unlocked emergency exit. She heard the photographer jogging to catch up.

'Hey, you!' the policeman called.

'Thanks, we won't disturb you any longer,' Annika called back, and waved without slowing down.

She held the door open for Henriksson and let it slam shut.

The photographer sat in silence as Annika drove back to the office. The snow was still falling, but at least there was proper daylight now. The traffic was even thicker, Christmas traffic was making it worse than usual. There were only three days left now.

'Where are you spending Christmas?' Annika asked, to break the silence.

'What are you going to do with that?' Henriksson replied.

Annika glanced at him, surprised.

'What? What do you mean?'

'Can we really publish any of that when we just walked in like that?'

Annika sighed.

'I'll talk to Schyman and explain what happened. I expect we'll end up with a picture of the men sitting in the stand, and something about them holding a minute's silence for Stefan. It won't be much more than a caption, really. In the article alongside we can add any information from the police and something about interviews with the builders and ongoing forensic work, blah, blah, blah. You know the sort of thing.'

'What about the woman?'

Annika bit her lip.

'I won't mention her. She's too unbalanced and didn't really add anything new. I didn't think she seemed all there. What did you make of her?'

'I missed the start,' Henriksson said. 'Did she spend the whole time talking about evil and guilt?'

Annika scratched her nose.

'Pretty much. That's why I won't be using her. She may have been in the building when the bomb went off, but she had nothing to say about that at all. You heard her. This is probably one of those instances where we ought to try to protect someone, even if she does want to get in the paper. She doesn't know what's best for her right now.'

'You said it wasn't up to us to decide who can cope with being in the paper,' Henriksson said.

'Yes, I did,' Annika said. 'But it is up to us to decide if a person is capable of understanding who we are and what we're saying. That woman was too weird. She's not going in the paper. But I'll write something about the project leader being in the building at the time of the explosion, that she's completely distraught after Stefan's death, and blames herself for his death. I just don't think we should publish her name or picture.'

They sat in silence the rest of the way back. Annika let Henriksson out at the main door before driving the car down into the garage.

41

Bertil Milander was sitting in front of the television in his magnificent art nouveau library. He could feel the blood pulse through his body; it bubbled and rushed in his veins. His breathing filled the room. He sensed that he was falling asleep. The volume of the television was turned down to a faint whisper, reaching him as irregular murmurs through the mechanical sounds of his body. A group of women were talking and laughing with one another, but he couldn't hear what they were saying. Every now and then banners listing various flags and phone numbers and currencies would appear on screen. He had no idea what was going on. The tranquillizers made everything so woolly. Occasionally he would let out a little whimper.

'Christina,' he muttered, and sobbed for a while.

He must have dozed off, then suddenly he was wide awake. He recognized the smell, and knew that it meant danger. The warning signs were so deeply imprinted in him that it reached him through sleep and drugs.

He struggled out of the leather sofa, his blood pressure sluggish, making him confused. He stood up, holding on to the back of the sofa, trying to work out where the smell was coming from. The drawing room. He moved carefully, holding on to the bookcases, until he felt his blood pressure rising.

His daughter was crouched in front of the stove, feeding the contents of a cardboard box into it.

'What are you doing?' Bertil Milander asked, bewildered.

The old stove was badly ventilated, and the smoke was drifting out into the room.

'I'm tidying up,' his daughter said.

He went over to the young woman and sat down beside her on the floor.

'You're lighting a fire?' he asked cautiously.

Lena looked at him.

'Not in the middle of the floor this time,' she said.

'Why?' he said.

Lena Milander stared at the flames as they slowly died away. She tore a new piece of cardboard and tried to get the fire going again. The flames caught hold and embraced it. For a few seconds it stood stiffly in the fire, then quickly rolled up and disappeared. Christina Furhage's smiling eyes vanished for ever.

'Don't you want to keep any memories of your mum?' Bertil asked.

'I'll always remember her,' Lena said.

She tore another three pages from the album and shoved them into the stove.

Eva-Britt Qvist looked up as Annika walked past her on her way to her office. Annika said a friendly hello, but Eva-Britt cut her off sharply.

'So you're back from the press conference already?' she said triumphantly.

Annika realized straight away what the secretary wanted her to say: 'What press conference?' Then Eva-Britt would be able to prove that she performed a vital role coordinating things in the crime unit.

'I didn't go,' she said, and gave an even broader smile as she went into her room and closed the door. There, she thought, that'll get you wondering where I've been.

Then she called Berit's mobile. The phone rang, but she was put through to voicemail. Berit's phone was always at the bottom of her bag, and she never managed to pull it out the first time you called. Annika waited thirty seconds, then called again. This time Berit answered straight away.

'I'm at the press conference in police headquarters,' the reporter said. 'You were out on a job, so I came down here with Ulf Olsson.'

Oh, thank you! Annika thought.

'What are they saying?'

'Some interesting stuff. I'll be back soon.'

They hung up. Annika leaned back in her chair and put her feet up on the desk. She found some half-melted chocolate in her drawer and broke it into smaller pieces. It was covered in sugar crystals, but was perfectly edible.

Even though she would probably not have dared to say so out loud in the office, she couldn't help thinking that the connection between these bombings and the Olympics was really tenuous. What if they were just two privately motivated attacks against two specific individuals?

Sätra Hall was as far as you could get from an Olympic arena. There had to be a lot of common denominators between Christina Furhage and Stefan Bjurling. Of course the connection could be the Olympics, but it didn't have to be. There was something in their past that linked them to the same killer, Annika was willing to bet on that. Money, love, sex, power, jealousy, hate, injustice, influence, family, friends, neighbours, holidays, school, children, transport – there were a thousand ways their lives could have collided. Out at the hall this morning there were at least ten people who had met both Stefan Bjurling and Christina Furhage. The victims didn't necessarily even have to have known each other.

She called her source.

He gave a deep sigh.

'I thought you and I had said all we have to say to each other,' he said.

'Well, look where that got us! How much are you enjoying this whole security debate? "Hello? Hello? Is there anyone here?"' she said, imitating the report on the radio that morning.

He sighed again and Annika waited.

'I can't talk to you any more.'

'Fine, okay,' Annika said quickly. 'I understand that you've got a lot to do, because I reckon you're all sitting there trying desperately to find some sort of common denominator between Stefan Bjurling and Christina Furhage. Maybe you've already found one. How many people do you think had access to the alarm codes, and knew Stefan as well?'

'We're trying desperately to fend off all these demands for more security guards . . .'

'I don't believe that,' Annika said. 'You're probably glad the focus has shifted away from the theory you believe in to an entirely irrelevant debate about security in the different venues.'

'You can't mean that,' her source said. 'When it comes down to it, security is always the responsibility of the police.'

'I'm not talking about the police as a whole, just about you and your friends sitting there trying to solve these murders. Because it's up to you lot, isn't it? If you sort this out, the security debate goes away.'

'If?'

'When. Which is why I think you ought to talk to me again. The only way to get ahead in life is by communicating.'

'Is that what you were doing inside Sätra Hall this morning, communicating?'

Fuck, he'd heard about that.

'Amongst other things,' Annika said.

'I'm going to hang up now.'

Annika took a deep breath and said, 'Christina Furhage had another child, a son.'

'I know that. Goodbye.'

He really was very angry. Annika hung up, and at that moment Berit walked in.

'Terrible weather,' she said, shaking her hair.

'Have they caught the killer, then?' Annika asked, holding out the chocolate. Berit looked at it in horror and declined the offer.

'Nah, but they think it's the same person. And they're still saying that there's no credible threat to the Games.'

'What's their argument?'

Berit picked up her notepad and leafed through it.

'There haven't been any public threats against any venue or person connected to the Games. Any threats that have been received have been of a personal nature, unconnected to either the venues or the Games themselves.'

'They're talking about the threat against Furhage. Were there any threats against Stefan Bjurling?'

'I'm hoping to find that out this afternoon, because I've arranged to meet his wife.'

Annika raised her eyebrows.

'Wow! She agreed?'

'Yes, she had nothing against seeing me. We'll have to

see if it gets us anything. She could well be too muddled and grief-stricken for us to write anything.'

'Well, it's still a great start. Anything else?'

Berit looked back at her notes.

'They're almost finished with the preliminary analysis of the explosive used in the first attack. They'll be distributing a press release right after lunch today, they reckon. They had thought it would be ready for the press conference, but there was some sort of delay in London.'

'So why was it sent to London in the first place?' Annika said.

Berit smiled.

'The equipment in the labs in Linköping was broken. As simple as that.'

'But why are they rejecting the sabotage theory so aggressively?'

'Maybe they just want some peace and quiet to work in?' Berit said.

'I don't know; I can't believe there's nothing more to it than that,' Annika said. 'I reckon they're on the brink of solving the murders.'

Berit stood up.

'I'm hungry. Are you?'

42

They went to the canteen, where Berit picked lasagne and Annika chicken salad. They had just got their food when Patrik came in. His hair was a mess and it looked like he'd slept in his clothes.

'Good morning,' Annika said. 'You did a damn good job last night. How did you manage to get hold of all his workmates?'

The young man grinned, embarrassed at the praise, then said, 'I just called and woke them up.'

Annika smiled.

They chatted a bit about Christmas, all the worry and presents and stress. Berit had finished her Christmas shopping before the start of Advent, Patrik hadn't started yet. And neither had Annika.

'I was thinking of doing some today,' she said.

'I'll get a box of chocolates for Mum on the plane,' Patrik said.

He was heading down to spend Christmas with his parents in Småland. Berit's grown-up children were coming to stay. She had a daughter in the USA and a son in Malmö.

'We've been working like hell recently. How about sorting out some time off amongst ourselves for the next few days?' Annika said.

'I'd like Thursday off, if possible,' Patrik said. 'Then I can get an earlier flight.'

'I could do with getting some cleaning done tomorrow, because Yvonne and her family are arriving on Thursday.'

'That works well. I'll leave early today, and as early as I can on Thursday.'

They left the canteen, agreeing to meet up again shortly in Annika's room for a run-through of what they had.

Patrik went off to get his own copy of the other evening paper.

Annika and Berit settled into their usual places, Berit in the armchair and Annika with her feet up on her desk. The next moment Patrik came rushing in.

'They know what made mincemeat of Furhage!'

He was waving the press release from Stockholm police headquarters.

'Great,' Berit said. 'So what does it say?'

Patrik read to himself for a few seconds.

'Normal dynamite,' he said, sounding disappointed.

'What do you mean, normal dynamite?' Annika said, reaching for the press release.

Patrik pulled it out of her reach.

'Calm down! It says: "The analysis of the explosive material used in the detonation at the Victoria Stadium in Stockholm at three seventeen, blah, blah . . . when the managing director of SOCOG, Christina Furhage, was killed is now complete. The substance was a gelatinous mixed explosive containing nitro-glycerine instead of just nitro-glycol. It is sold under the brand name MINEX, and is available in various different weights and shapes. The detonation in question is estimated to have contained approximately twenty-four kilos, divided into fifteen plastic casings measuring 50 by 550 millimetres—"'

'Twenty-four kilos? Isn't that a hell of a lot?' Annika said.

'Especially if you're using it above ground,' Berit said. 'No wonder it set off a shockwave that reached all the way to Södermalm.'

Patrik read on: '"The substance in question has been manufactured in Poland for the past three years. It is characterized by a high weight-to-strength ratio, high density, and speed of detonation. The consistency is soft and the smell relatively mild. The substance has a high degree of flegmentation . . ." What the hell does that mean?'

'Something to do with stability,' Berit said. 'It means it's a stable substance.'

'How on earth do you know that?' Annika said, impressed.

Berit shrugged. 'I'm good at crosswords.'

'"The energy content is high, gas volume slightly higher than normal, force 115 per cent of Anfo, and density approximately 1.45 kilos per cubic decimetre. The detonation speed can reach 5,500–6,000 metres per second."'

'Okay, and what does all that mean?' Annika wondered.

'Calm down, I'm getting to that. "Minex is one of the most common brands of dynamite in Sweden. The substance has been sold by an agent in Nora to over one hundred projects in the past three years. It has not proved possible to identify who the explosives in question were purchased by."'

'So, normal construction-use dynamite,' Berit said.

'What do you construct with dynamite?' Annika asked.

'Everything between heaven and earth. You use it to build roads, or down mines, in quarries, you make grit using dynamite, you level ground for building . . . We used dynamite when we were putting a sewage treatment unit in at our summer cottage. People use it every day.'

'I suppose so,' Annika conceded. 'They used a hell of a lot of explosives when they were building all that housing around St Erik's Hospital near me on Kungsholmen.'

'Listen, there's more: "The explosive was set off with the use of electronic detonators. These were linked to a delay mechanism in the form of a timer and connected to a car battery . . ."'

Patrik put the press release down and looked at his colleagues.

'Bloody hell,' he said. 'Pretty well thought out, then.'

They sat in silence for a few minutes, thinking through this new information. Annika pulled her feet off the desk and shook herself.

'God, what a job,' she said. 'So, who's doing what? Berit, you take the victim's family, and Patrik, will you do the analysis and the police investigation?'

The two reporters nodded, and Annika went on: 'I've written fifteen centimetres about the construction workers arriving at their workplace and having a minute's silence for their dead colleague. How much they miss their friend, and so on.'

'How bad was it out there?' Berit said.

'Oh, there was a woman in tears, completely inconsolable. She wasn't making much sense, going on about guilt and punishment and evil, it was a bit weird. I left her out of the article. It didn't feel right to expose her like that.'

'I'm sure that's the right thing to do,' Berit said.

'Have we missed anything? Is there anything else right now?'

The reporters shook their heads and went out to their phones and computers.

Annika moved her text onto the central filestore, put on her coat, and left. It was only half past one, but she had no intention of hanging around any longer.

43

It was still snowing when Annika walked out to the 56 bus-stop on Fyrverkarbacken. Because the temperature was only around zero, the flakes were transformed into a grey-brown sludge the moment they hit the ground. But for the time being they were settling on the grass near the Russian Embassy, forming a vaguely white covering.

She sat down heavily on the bench at the bus-stop. She was the only person there, which made her think she must have just missed a bus. She quickly realized that she was sitting on something wet, a puddle of water or a patch of snow. She put one of her gloves under her backside.

They would be spending Christmas in Stockholm – Thomas's parents were coming for Christmas Eve. She had very little contact with her own family. Her father was dead, and her mother still lived in Hälleforsnäs in Södermanland, where Annika had grown up. Her sister lived nearby, in Flen, doing some part-time work in Right Price. She hardly ever saw them. It didn't seem to matter. They had nothing in common any more, apart from the time they had spent together in a dying small industrial town. Sometimes Annika wondered if they had even been living in the same place, because their experiences of the little community were so utterly different.

The bus was almost empty. Annika sat at the back and went as far as Hötorget in the city centre. She went into the PUB department store and bought toys worth 3,218 kronor on her Visa card, consoling herself with the fact that she would get a lot of bonus points. She bought the *New Book of Sauces* and a designer shirt for Thomas, and a woollen shawl for his mother. Thomas would have to sort out his father. He usually only wanted cognac anyway.

She was back in the flat on Hantverkargatan by half past two. After a moment's hesitation she put everything at the back of her wardrobe. Kalle had actually found his presents there last year, but she couldn't be bothered to think of anywhere else to hide them right now.

She stepped out into the slush again, and was seized by a sudden impulse to go into the second-hand shop in the next block. It held Stockholm's largest assortment of fake jewellery, necklaces and earrings, the sort of things film stars wore in the forties. She went in and bought a gold-plated brooch with garnets for Anne Snapphane. The neat little man behind the counter wrapped it in shiny gold paper with shiny blue ribbons.

The children rushed towards her, delirious with joy, as she entered the nursery. Her guilty conscience stabbed at her heart. This was the sort of thing a proper mother would do every day, wasn't it . . . ?

They went into the supermarket on the corner of Scheelegatan and Kungsholmsgatan and bought marzipan, cream, syrup, chopped almonds, cookie dough and cooking chocolate. The children were chattering madly.

'What are we going to make, Mummy? Can we have sweets today, Mummy?'

Annika laughed and hugged them as they queued at the till.

'Yes, you can have sweets today. We're going to make our own sweets, that'll be fun, won't it?'

'I like Salty Cat liquorice,' Kalle said.

When they got home she put big aprons on the children, making up her mind not to care about the results and just let the children have fun. She started by melting the chocolate in the microwave, then let the children roll small pieces of marzipan in it. They didn't end up with many marzipan balls, and they weren't exactly beautiful. Annika's mother-in-law would probably turn her nose up at them, but the children enjoyed it, especially Kalle. She had planned to make toffee as well, but realized that she couldn't do that with the children, the mixture would be far too hot. Instead she put the oven on and got out the cookie dough. Ellen was beside herself. She rolled out the dough, cut out the biscuits and ate up the pieces between the shapes. In the end she was so full she could hardly move. But they ended up with a couple of trays of decent-looking biscuits.

'Aren't you clever!' she said to the children. 'Look what lovely Christmas biscuits you've made!'

Kalle was glowing with pride, and helped himself to a biscuit and a glass of milk, even though he really didn't have room for it.

She put the children in front of the television to watch a film while she tidied up in the kitchen. It took forty-five minutes. She sat between them on the sofa at the sad part when Simba's dad died. There was still part of *The Lion King* left when she had finished cleaning the kitchen, so she took the chance to call Anne Snapphane. Anne lived alone with her young daughter out on Lidingö, where they had the upper floor of a detached house. The girl, Miranda, lived with her dad every other week. They were both home when Annika called.

'I haven't done anything about Christmas yet,' Anne groaned. 'How come you always manage somehow and I never do?'

In the background Annika could hear the music to *The Hunchback of Notre Dame*. So Disney films were just as popular out on lovely posh Lidingö.

'I'm the one who never has any time,' she said. 'Your place is always so spotless. I always feel guilty when I'm round yours.'

'Three little words: Tonya from Poland,' Anne said. 'Is everything okay with you?'

Annika sighed. 'Things at work are a bit tough right now. There's a little gang who are constantly trying to undermine me.'

'It's a right arse when you're first put in charge, isn't it? When they made me a producer I spent six months thinking I was going to die, I was so miserable. There's always some bitter little bastard trying to ruin things.'

Annika bit her lip.

'Sometimes I wonder if it's worth it. This sort of thing is what you're supposed to do, isn't it, baking with the kids and being there for them when there's something horrid on television . . .'

'You'd go mad in a week,' Anne said.

'Oh, you're probably right. But the children are still the most important thing; you can't get away from that. That woman who was killed, Christina Furhage, had a son who died when he was five. She never got over it. Do you suppose her job and all that success ever managed to blot out the memory?'

'God, that's awful,' Anne said. 'What did he die of?'

'Malignant melanoma, skin cancer. Terrible.'

'No, Miranda, get down from there . . . How old did you say he was?'

'Five, the same age as Kalle.'

'And he died of malignant melanoma? Rubbish!'

Annika didn't follow.

'What?'

'He couldn't have died of a malignant melanoma if he was only five. That's impossible.'

'What do you mean?' Annika said, astonished.

'Do you think I've got a single mole left on my entire body? Well, do you? Or do you suppose I had every single last one removed before I was twenty? What do you think? Do you imagine that I of all people would be wrong about something like this? Oh, Annika . . .'

Annika was used to her friend's hypochondria, but could still feel her confusion growing. Could she have misunderstood Helena Starke?

'Why couldn't he have had malignant melanoma?' she asked, feeling foolish.

'Because the malignant bit, the fatal form of melanoma, never develops before puberty. He may have had a bloody early puberty, I suppose, some kids do. It's called . . .'

Annika was thinking so hard it hurt. Anne Snapphane was bound to be right. She was a total hypochondriac, there wasn't a disease on the planet that she hadn't at some time imagined that she had got, and there was no medical examination she hadn't been through. She'd been taken to Accident and Emergency at Danderyd Hospital by ambulance innumerable times, not to mention the number of times she had walked into the various emergency departments around the city, public and private alike. She knew everything about every form of cancer, and could list the differences between the symptoms of MS and primary amyloidosis in her sleep. There was no way she was wrong. So either Helena Starke was wrong or she was lying.

'. . . Annika?'

'Listen, I've got to go.'

She hung up, and felt a shiver down her spine. This was vitally important, she was sure of that. If Christina Furhage's son didn't die of malignant melanoma, maybe he had died of something else? Some other disease, or could he even have been murdered? Or maybe he hadn't died at all. Maybe he was still alive.

She got up, suddenly restless, and started to walk up and down the kitchen, adrenalin pumping. Bloody hell, she knew she was on to something here. She suddenly stopped. Her source! He knew that Christina had a son, he said so just before he hung up. Yes, that was it!

'Mummy, *The Lion King*'s over now.'

They came into the kitchen in a little procession, first Kalle, then Ellen a step behind. Annika forced her thoughts about Christina Furhage to the back of her mind.

'Was it good? Are you hungry? No, no more biscuits now. Spaghetti? Or how about a pizza?'

She called La Solo on the other side of the street and ordered one Capriccosa, one mince and garlic, and one folded pizza with steak. Thomas wouldn't be happy, but she couldn't help that. If he wanted something extravagant and time-consuming like elk stew, then he would have to come home at two o'clock to start browning the meat.

44

Evert Danielsson turned off the Sollentuna road into the petrol station at Helenelund. There was a large DIY carwash hall that he came to most weeks to take care of his car. His secretary had booked a three-hour slot from 7 p.m., although it wasn't strictly necessary – but he didn't want to take any chances. It could be difficult getting a slot as long as that if you didn't book.

He began by buying everything he needed from the shop: a bottle of stain remover spray, a bottle of wax-free carwash liquid, two bottles of original Turtle wax, and a pack of cloths. It cost him 31.50 kronor for the stain remover, 29.50 for the shampoo, and 188 kronor for the two bottles of wax. The three-hour slot cost 64 kronor an hour, so in total it cost him less than 500 kronor for a whole evening. Evert Danielsson smiled at the girl behind the counter and paid with the company card.

He went out and drove into the space he usually used and closed the door behind him, then took out his camping chair and put his small portable stereo on the bench in the corner. He picked out a CD of famous arias, from *Aida*, *The Magic Flute*, *Carmen* and *Madame Butterfly*.

As the Queen of the Night's powerful voice soared

into action he started to hose down the car. Small tides of mud, grit and ice ran down towards the drain. Then he sprayed the whole car in stain remover to get rid of any oil. While the spray was doing its work he sat on the camping chair and listened to Verdi's *La Traviata*. He didn't necessarily insist on listening to opera while he was washing the car: sometimes he played old R&B, like Muddy Waters, or some rockabilly, like Hank Williams. Every now and then he tried something more modern, such as Rebecka Törnqvist, or certain songs by Eva Dahlgren.

His thoughts started to wander, but soon enough they settled on the subject that occupied most of his time these days: the sort of work he would be doing in future. Earlier that day he had attempted to sort out some form of structure for his work, prioritizing the most urgent tasks. At some level he was actually relieved that Christina was gone. Whoever blew her up might well have done the world a big favour.

When the aria was finished he changed the disc and put on a CD of Satie's piano music. The mournful tones filled the hall as he grabbed hold of the hose again and started to rinse the car. All that mess with water wasn't much fun – the bit he looked forward to was the final stage, waxing and polishing the car until it positively shone. He stroked the roof of the car with his hand. He had a feeling that everything was going to be all right.

Thomas put the children to bed just after half past seven. Annika had read them a bedtime story, about a little girl and her mother going to nursery. In the story the mother tells the staff at the nursery how no one ever wants to do what their boss tells them, and all the grown-ups laugh.

'Great, so now it's okay to take the piss out of bosses even in kids' books,' Annika said.

'What do you mean?' Thomas said, opening the business section of *Svenska Dagbladet*.

'Look at this questionnaire,' Annika said, holding out a glossy women's magazine. 'It's supposed to tell you how well you're doing at work. Look at question fourteen. "What's your boss like?" The options are "feeble and incompetent", "pretentious and useless" or "arrogant". What's that all about? What sort of message does that send? And here, on the next page, it tells you what to do if you want to become a boss. The underlying message is that all bosses are idiots, and that everyone wants to become one. That's just plain wrong!'

'Of course it is,' Thomas said, turning a page of the paper.

'But our whole society is based on myths like this!'

'Well, you were pretty critical of your own bosses at the paper once upon a time, or have you forgotten that?'

Annika put the magazine down on her lap and looked at Thomas reproachfully.

'Yes, but, bloody hell, they were in the wrong jobs!'

'There you are, then,' Thomas said, and carried on reading.

Annika sat quietly, thinking, as John Pohlman read out the weather forecast for Christmas: a white Christmas all over the country, at least until Christmas Day, anyway. Then wet weather coming in from the west, bringing showers to the west coast late on Christmas Eve.

'You found things at the Association difficult until you settled in, didn't you?' Annika said.

Thomas put the newspaper down, switched off the television with the remote, and held out his arms to Annika.

'Come over here,' he said.

The silence after the television was deafening. Annika got up from her armchair and crept up onto the sofa and into Thomas's arms, nestling against his chest with her legs on the coffee table.

Thomas wrapped his arms around her and stroked her shoulders, blowing on her neck and kissing her collarbone. She felt a quivering in her groin, and wondered if they would have the energy to make love tonight.

At that moment Annika's mobile rang, the shrill tones finding their way out of her bag and into the television room.

'Don't answer,' Thomas whispered, nibbling at Annika's earlobe, but it was too late. The spell was already broken and Annika was now sitting stiff and tense.

'I'll just see who it is,' she muttered, scrambling to her feet.

'You really must change that ringtone,' Thomas called after her. 'What on earth is that tune supposed to be?'

Annika didn't recognize the number flashing on the display, and decided to answer.

'Annika Bengtzon? Hello, this is Beata Ekesjö. We met in Sätra Hall this morning. You told me to call if there was anything I wanted to say . . .'

Annika groaned silently to herself. Bloody business card.

'Of course,' she said curtly. 'What is it?'

'Well, I was just wondering, is there going to be anything about me in the paper tomorrow?'

The woman's voice sounded light and happy.

'How do you mean?' Annika asked, sitting down on the bench in the hall.

'Well, I just wondered; it feels important to get it right, that's all.'

Annika sighed.

'Can you be a bit more precise?' she said, looking at her watch.

'I could tell you a bit more about myself, about my work and so on. I've got a very nice house, you're welcome to come and take a look.'

Annika heard Thomas turn the television back on.

'That probably isn't necessary,' Annika said. 'We have very little space in the paper, as I'm sure you understand. In fact, we won't be quoting you at all.'

There was silence on the line for a few seconds.

'What do you mean?' the woman said finally. 'Aren't you going to write about me?'

'Not this time.'

'But . . . You talked to me! The photographer took pictures!'

'We talk to an awful lot of people that we never write about,' Annika said, making an effort to sound normal. 'Thanks again for letting us take up your time this morning, but we won't be publishing any of our conversation.'

The silence on the line grew.

'I want you to write about what I said this morning,' the woman said in a low voice.

'I'm sorry,' Annika said.

Beata Ekesjö sighed.

'Oh well,' she said. 'Thanks anyway.'

'Thank you, and goodbye,' Annika said, and hung up. She hurried back to Thomas on the sofa, took the remote out of his hand and turned off the television.

'Where were we?' she said.

'Who was that?' Thomas asked.

'A woman I met this morning, she seemed a bit crazy. Construction manager out at Sätra Hall.'

'She must have a pretty awful time of it, statistically, at any rate,' Thomas said. 'Young women in male-dominated workplaces have it worse than anyone.'

'Do you mean that? Is there any real proof?' Annika said, surprised.

'Yep. A big report has just come out. Numerous investigations show that women who take on male professions have the hardest task in the whole workforce. They get bullied, threatened and sexually harassed more often than any other group, male or female. Research from the nautical department of Chalmers University of Technology in Gothenburg showed that four out of five female sailors are bullied because of their gender,' Thomas said.

'How do you know all this?'

Thomas smiled.

'It's like you remembering the details of Berit Hamrin's articles. There are other examples, not least from the military. A lot of women leave early, even though they were volunteers. One of the main reasons is problems with their male colleagues. Female bosses suffer serious health risks, especially if they're under a lot of pressure from their colleagues.'

'But that's something we ought to write about,' Annika said, trying to get up.

'Yes, you should. But not right now, because I'm about to massage your shoulders. If we just take off your top, like that. And if we take this off too . . .'

Annika protested feebly as her bra came off.

'But the neighbours can see . . .'

Thomas got up and turned off the light. The only light in the room came from the street lamps swaying outside, far below. The snow was still falling, in huge, heavy flakes. Annika held out her arms to her husband and pulled him down to her. They took it slowly to start with, lying on the sofa and stroking each other and gently pulling off their clothes.

'You drive me crazy, you know that?' Thomas mumbled.

They moved onto the floor and started to make love, very slowly to start with, then hard and noisily. Annika cried out as she came. Thomas was slightly more restrained. Afterwards Thomas fetched a duvet and they stretched out together on the sofa again. Exhausted and relaxed, they lay there listening to the sounds of the big city outside in the evening darkness. Down below the number 48 bus pulled up, brakes shrieking; they could hear a neighbour's television, and someone was yelling out in the street.

'God, it'll be great to get some time off,' Annika said.

Thomas kissed her.

'You're the best in the whole world,' he said.

Lies

I was absolutely certain right from the start. The world was a stage set up to fool me, and the people around me were all actors in the play. The intention was to get me to believe that everything was real: the ground, the forest, the fields, Nyman's tractor, the village, the shop and the postman. The world beyond the blue slopes of Furuberget was just a vague backdrop. I listened intently for wrong notes, waited patiently for someone to give the game away. Whenever I left a room I would spin round in the doorway to get a glimpse of the people inside as they really were. It never worked. In winter I would clamber up on top of the snowdrifts outside the sitting-room window and look in. When I wasn't there people took off their masks, leaning their weary heads in their hands and relaxing. They chatted quietly among themselves, probably genuinely, naturally, confidentially, and truthfully. But when I went in again they were forced to adopt their uncomfortable disguises again, living lives that didn't suit them, with embittered faces and mendacious tongues.

I was convinced that this would all be revealed to me on the day of my tenth birthday. Everyone would come and see me that morning in their true, real bodies, and dress me all in white. Their faces would be relaxed and genuine. I would be carried in a procession off to the barn on the edge of the forest on the other side of the road. There the director of the play would be waiting at the door, and he would take my hand in his and lead me to the Kingdom of Enlightenment.

He would explain the way things really were to me.

Sometimes I would make my own way to the old barn. I can't say how old I was, but my legs were short, my woollen trousers were itchy, my boots made walking difficult. One time, I got stuck in the snow, right up to my waist.

The barn was tucked away on the edge of the forest, on what was left of an overgrown meadow. The roof had fallen in; the grey timber walls shone silver through the thickets. Part of one gable stuck up like a beacon against the sky.

The rectangular opening was in the far gable-end, and I would feel my way along the roughness of the walls as I went round towards it. The entrance was a little way up in the wall, and I had trouble clambering up to it.

Time stood still inside, dust hung in the air, and the light slanted in. The simultaneous sense of solid walls and open sky was intoxicating. The light filtered down through the branches of the surrounding thickets and the remnants of the roof. The floor had also started to give way, and I had to take care as I walked around.

Down there, beneath the floor, was the entrance to the stage. I knew that. Somewhere under those rotting boards the Truth lay in wait. Once I plucked up my courage and crept beneath the floorboards, exploring the ground to find the way to the Light. But all I found was hay and dead rats.

Wednesday 22 December

45

It was Annika's turn to take the kids to nursery, so she had time to lie and think for a bit after Thomas left for work. There were only two days left until Christmas Eve, so she was well and truly into the final straight. It was funny how little it took to get her back on her feet again. After an hour's shopping in town, a bit of baking and a decent shag, she was ready to face the vultures again. For once she had spent the night without either of the children in their bed, but now they were awake they came rushing into the bedroom. She gave them a hug and mucked about with them in bed until they were on the verge of being late. Ellen had invented something called the Meatball Game, which involved tickling each other's toes and shouting 'meatballs, meatballs' over and over again. And Kalle liked the flying game, which involved Annika lying on her back and balancing him on her feet up in the air. Every so often the plane would crash, much to everyone's delight. And finally they built a den with all the pillows and the duvet and Thomas's pyjamas. They ate a quick breakfast of strawberry yogurt and Sugar Puffs, while Annika made sandwiches. They almost made it in time for the register. Annika didn't stop today, but set off for work as soon as she had parked the children on the laps of two members of staff.

It was still snowing, and the filthy sludge lay in drifts along the pavements. Since the City Council introduced local management committees, you hardly ever saw a snowplough in the streets. She wished she had the energy to get involved in politics.

She got lucky with the number 56 bus, picked up a copy of the paper in reception, caught the lift, and said hello to the caretakers in their office just along from the door to the newsroom. She sent a silent prayer of thanks to Anders Schyman when she saw one of the caretakers dragging in the second post of the day. Life would be much easier now that Eva-Britt Qvist had started doing her job properly again.

She picked up a copy of the other evening paper and the morning papers at the news desk, and grabbed a cup of coffee from the machine on the way to her room. Eva-Britt was in her usual place, and said a grumpy hello. In other words, everything was the same as usual.

Berit had done a brilliant job with the wife of the murdered Stefan Bjurling. The article filled the centrefold, with a big picture of the woman and her three children, sitting in their brown leather sofa at home in Farsta. LIFE GOES ON was the headline. The woman, who was thirty-seven years old and called Eva, looked focused and serious. The children, eleven, eight and six years old, stared into the camera, wide-eyed.

'Evil appears in so many different ways in this world,' Eva said in the article. 'It's stupid to think that we're protected from it here in Sweden, just because we haven't had a war since 1809. You find violence and cruelty where you least expect it.'

Eva had been making pancakes when the police arrived to tell her that her husband was dead.

'You can't just fall apart when you've got three children,' she went on. 'We have to make the best of things and carry on with our lives.'

Annika stared at the picture for a long while. She had a vague sense that something wasn't right. Surely the woman was a bit too together? Why didn't she say anything about grief and despair in the article? Well, the text was good, the picture worked, and it was a successful spread. She pushed it away with a feeling of distaste.

As usual, Patrik had done a decent job with the technical analysis and the police hunt for the Bomber. The theory that the same man was responsible for the two explosions was still current, although they had said the substances used weren't identical.

'The explosive charge was much smaller this time,' the police spokesman said. 'Preliminary analysis indicates either that it was a different substance or that a much smaller quantity was used.'

During the next managerial meeting she would recommend that Patrik be given a permanent contract.

Her own piece with Johan Henriksson's picture of the construction workers had a page to itself. It had turned out pretty well.

She leafed through the rest of the paper, moving on from the Bomber and arriving at the 'Women and Knowledge' section. Predictably, these pages were only ever referred to as the Wank section in the office. Today the Wank team had gone for the age-old trick of writing about an American pop-psychology book for women, spiced up with a couple of famous Swedes. The book was *The Ideal Woman*, written by a woman with a double-barrelled surname and a very thin nose, the sort you only get if half of it has been removed. Apart from the little portrait of the author, the article was illustrated by a huge publicity shot of Christina Furhage. The text about the book explained that now, *finally*, all women could have the chance to be *the ideal woman*. A small box gave some basic facts about Christina Furhage, and Annika realized that the myth of the dead Olympic boss was already starting to develop. Christina Furhage was, the article claimed, a woman who had succeeded in everything. She had a fantastic career, a beautiful home, a happy marriage and a well-adjusted daughter. And she took care of her appearance, she was slim, in good shape, and she looked fifteen years younger than she really was. Annika got a bad taste in her mouth, not only from the cold coffee. None of this was exactly true. Christina's first marriage had collapsed, her first child had died or somehow disappeared, her second child was a pyromaniac, and she had ended up being blown to pieces in a deserted stadium by someone who hated her. Annika was convinced of that. And this person had evidently hated Stefan Bjurling as well; she was willing to bet on it.

She was about to go and get a fresh cup of coffee when the phone rang.

'Can you come over?' a man sobbed down the line. 'I want to tell you everything.'

It was Evert Danielsson.

Annika stuffed her notepad and pen in her bag and rang for a taxi.

Helena Starke woke up on the kitchen floor. At first she wasn't quite sure where she was. Her mouth was dry as sandpaper, she was freezing, and one of her hips ached. The skin on her face was taut from crying.

She struggled to get up, and ended up sitting with her back to the sink, looking out of the dirty window at the falling snow. She breathed slowly and deeply, forcing air into her lungs. Her throat felt raw, she wasn't used to smoking. It's odd, she thought. This feels like a completely new life. My brain is empty, the sky is white, my heart is calm. I've reached the bottom.

A sense of peace spread through her. She sat on the kitchen floor for a long time, watching the damp snow hitting the window. Memories of the past few days sailed through the back of her consciousness like grey ghosts. She wondered if she was hungry. As far as she could remember, she hadn't eaten anything for days, just drunk a bit of water and some low-strength beer.

The conversation with that woman from the paper on Monday had opened the floodgates. For the first time in her life Helena Starke experienced vast and genuine loss. The hours that followed had made her see that she had actually been in love, for the first time in her life. The realization that she was actually capable of love had gradually dawned on her during the long hours of last night, and had made her feel even more bereft.

Her confusion and loss at Christina's death had passed into a vast pit of self-pity, which she knew she would have to learn to live with. She was the classic mourning widow, with the big difference that she would never have the support and understanding of anyone around her. That was the preserve of established norms for relationships, and institutionalized heterosexual love.

Helena got to her feet with an effort; she really did feel incredibly stiff. She had sat for hours on the kitchen chair, chain-smoking one cigarette after the other, lighting one from the butt of the last. Sometime during the small hours she had given up trying to stay on the chair and had moved down onto the floor. Eventually she must have fallen asleep.

She found an old glass on the draining-board, rinsed it and drank some water, feeling her stomach knot inside her. She remembered what Christina used to say – she could practically hear her voice in her head: *You've got to eat, Helena; you have to take care of yourself.*

She knew she was important to Christina, maybe the most important person in her boss's life. But her awareness of the darker sides of Christina's life meant that she was under no illusions about what that actually meant. People were simply irrelevant to Christina.

She opened the fridge and, amazingly, found a small pot of yogurt that was only two days past its use-by date. She got a spoon and sat down at the table and started to eat. Vanilla: her favourite. She looked out at the snow. It really was desolate weather.

The traffic was rumbling down below on Ringvägen, she didn't know how she put up with it. All of a sudden she realized that she no longer had to. She was worth more than this. She had plenty of money, and could move wherever she wanted to, anywhere in the world. She put the teaspoon on the table and ate the last of the yogurt with her fingers.

It was time to leave.

46

The Sorbet restaurant lay on the eighth floor of the Luma Building in South Hammarby Harbour, serving both Swedish and Indian food. The owners weren't too fussy about opening times. They had let Evert Danielsson in for a cup of coffee even though there were still fifty minutes until they started serving food.

Annika found him behind a partition to the right of the door. His face was completely grey.

'What on earth's happened?' Annika asked, sitting down on the chair facing him. She pulled off her scarf, gloves and coat and threw them onto the chair beside her, along with her bag.

Evert Danielsson sighed, and looked down at his hands. True to form, they were clinging on to the edge of the table.

'They lied to me,' he said in a muffled voice.

'Who did?'

He looked up.

'The Board.'

'Meaning?' Annika said.

The man sniffed.

'And the Committee, and Hans Bjällra; they all lied. They told me I'd be given a range of other duties, that I would have the job of sorting out a load of practical details now that Christina is dead. But they tricked me!'

Annika looked around in frustration. She really didn't have time to hold his hand through all this.

'Just tell me what happened,' she said abruptly, and it had the desired effect. The man pulled himself together.

'Hans Bjällra, the Chairman of the Board, promised that we would work out my new responsibilities together, but that hasn't happened at all. This morning when I got to work there was a letter waiting for me. A courier had dropped it off first thing . . .' He fell silent and looked down at his white knuckles.

'And?' Annika said.

'It told me to clear my office by lunch. SOCOG had no plans to use my services in the future. I therefore did not need to remain at the disposal of the organization, but was free to seek alternative employment. My parachute payment will be paid on the twenty-seventh of December.'

'How big is the parachute?'

'Five times my annual salary.'

'Poor you,' Annika said sarcastically.

'Yes, it's not bad,' Evert Danielsson said. 'And as I was reading the letter one of the men from HR came in, he didn't even knock, just walked right in. He said he'd come to get my keys.'

'But you had until lunchtime, you said?'

'My car keys, they took my company car away.'

The man leaned over the table and wept. Annika looked at his greying hair in silence. It looked rather stiff, like he had blow-dried and sprayed it. She noted that he was starting to go thin on top.

'Surely you can use a bit of your parachute to buy a new car?' Annika suggested. But she realized at once that

302

it wasn't worth trying. You can't tell someone whose pet has just died that they can get another one.

The man blew his nose and cleared his throat.

'I've got no reason to show them any loyalty now,' Evert Danielsson said. 'Christina's dead, so I can't harm her any more.'

Annika pulled her notepad and pen out of her bag.

'So what do you want to tell me?' she said.

Evert Danielsson looked at her tiredly.

'I know almost all of it,' he said. 'Christina was never the obvious candidate to be head of SOCOG, or even of the campaign to bring the Games to Stockholm. There were plenty of other people, most of them men, who were regarded as more suitable.'

'How come you knew Christina?'

'She had a background in business and banking, you probably know that. I got to know her eleven years ago or so, when I was head of admin at a bank where she was deputy managing director. She wasn't very well liked by most of the employees; she was seen as rigid and unfair. The former was true enough, but not the latter. Christina was incredibly consistent, she never criticized anyone who didn't deserve it. But she did execute people in public, which meant that everyone was terrified of failure. Maybe that had a positive effect on the bank's profits, but it had a devastating effect on morale. The union was talking about a vote of no confidence in her, and things like that never usually happen in the banking sector. But Christina put a stop to it. The people in the union who were actively planning the revolt resigned and left the bank the same day. I don't know what she did to get rid of them, but the idea of a vote of confidence was never mentioned again.'

One of the waiters brought a cup of coffee for Annika and refilled Danielsson's cup. Annika thanked him, thinking that she'd seen his face before, from an advert for credit cards, perhaps? She had a good memory for faces, so she was probably right. The television production companies based in the building presumably used whatever extras they could get their hands on.

'How come she kept her position, if she was so unpopular?' Annika asked once the coffee man from the advert had disappeared.

'Yes, I wondered that as well. Christina had been deputy MD at the bank for almost ten years when I arrived. During that time there had been a couple of new managing directors, but Christina was never considered. She was firmly glued to her post, and she never got any higher.'

'Why not?' Annika wondered.

'I don't know. The glass ceiling, maybe. Or else the board were worried about what she might do if she got ultimate power. They must have known what she was like,' Evert Danielsson said, taking a lump of sugar. Annika waited as he stirred it into his coffee.

'Eventually Christina realized she wasn't going to get any further. When Stockholm City Council decided to submit a bid for the Olympic Games she made sure the bank got involved as one of the biggest sponsors. I think she already had her plan worked out.'

'Meaning . . . ?'

'That she was planning to take over the Games. She was heavily involved in the preparatory work. After a bit of negotiation she got leave from the bank and took on the work involved in the application as interim head of the Olympic bid. Her appointment wasn't particularly surprising, even though she was a relative unknown in a part-time post. The job was pretty badly paid, much worse than her job at the bank. That was why most other business leaders weren't interested. Besides, the job wasn't exactly guaranteed to lead to anything more prestigious – you probably remember the criticism and lack of enthusiasm at the start? The idea of hosting the Olympics was hardly popular with the public. And it was Christina who gradually changed that attitude.'

'Everyone says she did a great job,' Annika added.

'Of course,' Evert Danielsson said with a grimace. 'She was very good at lobbying, and at concealing the cost of that within various other sections of the budget. Changing Swedish popular opinion about hosting the Games was the biggest PR campaign ever mounted in this country.'

'I've never heard that before,' Annika said sceptically.

'Well, of course you haven't. Christina never let it leak out.'

Annika made some notes and thought for a moment.

'So when did you get involved with the Olympics?' she said.

Evert Danielsson smiled.

'You're wondering how much dirt I've got on my hands? How much shit I dealt with personally? Quite a bit. I stayed with the bank when Christina went off to run the Olympics campaign, taking over some of her responsibilities – mostly administrative matters. The fact that I started working for the Olympics happened entirely by chance.'

He leaned back in his chair, apparently in a much brighter mood now.

'Once Christina had secured the Games, things changed completely. The post of managing director of SOCOG was prestigious, all of a sudden. Everyone agreed that it should go to a competent individual with a wealth of business experience.'

'There were several people under consideration, weren't there? All men?' Annika said.

'Yes, and in particular one man who was in charge of one of the big nationalized companies at the time.'

Annika thought back, and conjured up an image of the man's jolly, smiling face.

'That's right, he pulled out for personal reasons, didn't he, and ended up being appointed a County Governor instead?'

Evert Danielsson smiled.

'Yes, that's precisely what happened. But those personal reasons were actually a receipt from a brothel in Berlin, which landed on my desk just after the Games were awarded to Stockholm.'

Annika looked up in surprise. The former chairman was enjoying himself now.

'I don't know how she did it, but somehow Christina found out that the man had taken several colleagues to a porn club during some big socialist conference in Germany. She dug out the credit-card bill, and of course it had been claimed on expenses, paid for by the tax-payer, and that was that.'

'How? And how did you get hold of it?'

Evert Danielsson pushed away his cup and leaned forward over the table.

'When the Games had been won, the plan was for Christina to return to the bank. The Swedish Olympic Committee were quick off the mark trying to get her contracted position to revert to us again, and because I had already taken on some of her formal duties, it was natural that I ended up dealing with any expenses and receipts that trickled in.'

'Did that really mean that you were authorized to open her mail?' Annika asked quietly.

The smile on the man's face stiffened.

'I'm not going to pretend that I'm pure as the driven snow,' he said. 'I passed on the original claim to Christina

306

without comment, but I made sure I took a copy first. The following day the man in question announced that he no longer intended to accept the offer to become managing director of SOCOG. And he recommended Christina Furhage for the job. Which was how it turned out, of course.'

'And when did you come into the picture?'

Evert Danielsson leaned back with a sigh.

'I was thoroughly sick of the bank by then. The fact that I had been given a lot of Christina's duties showed what the directors thought of me. I had no future there. So I showed Christina my copy of the receipt and said I wanted a job in the Olympic headquarters, a good job. And just one month later I was appointed chair of the committee.'

Annika looked down and thought for a moment. It made sense. If the director had indeed taken 'several colleagues' to a brothel after an international socialist conference, then his wasn't the only head on the block. The other men must have been influential socialists, so their careers and reputations were also at stake. They could well be local or national politicians, senior civil servants or union bosses. Whoever they were, they had a lot to lose from being revealed as brothel customers. They would lose their public responsibilities or get the sack, and they were almost bound to be charged with deception or false accounting. Their families would suffer, their marriages would probably collapse. For the director himself, the choice must have been fairly straightforward: step aside from leading the Olympic project or ruin his own and his friends' lives.

'Have you still got your copy of the receipt?' Annika asked.

Evert Danielsson shrugged.

307

'Sadly not. I had to give it to Christina in exchange for the job.'

Annika looked at the man in front of her. Maybe he was telling the truth, the story made sense and it wasn't exactly flattering to him. Then she suddenly remembered where she had seen the blackmailed director's happy, smiling face recently: standing next to Christina Furhage in one of the crop of memorial articles.

'Isn't the director on the Board?' she said.

Evert Danielsson nodded.

'Yes, but of course he's a County Governor these days.'

Annika felt suddenly uneasy. Evert Danielsson might simply be out for revenge. Maybe he was trying to trick her. As he had pointed out, it made no difference to Christina now, but he could still damage the members of the group that had fired him.

She decided to carry on with the conversation and see where it led.

'How did Christina handle the job?' she asked.

'Magnificently, of course. She knew all the tricks of the trade. She got on extremely well with several of the most important IOC delegates. I don't know exactly how she did it, but she got some serious support from them. I'd guess at sex, money or drugs, or maybe all three. Christina left nothing to chance.'

Annika was making notes, and trying to maintain a neutral expression.

'You indicated before that she had a lot of enemies.'

Evert Danielsson gave a short, dry laugh.

'Oh yes,' he said. 'I can think of a whole series of people, from our time in the bank onwards, who would be happy to see her brought down, or even dead. She could humiliate any man who tried to be macho in her presence, to the point where he would break down in public. Sometimes I think she actually enjoyed doing it.'

'Didn't she like men?'

'She didn't like people, but she preferred women. In bed, at least.'

Annika blinked.

'What makes you say that?'

'She had a relationship with Helena Starke; I'm absolutely convinced of it.'

'So you don't know for sure?'

The man looked at Annika.

'You can tell when two people have a sexual relationship. They stand in each other's personal space, a little too close; they accidentally touch each other while they're working. Little things, but they all add up.'

'But she didn't like all women?'

'No, not at all. She hated women who flirted. She crushed them under her heels, criticizing everything they did and bullying them until they resigned. Sometimes I think she enjoyed sacking people in public. One of the worst instances of that was when she attacked a young girl called Beata Ekesjö in front of loads of people.'

47

Annika's eyes opened wide.

'You mean that Beata Ekesjö hated Christina Furhage?'

'With a passion,' Evert Danielsson said, and Annika felt the hairs on the back of her neck stand up. Now she knew the man was lying. As recently as yesterday, Beata Ekesjö had said how much she admired Christina Furhage. Christina was her idol; she was devastated by her death. There was no doubt at all about that. Evert Danielsson was making a big mistake here, but of course he had no idea that Annika happened to know who Beata was.

By now it was half past eleven and the restaurant had started to fill with lunchtime customers. Evert Danielsson kept looking round uncomfortably; presumably a lot of his former colleagues from Olympic headquarters came here, and he evidently didn't want to be seen with a journalist.

Annika decided to ask a few final, decisive questions.

'Who do you think killed Christina, and why?'

Evert Danielsson ran his tongue over his lips and took hold of the edge of the table again.

'I haven't the faintest idea. But it was someone who

really hated her. You don't blow up half a stadium unless you're seriously angry.'

'Are you aware of any connection between Christina Furhage and Stefan Bjurling?'

Evert Danielsson looked bewildered.

'Who's Stefan Bjurling?'

'The second victim. He worked for one of your subcontractors, Bygg and Rör.'

'Right, they're one of the most reliable subcontractors. They've been involved in pretty much every construction project SOCOG has organized in the past seven years. So it was one of their men who died?'

'Don't you read the papers?' Annika countered. 'He was a foreman, thirty-nine years old, ash-blond hair, well-built . . .'

'Oh, him,' Evert Danielsson said. 'Yes, I do know who he is. Steffe. He's – or rather, he was – a really nasty piece of work.'

'His workmates said he was a happy, friendly man.'

Evert Danielsson laughed.

'Good grief, that's just what you have to say about the dead!'

'But was there any connection between him and Christina Furhage?' Annika repeated.

He pursed his lips, thinking. He caught sight of a group of people coming in and seemed to tense up, then relaxed again. It obviously wasn't anyone he knew.

'Yes, there was, come to think of it,' he said.

Annika waited, careful not to change the expression on her face.

'Christina was sitting next to Stefan at the big Christmas party last week. They sat and talked long after we'd finished the meal.'

'The party at the Basque restaurant?' Annika asked.

'No, no, that was the office party. This was the big

311

Olympic party, with all the delegates and volunteers, all the people employed by the subcontractors . . . We won't be doing anything on that scale again until after the Games are over.'

'So Christina Furhage and Stefan Bjurling knew each other?' Annika said in astonishment.

Evert Danielsson's face clouded over. It had suddenly dawned on him that he could no longer talk about 'we', and that he probably wouldn't be invited to any more Olympics parties.

'Well, I don't know if they really knew each other, but they sat and talked to each other that night. Look, I think I'm going to have to—'

'How come Stefan Bjurling ended up sitting next to the managing director?' Annika said quickly. 'Why wasn't she sitting next to the chairman of the Board or some other big name?'

Evert Danielsson looked at her in irritation.

'Well, they weren't there, were they? This was a party for the troops. Mind you, it was still a pretty smart affair. Christina had chosen the venue, the Blue Hall of the City Hall, where they have the Nobel dinner.'

He stood up, pushing his chair back with his knees.

'What do you think they talked about?'

'Haven't the faintest idea. I've really got to go now.'

Annika stood up as well, gathering up her things and shaking the former chairman by the hand.

'Call if there's anything you want to tell me,' she said.

The man nodded and hurried out of the restaurant.

Instead of leaving the building, Annika went down one floor to where Anne Snapphane worked. She was told that Anne had started her Christmas break early, which was obviously nice for her. The receptionist called a taxi for Annika.

She thought about what she had been told as the taxi drove through the slush back to the paper. She couldn't tell any of this to the police, because the confidentiality of her sources was protected by law, but she could use what Evert Danielsson had told her to ask questions, including questions that involved him.

48

Lena Milander could hear Sigrid, the home-help, humming in the kitchen as she put yesterday's dishes in the dishwasher. Sigrid was a little under fifty, and her husband had left her when their daughters had grown up and Sigrid had grown too large. She cleaned, washed up, did the shopping and laundry, and prepared meals – practically a full-time job – for the Furhage-Milander family. She'd been doing it for almost two years now.

Mum had been happy about the recession, because they used to have trouble finding and keeping decent help, but in recent years people knew better than to give up a job. To be honest, the various secrecy clauses and threats of legal action that Mum made them sign may have had a certain negative effect on their willingness to take the job in the first place. But Sigrid seemed happy enough, and she had never been happier than in recent days. She seemed to enjoy being at the centre of things, being able to move unhindered through the world-famous murder victim's home. She was probably bitterly regretting the confidentiality agreement she had signed, and would doubtless have sold her story to the press if she could. She had cried decorously to start with, the sort of tears people let fall for Princess Diana. Lena recognized the sort. Sigrid had hardly met Mum since she signed the confidentiality agreement, although she had wiped up her toothpaste stains and washed her dirty underwear for almost two years. Maybe that led to a certain level of intimacy.

Sigrid had brought in the first editions of both evening papers, putting them on the little mirrored table out in the hall. Lena took the papers with her into the library, where her poor father was lying asleep on the sofa, mouth open. She sat in an armchair and put her feet up on the antique table in front of her. The two rags were of course full of the new bombing, but there was a bit of new information about Mum's death as well. She couldn't help reading the details about the explosives now that the analysis was complete. Maybe the psychologist at Huddinge Hospital had been wrong after all when he decided she wasn't a pyromaniac. She was fully aware that she took pleasure in fires, and anything to do with explosions, and so on. And fire engines, extinguishers, hydrants, and gas masks all made her happy, sending a little quiver through her body. Well, they had decided she was better now, and she had no intention of telling the doctors that their diagnosis might be wrong.

She leafed through the paper, then moved on to the other one. When she reached the centrefold it was like a punch to her stomach. Mum was staring out at her from the paper, her eyes smiling, and beneath the picture it said in large letters, THE IDEAL WOMAN. Lena cast the paper aside and screamed, a howl that echoed through the peace and quiet of the apartment. Poor Dad woke up and looked around, bewildered, saliva dribbling from the corner of his mouth. She stood up, overturning the table and grabbing hold of the nearest bookcase. The whole thing came crashing down, shelves and books hitting the floor with a terrible noise, smashing the television and stereo on their way down.

'Lena!'

She heard her father's despairing cry through a fog of hate, and came to her senses.

'Lena, Lena, what are you doing?'

Bertil Milander held out his arms to his daughter, the look of pain on his face making the young woman's own despair burst from her chest.

'Oh, Daddy!' she said, throwing herself into his arms.

Sigrid carefully closed the door on the father and daughter and went to fetch bin-bags, a brush and the vacuum cleaner.

When Annika arrived back at the office she ran straight into Patrik and Eva-Britt Qvist. They were on their way down to the canteen, and Annika decided to go with them. She could see the secretary wasn't happy, presumably because she had been hoping to talk about her. The staff canteen was called 'The Three Crowns', but was usually known as 'The Seven Rats' after a rumoured health and safety inspection. It was so full when they got there that there was hardly room for even a very small rat.

'Yesterday's work turned out really well,' Annika said to Patrik as she picked up an orange plastic tray from the end of the self-service counter.

'Do you think? Great!' the reporter said, lighting up.

'You made the analysis interesting, even though it was so technical. Where on earth did you find that explosives expert, the one who gave you all that stuff about different types of dynamite?'

'Yellow Pages, under "explosives". He was great! Do you know what he did? He let off three different charges while I was on the phone so I could hear the difference between different brands.'

Annika laughed. Eva-Britt Qvist didn't.

Dish of the day was herring salad with ham and stockfish, traditional Christmas fare. Annika got a cheeseburger and French fries. The only spare table was at the far end of the canteen, in the smokers' section. So they ate quickly without talking, then went up to the newsroom to talk about today's work over coffee.

On the way up they bumped into Nils Langeby. He was back at work after taking the time in lieu that he had accumulated over the weekend. He straightened when he caught sight of Annika and the others.

'Are we going to have a run-through today, or what?' he challenged.

'Yes, in quarter of an hour. My office,' Annika said.

She wanted to go to the toilet and work out her thoughts first.

'Right, good. We've been far too sloppy with run-throughs recently,' Nils Langeby said. Annika pretended she hadn't heard and carried on towards the ladies' bathroom. She really had to make an effort not to say something crushing to the older reporter. In Annika's opinion, he was incredibly fucking bitter, mean and mad. But he was part of the team she was responsible for, so she had to find a way of working with him. She was aware that he was trying to provoke her into making a mistake, and she had no intention of providing him with one.

Nils Langeby had already made himself comfortable on the sofa in Annika's office when she got back from the toilet. The fact that he had gone into her room while she wasn't there annoyed her, but she decided not to show it.

'Where are Patrik and Eva-Britt?' she asked instead.

'Surely you should know that. I thought you were in charge here, not me?' Nils Langeby said.

She went out and asked Patrik and Eva-Britt to come

to her room, then went over to Ingvar Johansson, the editor, and asked him to come along as well. On the way back she picked up a cup of coffee.

'Didn't you get me a cup?' Nils Langeby teased as she entered the room.

Deep breaths, she thought, sitting down behind her desk.

'No,' she said, 'I didn't know you wanted coffee. But you've got time to get some if you hurry.'

He didn't move. The others came in and sat down.

'Okay,' Annika said. 'Four pieces. The hunt for the Bomber: the police have to have some new ideas by now. We need to try to crack that today. Has anyone got anything good on that?'

She left the question open, looking round at her colleagues: Patrik, thinking so hard you could almost hear it; Ingvar Johansson, sceptical but detached, and Eva-Britt Qvist and Nils Langeby, who were just waiting for her to mess up.

'I can do a bit of digging,' Patrik said.

'What were the police saying last night?' Annika wondered. 'Did you get the impression that they're looking for a connection between the two victims?'

'Definitely,' Patrik said. 'It could be anything, maybe just the Games alone, but something makes me think the police have got more than they're saying. They seem really focused, and they're not saying much, which might mean they're about to arrest someone.'

'We'll have to keep a close eye on that,' Annika said. 'It's not enough to listen to police radio and rely on tip-offs, we've got to try to work out if they're about to arrest someone. Pictures of the Bomber being led to a police car in handcuffs would be a worldwide scoop.'

'I'll try to find something out,' Patrik said.

'Good. I'll make some calls as well. Number two: I

know there's a link – the victims knew each other. They sat next to each other at a Christmas party last week, and evidently had a good chat.'

'Bloody hell,' Patrik said. 'That's brilliant!'

Ingvar Johansson came to life as well.

'What if there are pictures!' he said. 'Stunning! Imagine the picture, bomb victims embracing beneath the mistletoe, and the headline: NOW THEY'RE BOTH DEAD!'

'I'll try to find out if there are any pictures,' Annika said. 'There may be more than one link between the victims. I met Evert Danielsson this morning, and when I described Stefan Bjurling he knew exactly who he was. He even called him "Steffe". So Christina Furhage may have known him as well, even before the Christmas party.'

'Why did you meet Danielsson?' Ingvar Johansson wondered.

'He wanted to talk,' Annika said.

'What about?' Johansson said, and Annika realized that she'd walked into a trap. She would have to say something, otherwise she would be in the same position as at the editorial meeting on Monday evening, and she certainly didn't want that, especially not when Nils Langeby and Eva-Britt Qvist were here. So she said, 'He thought Christina Furhage was a lesbian. He thought she was having an affair with a woman in the office, Helena Starke, but he had no proof. It was just a feeling, he said.'

No one said anything.

'Three: had any threats been made against Stefan Bjurling? Has anyone heard anything? No? Okay, I'll check up on that. And finally, four: what happens next? Security, the Games, will everything be ready in time, terrorist groups under observation, etc, etc. Are you covering all that out in the newsroom?'

319

Ingvar Johansson sighed. 'No, there's hardly a single reporter in today. They've all taken time off before Christmas.'

'Nils, can you look into that?' Annika said.

It was framed as a question, but was actually an order.

'Well,' Nils Langeby said, 'I'm just wondering how much longer the rest of us are going to have to sit and listen to this?'

'What do you mean?' Annika said, straightening up.

'Are we really supposed to sit here like schoolchildren while you ram jobs down our throats? Where the hell is our analysis? What about reflection, afterthought? That used to be the hallmark of the *Evening Post*, didn't it?'

Annika wondered how best to react for a moment. She could take hold of the situation, ask Nils Langeby to be more specific, then nail him when he failed, and force him into a corner like a scared animal. But that would take at least an hour, and every bone in her body told her she didn't have the energy for that.

'Okay, you can take care of that, can't you?' she said instead, and stood up. 'Was there anything else?'

Ingvar Johansson and Patrik left first, followed by Eva-Britt Qvist and Nils Langeby. But Nils Langeby stopped and turned round in the doorway.

'I think it's a real shame how the crime section has deteriorated,' he said. 'All we do is crap these days. Haven't you noticed how we're being overtaken by all the other media?'

Annika went up to him and took hold of the door.

'I haven't got time for this right now,' she said breathlessly. 'Go away.'

'I think it's rather pathetic when the head of department can't handle a simple discussion,' Nils Langeby said.

320

He walked away, provocatively slowly.

'I swear I'm going to do that man some serious damage one day,' Annika said. 'The next time he starts whining I'll kick his teeth in.'

She shut the door so she could think, and went back to her desk. She looked up Bygg & Rör, the building company that Stefan Bjurling worked for, in the phone book and found a mobile number in the list. It turned out to be the managing director's number, a man in early middle-age, who was evidently out at a site somewhere.

'Yes, I was at the Christmas party,' he said.

'I don't suppose you happened to have a camera with you?' Annika asked.

The man said something to someone standing next to him.

'A camera? No, I didn't. Why?'

'Do you know if anyone else did? Anyone who took pictures at the Christmas party?'

'What? It's over there, behind the scaffolding! Pictures. Hmm . . . There must have been someone. Why do you ask?'

'You don't know if Stefan Bjurling had a camera with him?'

The man was quiet for a moment, she could hear nothing but the noise of a truck in the background. When he spoke again his voice had changed tone.

'Listen, young lady, where did you say you were calling from?'

'The *Evening Post*, my name's Annika Bengt—'

He hung up.

Annika put down the phone and thought for a minute. Who was most likely to have taken a picture of Stefan Bjurling together with the world-famous head of the Games?

49

She took several deep breaths and then dialled Eva Bjurling's number out in Farsta. The woman sounded tired but composed when she answered. Annika said all the usual sympathetic phrases, but the woman interrupted her.

'What do you want?'

'I was wondering if either you or your husband knew the head of SOCOG, Christina Furhage, personally?' Annika said.

The woman thought.

'Well, I didn't,' she said. 'But Stefan must have met her; he used to mention her occasionally.'

Annika started her tape-recorder.

'What did he say about her?'

'I don't know,' the woman said with a sigh. 'He just talked about her, said she was a tough cookie, stuff like that. I don't really remember . . .'

'But you got the impression they knew each other personally?'

'Well, I wouldn't really say that. Why, do you think they might have?'

'I was just wondering. They sat next to each other at the Christmas party last week.'

'Did they? Steffe didn't mention that. He said it was a pretty dull event.'

'Did he happen to have a camera with him at the party?'

'Steffe? No, definitely not. He thought cameras were a bit stupid.'

Annika hesitated a few seconds, then decided to ask what she was actually thinking.

'I'm sorry if this upsets you, but I'm just wondering how you're managing to sound so together?'

The woman sighed again.

'Well, obviously I'm sad, but Steffe wasn't exactly an angel,' she said. 'Being married to him was pretty hard work. I was on the point of divorcing him twice, but changed my mind. I couldn't get rid of him. He always came back, and he never gave up.'

It sounded like a very familiar situation. Annika knew what her next question had to be.

'Did he abuse you?'

The woman hesitated a moment, then evidently made up her mind to be honest.

'He was found guilty of actual bodily harm and making unlawful threats once. The judge issued a restraining order, but he just kept breaking it. In the end I couldn't be bothered to fight any more, and took him back,' the woman said calmly.

'Did you think he'd get better?'

'He'd stopped promising to change; we were way past that stage. But it did actually get better. This past year hasn't been too bad.'

'Did you ever try a women's refuge?'

The question came out quite naturally; Annika must have asked it a hundred times or more over the years. Eva Bjurling hesitated once more, but decided to answer.

'A couple of times, but it was hard for the kids. They couldn't go to nursery and school as usual, it just got too messy.'

Annika waited without saying anything.

'So you're wondering why I'm not in pieces?' Eva Bjurling said. 'Of course I'm sorry, mostly for the kids' sake. They loved their dad, but life will be easier now he's not here. He used to drink a lot. So it's . . .'

They were silent for a few moments.

'Well, I won't take up any more of your time,' Annika said. 'Thank you for being so honest. It's important to get the facts straight.'

The woman suddenly got worried.

'You're not going to write about this? The neighbours round here don't know any of this.'

'No,' Annika said. 'I'm not going to write about it, but I'm glad I know, because it might stop me getting things wrong later on.'

They hung up and Annika turned off the tape-recorder. She sat at her desk staring into thin air for a while. Women were being abused all over the place; she had learned that over the years. She had written several series of articles about women and the violence they suffered, and as her thoughts roamed freely she realized that this was another factor the victims had in common. People who didn't know them particularly well heaped praise on them, then they turned out to be real bastards. As long as Evert Danielsson wasn't lying about Christina.

She sighed and switched on her Mac.

It was just as well to get everything written down while it was still fresh in her head. As the various programs started up on the computer she fished her notepad out of her bag. She really wasn't sure what to make of Evert Danielsson. One moment he seemed professional and competent, and the next he was crying because they'd taken his company car away. Were men in positions of power really so sensitive and naïve? The answer was probably yes. Men in positions of power were no more unusual than any others. If they lost their job or anything else they cared about, they had a crisis. A person under pressure and in a crisis doesn't act rationally, no matter what title they happen to have.

She had almost written up all her notes when the phone rang.

'You said I should get in touch if you got anything wrong,' a voice said.

It was a young woman's voice, but Annika couldn't place it.

'Of course,' she said, trying to sound neutral. 'How can I help you?'

'You said it when you came to see us on Sunday. That I should call you and tell you if there was anything wrong with anything in the paper. Well, you've really messed up big time.'

It was Lena Milander. Annika's eyes opened wide and she fumbled with the tape-recorder.

'How do you mean?' she said.

'You must have read your own paper. You've got a huge picture of Mum, and underneath it you put *the ideal woman*. How the hell would you know?'

'What do you think we should have written, then?' Annika said.

'Nothing at all,' Lena Milander said. 'Leave Mum alone. We haven't even buried her yet.'

'As far as we know, your mum was an ideal woman,' Annika said. 'How can we say anything else if no one tells us otherwise?'

'Why do you have to go on writing anything at all?'

'You mum was a public figure. She chose that for

325

herself. She helped create the public image of her. If no one tells us otherwise, then that's all we've got to go on.'

Lena Milander was silent for a while, then she said, 'Meet me at the Pelican on Södermalm in half an hour. Afterwards you'll be promising me never to write this sort of rubbish again.'

Then she hung up, leaving Annika staring at the receiver in surprise. She quickly saved the file of notes from her meeting with Evert Danielsson onto a USB stick, deleted the document from the computer, grabbed her bag and coat and hurried out.

50

Anders Schyman was sitting in his office going through the sales figures for the past weekend. He felt good; this was what it should look like. On Saturday the competition had beaten them, as they usually did. But on Sunday they had bucked the trend. The *Evening Post* had won the sales war for the first time in over a year, even though their supplement was neither as big nor as expensively produced as the other evening paper's. It was their coverage of the bombing at Stockholm's Victoria Stadium that had driven up sales, and the defining article was obviously the one on the front, Annika's discovery that Christina Furhage's life had been threatened.

There was a knock on the door. It was Eva-Britt Qvist.

'Come in, come in,' the editor-in-chief said, gesturing towards the chair on the other side of the desk.

The secretary smiled fleetingly, adjusted her skirt and cleared her throat.

'Well, there's just something I'd like to talk to you about.'

'By all means,' Anders Schyman said, leaning back in his chair. He put his hands behind his head and looked at Eva-Britt Qvist through half-closed eyelids. He was willing to bet that this was going to be unpleasant.

'There's a really bad atmosphere in the crime team these days,' the secretary said. 'No one enjoys working there any more. I've been here a long time, and I don't think we should just accept that's the way it has to be.'

'No, of course we shouldn't,' Anders Schyman said. 'Can you give me a concrete example of what you mean?'

The secretary shifted on her seat and tried to think.

'Well, it's not nice to be ordered to come into work when you're in the middle of baking, just before Christmas and everything. There has to be a degree of flexibility in a team like this.'

'Were you called into work when you were in the middle of baking?' Schyman said.

'Yes, by Annika Bengtzon.'

'Was it to do with the Bomber, by any chance?'

'Yes, and I think she handled it incredibly badly.'

'So you don't think it's right that you should have to put in extra hours when everyone else is?' he said calmly. 'Tragic events on this scale happen very rarely in this country, thank goodness.'

The woman was starting to blush, and decided to go on the attack.

'Annika Bengtzon has no idea how to behave! Do you know what she said after lunch today? That she wanted to kick Nils Langeby's teeth in!'

Anders Schyman had difficulty not laughing.

'I see,' he said. 'Did she really say that to Nils Langeby?'

'No, not to anyone, more to herself, but I still heard it. And it was quite unreasonable; you really shouldn't say things like that at work.'

The editor-in-chief leaned forward, his clasped hands almost reaching the far side of the desk.

'You're quite right, Eva-Britt, that sort of thing isn't

appropriate. But do you know what I think is considerably worse? When workmates keep running to the boss to tell tales.'

Eva-Britt Qvist's face went completely white, then flaming red. Anders Schyman didn't take his eyes off her. She looked down at her lap, looked up, then down again, then got up and walked out. She would probably spend the next fifteen minutes crying in the toilet.

The editor-in-chief leaned back and sighed. He hoped he'd done his share of playground management for the week, but somehow he doubted it.

Annika jumped out of the taxi outside number 40 Blekingegatan, momentarily bewildered by little Miss Milander from lovely Östermalm's choice of meeting-place. The Pelican was an old-fashioned beer hall, with tall ceilings, good traditional food and fairly raucous noise levels in the evenings. At the moment it was relatively quiet in the main hall, just a few people sitting around the walls and chatting over a beer or a sandwich. Lena Milander had just arrived, and was sitting with her back to the far wall, taking deep drags on a hand-rolled cigarette.

Lena Milander fitted in perfectly here, with her short hair, black clothes and sombre facial expression. She could easily have been a regular. That theory turned out to be accurate when the waitress came over to take their order, saying: 'The usual, Lena?'

Annika ordered a cup of coffee and a cheese and ham sandwich; Lena a beer and a plate of hash. The young woman stubbed out her half-smoked cigarette, looked at Annika and gave her a crooked smile.

'I don't really smoke, but I like lighting cigarettes,' she said, studying Annika intently as she said it.

'Yes, I know you like setting fire to things,' Annika

said, blowing on her coffee. 'The children's home in Botkyrka, for instance.'

Lena's expression didn't change.

'How long are you going to go on lying about Mum?'

'Until we know better,' Annika said.

Lena lit the cigarette again and blew smoke in Annika's face. Annika didn't blink.

'Have you bought any Christmas presents yet, then?' Lena said, pulling a strand of tobacco from her teeth.

'Some. Have you got one for Olof?'

Lena's eyes glazed over slightly, and she took a deep drag on the cigarette.

'Your brother, I mean,' Annika went on. 'We may as well start with that, don't you think?'

'I don't have any contact with him,' Lena said, looking out of the window.

Annika felt a shiver run down her spine. Olof was alive!

'Why not?' she asked, as blankly as she could.

'We never have had. Mum didn't want us to.'

Annika took out her pad and pen, as well as the copy of the family portrait taken when Olof was two years old, and put it on the table in front of Lena. The girl stared at it for a long time.

'I've never seen this before,' she said. 'Where did you find it?'

'It was in the archive. You can have it if you like.'

Lena shook her head.

'There's no point, I'd only set fire to it.'

Annika put it back in her bag.

'So what did you want to tell me about your mum?' she said.

Lena fingered her cigarette.

'Everyone keeps saying that she was so wonderful.

In your paper today she's practically a saint. But Mum was a really tragic person. She failed at loads of things. And she hid all the failures by threatening and betraying people. Sometimes I think there was something wrong with her, she was so fucking mean.'

The young woman fell silent and looked out through the window again. It was starting to get dark already, and the snow looked like it was never going to stop falling.

'Can you tell me what you mean by that?' Annika said carefully.

'Take Olof, for instance,' Lena went on. 'I didn't even know he existed until Grandma mentioned him. That was when I was eleven.'

Annika was making notes, waiting for her to go on.

'Grandpa died when Mum was little. Grandma sent her to stay with family in upper Norrland. That was where she grew up. The relatives up there didn't like her, but Grandma was paying them.

'When she was twelve she was sent to boarding school, and she stayed there until she got married to Carl. The old man in the photograph. He was almost forty years older than Mum, but he came from a very good family. Grandma thought that sort of thing was important. She was the one who arranged it.'

Lena started rolling a new cigarette. She did it by hand, and wasn't very good at it, scattering tobacco on her untouched plate of food.

'Mum was only twenty when Olof was born, and old Carl liked showing off his new family. Then his business went bust and the money ran out. Suddenly it was no fun having a penniless child-bride any more, so the old bastard dumped Mum and Olof and got married to an old bag who was loaded.'

'Dorotea Adelcrona,' Annika said, and Lena nodded.

'Dorotea was an old forestry owner's widow from somewhere near Sundsvall. She was rolling in money, and Carl was keen to get his hands on it. The old bag died a year or so later, and Carl was suddenly the richest widower in Norrland. He set up some sort of big award for daft forestry stuff.'

Annika nodded. 'That's right. It still gets awarded every year.'

'Whatever. Mum didn't get a penny. And of course she was a social pariah. In the fifties, a poor, divorced single mother wasn't exactly the most popular person to have around, and Mum always set great store by that kind of thing. She had some sort of business qualification from boarding school, and moved to Malmö where she got a job as a secretary for someone running a scrap business. She left Olof with an old couple out in Tungelsta.'

Annika looked up from her notes.

'She gave him away?'

'Yep. He was five years old. I don't know if she ever saw him again.'

'Why?' Annika said, slightly shocked. The thought of giving away Kalle made her feel sick.

'He was too much trouble, she said. But the real reason was that she wanted to work and not have to drag a child around with her. She wanted a career.'

'Yes, and she certainly managed that,' Annika muttered.

'Things were pretty bad to start with. Her first boss forced himself on her and she got pregnant, or at least that's what she said. She went to Poland to have an abortion, and ended up getting really ill afterwards. The doctors didn't think she'd ever be able to have children again. She got fired, of course, but found a new job in a bank in Skara. She stayed there until she got a job in head office in Stockholm. She climbed the greasy ladder pretty quickly; and somewhere along the way she met Dad, and he fell head over heels in love with her. They got married a couple of years later, and then Dad started going on about wanting children. Mum said no, but stopped taking the pill to make him happy. Presumably she didn't think she could get pregnant again.'

'But she did,' Annika said.

Lena nodded.

'She was over forty. You can imagine how angry she was. Abortions were legal by then, but for once Dad stood up to her. He refused to let her have an abortion, and threatened to leave her if she went ahead anyway. So she bit the bullet and gave birth to me.'

The young woman made a face and drank some beer.

'Who told you all this?' Annika asked.

'Mum, of course. She made no bones about what she thought of me. She always said she hated me. My earliest memory is Mum pushing me away so hard that I fell over and hurt myself. Dad liked me, but he never had the courage to show how much. He was pretty scared of Mum.'

She thought for a moment, then went on: 'I think most people were scared of Mum. She had a way of frightening people. Anyone who ever got close to her had to sign a confidentiality agreement. They were never allowed to talk about Christina in public without her approval.'

'Is that even legal?' Annika said.

Lena Milander shrugged. 'Doesn't matter. People believed it, and were scared into silence.'

'It's hardly surprising we never really found out much at the paper, then,' Annika said.

'Mum herself was only frightened of two people: me and Olof.'

How sad, Annika thought.

'She was worried I'd set fire to the house,' Lena said with a wry smile. 'Ever since I set fire to the parquet floor in the sitting room out in Tyresö she was terrified of me getting hold of a box of matches. She sent me to a clinic for "disturbed children", the children's home, but when I burned that down I was sent home again. That's what happens to children who are out of control. When the Social Services can't be bothered to try any more, the parents get their little brats back again.'

She lit a fresh, crumpled cigarette.

'Once I was experimenting with homemade explosives out in the garage. It detonated too soon and blew the garage door off. I got shrapnel in my leg. Mum was convinced I was going to blow her up with a car-bomb, and after that she had a massive complex about car-bombs.'

She laughed humourlessly.

'How did you learn how to make explosives?' Annika asked.

'Oh, there are various recipes floating around on the internet, it's not that difficult. Do you want to know how?'

'No thanks. So why was she frightened of Olof?'

'I don't really know, she never said. She just said I should watch out for Olof, that he was dangerous. He must have threatened her somehow, I suppose.'

'Have you ever met him?'

The young woman shook her head, her eyes moist. She blew out a plume of smoke and tapped a long pillar of ash onto the side of her plate.

'I don't know where he is,' she said.

'But you think he's still alive?'

Lena took a deep drag on the cigarette and looked at Annika.

'Why else would Mum have been so frightened?' she said. 'If Olof was dead then we wouldn't have to keep our identities secret.'

That makes sense, Annika thought. She hesitated for a moment, then asked a difficult question. 'Do you think your mum ever met anyone else that she fell in love with?'

Lena shrugged.

'I don't give a shit,' she said. 'I doubt it, though. Mum hated men. Sometimes I think she hated Dad too.'

Annika dropped the subject.

'So as you can see, she wasn't exactly "the ideal woman",' Lena said.

'No, she wasn't,' Annika said.

'So will you be printing that again?'

'I hope we can avoid that in future,' Annika said. 'But it sounds to me as though your mum was a victim as well.'

'How do you mean?' Lena said, suddenly wary.

'Well, she got sent away, just like Olof.'

'There was a big difference. Grandma couldn't look after her, there was a war on, and Grandma did really love her. It was Grandma's biggest regret that Christina didn't grow up with her.'

'Is your grandmother still alive?'

'No, she died last year. Mum actually went to the funeral, probably because it would have looked bad if she didn't. But Grandma saw Mum every school holiday when Mum was little, and always spent Mum's birthday with her.'

'It sounds like you can forgive your grandmother, but not your mum,' Annika said.

'When did you get to be a fucking psychiatrist?'

Annika held her hands up. 'Sorry.'

Lena looked at her suspiciously.

'Okay,' she eventually said, downing the last of the beer. 'I'm going to sit here and get drunk. Do you want to join me in my search for oblivion?'

Annika smiled weakly.

'I'm afraid I can't,' she said, gathering up her things. She put on her coat and scarf, and hoisted the bag onto her shoulder. Then she stopped and said, 'Who do you think killed your mother?'

Lena's eyes narrowed.

'Well, it wasn't me,' she said.

'Did she know anyone by the name of Stefan Bjurling?'

'The latest victim? Haven't a clue. Just don't write any more crap from now on,' Lena Milander said, then demonstratively turned her head away.

Annika took the hint, turned to the waitress and paid for their order, then walked out.

51

The woman walked into the ultra-modern entrance to the *Evening Post*, trying to look as though she belonged there. She was wearing a straight, calf-length woollen coat that shifted between turquoise and lilac depending on the light, and her hair was hidden under a brown beret. On her left shoulder she had a replica Chanel bag, and in her right hand she was carrying a leather brief-case. She was wearing gloves.

As the outer doors slid shut behind her she stopped and looked round, her eyes fixing on the glassed-in reception desk in the left-hand corner. She adjusted the thin strap of her bag and set off towards the glass booth.

One of the caretakers, Tore Brand, was sitting inside. He had stepped in while the usual receptionist went off for a cup of coffee and a cigarette.

Tore Brand pressed the button to open the hatch when the woman had almost reached the desk. He adopted an official expression and asked curtly: 'Yes?'

The woman hoisted her bag up onto her shoulder once again and cleared her throat.

'Yes, I'm looking for one of your reporters, an Annika Bengtzon. She works in—'

'Yes, I know,' Tore Brad interrupted. 'She's not here.'

The caretaker's finger was about to press the button

to close the hatch. The woman fingered the handle of the briefcase nervously.

'I see, not here . . . When will she be back?'

'Difficult to say,' Tore Brand said. 'She's out on a job and you never know what might happen or how long it's going to take.'

He leaned forward and added confidentially, 'This is a newspaper, you know.'

The woman laughed in a slightly forced way.

'Thanks, I know. But I'd really like to see Annika Bengtzon. There's something I want to give her.'

'I see. What?' the caretaker asked curiously. 'Is it anything I can pass on to her?'

The woman took a step back.

'It's for Annika, no one else. We spoke yesterday, it's quite important.'

'If you want to leave any files or documents with me I'll see that she gets them.'

'Thanks, but I think I'll come back another time.'

'We get people bringing boxes full of stuff every day, leaflets and insurance offers and all sorts, and we take them all. If you want to leave anything with me I'll take care of it.'

The woman turned on her heel and almost ran for the door. Tore Brand shut the hatch, thinking how much he wanted a cigarette.

Annika was forcing her way through the crowds of Christmas shoppers on Götgatan after leaving the Pelican when she suddenly realized that she was only a couple of blocks from where Helena Starke lived. Instead of fighting against the tide coming out of the underground station at Skanstull, she turned round and let herself be carried along with the flow.

She slipped and slid her way along Ringvägen: they

were just as bad at clearing the roads here as over on Kungsholmen. Her memory for numbers didn't let her down as she typed in the door-code, and she was soon inside number 139. This time Helena Starke opened her door after just one short ring.

'You don't give up, do you?' she said as the door opened.

'Can I just ask a couple of questions?' Annika implored.

Helena Starke sighed loudly.

'What is it with you? What the hell do you want from me?'

'Please, not here in the stairwell—'

'I don't care any more; I'm moving.'

She yelled the last word so that anyone listening would hear. That would give them something to talk about.

Annika glanced past the woman's shoulder, and it certainly looked as though she was packing her belongings. Helena Starke shrugged.

'Oh, come in then, but you'd better be quick. I'm leaving tonight.'

Annika decided to get straight to the point.

'I know you were lying about the boy, Olof, but that's fine. I'm here to ask if it's true that you were having a relationship with Christina Furhage.'

'If I was, what the hell is it to do with you?' Helena Starke said calmly.

'Nothing, I'm just trying to piece everything together. So were you?'

Helena Starke sighed.

'If I say I was, it would end up on posters outside newsagents and kiosks all over the country tomorrow, wouldn't it?'

'Of course not,' Annika said. 'Christina's sexuality had nothing to do with her public duties.'

'Okay,' Helena Starke said, almost amused by this. 'In that case, yes. Happy now?'

Annika was a little taken aback.

'So what else do you want to ask?' Helena Starke said sharply. 'What we did when we fucked? If we used dildos or fingers? If Christina screamed when she came?'

Annika lowered her eyes, feeling like an idiot. This really wasn't any of her business.

'Sorry,' she said. 'I really didn't mean to be intrusive.'

'No, but you were, weren't you?' Starke said. 'Was there anything else?'

'Did you know Stefan Bjurling?' Annika said, looking up again.

'He was a real bastard,' Starke said. 'If anyone ever deserved to get their kidneys blown out, he did.'

'Did Christina know him?'

'She knew who he was.'

Annika closed the door, which had been open since she came in.

'Please, can you tell me what Christina was really like?'

'Bloody hell, you've been filling the papers with articles about what she was like all week!'

'I mean Christina the person, not the public façade.'

Helena Starke leaned against the frame of the living-room door and looked at Annika with interest.

'Why are you so keen to find out?' she said.

Annika breathed in through her nose. The flat really did smell awful.

'Every time I talk to someone who knew Christina, the picture changes. I think you were the only person who was really close to her.'

'You're wrong,' Helena Starke said. She turned and

walked away, sitting down in the sofa in the small living room. Annika followed her in without being asked.

'So who did know her, then?'

'No one,' Helena said. 'Not even her. Sometimes she got scared by who she was, or rather the person she had become. Christina carried a lot of demons around with her.'

Annika looked at the woman's face, half turned away from her. The light from the hall was on her neck and her classical profile. Helena Starke was actually strikingly beautiful. The rest of the room was in darkness, and outside the traffic thundered along Ringvägen.

'What form did those demons take?' Annika asked quietly.

Helena Starke sighed.

'She had a hell of a life, from childhood onwards. She was extremely intelligent, but that never seemed to count for anything. People were always messing her about, and she dealt with it by becoming cold and remote.'

'What do you mean, messing her about?'

'She was a real trail-blazer as a female manager in the private sector, in the banking industry and in the board-room. People were always trying to bring her down, but they never succeeded.'

'Well, maybe they did actually manage to anyway, in spite of everything,' Annika said. 'People sometimes crack, even though the exterior looks intact.'

Helena Starke didn't reply. She was staring blankly into the darkness. After a while she raised a hand to her eye to wipe something away.

'Did people know that you . . . were together?'

Helena Starke shook her head.

'No, not a single person. There was probably gossip, but no one ever asked us straight out. Christina was frightened it would get out, so she changed her driver

341

every eight weeks so they would never work out why she came here so often.'

'Why was she worried about it? There are loads of people in public life who are open about their sexuality these days.'

'It wasn't just that,' Helena Starke said. 'Relationships of any sort weren't allowed inside the Olympic office; Christina had brought in that rule. If our relationship became public, I'd have to leave. And she probably wouldn't have been able to hang on as managing director if she was seen to have broken one of her own big rules.'

Annika let the words sink in. Yet another thing that Christina Furhage was afraid of. She looked at Helena Starke's lowered face in profile and realized the paradox. Christina Furhage had risked everything she had spent all her life fighting for, for the sake of this woman.

'She was here that last night, wasn't she?'

Helena Starke nodded. 'We took a taxi; I think Christina paid cash. I don't really remember, but that's what she usually did. I was really drunk, but I remember that Christina was angry. She didn't like me drinking and smoking. We made love, fairly roughly, and then I went out like a light. When I woke up she was gone.'

She stopped and thought for a moment.

'Christina was already dead when I woke up,' she said.

'Do you remember her leaving?'

The woman sighed into the darkness.

'No, but the police say she got a call on her mobile at two fifty-three. She answered and spoke for three minutes. And that must have been after we finished fucking, because Christina could hardly have been on the phone while we were . . . '

She turned to look at Annika with a wry smile.

'Is it uncomfortable talking openly about what you felt?' Annika said.

Helena Starke shrugged. 'When I fell in love with Christina I knew what to expect. It wasn't easy, getting her to open up. It took more than a year.' She gave a short little laugh.

'Christina was really inexperienced. It was like she'd never enjoyed sex before, but once she realized it could be fun, she couldn't get enough. I've never had such a wonderful lover.'

Annika was feeling uncomfortable. This was none of her business. She didn't want to think of them together, this beautiful forty-year-old making love to a sixty-year-old ice-maiden. She tried to shake off the image.

'Thank you for telling me,' she said simply.

Helena Starke didn't reply. Annika turned and started to walk to the door.

'Where are you moving to?' she said.

'Los Angeles,' Helena Starke said.

Annika stopped and looked over her shoulder.

'Isn't that a bit sudden?' she said.

Helena Starke was peering round the door-frame, looking at her intently.

'It wasn't me who blew them up,' she said.

52

Annika was back in the office again in time for the 4.45 news on the radio. The broadcast opened with a scoop, at least on their terms. They had got hold of the government proposal on regional politics that was due to be published at the end of January. The proposals didn't seem particularly remarkable to Annika, but the next item was more interesting. They had received a copy of the preliminary report into the explosives used in the murder of Stefan Bjurling. The constituent parts were most probably the same as the ones used at the stadium: a high-density mixture of nitro-glycerine and nitro-glycol, but the dimensions and packaging were different. According to the radio report, the explosives were packed in small cardboard tubes with a diameter of 22 to 29 millimetres. The police were making no comment on the leak, merely saying that their technical analysis was far from complete.

Well, Patrik can take care of that, Annika thought, making a note in her pad.

There was nothing else of interest to her in the news so she switched off the radio and started making phone-calls. The builders who worked with Stefan Bjurling ought to be home by now. She checked the caption to the picture accompanying her own article, then dialled Directory Inquiries. Several of the men had very common names, like Sven Andersson, which made them impossible to track down, but five of them were sufficiently unusual to save her dialling fifty different numbers to find the right person. Someone answered the fourth number she called.

'Yes, I had my camera with me,' Herman Ösel, one of the plumbers, said.

'Do you remember if you took any pictures of Christina Furhage?'

'Definitely, yes I did.'

Annika felt her heart start to beat faster.

'Did you take any pictures of Stefan Bjurling?'

'Well, not of him on his own, but I think he was in one of the pictures with Christina Furhage.'

Incredible, what a stroke of luck, Annika thought.

'But you're not sure?' she asked.

'Well, I haven't uploaded them yet. I thought I'd take a few pictures of the grandchildren over Christmas . . . '

'Herman, do you think you might be able to email those pictures over to me at the *Evening Post*? And if there were any pictures that we might want to publish, do you think you might be interested in selling them to us?'

'Well, I don't know . . .'

Annika quietly took a deep breath.

'It's like this, you see,' she said. 'At the *Evening Post* we think it's really important that the bomber who killed Christina Furhage and Stefan Bjurling is caught and put in prison. It's important to everyone, Christina and Stefan's families and the people they worked with, but also the whole country, the whole world even. The Games are under threat, we have to realize that. And the best way to spread information and influence the way people think is for the mass media to do the socially responsible thing. For us at the *Evening Post*, that means writing about the victims and the work the police are doing, but it also means working on our own journalistic stories. Like talking to people who worked with the victims, for instance. That's why I was wondering if we could publish a picture of Christina and Stefan together, if you've got a picture like that . . .'

Her throat was dry after this little speech, but it seemed to have worked.

'Well, I suppose that would be okay. How do we go about it?'

Annika gave the man her email address and hung up.

Tore Brand looked up from his desk as Annika was leaving. 'By the way, someone was looking for you earlier today,' he said.

'Oh, who?'

'She didn't say. She wanted to give you something.'

'Really? What?'

'She didn't tell me that either. She said she'd come back another time.'

Annika smiled, groaning to herself. The caretakers really had to learn to take more information than that. One day it could turn out to be really important.

She went back to her office via Patrik's desk, but he was out. She'd have to call him on his mobile to arrange a meeting before the six o'clock editorial conference. As she passed Eva-Britt Qvist's desk she heard the phone in her office start to ring. She ran the last few steps. It was Thomas.

'When will you be home?'

'I don't know. I expect I'll be late. Somewhere around nine, I should think.'

'I have to get back to work; we've got a meeting at six.'

346

Annika could feel herself getting annoyed.

'At six o'clock? But I'm at work! That's when we have our meeting! Why didn't you call earlier?'

Thomas sounded calm, but Annika could tell from his voice that he was getting angry as well.

'Radio news have somehow managed to get hold of the government's proposal about regional politics, and it's like a bomb has gone off at the Association. Several politicians involved in the inquiry are on their way already. You have to see that I've got to be there, surely?'

Annika took a deep breath and closed her eyes. Fuck, fuck, she had to go home.

'We agreed that I'd work late Monday and Wednesday, and you'd have Tuesday and Thursday,' she said. 'I've kept my part of the bargain. My job is just as important as yours.'

Thomas started pleading instead.

'Darling, please,' he said. 'I know you're right. But I have to go back in. This is a damage limitation meeting, it shouldn't take long. I've got dinner ready – if you can come home and eat with the kids, I'll be back as soon as the meeting's over. We should be done by eight, there's not really that much to say. You can go back to work once I'm home again.'

She sighed, shutting her eyes, pressing one hand to her forehead.

'Okay,' she said. 'I'll get a taxi right away.'

She went out to tell Ingvar Johansson about Herman Ösel's picture, but he wasn't at his desk. At the picture desk Pelle was on the phone, so she stood there waving in front of his face.

'What is it?' he said crossly, holding the receiver to his shoulder.

'We're getting some pictures from Vallentuna, of

Christina Furhage and Stefan Bjurling together. Print some copies off once they come through. I have to go now, but I'll be back around eight, okay?'

Pelle nodded and went back to his phone-call.

She didn't bother calling for a taxi, just took one in the queue at the taxi rank on Rålambshovsvägen. She could feel the stress growing into a big lump in her stomach, until she started having trouble breathing. She really didn't need this right now.

When she got home the children rushed towards her and she was showered in kisses and drawings. Thomas gave her a quick peck on the way out, and picked up the same taxi she had arrived in.

'Right, you've got to let me take my coat off, just calm down . . .'

Ellen and Kalle stopped, surprised that she sounded so irritable. She leaned over and hugged them, too hard and too quickly, then went over to the phone. She called Ingvar Johansson, but he had already gone into the editorial meeting. Damn, now she hadn't had time to tell anyone what her team had been doing today. Oh well, she'd just have to talk to Spike later.

Dinner was on the table, and the children had already eaten. She sat down and tried to eat some of the chicken, but it seemed to grow in her mouth until she had to spit it out. She ate a little rice, then threw the rest away. She could never eat when she was this stressed.

'You ought to eat up all your dinner,' Kalle said reproachfully.

She parked them in front of Swedish Television's series of Advent programmes for children, shut the sitting-room door and called Patrik.

'The Tiger's called,' the reporter yelled. 'He's really angry.'

'Why?' Annika asked.

'He's on his honeymoon in Tenerife, Playa de las Americas. He's been there since Thursday, coming home tomorrow. He says the police knew perfectly well where he was, because they'd already checked all flights out of Arlanda and he was on the list. But the Spanish police got hold of him and forced him to sit through a whole afternoon of questioning. They made him miss the barbecue and a free drink by the pool. Can you believe they'd do anything so cruel?'

Annika smiled weakly.

'Are you going to put something together about it?'

'Of course.'

'Did you hear the piece on the radio about the explosives?'

'Yes, that's what I'm working on at the moment. Ulf Olsson and I are in an explosives store, taking pictures of different types of dynamite. Do you know, they look just like big sausages!'

Bless him! He had a capacity for relentless enthusiasm under all circumstances, and at the same time always managed to get a good angle to his stories.

'Have you got anywhere with the police hunt for the Bomber?'

'Nope, it's all gone very quiet. I think they must be getting close to the bastard.'

'We need to get some sort of confirmation. I'll try to sort that tonight,' Annika said.

'Right, well, we've got to get out of here now, or else we'll get a serious headache, according to our expert. Speak to you later.'

The television programme had evidently finished, because the children were fighting over a comic. She went in and changed channels, and waited for the regional news to start.

'Can we do a jigsaw, Mummy?'

They sat on the floor and tipped out a twenty-five-piece wooden jigsaw. Annika sat down and moved the pieces around absent-mindedly. They sat like that until the local news started at ten past seven. She told them to go and brush their teeth while she checked what the news team had come up with. They had been out to Sätra Hall and had been allowed into the referees' changing-room. The pictures weren't terribly dramatic; the room itself didn't seem to have suffered much damage. Every trace of poor Steffe had been carefully scrubbed away. There was no indication that an arrest was imminent. She went into the bathroom and helped the children brush their teeth while the local news moved on to a report about Christmas shopping.

'Put on your pyjamas and we'll read Peter No-Tail. Don't forget your fluoride pills.'

She left them arguing as the main television news got underway. They were pushing hard with the story of the government proposal for regional politics. Nothing she needed to watch, in other words. She read the children their story and tucked them up in their beds, as they protested and said they weren't tired.

'It'll soon be Christmas Eve, and children have to be very good, because otherwise Father Christmas won't come.'

That worked, and soon they were asleep. She called Thomas at work and on his mobile, but of course he didn't answer. She started up the old PC in their bedroom and quickly typed up what she had learned from her conversation with Helena Starke from memory. She saved the file on a USB stick, all the while growing more anxious. Where the hell had Thomas got to?

He arrived just after half past eight.

'Thanks, darling,' he panted as he came through the door.

'Did you ask the taxi to wait?' she asked curtly.

'Shit, no, I forgot.'

She rushed down the stairs to catch the car, but of course it had driven off. She walked down to Kungsholmstorg, but naturally there were no cars waiting at the taxi rank. She carried on past the chemist, down towards Kungsholmsgatan: there was another taxi rank on Scheelegatan. There was a single car standing there, from some unfamiliar firm out in the suburbs. She got back to the office at five to nine. Everything was quiet and deserted. Ingvar Johansson had long since gone home and the night team were down in the canteen. She went into her room and started making phone-calls.

'This is starting to get bloody monotonous,' her source said.

'Stop being so grouchy,' she said tiredly. 'I've been on the go for fourteen hours and I'm starting to get fed up. You know who I am and what I'm about, so come on . . . Ceasefire?'

The policeman on the other end gave a deep sigh.

'You're not the only person who's been at it since seven this morning.'

'You're closing in on him, aren't you?'

'What makes you think that?'

'You usually stick to your allocated hours, especially ahead of public holidays. Something's going on.'

'Of course it is. There's always something going on.'

Annika groaned out loud.

'Jesus Christ,' she said.

'Look, we can hardly leak information that we're closing in on the Bomber, can we? Surely you can see that? He'd just take off.'

'But you're close?'

'I didn't say that.'

'But you are?'

The man didn't reply.

'How much can I write?' Annika asked cautiously.

'Not a single bloody line, otherwise it'll go to hell.'

'When are you planning to arrest him?'

The policeman was silent for a few seconds.

'As soon as we've found him.'

'Found?'

'He's disappeared.'

53

The hairs on the back of Annika's neck stood up.

'So you know who it is?'

'We think so, yes.'

'Bloody hell,' Annika whispered. 'How long have you known?'

'We've had a good idea for a couple of days, but now we're sure enough to want to bring the individual in for questioning.'

'Can we come with you?' she asked quickly.

'For the arrest? I doubt it. We haven't got a fucking clue where he is.'

'How many have you got out looking for him?'

'Not many, we haven't put out a regional alert yet. We want to check the locations we know about first.'

'When will you be putting out the alert?'

'Don't know.'

Annika was thinking so hard it hurt. How could she write about this without writing about it?

'I know what you're thinking,' the policeman said. 'Look upon this as a test. I've given you confidential information, so think bloody carefully before you do anything with it.'

The conversation ended, and Annika was left sitting

in her dusty room, her heart thudding. She could well be the only journalist who knew this, and she couldn't do anything with it.

She went out into the newsroom to calm down, and to have a word with Spike. The first thing she saw was a black-and-white printout of the next day's newsbill. It said: CHRISTINA FURHAGE LESBIAN – LOVER TALKS ABOUT HER FINAL HOURS.

Annika felt the room start to spin. This can't be true, she thought. Good grief, where had it come from? With something approaching tunnel vision, she walked over to the printout, grabbed it, and slapped it down on the desk in front of Spike.

'What the hell is this?' she said.

'Our best story tomorrow,' the night-editor said, non-chalantly.

'But we can't publish this,' Annika said, unable to control her voice. 'This is irrelevant. Christina Furhage never spoke openly about her sexuality. We've got no right to put her on display like this. She didn't want to say anything while she was alive, so we don't have any right to do it now that she's dead.'

The editor stretched his back, and put his hands behind his head. He leaned back, almost overturning his chair.

'It's nothing to be ashamed of, is it, liking women. Hell, I do too.' He grinned. He looked over his shoulder to get support from the rest of the formatting team around the desk behind him. Annika forced herself to stick to the facts.

'She was married and had children. Do you fancy volunteering to look her family in the eye tomorrow if you print this?'

'She was a public figure.'

'That doesn't make any fucking difference!' Annika

354

said, unable to keep calm any longer. 'The woman was murdered! So, who the hell wrote the article?'

The night-editor got to his feet with an effort. Now he was angry as well.

'Nils has got hold of some good information. He's got confirmation from a named source that she was a lesbian. She had a relationship with that macho dyke, Starke—'

'But that's my information!' Annika yelled, furious now. 'I mentioned it as gossip at our run-through after lunch. So who's the named source?'

The editor stood with his face inches from Annika's.

'I don't give a damn where the information comes from,' he snarled. 'Nils has come up with our best story for tomorrow. If you had that information, then why the hell didn't you write the article? Don't you think it's about time you grew up?'

Annika felt the words hit home. They struck her in the stomach, where the lump of stress expanded and made her lungs feel too small. She forced herself to steer away from the personal attacks and concentrate on the journalistic facts. Was she actually wrong about this? Was Christina Furhage's sexuality really the most important story of the day? She pushed the thought aside.

'Who Christina Furhage was fucking is completely irrelevant,' she said in a low voice. 'The interesting thing is who murdered her. Another interesting thing is how this affects the Olympic Games, sport generally, and Sweden's international reputation. And it's important to find out why she was killed, to work out who the killer is, and what his motivations were. I don't give a shit about who she was sleeping with, as long as it doesn't have anything to do with her death. And that's really what you should be concentrating on too.'

The night-editor breathed in through his nose, making a noise like an air-conditioning unit whirring into life.

'Do you know what, esteemed head of crime? You are completely fucking wrong. You should have made sure you could fill those boots before you put them on. Nils Langeby is right: you aren't up to the job. Can't you see how pathetic you are?'

The lump of stress exploded inside her, a physical sensation of falling apart. All sound vanished, and she saw flashes of light in front of her eyes. To her surprise she realized that she was still standing, that she was aware of what was happening around her, and that she was still breathing. She turned on her heel and went into her room, concentrating hard on crossing the floor of the newsroom, feeling the other journalists' eyes on her back like arrows. She made it to her office and shut the door. She slumped to the floor inside the door, her whole body shaking. I'm not dying, I'm not dying, I'm not dying, she thought. This will pass, this will pass, this will pass. She felt short of air and was panting for breath, but the air wasn't reaching her lungs. She took another deep breath, then another, until she started to get cramp in her arms. She realized she was hyperventilating and had too much oxygen in her blood. She struggled to her feet and staggered to her desk, pulled a paper bag out of the bottom drawer and started breathing into it. She conjured up Thomas's voice, calm and soothing, calm and soothing, calm and soothing, it'll be all right, darling, just breathe; you're not falling apart, little Anki, calm and soothing, calm and soothing . . .

The shaking subsided and she sat on her chair. She had a strong urge to cry, but suppressed it and called Anders Schyman at home. His wife answered and Annika did her best to sound normal.

'He's at the Christmas dinner in the executive suite,' Schyman's wife said.

Annika called reception and asked them to put her through to the directors' floor. She realized that she was no longer sounding coherent, and was hardly making herself understood. After several minutes of nothing but background conversation and the sound of serving dishes rattling, she heard Anders Schyman's voice.

'Sorry, sorry . . . to disturb you in the middle of dinner,' she said quietly.

Chatter and laughter in the background.

'And sorry I wasn't able to make it to the six o'clock meeting this evening, but there was a crisis at home—' She started to sob loudly and uncontrollably.

'What on earth's happened? Has something happened to the children?' Anders Schyman said, sounding horrified.

'No, no, it's nothing serious, but I have to ask – did you discuss what Spike is leading with tomorrow, about Christina Furhage being a lesbian?'

Annika heard nothing but chatter and laughter for several seconds.

'About what?' Anders Schyman said eventually.

She put a hand to her chest and forced herself to breathe normally and calmly.

'Her lover speaking out about their last hours together, according to the newsbill.'

'Bloody hell. I'm on my way down,' the editor-in-chief said, and hung up.

She put the receiver down, leaned over her keyboard and wept. Her mascara made a mess of her notes, and her whole body was shaking. I can't do this, I can't do this, I can't do this, she thought.

She knew that she was making a fool of herself, that she was burning her bridges, that she was finished in this job. The sound of her despair seeped under the door and out into the newsroom. Everyone could see that she couldn't take the pressure, that she shouldn't have been given the job, that her promotion had been a disaster. This realization did nothing to help, and she couldn't stop crying. The great lump of stress and tiredness had finally taken over her whole body, and there was nothing she could do to stop the shaking or the tears.

She felt a hand on her shoulder and a soothing voice from up above her.

'Annika, Annika, it's all right now. Whoever's behind this, we'll sort it out. Annika, do you hear what I'm saying?'

She held her breath and looked up. Her head was aching badly and her eyes were still seeing flashes of light. It was Anders Schyman.

'Sorry, I . . .' she said, trying to wipe away the make-up from her face with the back of her hand. 'Sorry . . .'

'Here, use my handkerchief. Sit up properly and clean yourself up, I'll go and get a glass of water.'

The editor-in-chief disappeared through the door and Annika mechanically did as she was told. Anders Schyman returned with a plastic cup of cold water and closed the door behind him.

'Drink some of this, then tell me what's happened.'

'Have you spoken to Spike about the newsbill?' she said.

'I'll do that later, that's not so urgent. I'm worried about you. Why are you so upset?'

She started crying again, quietly this time. The editor-in-chief waited in silence.

'I'm probably just worn out,' she said once she'd pulled herself together again. 'And then Spike said all those things you only hear in nightmares, that I'm a worthless idiot who isn't up to the job, all that . . .'

She leaned back in her chair, she'd said it, and oddly enough, it made her feel calmer.

'He has absolutely no confidence in my ability to do this job, he made that very clear. There are probably loads of people who think the same.'

'That's possible,' Anders Schyman said, 'but that's not really very interesting. What's important is that I have faith in you, and I'm absolutely convinced you're the right person for the job.'

She took a deep breath.

'I want to leave,' she said.

'I won't let you,' he said.

'I'll resign,' she said.

'I won't accept your resignation.'

'I'll go now, tonight.'

'You can't. I was planning to promote you.'

She lost her thread and stared at him.

'What?' she said in astonishment.

'I wasn't going to tell you just yet, but sometimes plans have to change. I've got big ambitions for you, Annika. I suppose I might as well tell you about them now, before you make up your mind to leave the paper for good.'

She stared at him sceptically.

'This newspaper is facing some big changes,' the editor-in-chief said. 'Right now I don't think anyone who works here appreciates just how big the challenge is. We have to adapt to entirely new ways of doing things, with all the technological changes and the competition from the free papers. And, above all, we have to keep pushing ahead with our journalism. To do all that, we need editorial leadership that's capable of managing a whole range of different areas. And people who can do that don't grow on trees. Either we can sit here with our fingers crossed, hoping that someone like that turns up, or we can make sure that the people we have most faith in are prepared for the changes well in advance.'

Annika was listening, wide-eyed.

'I've got at most another ten years in me, Annika, maybe no more than five. We have to make sure there are people ready to take over after me. I'm not saying that it's going to be you, but you're one of three people I think might be suitable. There's an awful lot you'd need to learn before then, not least how to control your moods. But that's just a bit of fine-tuning – otherwise, I think you're the most suitable candidate to succeed me. You're creative and you think on your feet – I don't think I've ever come across anyone as good as you are at that. You take responsibility and deal with conflicts with the same authority, you're organized, competent and you show a lot of initiative. I'm not going to let some idiotic night-editor drive you away, I hope you realize that. It's not you who should leave, but them.'

The potential future editor-in-chief blinked in surprise.

'I'd be grateful if you could delay your resignation until after the New Year,' Schyman went on. 'There are a couple of people in this newsroom who mean you no good, and it's very difficult to defend yourself against that sort of antipathy. It has to be rooted out. Let me take a few measures first, then we can talk again once this business with the Bomber has calmed down. I'd also like to talk about your background and discuss what additional training might be appropriate for you. We ought to put together a plan about which posts you should have experience of before the time comes. It's important that you learn about all the different aspects of the newsroom. You'll need to have a good grasp of the technical stuff and the organization of the rest of the company. You need to be respected and accepted everywhere, that's vital, and you will be if we do this the right way.'

Annika's mouth was hanging open. She couldn't believe her ears.

'You've really thought about this, haven't you?' she said, amazed.

'Well, this isn't an invitation to become editor-in-chief, it's a challenge to you to educate yourself and gain the experience necessary so that you would be eligible for the job in the future. I'd prefer it if you didn't mention this to anyone else just yet, apart from your husband. What do you say?'

Annika shook herself.

'Thank you,' she said.

Anders Schyman smiled.

'Take some time off now, until New Year. You must have a mountain of time owing as big as the Himalayas.'

'I was thinking of working tomorrow morning, and I don't want to change that just because of Spike. I hope I can get my picture of Christina Furhage's life-story sorted out by then.'

'Anything we can publish?'

She shook her head sadly. 'I don't actually know. We'll have to talk it through properly. It's a really tragic story.'

'Which makes it all the more interesting. Well, let's talk about that later.'

Anders Schyman got up and walked out. Annika stayed where she was, overcome by a vast sense of peace and surprise. How easy it was to feel good again, how little it took to get rid of all that dark despair. One serious bolstering session, and it was like the public humiliation had never happened.

She put her coat on and went out the back way, picked up a taxi at the taxi rank and went home.

Thomas was asleep. She washed off the last of her make-up, brushed her teeth, and crept into bed beside her husband. Only then, in the darkness, staring up at the ceiling through the gloom, did she remember what she had learned from the police that evening: they knew who the Bomber was, and they were about to arrest him.

Evil

My intuition told me very early on that there was such a thing, and that it was strong. Accepted wisdom, in the form of fairy tales and grown-ups, tried to shake my certainty. 'It's only make believe,' they said. 'It isn't like that in real life, and good always wins in the end.' I knew that was a lie, because I had heard the story of Hansel and Gretel. Evil was victorious there, even if the narrative suggested that it all ended on terms dictated by goodness. Evil forced the little children into the forest, evil fattened Hansel up and heated the oven, but Gretel turned out to be most evil of all, because she was the only one who actually killed anyone.

Stories like that never frightened me. Things you know well rarely scare you. That gave me an advantage over the world around me.

Later experience naturally proved that I was right. In this country we have made the grave mistake of abolishing evil. Officially it doesn't exist. Sweden is a constitutional state, where understanding and logic have taken the place of evil. This meant that evil was forced underground, and there, in the darkness, it thrived better than ever. It grew on a diet of jealousy and suppressed hate, it became impenetrable and, over the course of time, so dark that it couldn't be seen. But

I recognized it. Anyone who has ever got to know it can sniff it out wherever it is.

Anyone who has learned from Gretel knows how to deal with evil. Evil must be fought with evil, nothing else has any effect. I saw evil in the malevolent faces at work, in the eyes of committee members, in the fixed smiles of colleagues, and I smiled back. Its hydra-headed form was nowhere to be seen, it was hiding behind union negotiations and formal discussions. But I knew, and I played along. It couldn't fool me. I held up a mirror and reflected its power back at it.

But I watched it make progress elsewhere in society. I saw how violence against several of my employees was disregarded by the police and the legal system. A woman in my department reported her ex-husband twenty times or more, and the police filed every report under 'domestic incident'. Social Services appointed a mediator, but I knew there was no point. I could smell the stench of evil, and knew its time had come. The woman was going to die because no one took evil seriously. 'He didn't mean any harm, he just wanted to see the children,' I once overheard the mediator say. On that occasion I told my secretary to close the door, because human inertia always puts me in a bad mood.

The woman eventually had her throat cut with a bread-knife, and everyone was surprised and upset. They tried to find an explanation, but ignored the most obvious one.

Evil had got away with it, yet again.

Thursday 23 December

54

The apartment was empty by the time Annika woke up.
It was half past eight and light was just starting to fall
through the bedroom window. She got up and found
a large note on the fridge door, held by magnets in the
shape of Christmas elves:

Thanks for being you.
Love and kisses from your husband.
PS. I'm taking the kids to nursery, your turn to
pick up.

She ate a cheese roll as she leafed through the morning papers. They were all focusing on the government's
plans for regional politics, and had started to run their
Christmas material: historical overviews of Christmas
through the ages, and so on. There was nothing new
about the Bomber. She took a quick shower, heated some
water in the microwave and made some instant coffee
that she drank as she was getting dressed. She took the
number 62 bus to the morning paper's old entrance and
went up the back stairs to the newsroom. She didn't
want to meet anyone until she found out what they had
published about Christina Furhage's sexuality.

There wasn't a single disrespectful remark about

Christina Furhage or Helena Starke in the paper. Annika switched on her computer and went into something called the 'historical list'. It was where articles that had been deleted were stored for twenty-four hours after they were dumped.

And there it was. Nils Langeby had indeed written an article under the title 'Furhage Lesbian'. The article had been dumped at 22.50 the previous evening. Annika opened the file and quickly scanned the article. What she read made her feel sick. The source, named in the article, who was supposed to have confirmed that Christina Furhage was a lesbian, was a woman from Olympic headquarters who Annika had never heard of. The woman said: 'Of course we wondered. Christina always wanted to work with Helena Starke, and a lot of people thought that was a bit strange. Because everyone knew that Helena was one of those . . . Several of us thought they were having a relationship.' The reporter went on to quote a couple of unnamed sources who said they had seen the women out together.

At the bottom was a quote from Helena Starke herself: 'The last time I saw Christina was in the Vildsvin restaurant on Fleminggatan on Friday evening. We left the restaurant together at midnight. We went our separate ways home.'

That was all. No wonder Schyman had pulled the article.

Annika read on, and was struck by an uncomfortable thought: how the hell had Nils Langeby managed to get hold of Helena Starke's ex-directory number, if he had actually spoken to her at all?

She opened the shared database of telephone numbers and realized she had made a mistake when she had entered the woman's private number on the computer. Instead of putting it in her own private file, she had entered it in the shared database. Without stopping to think, she dialled Helena's number to apologize on Nils Langeby's behalf. But all she got was an automatic message: 'This number is no longer in use. Please hang up.' Helena Starke had left the country.

Annika sighed and looked through what they had actually published. They had chosen to lead with something other than the Bomber, a celebrity revealing all about his incurable illness. It was one of the television sports presenters who suffered from gluten intolerance. In other words, he was allergic to flour. He talked about how his life had changed in the year since the diagnosis. Perfectly okay as a lead story on a day like this, the day before the big day. Anne Snapphane would be delighted with it. Herman Ösel's picture of Christina Furhage and Stefan Bjurling was terrible, but it worked well enough. The two murder victims were sitting next to each other in a dimly lit room, the flash giving Christina red eyes and making her teeth glow. Stefan Bjurling was pulling some kind of face. The focus was a bit blurred. It was on the page six and seven spread, next to Patrik's piece about the police. The headline was the one Ingvar Johansson had come up with earlier on the spur of the moment: NOW THEY'RE BOTH DEAD. Patrik's article about the explosives was on page eight. She made a mental note to tell him how good his work was next time she saw him.

Annika leafed through the other evening paper, which had chosen to lead with financial advice: DO YOUR TAX RETURN NOW AND SAVE MONEY! They always ran something like that at the end of December, because there was always some change to the tax regulations coming in at the turn of the year. Annika didn't bother reading it. It didn't affect her, or people like her, who didn't have a portfolio of shares or property, or drove a company car for work. She knew that sort of story sold well, but always felt they should be used with caution.

She pulled the USB stick containing what Christina Furhage's lover had really said about their last hours together out of her bag, and put it with the rest of her more sensitive material. She called her source, but he was at home, probably asleep. Feeling suddenly restless, she went out into the newsroom, but Berit hadn't arrived yet. She asked the picture desk to call Herman Ösel about payment, fetched a cup of coffee, and said hello to Eva-Britt Qvist.

'What was all the fuss about yesterday?' the secretary asked, trying to hide her glee.

'What fuss?' Annika said, pretending to think. 'What do you mean?'

'You know, here in the newsroom. With you and Spike?'

'Oh, you mean Spike's ridiculous newsbill about Christina Furhage being a lesbian? Yes, I don't know what happened, but Anders Schyman must have put a stop to it. Poor Spike – such a bad mistake,' Annika said as she went into her office and shut the door. She couldn't resist being a bit cruel.

She drank her coffee and started to sketch a plan of the day's work. There was a chance the police would be arresting the Bomber today, but they probably wouldn't mention it over their radio channels. So they'd have to rely on other sources, not the usual tip-off agents. She would have to talk to Berit and Ingvar Johansson about that. She was thinking of trying to pull together her overview of Christina Furhage's past, so would have to try to get hold of her son, Olof.

She closed her notepad and went on the internet. When she had time she preferred to look things up online rather than calling Directory Inquiries, where the operators sometimes managed to miss the most obvious details. She did a national search for Olof Furhage, and the computer checked through the databases. Bingo! Just one result, living in Tungelsta, south of Stockholm.

'Got you!' Annika said.

Christina Furhage had left her five-year-old son in Tungelsta almost forty years ago, and there was still a man with that name living there today. She wondered for a moment if she should call him first, but decided to make the trek out instead. She needed to get out of the office.

At that moment there was a knock on her door. It was the editor-in-chief, holding a large jug of water. He looked terrible.

'What's happened?' Annika said, concerned.

'Migraine,' Anders Schyman said curtly. 'I drank a glass of red wine with my venison last night, so I've only got myself to blame. How are you feeling today?'

He closed the door behind him.

'Thanks, I'm good,' Annika said. 'I gather you stopped the newsbill about Christina's lesbian adventures.'

'It wasn't too difficult; the article it was based on was very thin.'

'Did Spike explain why he chose that for the news-bill?' Annika asked.

The editor-in-chief sat down on Annika's desk.

'He hadn't read the article, just heard Nils Langeby describing it. When we went to Langeby and asked to see the text, the matter was sorted. There was no information, and even if there had been we wouldn't have published it. It would be another matter if Christina had told the world about her love life, but writing about a dead person's most personal activities has to be the worst possible infringement of the sanctity of private life. Spike realized that, once I'd explained it to him.'

Annika bowed her head, relieved that her gut instinct had been right.

'It was true,' she said.

'What was?'

'They had a relationship, but no one knew about it. Helena Starke is in pieces. She's just left for the US.'

'Wow,' the editor-in-chief said. 'So what else have you found out that we can't print?'

'Christina hated her children and terrified everyone around her. Stefan Bjurling was a drunk who beat his wife.'

'What a pair. What are you up to today?' the editor-in-chief asked.

'I'm heading out to talk to someone, then I need to check something with my source. They're closing in on the Bomber.'

Anders Schyman raised his eyebrows.

'Will we be able to put that in tomorrow's paper?'

'I hope so,' she said, smiling.

'What did your husband say about our plans for the future?'

'I haven't spoken to him yet.'

The editor-in-chief got up and left. Annika put her notepad and pen in her bag, and noticed that her mobile was almost out of battery. Just to be sure, she put the charger in her bag.

'I'm going out for a while,' she said to Eva-Britt, who was almost hidden behind the pile of post.

She picked up the keys to a fairly nondescript car and went down to the garage. It was a beautiful winter's day. The snow was several inches thick, making the city look picture-postcard pretty. As long as we get a white Christmas, so the kids can go sledging in Kronoberg Park, she thought.

55

She turned on the car radio, found one of the commercial stations, and set off along the Essinge motorway towards the Årsta link road. They were playing an old Supremes classic.

Annika sang along at the top of her voice as the car headed towards the Huddinge junction. She took the Örby link road as far as the Nynäshamn junction, singing along merrily to old classics and laughing all the way. Everything was white and crystal clear, and she was soon going to be away from work for more than a week, and she was going to be editor-in-chief! Well, maybe not, but she was going to get training, and her superiors believed in her. She would doubtless have more setbacks along the way, but you just had to roll with them. She turned up the volume to Simon and Garfunkel.

Tungelsta was an old garden suburb some 35 kilometres south of Stockholm, and it was like a gentle oasis after the concrete desert of Västerhaninge. Building had started in the 1910s, and it didn't look much different today from many other places built at the same time, with one exception: every garden had a greenhouse, or the remains of a greenhouse. Some had been beautifully well kept, but a few were just spiky skeletons.

Annika arrived early in the morning. Old men were clearing snow, and waved cheerily as she drove past. Olof Furhage lived on Älvvägen, and Annika had to pull up outside a pizzeria and ask for directions. An elderly man who turned out to have been the local postman talked animatedly about the original plan for the place, and knew exactly where Olof Furhage lived.

'A blue cottage with a big greenhouse,' he said.

She drove across the railway line and could see, even from a distance, that she was on the right track. The greenhouse was close to the road, and further up towards the forest lay a blue-painted detached house. Annika pulled into the drive, stopping the car in the middle of an Abba song, hoisted her bag on her shoulder and got out. She had put her mobile phone on the passenger seat in case it rang, and she saw it was still there, but decided not to take it.

She stopped and looked up at the house. The design reminded her of a much older sort of building, but the windows and façade made her think it must have been built in the 1930s. It had a tiled, hipped roof, and generally looked well-kept and neat.

'Can I help you?'

It was a man in his forties, with medium-length brown hair and bright blue eyes. He was wearing a knitted sweater and dirty jeans.

'I hope so. I'm trying to find someone called Olof Furhage,' Annika said, holding out her hand in greeting. The man smiled and shook her hand.

'Well, you're in the right place. I'm Olof Furhage.'

Annika smiled back. This next bit was going to be a bit tricky.

'I'm from the *Evening Post*,' she said. 'I was wondering if I could possibly ask you a few rather personal questions.'

The man laughed.

'I see! What sort of questions?'

'I'm trying to track down the Olof Furhage who's the son of the managing director of the Stockholm Olympics, Christina Furhage,' she said as neutrally as she could. 'Would that be you, by any chance?'

The man looked down at the ground for a moment, then looked up and brushed his hair back.

'Yes,' he said, 'that's me.'

They stood in silence for a few seconds. The sun was shining right in their eyes. Annika could feel the cold coming through the thin soles of her shoes.

'I don't want to be intrusive,' she said, 'but I've spoken to a lot of people who knew Christina Furhage in recent days. It felt important to talk to you as well.'

'Why have you been doing that?' the man said, wary, but not hostile.

'Your mother was a very well-known woman, and her death has repercussions for the whole world. But even though she was such a public figure, she was almost completely anonymous as a private person. Which is why we've been talking to the people closest to her.'

'Why, though? Presumably she wanted to be anonymous. Can't you respect that?'

The man wasn't stupid, that much was clear.

'Of course,' Annika said. 'It's out of respect for those close to her, and her own desire to be anonymous, that I'm doing this. Because we don't know anything about her, there's a risk that we'll make basic mistakes in what we write about her, the sort of thing that might upset her family. I'm afraid we've done that once already.

'Yesterday we printed a big article in which your mother was described as the ideal woman. That upset

375

your sister Lena quite badly. She called me yesterday, I met her and we had a long talk. I want to make sure we don't do the same thing to you.'

The man was looking at her, bemused.

'Quite a speech,' he said, impressed. 'You could talk the hind legs off a donkey, couldn't you?'

Annika wasn't sure whether she should smile or be serious. The man saw her confusion and laughed.

'It's okay,' he said. 'I'll talk to you. Do you want coffee, or are you in a hurry?'

'Both, really,' Annika said, laughing back.

'Would you like to take a look at the greenhouse first?'

'I'd love to,' Annika said, hoping it was warmer in there.

It was. The air was mild and smelled of compost and fruit. It was an old-fashioned design, and big, at least fifty metres long and ten wide. It was completely empty; the ground was covered in an enormous sheet of dark-green plastic. Two paths ran down the entire length of the greenhouse.

'I grow organic tomatoes,' Olof Furhage said.

'In December? Wow,' Annika said.

The man laughed again – he clearly laughed easily.

'No, not right now. I pulled the plants up in October, then the ground rests over winter. When you grow organically, it's important to keep the greenhouse and the soil free from bacteria and mould. Modern growers often use rockwool or peat, but I stick to soil. Come and have a look.'

He went quickly down the path and stopped at the far end of the greenhouse.

'This is a steam machine,' Olof Furhage said. 'I force steam in through these thick tubes, and they run underground and heat up the soil. And that kills the mould.

I've had it on this morning, which is why it's so warm in here.'

Annika looked on with interest. There was a lot she didn't know anything about.

'So when do you get tomatoes?' she asked politely.

'You don't want to force your tomatoes too early; they get really straggly if you do. I start towards the end of February, and by October the plants are up to six metres long.'

Annika looked round the greenhouse.

'But how does that work? There's not enough room in here?'

Olof Furhage laughed again.

'Well, you see that wire there? When the plant gets that tall you bend it over the wire. There's another wire fifty centimetres from the ground, and you do the same thing again, bend the stem over and up it goes again.'

'Ingenious,' Annika said.

'Well, what about coffee?'

They left the greenhouse and went up to the house.

'You grew up here in Tungelsta, didn't you?' she said.

The man nodded as he held the outer door open for her.

'Feel free to take your shoes off. Yes, I grew up on Kvarnvägen, not far from here. Hello! How are you getting on?'

This last part was shouted into the house, and a young girl's voice replied from upstairs: 'Okay, Daddy, but I don't think I can get any further. Can you help me?'

'Yes, but in a little while. I've got a visitor.'

Olof Furhage pulled off his heavy boots.

'She's had flu, was really quite ill. I bought her a new computer game as consolation. Please, go in . . .'

A small face peered down from the staircase.

'Hello,' the girl said. 'My name's Alice.'

She was nine or ten years old.

'My name's Annika,' Annika said.

Alice disappeared to play her computer game again.

'She lives with me every other week, and her sister Petra lives here full time now. Petra's fourteen,' Olof Furhage said as he filled the coffee-machine.

'You're divorced?' Annika asked, sitting down at the kitchen table.

'Yes, two years ago. Milk or sugar?'

'No thanks.'

Olof Furhage finished making the coffee, set the table, then sat down opposite Annika. It was a nice kitchen, with a wooden floor, mirrored cupboard doors, a red gingham tablecloth and an Advent star in the window. There was a fine view of the greenhouse.

'How much do you know?' the man asked.

Annika took her notepad and pen out of her bag.

'Do you mind if I make notes? Well, I know that your father's name was Carl, and that Christina left you with a couple in Tungelsta when you were five years old. I know you were in touch with Christina a couple of years ago. She was very scared of you.'

Olof Furhage laughed again, but this time it was sad laughter.

'Yes, poor Christina. I never understood why she got so terrified,' he said. 'I wrote her a letter just after the divorce, mainly because I felt so bloody awful. I wrote and asked those questions I had always wondered about, but never had any answers to. Why she gave me away, whether she had ever loved me, why Gustav and Elna weren't allowed to adopt me . . . She never replied.'

'So you went to see her?'

The man sighed.

'Yes, I started going out to Tyresö and sitting outside

378

the house in the weeks when the girls were with their mother. I wanted to see what she looked like, where she lived, what her life was like. She was famous by then – now that she was head of the Olympics, she was in the paper every week.'

The coffee-machine hissed and Olof Furhage stood up and brought the jug over to the table.

'I'll let it settle for a few moments,' he said, slicing some cake and putting it on a plate. 'One evening she came home alone. I remember it was spring. She was heading towards the door when I got out of the car and walked up to her. When I said who I was she almost fainted. She stared at me like I was a ghost. I asked her why she'd never answered my letter, but she didn't answer. When I began asking the questions I had written in the letter she turned away and carried on walking to the door, still without saying a word. I got angry and started shouting at her. "Fucking bitch," I yelled, "surely you could let me have just one minute of your time?" or something like that. She started to run, and stumbled on the steps up to the door. I ran after her and grabbed her, spun her round and shouted "Look at me!" or something similar.'

The man lowered his head, as if pained by the memory.

'And she said nothing?' Annika asked.

'Yes, she said two words: "Go away!" Then she went in and locked the door and called the police. They picked me up here later that evening.'

He poured the coffee and helped himself to a lump of sugar.

'You'd never had any contact with her?'

'Not since she left me with Gustav and Elna. I can still remember the night I arrived at theirs. We took a taxi, Mum and I, and it felt like a really long journey. I was happy; Mum had explained it all as a big adventure, a nice outing.'

'Did you like your mother?' Annika asked.

'Of course I did. I loved her. She was my mum; she read me stories and sang to me, gave me lots of hugs and said my prayers with me every evening when I went to bed. She was as small and bright as an angel.'

He stopped and looked down at the table.

'When we got to Gustav and Elna's we had something to eat, sausage and mash. I still remember that. I didn't like it, but Mum said I had to eat it up. Then she took me out into the hall and said I had to stay with Gustav and Elna, because she had to go away. I was hysterical. I suppose I must have been very close to her. Gustav kept hold of me while Mum grabbed her things and ran out. I think she was crying, but I might have got that wrong.'

He drank some coffee.

'I lay awake shaking all night long, screaming and crying whenever I had the energy. But things got better as time passed. Elna and Gustav were both over fifty, and had never had any children of their own. There's no question that they spoiled me rotten. They loved me above everything else on earth, you couldn't wish for better parents. They're both dead now.'

'And you never saw your mother again?'

'Once, when I was thirteen. Gustav and Elna had written to her saying they wanted to adopt me. I sent a letter and a drawing as well, I remember. She came out here one evening and told us to leave her alone. I recognized her straight away, even though I hadn't seen her since I was little. She said there was no question of me being adopted, and that she didn't want any letters or drawings in future.'

Annika suddenly felt at a complete loss for words.

'Good grief,' she said simply.

'I was crushed, naturally. What child wouldn't be? She married soon after she came out to see us; maybe that was why she was stressed.'

'Why weren't your foster-parents allowed to adopt you?'

'I've wondered about that as well,' Olof Furhage said, pouring more coffee for both of them. 'The only reason I can think of is that I would soon be inheriting a great deal of money. Carl Furhage had no other children apart from me, and after his third wife died he was really loaded – maybe you know that? Well, you'll also know that he set up a foundation with most of his money. I got my legal share, which was to be administered by Mum. And she certainly did that. There was practically nothing left when I came of age.'

Annika could hardly believe her ears.

'Is that true?' she said.

Olof Furhage sighed.

'Yes, unfortunately. There was enough money left for this house and a new car. The money came in very useful, I was at college and had met Karin. We moved in here and started to do it up; it was practically uninhabitable when we bought it. When we got divorced Karin let me keep the house. I suppose it was a fairly amicable break-up really.'

'But you should have sued your mother!' Annika said, worked up. 'She'd embezzled your money!'

'To be honest, I didn't care,' Olof said with a smile. 'I didn't want anything to do with her. But when I got divorced my childhood bubbled up to the surface again. I suppose I was trying to work out why I'd failed – what it was in my background that made it all go wrong. That was why I got back in touch with Mum again. It didn't make things any better, of course, as you've probably worked out by now.'

'How did you get over it?'

'In the end I took the bull by the horns and got some counselling. I wanted to break the vicious circle of bad parenting in the family.'

At that moment Alice came into the kitchen. She was wearing pink pyjamas and a dressing gown, and was carrying a Barbie doll. She looked quickly and shyly at Annika, then crept up into her dad's lap.

'How are you feeling?' Olof Furhage said, kissing the child on the head. 'Have you been coughing as much today?'

The girl shook her head and burrowed her face into her father's knitted sweater.

'I think you're getting a bit better, aren't you?'

The child took a piece of cake and ran out into the sitting room. Soon they heard the theme tune of *The Pink Panther* through the open door.

'I'm glad she's well enough to join in with Christmas Eve,' Olof said, taking a piece of cake for himself. 'Petra made it, it's not bad – try a bit!'

Annika took a piece. It was very good.

'Alice arrived on Friday after school, and got sick that night. I called the doctor at midnight, when her temperature was over forty-one degrees. I sat with her burning up in my lap until ten past three the next morning, until the doctor finally arrived. When the police turned up on Saturday afternoon at least I had a watertight alibi.'

She nodded: she had already come to the same conclusion. They sat in silence for a moment, listening to the sound of the television.

'Well, I really ought to be getting back,' Annika said. 'Thank you very much for taking the time to talk to me.'

Olof Furhage smiled.

'Don't mention it. As a tomato grower I don't have much to do in winter.'

'Do you make a living from that?'

The man laughed.

'No, it hardly covers its costs. It's practically impossible to make any money from growing vegetables under glass. Not even the companies that grow them way down south with grants, decent heat and cheap labour manage to make much of a profit. I do it because I enjoy it; it costs me nothing but time and labour. And I suppose I do it for the sake of the environment.'

'So what do you live off?'

'I'm a researcher at the Royal Institute of Technology, in waste product technology.'

'Compost and all that?'

He smiled.

'Among other things.'

'So when do you get to be a professor?' Annika asked.

'Probably never. One chair has just been appointed, and the only other one is up at Luleå Technical College and I wouldn't want to move that far, because of the girls. You never know, things might even work out between me and Karin in the end. Petra is at hers right now, we're all going to celebrate Christmas together.'

Annika smiled, and her smile came from somewhere deep inside.

56

Anders Schyman was sitting in his room with his elbows on the desktop and his hands clutched to his head. He had the most unbelievable headache. He got migraines a couple of times a year, always when he started to relax after a particularly stressful period. And yesterday he had made the mistake of drinking red wine as well. Sometimes that wasn't a problem, but drinking wine just ahead of a few days off was a big mistake. So now he felt terrible, not just because of his headache, but because of what he was about to do. He was on the brink of doing something he'd never done before, and it was unlikely to be pleasant. He had been on the phone half the morning, first to the managing director, and then to the newspaper's lawyers. His headache had got worse as the conversations went on. He sighed and dropped his hands onto the heaps of papers on his desk. His eyes were bloodshot and his hair was a mess. He stared vacantly ahead of him for a while, then reached for a box of pills and took another Distalgesic. There was no way he'd be able to drive home now.

There was a knock on the door and Nils Langeby put his head in.

'You wanted to see me?' he said cheerfully.

'Yes, come in.' Anders Schyman stood up with an effort. He went round the desk and gestured to the reporter to have a seat on one of the sofas. Nils Langeby sat down in the middle of the largest sofa and made himself at home. He seemed nervous, but was trying hard to hide it. He was looking at the low coffee table in a slightly perplexed way, as if he were expecting a cup of coffee and a pastry. Anders Schyman sat down in an armchair facing him.

'I wanted to talk to you, Nils, because I want to make you an offer . . .'

The reporter brightened up, and a light went on behind his eyes. He presumed he was going to be promoted, that he was about to get some sort of recognition. The editor-in-chief realized this and felt he was being a real bastard.

'I see,' Nils Langeby said when his boss had been silent for a short while.

'I was wondering what you'd think about continuing to work for the paper on a freelance basis?'

There, he'd said it. It sounded like a normal question, spoken in a normal tone of voice. The editor-in-chief made an effort to appear calm and collected.

Nils Langeby clearly didn't understand.

'Freelance? But . . . why? Freelance . . . how . . . ? I've already got a fixed contract!'

The editor-in-chief stood up and went over to fetch the glass of water on his desk.

'Yes, I know you've got a fixed contract, Nils. You've been employed here for quite a number of years now, and you could stay on for another ten, twelve years, until you retire. What I'm offering you now is a way of working in a less rigid way for the rest of your working life.'

Nils Langeby's eyes were darting about.

'What do you mean?' he said. His chin had dropped, turning his mouth into a black hole. Schyman sighed and sat down in the armchair again with the glass in his hand.

'I'm asking if you'd like to enter into a preferential freelance contract with the paper. We could help you set up as self-employed, maybe even help you start your own business, then you could work for us on a less formal basis.'

The reporter gawped and blinked a couple of times. He reminded Schyman of a fish out of water.

'What?' he said. 'What the hell's going on?'

'Just as I say,' the editor-in-chief said tiredly. 'An offer of a new way of working. Have you never given any thought to moving on?'

Nils Langeby closed his mouth and pulled his legs in under the edge of the sofa. While the significance of what was being said sank in, he turned to look at the office-block outside the window, clenched his teeth and swallowed.

'We could help you to set up an office in the city. We would guarantee you the income from five days' freelance work each month, plus tax and holiday pay, for five years. You'd continue to cover the areas you're already working on, crime in schools and—'

'It's that fucking bitch, isn't it?' Nils Langeby said angrily.

'Sorry . . . ?' Schyman said, losing a little of his calm façade.

Langeby turned back to face the editor-in-chief, and Schyman was taken aback by the hatred in his eyes.

'That bitch, that fucking cow. She's behind this, isn't she?'

'What on earth are you talking about?' Schyman said, and realized he was raising his voice.

The reporter clenched his fists and was breathing hard through his nose.

'Fuck, fuck, fuck,' he said. 'That bitch wants to get me fired!'

'I haven't said anything about firing you,' Schyman started.

'Bollocks!' Langeby yelled, standing up so fast that his gut wobbled. His face was deep red and he was waving his fists in the air.

'Sit down,' Schyman said, quietly and calmly. 'Don't make this any more unpleasant than it already is.'

'Unpleasant?' Langeby roared, and Schyman stood up as well. The editor-in-chief took two steps towards Langeby and stopped right in front of his face.

'Sit down, man; I haven't finished!' he snarled.

Langeby ignored him and went over to the window, and just stared out through the glass. The air was clear and cold, the sun shining over the Russian Embassy.

'Who are you referring to with all that misogynistic swearing?' Schyman asked. 'Your line manager, Annika Bengtzon?'

Langeby let out a short, pathetic little laugh.

'My line manager? Yes, for fuck's sake, of course I mean her. The most incompetent bitch I've ever met. She has no idea! She can't do anything! Everyone finds her utterly impossible to deal with. Eva-Britt Qvist thinks exactly the same as me! She yells and shouts at people. No one can understand how she got that job. She has no authority, no legitimacy and no editorial experience.'

'Editorial experience?' Anders Schyman. 'What's that got to do with anything?'

'Everyone knows about that man who died, you know. She never mentions it, but everyone knows.'

The editor-in-chief took a deep breath, and his nostrils flared.

'If you're referring to what happened before Annika Bengtzon became a permanent employee here, the court made it very clear that that was an accident. Dragging that up now is pretty low,' he said coldly.

Nils Langeby said nothing, just rocked on his heels, trying to hold back the tears. Schyman decided to stick the knife in and give it a good twist.

'I think it's quite remarkable of you to express yourself in this way about your boss,' he said. 'Outbursts of the sort you just made are grounds for a written warning.'

Nils Langeby didn't react, merely carried on rocking over by the window.

'We have to discuss your work here at the paper, Nils. Your so-called article yesterday was an absolute disaster. That in itself isn't enough to justify a warning, but recently there have been numerous occasions when you have shown shockingly poor judgement. Take your article on Sunday about the police suspecting that the first explosion was the work of terrorists, for instance. You weren't able to identify a single source.'

'I don't have to reveal my sources,' Nils Langeby said breathlessly.

'Yes you do, to me at least, because I'm the fucking publisher of this paper. If you're wrong, I'm the one who takes the fall. Or maybe you never grasped that in all your years here?'

Langeby carried on rocking.

'I haven't been in touch with the union about this yet,' Schyman said. 'I wanted to talk to you first. We can do this however you want to, with or without the involvement of the union, and with or without open hostility. It's up to you.'

The reporter raised his shoulders, but said nothing.

'You can carry on standing there, or you can sit down and let me tell you what I have in mind.'

Langeby stopped rocking, hesitated for a moment, then slowly turned round. Schyman could see that he had been crying. The two men took their seats again.

'I have no wish to humiliate you,' the editor-in-chief said quietly. 'I want to make this as dignified as possible.'

'You can't fire me,' Nils Langeby sniffed.

'Yes, I can,' Schyman said. 'It would cost three years' salary at an industrial tribunal, maybe four. That would be a horribly messy and unpleasant orgy of recrimination and accusation, and neither you nor the paper deserves that. You'd probably never work again afterwards. The paper would end up looking like a harsh and heartless employer, but that wouldn't be particularly damaging. It might even be good for our reputation. We would be able to give very good justifications for firing you. You would receive a formal written warning immediately, today, and we would refer to that in our case.

'We would claim that you have sabotaged our work, have bullied and undermined your line manager with crude sexual insults. We would provide evidence of your incompetence and poor judgement – we would only have to refer to what has happened in recent days, and count the number of articles in the archive that have been written by you. How many have there been in the past ten years? Thirty? Thirty-five? That's three and a half articles per year, Nils.'

'You said . . . you said on Sunday that I could carry on working on lead articles for the *Evening Post* for years . . . Was that just crap?'

Anders Schyman sighed.

'No, not at all. That's why I'm making you this offer, to carry on working for the paper in a different way. We'll set up a company and premises for you, and purchase five days of your time each month for five years, on a freelance rate, plus tax and holiday pay. That would provide more than half your current salary for five years, and would leave you free to do as much work as you like elsewhere.'

Langeby wiped the snot from his upper lip with the back of his hand, and stared down at the carpet. After a couple of minutes' silence he said, 'And if I get another job?'

'Then we'd arrange to pay the same amount as retirement compensation. We can't give more than that.'

'You said five years!' Langeby said, suddenly combative.

'Yes, but that's if you're producing work for us. The freelance contract isn't a parachute payment. We expect you to continue to work for us, just on new terms.'

Langeby looked down at the floor again. Schyman waited for a few minutes, then moved on to his next point: tidying up the mess.

'I know you haven't been happy here for a while, Nils. You haven't really come to terms with the new culture. I don't like the idea of you being unhappy with developments in your place of work. This is a very good way for you to build a solid foundation for your own business, and get going on a whole new stage of your career. You don't like working under Annika Bengtzon, and I think that's a shame. But Annika isn't going anywhere; I've got big plans for her. I don't agree with your evaluation of her at all. I think she's courageous, and highly intelligent. She flares up a bit too easily sometimes, but that will wear off with time. She's been under a lot of stress recently, and a lot of that is down to you, Nils. I want to keep the skills that you both have here at the paper, and I think that this sort of offer is the best way of achieving that for all concerned . . .'

'That's only twice my annual salary,' Nils Langeby said.

'Yes, it's twice your full salary, and you get that with no strings attached. No one even has to know about it. You can just say that you're moving on in your career and starting up your own business as a freelance journalist. The paper will express its sorrow at losing such an experienced colleague, but is happy that you will continue to work for us under the terms of a new fixed contract . . .'

Nils Langeby looked up at the editor-in-chief with an expression of intense loathing.

'Fucking hell,' he said. 'What a devious fucking snake you are. Fuck you!'

Without another word Nils Langeby got up and walked out. He slammed the door hard behind him, and Anders Schyman listened to his footsteps as they blended into the noise of the newsroom.

The editor-in-chief went over to his desk and drank another glass of water. The last tablet had taken the edge off his headache, but his forehead was still throbbing angrily. He gave a deep sigh. That had gone pretty well, all things considered. He might even have won already. One thing was certain: Nils Langeby was on his way out. He would be gone from the newsroom, and would never be allowed to set foot here again. Sadly there was no way he would ever resign voluntarily. He would carry on poisoning the atmosphere in the newsroom for another twelve years, doing nothing but sabotaging their efforts.

Schyman sat down behind his desk and looked out over the embassy complex. Some children were trying to sledge down the mud on the slope in front of it.

That morning the managing director had promised Schyman that he could reallocate a couple of posts in his budget, and use the money to buy out Nils Langeby – offering him up to four times his annual salary. Which was cheaper than paying for twelve years, which they would have to do if he stayed. If Nils Langeby was smart, which of course he wasn't, he would take what was on offer. If he didn't, there were other, more drawn-out, methods available. He could be moved to an early-morning post doing proof-reading. That would mean industrial relations trouble, but the union wouldn't be able to stop it. They'd never be able to prove that the company had done anything wrong. Reporters were assumed to be competent proof-readers, so there wouldn't be any formal grounds for complaint.

The union wouldn't really have much of a case. Anders Schyman had simply made the reporter an offer. People were often offered this sort of deal when they approached retirement, even if it didn't happen very often at this paper. All the journalists' association could do was support its members through the negotiations and make sure they got as good a deal as possible.

But if everything fell apart, one of the paper's lawyers, an expert in employment law, was ready to launch proceedings in an industrial tribunal. An ombudsman from the journalists' association would represent Langeby in court, but there was no way the paper could lose. Schyman's one and only aim was to get rid of the bastard, and he was going to get his way, come what may.

The editor-in-chief took another sip of water, then picked up the phone and asked Eva-Britt Qvist to come and see him. He had torn Spike off a strip last night, and was pretty sure he wouldn't be a problem in future. It was just as well to deal with the whole lot of them in one go.

*　　　*　　　*

The call from Leif, the tip-off merchant, came at 11.47, just three minutes after it had happened. Berit took the call.

'Stockholm Klara has been blown up, at least four people injured,' Leif said, and hung up. Before the information sank into Berit's brain, Leif had already called the next paper. He had to be first with the information – otherwise he wouldn't get paid for it.

Berit held on to the receiver, but pressed the cradle to end the call, then dialled the direct number to police central control.

'Is it true there's been a bomb in the central sorting office?' she asked quickly.

'We don't know anything yet,' an extremely stressed police officer said.

'Is it true? Has there been another explosion?' Berit said.

'It looks like it,' the policeman said.

They hung up and Berit threw the remains of her lunch in the bin.

At noon, Radio Stockholm were the first to announce the news publically.

57

Annika left Tungelsta with a warm feeling in her soul. The human psyche had a wonderful capacity for healing itself. She waved to Olof Furhage and Alice as she pulled out onto Älvvägen, heading towards Allévägen. She cruised slowly through the charming streets towards the main road. She could actually imagine living out here. She drove past Krigslida, Glasberga and Norrskogen on her way back to the Västerhaninge junction and the motorway up to Stockholm.

Once she was safely in the right lane on the Nynäshamn road, she picked up her mobile from the passenger seat. The display read '1 missed call', so she clicked to see the number. The call was from the paper. She sighed and put the phone back on the seat. Thank goodness it was nearly Christmas.

She switched on the radio and sang along to Alphaville's 'Forever Young'.

Just after the Dalarö junction the mobile rang again. She sighed and turned the radio down, put in her earpiece and pressed 'answer'.

'Annika Bengtzon? Yes, hello, this is Beata Ekesjö, we spoke on Tuesday. We met out at the sports centre and then I called you that evening . . .'

Annika groaned silently to herself. Great, the crazy construction manager.

'Hello,' Annika said, overtaking a Russian lorry.

'I was wondering if you've got time for a chat . . .'

'Not really,' Annika said, pulling in ahead of the lorry.

'It's important,' Beata Ekesjö said.

Annika sighed again.

'I see. What's it about?'

'I think I know who killed Christina Furhage.'

Annika came close to driving off the road.

'Really? How could you possibly know that?'

'I've found something,' Beata Ekesjö said.

Annika's brain was working overtime.

'What?'

'I can't say.'

'Have you told the police?'

'No, I wanted to show you first.'

'Me? Why?'

'Because you've written about all this.'

Annika slowed down to give herself space to think, and was overtaken by the Russian lorry. A swirl of snow kicked up in its wake covered the road.

'But I'm not the one investigating the murder, that's the police's job,' she said.

'Don't you want to write about me?'

The woman wasn't giving up; she was evidently desperate to get in the paper.

Annika weighed up the pros and cons. The woman was crazy, and probably didn't have anything, and she just wanted to get home. But at the same time you couldn't just hang up when someone said they could give you the solution to a murder.

'Tell me what you've found and I'll tell you if I'm going to write about it.'

The snow being kicked up by the lorry was a real nuisance, so Annika pulled out and overtook it again.

'I can show you.'

Annika groaned silently and looked at the time. Quarter to one.

'Okay, so where is it?'

'Here, at the Victoria Stadium.'

Annika was driving past Trångsund; she would practically be driving right past the Victoria Stadium on her way back to the paper.

'Okay,' she said. 'I can be there in quarter of an hour.'

'Great,' Beata said. 'I'll be waiting for you out in front—'

The telephone gave three short bleeps and the call was cut off. It was out of battery. Annika found the in-car phone charger in the bottom of her bag and plugged it in. She turned up the volume again and discovered to her great delight that they had just started playing Gloria Gaynor's old feminist anthem, 'I Will Survive'.

58

A group of journalists and reporters had already gathered at the central sorting office by the time Berit and Johan Henriksson arrived. Berit looked up at the futuristic façade, the sun glittering in the glass and chrome.

'So our bomber is ringing the changes,' she said. 'He's never used letter bombs before.'

Henriksson checked his cameras as they climbed the steps up to the main doors. The other journalists were standing in the airy entrance hall. Berit looked round as she walked in. The building was a fairly typical 1980s construction: marble, escalators, ridiculously high ceilings.

'Is there anyone from the *Evening Post* here?' asked a man over by the lifts.

Berit and Henriksson looked at each other in surprise.

'Yes, here,' Berit said.

'Would you mind coming with me?' the man said.

The cordons had been removed, the approach road had been cleared of snow, and Annika was able to drive right up to the steps in front of the stadium. She looked around, the sun making her squint, but she could see no signs of life anywhere. She sat in the car for a while with

the engine idling, listening to the end of Dusty Spring-
field's 'I Only Want To Be With You'. When there was
a knock on the window she almost jumped out of her
skin.

'God, you scared me,' Annika said as she opened the
door.

Beata Ekesjö smiled.

'No need to worry,' she said.

Annika turned off the engine.

'You can't park here,' Beata Ekesjö said. 'You're
bound to get a ticket.'

'I wasn't planning to stay long,' Annika protested.

'No, we have to take a bit of a walk. There's a nine-
hundred-kronor fine for parking here.'

Annika groaned to herself.

'Where should I park, then?'

Beata pointed.

'Over there, on the other side of the walkway. I'll wait
for you here.'

Annika got back in the car. Why do I let people mess
me about? she thought as she drove back the way she
had come and parked among the other cars alongside
a residential block. Oh well, a short walk in the sun-
shine would do no harm, it didn't exactly happen every
day. The main thing was to make sure she wasn't late
picking the children up. Annika unplugged her mobile.
The battery showed it was a quarter full, as the screen
flashed up '1 new message'. She pressed 'c' to clear the
screen and called the nursery. They were closing at five,
an hour earlier than usual, but still later than she had
thought.

She breathed out a sigh of relief and started to cross
the walkway.

Beata was waiting for her, her breath hanging in the
air around her.

'So what do you want to show me?' Annika said, aware that she sounded irritable.

Beata was still smiling.

'I've found something very strange over there,' she said, pointing. 'It won't take too long.'

Annika sighed quietly and set off. Beata followed her.

59

As Berit and Henriksson were stepping into the lift in the sorting office, Chief Prosecutor Kjell Lindström was making a call. He asked to speak to the paper's editor-in-chief, but was put through to his secretary.

'I'm afraid he's gone to lunch,' the secretary said, as Schyman waved to her to hold him off. 'Can I take a message? I see. Hold on a moment, and I'll see if I can get hold of him . . .'

Schyman's migraine was still lingering. Right now, all he wanted to do was lie down in a darkened room for an hour and go to sleep. In spite of the headache, he had accomplished a number of constructive things that morning. His conversation with Eva-Britt Qvist had gone surprisingly smoothly. The secretary had said she thought Annika Bengtzon showed a lot of promise as head of section, and that she wanted to support her in any way she could. She definitely wanted to help make the crime team work under Annika's leadership.

'It's one of the state prosecutors, and he's *very* insistent,' Schyman's secretary said, emphasizing the 'very'.

Anders Schyman groaned and took the call.

'So, the forces of law and order are still on high alert on a day like today, a day before Christmas Eve.

Although I have to say this is all the wrong way round, we're supposed to chase you—'

'I'm phoning about the explosive device that detonated in Klara sorting office,' Kjell Lindström interrupted.

'Yes, we've got a team on their way—'

'I know, we're talking to them now. The device was addressed to one of your employees: a reporter by the name of Annika Bengtzon. We have to get her under protection immediately.'

The words found their way into Anders Schyman's brain through a cloud of painkillers.

'Annika Bengtzon?'

'The package was addressed to her, but was set off accidentally in the sorting office. We think it was sent by the person behind the bombings at the Victoria Stadium and the sports hall in Sätra.'

Anders Schyman felt his knees buckle beneath him, and sat down heavily on his secretary's desk.

'Bloody hell,' he said.

'Where's Annika Bengtzon at the moment? Is she in the office?'

'No, I don't think so. She went out this morning, to interview someone. I don't think she's back yet.'

'Man or woman?'

'What, the person she was going to meet? Man, I think. Why?'

'It's vitally important that Annika Bengtzon is put under protection immediately. She has to stay away from home and work until the person in question is caught.'

'How do you know the bomb was addressed to Annika?'

'It was sent by registered post. We're looking into the details at the moment. Right now, the most important thing is to get Annika Bengtzon to a place of safety. We're sending a couple of patrols over to you at the paper; they should be with you shortly. They'll make sure she's taken to a safe house. Has she got family?'

Anders Schyman shut his eyes and ran a hand over his face. This can't be happening, he thought, feeling all the blood draining from his head.

'Yes, a husband and two young children.'

'Do the children go to a nursery? Which one? Is there anyone there who can tell us? Where does her husband work? Can you get hold of him?'

Anders Schyman promised personally to make sure that Annika's family were informed and taken care of. He gave the police Annika's mobile number and asked them to do everything they could.

60

They walked away from Sickla canal and past a small clump of trees close to the stadium. The slender pines had been damaged by the explosion, one was lying with its roots exposed, and the others all had split and shredded branches. The snow was almost twenty centimetres thick. Annika got snow in her shoes.

'Is it far?' she asked.

'Not much further,' Beata said.

They trudged on, with Annika getting increasingly irritated. The training ground was looming alongside them, and Annika could see the upper floors of the media centre in the distance ahead of them.

'How do you get in, there don't seem to be any steps?' she said, looking at the three-metre-high concrete wall that ran alongside the length of the track.

Beata caught up with her and stopped beside her.

'We're not going up there. Just keep following the wall.'

She pointed and Annika trudged on. Stress was starting to bubble through her veins, she had to finish her article about how close the police were to catching the Bomber before she went home, and she still had to wrap up the children's presents. Well, she could always do that this evening, once they were asleep. Beata's discovery might even be enough to make the police talk.

'You see where the wall stops over there?' Beata said behind her. 'You can get a couple of metres in under the stadium, that's where we're going.'

Annika shivered, it was cold in the shadow of the wall. She could hear the sound of her breathing over the noise of traffic on the southern link road behind her, but otherwise everything was quiet. At least she knew where they were going now.

The police patrols consisted of two uniformed policemen and two plain-clothed officers. Anders Schyman received them in his office.

'We've got two bomb units with sniffer-dogs on their way here,' one of the officers said. 'There's a serious risk that there are more bombs, maybe even here. We have to evacuate the building immediately and conduct a thorough search.'

'Is that really necessary, we haven't received any threats?' Anders Schyman said.

The policeman looked at him sternly.

'She hasn't sent any warnings before.'

'She?' Schyman said.

The other officer stepped forward.

'Yes, we believe the Bomber could well be a woman.'

Anders Schyman looked from one to the other.

'Why do you think that?'

'I'm afraid we can't tell you that at the moment.'

'So why haven't you arrested her?'

'She's vanished,' the first officer said, then changed the subject. 'We haven't managed to get hold of Annika Bengtzon. Have you any idea where she might be?'

Anders Schyman shook his head. His mouth was completely dry.

'No. She just said she was going out to do an interview.'

'Who with?'

'She didn't say.'

'Has she got her own car?'

'I don't think so.'

The policemen exchanged a look. This man didn't seem to know very much.

'Okay, we need to find out what vehicle she's driving and put out an alert for it. And we have to start clearing the building.'

'Up above is where the competitors will warm up before the different events,' Beata said once they were under the training ground. It was gloomy, almost dark, under the concrete roof. Annika looked back through the long, low opening. On the far side lay the Olympic village, its white buildings shining in the sun. The windows were sparkling, they were all new. Putting in new glass had been a priority after the explosion, otherwise the plumbing might have frozen and burst.

'The competitors have to be able to get to the Victoria Stadium quickly,' Beata said. 'This area will be open to the public, so to stop the athletes having to queue at the main entrance to get in and compete, we built an underground tunnel from here right up into the stadium itself.'

Annika turned round and peered into the darkness.

'Where's the tunnel?' she asked, surprised.

Beata smiled.

'Well, we didn't exactly want to make it obvious,' she said. 'Otherwise the public would be able to get in through the tunnel as well. Over here in the corner. Look, I'll show you.'

405

They went further in, and Annika blinked to get her eyes accustomed to the darkness.

'Here it is,' Beata said.

Annika was facing a grey-painted metal door, hardly visible in the darkness. There was a thick iron bar across it. It looked like a normal waste-disposal room for bins and rubbish. Next to the metal bar was a small box, which Beata opened. Annika watched her pull a card from her pocket and run it through the electronic reader inside the box.

'You've got a card?' Annika said in surprise.

'Everyone has,' Beata said, lifting the metal bar.

'What are you doing?' Annika said.

'Opening the tunnel,' Beata said, pulling the door open. The hinges made no sound at all. The darkness inside was impenetrable.

'But is this allowed? Isn't it alarmed?' Annika said, feeling more and more uncomfortable with the situation.

'No, the alarms aren't on in the middle of the day. They're working like crazy up in the stadium. If you go in you'll find something really strange. Hang on, I'll get the lights.'

Beata pulled a large circuit-breaker beside the entrance and a series of strip-lights lit up in the roof. The tunnel had concrete walls and a plain yellow linoleum floor. It was approximately two and a half metres high. It went straight on for some twenty metres, then curved to the left and disappeared up towards the Victoria Stadium. Annika took a deep breath and walked into the tunnel. She turned round, to see Beata closing the door.

'It's against regulations to leave it open,' Beata said, smiling once more.

Annika smiled back, turned round and carried on into the tunnel.

'Is it up here?' she said.

'Yes, just round the corner,' Beata said.

Annika felt her blood start to race: this was actually pretty exciting. She quickened her pace, her heels echoing in the tunnel. She turned the corner, and caught sight of a heap of clutter up ahead.

'There's something up there!' she said, turning to face Beata.

'Yes, that's what I wanted to show you. It's really interesting.'

Annika hoisted her bag further onto her shoulder and started jogging. It was a mattress, two plain folding chairs, a camping table and a coolbox. Annika walked closer and stared at the objects.

'Someone's been sleeping here,' she said. At that moment she caught sight of the box of dynamite. It was small and white, and had the word 'Minex' printed along the side. She gasped, and the next moment felt something round her neck. Her hands flew up to her throat, but couldn't get any grip. She tried to scream, but the rope was already too tight. She began thrashing and pulling, trying to run, sank to the floor and tried to crawl away, but the rope just kept getting tighter and tighter.

The last thing she saw before everything went black was Beata holding the rope in her gloved hands, hovering far above her under the concrete ceiling.

61

The evacuation of the building housing the *Evening Post* took place relatively quickly and efficiently. They set the fire alarm off and nine minutes later the building was completely empty. Last out was Ingvar Johansson, the editor, who made it very clear that he had more important things to do than take part in a fire drill. When the editor-in-chief roared at him over the phone he left his post, albeit under protest.

The staff remained relatively calm. They had no idea that the bomb in the central sorting office was intended for one of their colleagues, and now they were being offered coffee and sandwiches in the staff canteen of the neighbouring building. As they did so, the police bomb detection squads searched through the newspaper's premises.

Anders Schyman suddenly realized that his migraine had vanished. His blood vessels had shrunk to their normal size and the pain had subsided. He was sitting with his secretary and the head telephonist in an office next to the kitchen in the neighbouring building. Getting hold of Annika's husband was easier said than done. The switchboard at the Association of Local Councils had closed at one o'clock and no one on the paper had Thomas's office phone number. Nor did anyone know his mobile number. None of the main phone companies had a Thomas Samuelsson living on Hantverkargatan on their books. And Anders Schyman had no idea which nursery the children went to. His secretary was calling all the nurseries within social service district 3, which covered Kungsholmen, asking if the Bengtzon children were there. What she didn't know was that the nursery never gave out any information about Annika's children. They weren't even on the list of phone numbers handed out to other parents. After a series of articles about an organization known only as the Paradise Foundation, Annika had received death threats. Ever since that, she and Thomas had been very careful with their personal details. The nursery staff had obviously been made aware of this, so when Schyman's secretary phoned she was blithely told that the children weren't there. Then the manager called Annika on her mobile at once to tell her, but got no answer.

Anders Schyman could practically taste the metallic tang of stress in his mouth. He asked the head telephonist to try every conceivable number on the Association of Local Councils switchboard, starting from the main public number, then 01, 02, and so on, until she reached someone who could get hold of Thomas. The police already had a patrol waiting outside Annika's home address. Beyond that, the editor-in-chief didn't know what he could do. He went over to the police to find out how they were getting on.

'So far we haven't found anything. We should be done in half an hour or so,' the officer in charge said.

Anders Schyman went back to help his secretary call every nursery on Kungsholmen.

Annika slowly became aware that she was awake. She could hear someone groaning, and realized after a while that it was her making the noise. When she opened her eyes she was struck with a sense of total panic. She was blind. She screamed like someone possessed, opening her eyes as wide as she could against the impenetrable darkness. Her fear multiplied when the only sound that came out was a falsetto croak. The sounds were echoing in the dark, bouncing back like frightened birds against a window, and she suddenly remembered the underground tunnel beneath the Victoria Stadium. She stopped screaming and listened for a minute to her own panic-stricken breathing. She was still in the tunnel. She concentrated on her body, trying to feel if everything was still there, and still working. She started by raising her head, which hurt, but wasn't obviously injured. She realized that she was lying down, and that whatever she was lying on was relatively soft, probably the mattress she had seen before . . .

'Beata,' she whispered.

She lay still in the darkness. Beata had put her here and had done something to her; that was it. Beata had put a rope round her throat, and now she was gone. Did Beata think she was dead?

Annika became aware that one of her arms was hurting, the one that was squashed beneath her. When she tried to move it she realized it was tied down. Her hands had been tied behind her back. She was lying on her side with her arms behind her. She tried to lift her legs and found the same thing. They had been tied up as well, not just together, but to the wall alongside. When she moved her legs she realized something else. Her bladder and bowels had emptied themselves of their contents while she was unconscious. The urine was cold and the faeces sticky. She started to cry. What had she done? Why was this happening to her? She cried so hard she was shaking. The tunnel was cold, and her crying seeped out through the cold and into the darkness. She rocked gently on the mattress, back and forth, back and forth, back and forth.

I don't want to, she thought. Don't want to, don't want to, don't want to . . .

Anders Schyman was back in his office again, staring out over the dark façade of the Russian Embassy. No bomb had been found on the premises. The sun had gone down behind the old tsarist flag, leaving the sky glowing red for a few minutes. The paper's staff were back at their desks, but only he, his secretary, and the head telephonist knew that the bomb in Klara sorting office had been intended for Annika. Anders Schyman had been given some basic information about the bomb, but all the police knew so far merely proved that the Bomber was a cold-hearted killer.

The package containing the explosive device had arrived at the sorting office in the Klara district of central Stockholm at 18.50 on Wednesday evening. It had been sent by registered mail from postal district 17 in Stockholm at 16.53. District 17 meant the local post office on Södermannagatan, on Södermalm. Because the package had been registered, it was treated as valuable and had not been picked up by the usual truck, but by a special van that arrived slightly later.

The brown package hadn't aroused any particular interest. Stockholm Klara is the largest sorting office in Sweden, on the Klaraberg Viaduct in the middle of the city centre. It occupies eight floors of an entire city block between the City Coach Terminal, the City Hall and the Central Station. One and a half million items pass through its premises every day.

After it arrived at one of the office's four loading bays, the package had ended up on the fourth floor with the other registered post. Specially trained staff there dealt with all manner of valuable items.

Because the *Evening Post* had its own postcode, notifications of registered mail were sent to the newspaper's normal postbox. The box was emptied several times each day and the contents driven up to the editorial offices out in Mariaberg on Kungsholmen. The paper's caretakers were authorized to pick up items needing signatures even though they were addressed to other people at the paper. These were picked up once a day, usually just after lunch.

On Thursday morning there were a number of registered items in the first post, because of Christmas. The notification of the package addressed to Annika Bengtzon had been one in a pile of others left with the caretakers.

The explosion had gone off when Tore Brand had gone to pick up the registered post. One of the postal employees had stumbled and happened to drop the package.

It couldn't have fallen more than half a metre, and it tumbled back into the tray it had been in all night, but that was enough to trigger the detonator.

Four people were injured, three of them seriously. The man closest to the explosion, the one who had dropped it, was in a critical condition.

Anders Schyman sighed. There was a knock on his door and one of the police officers walked in without waiting for a response.

'We can't get hold of Thomas Samuelsson either,' he said. 'We sent officers to the Association of Local Councils, but he wasn't there. People there think he went to meet a local politician involved in a committee report they're both working on. We've tried calling his mobile number, but so far he hasn't answered.'

'Have you found Annika or the car?' Schyman asked.

The police officer shook his head.

The editor-in-chief turned away and stared at the embassy roof again.

Dear God, he prayed, please don't let her be dead.

62

Suddenly her sight returned. The strip-lights flickered on with a buzz, and for a moment Annika was blinded and couldn't see a thing. A clatter of heels approached in the tunnel and Annika rolled into a little ball and shut her eyes tight. The steps came closer and stopped next to her ear.

'Are you awake?' a voice said above her.

Annika opened her eyes and blinked. She could see the linoleum floor and the toes of a pair of Pertti Palmroth designer boots.

'Good. We've got things to do.'

Someone grabbed her and sat her up against the concrete wall with her legs bent at the knees and sticking out to one side. It was extremely uncomfortable.

Beata Ekesjö leaned over her, sniffing.

'Have you shat yourself? Eurgh, how disgusting!'

Annika didn't react. She was staring at the concrete wall opposite, whimpering quietly.

'Right, let's get you ready,' Beata said, grabbing Annika under the arms. With a combination of shoves and tugs she managed to make Annika lean forward with her head between her knees.

'This worked well last time,' Beata said. 'It's nice when you start to get used to things, isn't it?'

Annika couldn't hear what the woman was saying. Her terror was muffling everything around her, killing all activity in her brain. She didn't even notice the smell from her lower half. She cried silently as Beata fiddled with something next to her. Beata was humming some old song. Annika tried to join in but couldn't.

'Don't try to talk yet,' Beata said. 'The rope dug into your larynx. Here, look at this!'

Beata stood up in front of Annika. She was holding a roll of duct tape in one hand and a pack of what looked like red candles in the other.

'This is Minex, twenty cardboard charges, 22 by 200 millimetres, each weighing 100 grams. Two kilos. That's enough. It was enough for Stefan. He ended up in pieces.'

Annika realized what the woman was saying. She realized what was happening and leaned over and threw up. She vomited until her whole body was shaking and nothing but bile was coming out.

'What a mess you're making!' Beata said reproachfully. 'I really ought to make you clean that up.'

Annika was panting heavily. She could feel the bile dribbling from her mouth. I'm going to die, she thought. How has it come to this? This isn't the way things end in the movies.

'What the fuck do you expect?' Annika croaked.

'Ah, you're starting to get your voice back now,' Beata said happily. 'That's great, because I've got a few questions I'd like answers to.'

'Fuck you, you bitch,' Annika said. 'I'm not talking to you.'

Beata didn't answer, merely leaned forward and attached something to Annika's back, just below her ribcage. Annika thought, breathed, and thought she could smell a mixture of fear and explosives.

415

'Dynamite?' she asked.

'Yep. I'm using the duct tape to hold it.'

Beata rolled the tape round Annika's body a couple of times, wrapping her arms round her as she did so. Annika knew that this was an opportunity to get free, but couldn't work out what to do. Her hands were still tied behind her back, and her feet were still chained to the wall.

'There, now you're ready,' Beata said, standing up again. 'The explosive is stable enough, but the detonator can be a bit sensitive, so we'll have to be careful. I've got the wire, can you see? This is what I use to set off the explosion. I take it over here, and do you see this? An ordinary little torch battery. That's enough to set it off. Isn't that great?'

Annika looked at the thin yellow and green wire snaking over to the little camping table. She didn't know anything about explosives, so had no way of knowing if Beata was bluffing or telling the truth. She had used a car battery for Christina's murder. Why, if a small torch battery would do the job?

'It's a shame it had to turn out like this,' Beata said. 'If you'd stayed at work yesterday afternoon we wouldn't have to bother with all this. That would have been much better for all concerned. Climaxes should happen in the right place, which in your case would be the *Evening Post*'s newsroom. But it went off in the sorting office instead, which, frankly, was a real shame.'

Annika stared at the woman, she really was completely mad.

'What do you mean? Has there been another explosion?'

The Bomber sighed.

'Yes, I haven't dragged you out here for the fun of it, you know. Well, we'll just have to make do with this instead. I'm going to leave you for a little while. If I were you, I'd try to get some rest. But don't lie on your back, and don't try to pull the chain from the wall. Sudden movements can set off the explosives.'

'But why . . . ?' Annika said.

Beata stared at her with a look of complete indifference for several seconds.

'See you in a couple of hours,' she said, and headed off, heels clicking, back towards the training ground.

Annika heard her steps disappear round the corner, then the lights went out again.

Annika turned carefully, away from the vomit, and lay down incredibly slowly on her left side. She had her back to the wall and was facing the darkness, almost afraid to even breathe. Another explosion, then. Had anyone been killed? Was the bomb meant for her? How on earth could she possibly get out of this?

The stadium was crawling with people, Beata had said. They ought to be at the far end of the tunnel. If she shouted loudly enough maybe they'd hear her.

'Help!' Annika screamed as loudly as she could, but her voice was still weak.

She waited a few seconds, then screamed again. She realized the sound wouldn't travel far enough.

She lay her head down and felt panic rising. She thought she could hear animals moving around her, but realized that it was just the sound of the chain around her ankles. If Beata had left the light on she might have been able to get them loose.

'Help!' she screamed again, but with even poorer results.

Don't panic, don't panic, don't panic . . .

'Help!'

She was breathing fast and deep. Don't breathe too fast, or you'll get cramp, take it easy, hold your breath, one two three four, breathe, hold your breath, one two three four . . . It'll be fine, take it easy, you can do this, it can all be sorted out . . .

Suddenly Mozart's Symphony No.40, the first movement, started peeping electronically in the dark. Annika stopped hyperventilating out of sheer shock.

Her mobile phone! It still worked down here! Oh, God bless her network! She got to her knees. The music went on. She was the only person in the city who used this particular ringtone. Carefully she started to crawl towards the sound as the tune began again. She knew her time was almost out. The call would go to voicemail any second. At that moment she reached the end of the chain. And she couldn't reach her bag.

The telephone fell silent. Annika was panting loudly in the darkness. She knelt on the yellow linoleum floor for a minute or so, thinking. Then she started to go back to the mattress again. It was warmer and more comfortable there.

'This will be fine,' she said out loud to herself. 'As long as that madwoman isn't here, everything's fine. Not very comfortable, admittedly, but as long as I move very carefully there's no danger. It's going to be fine.'

She lay down and, like a form of incantation, started quietly singing the first lines of 'I Will Survive'.

Then she started to cry softly, into the darkness.

63

Thomas was striding out of the Central Station when his mobile rang. He got it just in time before voicemail took the call.

'We did tell you we'd be closing at five o'clock today,' one of the male nursery teachers said. 'Are you on your way?'

The traffic on Vasagatan was so noisy that Thomas could hardly hear what he said, and went into the doorway of a fur shop to ask what the matter was.

'Are you on your way, or what?' the man said again.

Fury hit Thomas in the guts with a force that surprised him. Bloody Annika! He had let her sleep late that morning, he had taken the kids and was on his way home on time, despite the fact that the regional government proposal had been leaked, and she couldn't even be bothered to pick up her own kids from nursery on time.

'I'm sorry we're late. I'll be there in five minutes,' he said, and ended the call.

Furious, he marched off towards Kungsbron. He went past Burger King and almost collided with a pushchair full of Christmas parcels, and hurried past Oscars Theatre. A group of black men were standing on the pavement outside Fasching's jazz club and Thomas stepped onto the road to get past them.

This was what he got for being so reasonable, such a New Man: his children were left waiting in an educational institution the day before Christmas Eve because his wife who was supposed to pick them up put her job ahead of her family.

They had had this discussion before. He could hear her voice over the noise of the city.

'My job is important to me,' she always said.

'More important than the children?' he had shouted on one occasion. She had gone completely pale and said 'of course not', but he wasn't sure he believed her. They had had a couple of really serious arguments about it, one when his parents had invited them out to their summer cottage out in the archipelago for Midsummer. There had been a murder somewhere and she had to mess up all their plans and leave.

'I don't do this just because I think it's fun,' she said. 'Yes, it is fun having an interesting story to work on, but this time I've negotiated to get a whole week off instead if I cover this job.'

'You never think of the children,' he had raged, and she had gone all cold and dismissive.

'Now you're just being unfair,' she'd said. 'I'll get a whole week's extra holiday with them now. They won't miss me at all out there on the island, there'll be loads of people there. You'll be there, and Grandma and Grandpa and all their cousins . . .'

'You really are selfish,' he had said.

She had been completely calm when she replied. 'No, you're the one being selfish now. You want me out there so you can show your parents what a lovely family you've got, and to prove that I don't work all the time. Yes, I know that's what your mother thinks. And she thinks the children spend far too much time at nursery, don't tell me she doesn't. I heard her say it.'

'Your job's more important to you than your family,' he had shouted after her, trying to hurt her.

She had stared back at him with distaste, and then said, 'Who took two years off to be with the children when they were tiny? Who stays at home with them when they're ill? Who takes them to nursery every day, and who picks them up most days?'

She had walked right up to him. 'Yes, Thomas, you're absolutely right. I'm going to let my job take priority over my family this time. For once I'm actually going to do it, so you're just going to have to put up with it.'

Then she had turned on her heel and walked out through the door without taking so much as a tooth-brush with her.

Of course the whole Midsummer weekend was ruined, for him, not the children. They didn't miss Annika for a second, just as she had said. Instead they were overjoyed when they got back home and Mummy was already there with meatballs and presents at the ready.

In hindsight he had to admit she had been right. She didn't put her job ahead of her family very often, just occasionally, just the same as him. But this didn't stop him from feeling absolutely livid right now. For the past two months, everything had been about the damn newspaper. This new job wasn't good for her, the others were pushing her too hard and she hadn't been prepared for it.

He had noticed other signs that she wasn't happy. She had started eating badly again, for instance. After one particular mass murder, when she was away for eight days, she had lost five kilos. It took five months for her to put the weight back on again. The occupational health advisor had warned her about being underweight. She saw this as praise, and proudly told all her friends over the phone. But in spite of that, she still got it into her head that she ought to diet occasionally.

He turned off Fleminggatan and went down the steps beside the Klara Sjö restaurant, to the waterside walk along Kungsholms Strand, which took him to the rear entrance of the nursery. The children were sitting in their coats beside the door, tired and hollow-eyed. Ellen was clutching her blue teddy bear.

'Mummy's coming to get us today,' Kalle said dismissively. 'Where's Mummy?'

The teacher who had stayed with the children was properly annoyed.

'I won't get this quarter of an hour back, you know,' he said.

'I really am very sorry,' Thomas said, noticing how out of breath he was. 'I don't know where on earth Annika could have got to.'

He hurried away with the children, and after a quick run they caught the number 40 bus outside the Pousette å Vis bar.

'You shouldn't run to catch the bus, you know,' the driver said crossly. 'How can we teach the kids not to when their parents do it?'

Thomas felt like hitting the man. He held up his card and herded the children back through the bus. Ellen fell over and started to cry. Give me strength, Thomas thought. They had to stand in the middle, among the Christmas presents, dogs and three pushchairs. When they tried to get out at Kungsholmstorg they almost didn't make it. He groaned out loud as he pushed open the door to number 32 Hantverkargatan. As he was stamping the snow off his shoes on the mat inside the door he suddenly heard voices behind him.

422

He looked up and saw two uniformed policemen coming up the steps.

'Thomas Samuelsson? I'm afraid I must ask you and the children to come with us.'

Thomas stared at them.

'We've been trying to get hold of you all afternoon. You haven't received any messages from us or the paper?'

'Daddy, where are we going?' Kalle said, taking Thomas's hand.

The realization that something was terribly wrong dawned on Thomas all of a sudden. Annika! Oh God!

'Is she . . . ?'

'We don't know where your wife is. She disappeared this afternoon. Our detectives will tell you more. If you could just come with us . . .'

'Why?'

'We're afraid that your home may have been interfered with.'

Thomas leaned down and took the two children in his arms.

'Let's get away from here,' he said quietly.

64

The six o'clock meeting at the paper was the strangest for many years. Anders Schyman could feel panic bubbling under the surface, his instinct told him that the paper shouldn't be published, that they should be out looking for Annika, supporting her family, hunting for the Bomber. Anything, really.

'We're going to sell a hell of a lot of papers,' Ingvar Johansson said as he entered the room. He sounded neither happy nor triumphant, just flat and sad, as if he were merely stating a fact. But Anders Schyman exploded.

'How dare you?' the editor-in-chief roared, grabbing hold of Ingvar Johansson, making him spill his coffee down one trouser leg.

Ingvar Johansson didn't even feel the burning coffee on his thigh, he was so shocked. He had never seen Anders Schyman lose control. The editor-in-chief glared right into the other man's eyes for a moment, then pulled himself together.

'Sorry,' he said, letting go and turning away with his hands over his face. 'I'm not myself today. Sorry.'

Jansson came into the room, last as usual, but without making his usual fuss. The night-editor looked pale and focused. This would be the hardest edition he had ever produced, he was fully aware of that.

'Okay,' Schyman said, looking at the few faces round the table: Picture-Pelle, Jansson and Ingvar Johansson. Entertainment and Sport had gone home. 'What are we going to do?'

Silence filled the room. They all had their heads bowed. The chair where Annika usually sat seemed to grow and fill the whole room. Anders Schyman turned away towards the night sky outside.

Ingvar Johansson started to speak, quietly and intently.

'Well, what we've got so far is a sort of embryonic stage, I suppose. There are a lot of editorial decisions to be taken on this edition . . .'

He leafed uncertainly through his notes. The situation felt absurd, unreal. It was very rare for the people in the room to be personally affected by the subject under discussion. But now the discussion was about one of them.

As Ingvar Johansson went slowly through his list, talking about what they had, the men seemed to find strength in their own routines. There was no escaping this, so the best thing they could do right now was to continue to do their jobs as well as they could. So this is what it feels like to be the colleagues of one of the victims, Anders Schyman thought as he stared out through the glass. It might be worth remembering how it feels when we come to cover other stories.

'Well, we've got the Klara bombing; we have to cover that,' Ingvar Johansson said. 'One article about the victims. The man who was most badly injured died an hour ago. He was single, lived in Solna. The others are out of danger. Their names will be released this evening

425

or later tonight, and we should be able to get passport photographs of them. Then we've got the damage to the room—'

'Leave the relatives alone,' Schyman said.

'What?' Ingvar Johansson said.

'The injured post office workers. Let's leave their relatives alone.'

'We don't even have their names yet,' Ingvar Johansson said.

Schyman turned towards the table. He ran his hands despairingly through his hair.

'Okay,' he said. 'Sorry. Go on.'

Ingvar Johansson took several deep breaths, collected himself, and went on. 'We've been inside the room damaged by the bomb in the sorting office. I don't know how Henriksson did it, but he got in and took a lot of pictures of the devastation. That room isn't usually accessible even to the normal staff there. They only deal with registered mail. But we've got the pictures.'

'We can add a discussion of principle to that,' Schyman said, walking slowly round the room. 'How far is the Post Office responsible for something like this? How carefully do they check parcels? Here we have the classic compromise between public integrity and the safety of Post Office staff. We'll have to talk to the general director of the Post Office, the union, and the minister responsible for the Post Office.'

The editor-in-chief stopped by the window, staring out at the darkness again. He listened to the hum of the ventilation unit, and tried to make out the sound of the traffic far below. It was quite soundless. Ingvar Johansson and Jansson were making notes. After a while the head of news went on with his run-through.

'Then there's our involvement. The fact that the bomb was addressed to the head of our crime team. We'll have

426

to cover that, everything from lunchtime when Tore Brand went to fetch the package to the work the police are doing to trace the source of the parcel.'

The men made notes; the editor-in-chief listened with his back to the table.

'Annika has disappeared,' Ingvar Johansson said quietly. 'We have to accept that now, and I suppose we should write about it . . .'

Anders Schyman turned round. Ingvar Johansson looked uncertain.

'The question is: can we write anything at all about the bomb being meant for us?' the news-editor went on. 'We may end up drowning in letter bombs if we do. We might encourage a gang of copycats to start kidnapping our reporters and threatening to send bombs . . .'

'We can't think like that,' Schyman said. 'If we did, we'd never be able to cover anything that affected anyone at all. We have to give an account of everything that's happened, including the parts that affect us and our head of crime. But I need to talk to Thomas, Annika's husband, about what we're going to write about her as a private person.'

'Does he know yet?' Jansson asked, and Anders Schyman sighed.

'The police got hold of him just after half past five. He'd been up in Falun all day, and had his mobile switched off. He had no idea what Annika was planning to do today.'

'So we've got an article about Annika going missing?' Jansson said.

Schyman nodded and turned away again.

'We give an outline of her work, but we have to be careful with any personal information about her,' Ingvar Johansson summarized. 'The next piece ought to be what the police think was the motive for Annika being . . . targeted.'

'Do they know why?' Pelle Oscarsson said, and the news-editor shook his head.

'There's no connection between her and the other victims, they'd never met. Their theory is that Annika was stirring things up so much that she had found out something she shouldn't have. She was ahead of the pack on this story from the start, so the motive has to lie somewhere in there. Quite simply, she knew too much.'

The men fell silent, each listening to the sound of the others breathing.

'That needn't necessarily be the case,' Schyman said. 'This bitch isn't rational. The bomb may well have been sent for a reason that makes no sense to anyone except the Bomber herself.'

The other men all looked up at the same time. The editor-in-chief sighed.

'Yes, the police think it's a woman. I think we should go ahead and publish that, sod them and their damn investigation. Annika knew this morning that the police were closing in on the woman, but they didn't tell her who it was. We'll say that the police are searching for a suspect, a woman that they haven't been able to trace.'

Anders Schyman sat down at the table with his hands over his face.

'What the hell do we do if the Bomber's got hold of her?' he said. 'What do we do if she dies?'

The others didn't answer. Somewhere out in the news-room came the sound of the television news, they could hear the newsreader's voice through the thin walls.

'We ought to run something about all the bombings so far,' Jansson said, taking over. 'Someone will have to have a serious talk with the police about how they managed to identify this particular woman. There must be details there that we should . . .'

He fell silent. All of a sudden it was no longer obvious what was interesting and what wasn't. The horizon was blurred, and there were no longer any fixed points of reference, no clear focus.

'We have to try to deal with this as normally as possible,' Anders Schyman said. 'Do what you always do. I'll be staying on tonight. What pictures have we got for all this?'

The picture editor explained the options.

'We haven't got many pictures of Annika, but we did take one last summer for the display of staff pictures. That should work okay.'

'Have we got any pictures of her working?' Schyman asked.

Jansson clicked his fingers.

'There's a shot of her at Panmunjom, in the demilitarized zone between North and South Korea, standing next to the American president. She was there on some sort of grant, with the press delegation ahead of the four-party talks in Washington in the autumn. Do you remember? She happened to be getting off the coach just as the president got out of his limo, and AP took a shot of them next to each other . . .'

'Okay, we'll take that,' Schyman said.

'I've dug out pictures of the ruined stadium, Sätra Hall, Furhage and the construction worker, Bjurling,' Pelle said.

'Okay,' Schyman said. 'What have we got for the front?'

They waited in silence, hoping the editor-in-chief would say it out loud.

'A portrait of Annika, preferably one where she looks nice and happy. She's the story now. The bomb was aimed at her, and now she's vanished. And only we know that. I think we should tackle it logically and chronologically: on six and seven, the bomb in the sorting office; eight and nine, the new victims; ten and eleven, our reporter is missing; twelve and thirteen, the Bomber is a woman, the police are closing in; fourteen and fifteen, reminder of events so far, discussion of Post Office security versus confidentiality; centrefold, the article about Annika and her work, with the Korean picture . . .'

He stood up, nauseated by his own decisiveness. Once again, he looked out over the darkened Embassy. They really shouldn't be doing this. The paper really shouldn't publish tomorrow. They really ought to shut down their coverage of the Bomber for the time being. He felt like a monster.

The others ran through the rest of the paper quickly. None of them said anything as they left the room.

65

Annika was freezing. It was cold in the tunnel; she guessed it was between eight and ten degrees. Fortunately she had put on a pair of long-johns that morning because she had planned to walk home from work. At least she wouldn't freeze to death. But her socks were wet from the trudge through the snow, making her feet cold. She tried wriggling her toes to warm them up. She was doing everything gently, trying not to move her feet too much, desperate not to set off the explosives on her back. She changed position every now and then, putting her weight on different parts of her body. If she lay on her side one of her arms got squashed, if she lay on her stomach her neck ached, kneeling and crouching made her legs go numb. She cried intermittently, but the more time passed, the more composed she became. She wasn't dead yet.

Her panic had subsided, and she had regained the power of thought. She was trying to think of a way out of this situation. It wasn't very realistic to imagine that she could get loose and escape, certainly not at the moment. And attracting the attention of anyone working in the stadium seemed unlikely. Beata had probably been lying when she said they were hard at work up there. Why would they start reconstruction the day before Christmas Eve? Besides, Annika hadn't seen a single vehicle or person near the stadium. If the builders really had started work, there would have been various different vehicles parked by the stadium, and there hadn't been any. Anyway, they would all have gone home by now, it was already evening. Which meant that they should have started looking for her by now.

She started to cry again when it dawned on her that no one had picked up the children from nursery. She knew how cross the staff there could get; Thomas had borne the brunt of that a year or so ago. The children would be sitting there waiting, eager to get home and decorate the tree, and she couldn't get to them. Maybe she'd never get home again. Maybe she'd never see them grow up. Ellen probably wouldn't even be able to remember her. Kalle may have some vague memories of his mum, especially when he looked at pictures of them out at the cottage last summer. She started crying helplessly, it all seemed so incredibly unfair.

After a while her tears dried up, she seemed to have run dry. She mustn't start thinking about death, because that could well become a self-fulfilling prophecy. She was going to make it. She should have been at the nursery at five o'clock. But it wasn't too late for Christmas. She was sure the Bomber had some sort of plan for her – otherwise she would be dead already. And the paper and Thomas would have realized she was missing, and the police were bound to be looking for her car. Which was parked legally and discreetly in a row of other cars in a residential car park half a kilometre from the stadium. And who would ever think of looking in this tunnel? No one had found it so far; otherwise they would have discovered this little hiding place. How could the police have missed it? The entrance up in the stadium must be very well concealed.

Her mobile rang at regular intervals. She had tried to find a stick or something that she could use to reach her bag, but hadn't found anything. Her range of movement was restricted to three metres in all directions, and it sounded as though the phone was about ten metres away. Well, at least it proved that they were trying to find her.

She had no real idea of what time it was, or how long she had been in the tunnel. It wasn't quite half past one when she came down here, but she didn't know how long she had been unconscious. And she had lost all track of time during her first panicked reaction. But at least five hours must have passed since then. As far as she could guess, it ought to be at least half past six now. But it could be much later, half past eight, nine o'clock. She was hungry and thirsty, and had wet herself once more. There hadn't been any choice. The faeces had started to dry up and itch, it really was very uncomfortable. This must be what it's like for little children in nappies, she thought. Mind you, at least they got changed regularly.

Suddenly another thought struck her: what if Beata doesn't come back! What if she was left here to die! No one would think of coming down here over Christmas.

Human beings only survive a couple of days without water. By Boxing Day it would be too late. She started to cry again, quietly and tiredly. Then she made herself stop. The Bomber would come back. She had a reason for holding Annika captive here.

Annika changed position again. She had to try to think clearly. She had met Beata Ekesjö before; she had to work with what she knew about her as a person. During their short conversation in Sätra Hall, Beata had been highly emotional. She had been genuinely upset about something, whatever it might be, and she had been keen to talk. Annika could exploit that. The only question was, how? She had no idea what you were supposed to do when you were held prisoner by a madman. She vaguely recalled hearing that you could go on courses about this sort of thing, unless she had read it somewhere? Or seen in on television? Yes, on television!

In an episode of the old detective series, *Cagney & Lacey*, one of the female cops had been held prisoner by a madman. Cagney – unless it was Lacey? – had been on a course about how to behave if you were taken hostage. She talked all about herself and her children, her dreams, her loves, anything to arouse some sort of empathy in her kidnapper. If she was talkative and friendly enough, it would be harder for the kidnapper to kill her.

Annika changed position again, getting to her knees this time. Maybe that would work with a normal person, but the Bomber was insane. She had already blown people up. Maybe talking about children would have no effect on Beata – she hadn't shown much sympathy for anyone's children or family so far. She would have to think of something else, based on what Cagney had done, and try to establish some form of communication with her kidnapper.

What had Beata actually said? That Annika had misunderstood her emotional response? Was that really why she was here? She'd have to try to read the Bomber better from now on. She had to listen carefully to what the woman said and follow her reasoning as well as she could.

And she would. She would conduct a dialogue with the Bomber, and pretend to understand and agree with her. She would stop protesting and just go with the flow.

She lay down on the mattress again, on her right side, facing the concrete wall, and made up her mind to try to get some rest. She wasn't afraid of the dark, so the darkness around her didn't scare her. Soon she felt her body give that familiar little twitch, and shortly afterwards she was asleep.

Death

I went to school in a wooden, three-storey building. The older we got, the higher up the building our classroom was. Once each year, in the spring, the whole school took part in a fire drill. In those days old schools went up like tinderboxes, and everyone had to take the drills very seriously, with no exceptions.

In my class we had a boy who was epileptic, I forget his name. For some reason he couldn't raise his hands above his head. Even so, he took part in the fire drill the year after the end of the war. I remember that day quite clearly. The sun was shining with a cold, pale light, and the wind was sharp and gusty. I hate heights, always have done, so I was stiff with terror when I got onto the fire-escape. The world over by the river seemed to tip, and I clung to the rungs. Slowly I turned my head and stared at the red-stained wood of the school building, and I struggled down every rung with the same cramped grip. I was shattered when I finally reached the ground. My legs were shaking, and I stood there trying to pull myself together while my classmates headed back to our classroom. When I looked up I saw the epileptic boy slowly climbing down the ladders. When he reached the last platform I heard him say: 'I can't go any further.'

He lay down, turned his face to the wall, and died in front of our eyes.

An ambulance came to fetch him. I'd never seen one before. I stood in the doorway as they put him on a stretcher. He looked the same as usual, just a bit paler, his eyes were closed and his lips were blue. His arms shook a little as the stretcher was pushed inside the ambulance, and a last breeze ruffled his blond curls before the doors closed.

I can still remember my surprise at the fact that I wasn't afraid. I saw a dead person, no older than me, and it didn't upset me. It wasn't unpleasant, or tragic, he was just completely still.

Since then I have often wondered what it is that makes a person alive. Our consciousness is really nothing but signal substances and electricity. The fact that I still think about the epileptic boy to this day means that he is actually still here. He is present in the dimension that we call reality, not in the form of his own signal substances, but in mine.

The question is whether we can't do worse things to people than merely kill them. Sometimes I suspect that I have destroyed people in other ways, not like the teacher who forced the boy down the ladders.

The ultimate question, then, is whether or not I require absolution, and, if so, from whom?

Friday 24 December

66

Thomas was sitting by the window looking out at Strömmen. It was clear and cold; the water was frozen and lay like a black mirror down below. The grey-brown façade of the Royal Palace was lit up, and looked like a stage-set against the winter sky. Over on Skeppsbron taxis glided past on their way to Gamla Stans Bryggeri. He could see the queue waiting to get into Café Opera.

He was in the sitting room of a corner suite on the fifth floor of the Grand Hotel. The suite was the size of a normal two-room apartment, with a hall, sitting room, bedroom, and an enormous bathroom. The police had brought him here. They regarded the Grand Hotel as the best place in Stockholm to protect people under threat. Kings and presidents on state visits often stayed here. The staff were used to dealing with unusual situations. Naturally, Thomas was not booked in under his own name. In the room next door there were currently two bodyguards.

About an hour ago the police had said that they hadn't found any trace of explosives in the flat on Hantverkargatan. But they would still have to stay hidden until the Bomber was caught. Anders Schyman had decided that, if need be, Thomas and the children should spend Christmas in the hotel at the paper's expense. Thomas turned away from the view and let his eyes sweep over the darkened room. He wished Annika was here, so they could enjoy the luxury together. The furniture was shiny and expensive, the green carpet thick as a mattress. He stood up and went in to see the children sleeping in the bedroom. They were sound asleep, snuffling slightly, exhausted after the excitement of this little holiday. They had had a bath in the beautiful bathroom, and had splashed water all over the floor. Thomas hadn't bothered to mop it up. At midnight they had eaten meatballs and mashed potato, delivered by room service. Kalle thought the mash was disgusting. He was used to the powdered version that Annika served. Thomas didn't like Annika serving hotdogs and mash for dinner, and had once described it as pigswill. As he remembered their stupid argument about it, he started to cry, something he very rarely did.

The police had found no trace of Annika at all. It was as if she'd disappeared into thin air. The car she'd been driving was also gone. The woman they suspected of being the Bomber hadn't been seen at her home since they began to suspect her, on Tuesday evening. A regional alert had now been issued. The police hadn't yet named the woman, merely saying that she had been project leader on the construction of the Victoria Stadium in South Hammarby Harbour.

He wandered aimlessly back and forth across the thick carpet for a while, then forced himself to sit down and watch television. Of course there were seventy channels, plus a whole series of internal film channels, but Thomas couldn't settle to watch anything. He went out into the hall instead, then into the bathroom where he threw a towel onto the wet floor. He washed his face in ice-cold water and brushed his teeth with a brush provided by the hotel. The thick towelling beneath his feet sucked up the water. He went out, undressing on his way to the bedroom and throwing his clothes in a heap on a chair in the hall, and went in to the children. As usual, they had kicked off the duvet. Thomas looked at them for a while. Kalle had his arms and legs stretched out, taking up most of the double bed. Ellen was curled up among the pillows.

One of the bodyguards had gone shopping in Åhléns for pyjamas and Gameboys. Thomas tucked Kalle's limbs in and pulled the duvet up, then went round the bed and crept in next to Ellen. He put his arm carefully under the girl's head and pulled her to him. She moved in her sleep and put her thumb in her mouth. Thomas let it be. Inhaling his daughter's sweet scent, he started to cry.

Work in the newsroom was carrying on under intense concentration and in almost total silence. Everyone was gathered around the formatting table. Jansson was permanently on the phone, as usual, but quieter and more subdued. Anders Schyman had barricaded himself into the place where the editor of the comment pages sat during the day. He was doing very little, mostly staring into space or talking quietly on the phone. Berit and Janet Ullberg's normal workplaces were deep in the corners of the newsroom, but now they were typing at the night-editors' desk so they could follow developments. Patrik Nilsson was there too. Ingvar Johansson had called his mobile during the afternoon. The reporter had been sitting in a plane on his way down to Jönköping, but he had still answered.

'You're not allowed to have your mobile on during a flight,' Ingvar Johansson had told him.

'I know that!' Patrik had yelled with evident delight. 'I

just wanted to see if it's really true that the plane crashes if you leave it switched on.'

'So is it crashing?' Ingvar Johansson had asked sardonically.

'Not yet, but if it goes down anytime soon you'll have a great scoop. "*Evening Post* reporter in Flight Drama – His Final Words".'

He had laughed hysterically and Ingvar Johansson had merely raised his eyebrows.

'Maybe we'll hold back on your flight drama, because we've already got one reporter in a leading role in a story about explosions. How soon can you be here?'

Patrik had stayed on the plane and returned to Stockholm with it. He reached the newsroom at five in the afternoon. Now he was writing the article about the police hunt for the Bomber. Anders Schyman was watching him surreptitiously. He was astonished at the young man's speed and engagement; there was something almost unreal about him. The only thing he had going against him was his almost ghoulish delight in accidents, murders and other tragedies. But a bit more life experience would probably tone that down. In time he would be an excellent reporter.

Anders Schyman got up to get more coffee. He felt slightly sick from the amount he had already drunk, but he needed to move about. He turned away from the formatting table and began to walk slowly towards the row of windows beyond the sports desk, where he stopped and looked out at the neighbouring blocks of flats. The lights were on in several windows, even though it was after midnight. People were still up, watching some thriller on television and drinking mulled wine, or wrapping the last of their presents. Some of the balconies had been decorated with trees, and Christmas lights shone in most windows.

Anders Schyman had spoken to the police several times that evening. He had become the natural link between the newsroom and the investigating team.

When Annika failed to appear at the nursery by five o'clock, the police began to treat the case as a missing person inquiry. After talking to Thomas, they realized there was no way she would have vanished of her own accord. Her disappearance had been classified as a kidnapping since the middle of the evening.

Earlier on the police had told them not to call Annika's mobile. Anders Schyman had asked why, but hadn't received an answer. But he had passed the order on, and as far as he knew no one had tried to call since then.

The staff were shaken and upset; Berit and Janet Ullberg had been in tears. It's strange, Anders Schyman thought. We write about things like this every day, we use suffering to spice things up a bit. Yet we're still completely unprepared when it happens to us.

He headed off to get another cup of coffee.

67

Annika woke up as a cold draught blew through the tunnel. She knew immediately what that meant: the metal door under the training ground had been opened; the Bomber was on her way back. Fear made her curl into a ball on the mattress again, and she lay there panting for breath as the strip-lights came back on.

Her subconscious kicked into gear, whispering: Take it easy, listen to the woman, see what she wants, do as she says, try to win her trust.

The clicking of heels came nearer. Annika sat up.

'Aw, how lovely, you're awake,' Beata said, going over to the camping table. She began unpacking various groceries from a 7-Eleven bag, lining them up around the torch battery and the timer. Annika caught sight of several cans of Coca-Cola, a bottle of Evian, some sandwiches and a bar of chocolate.

'Do you like Fazer's Blue chocolate? It's my favourite,' Beata said.

'Mine too,' Annika said, trying to keep her voice steady. She didn't like chocolate, and had never even tasted Fazer's Blue.

Beata folded the bag and put it in her pocket.

'Well, we've got a lot to do,' she said, sitting down on one of the folding chairs.

Annika tried to smile.

'Oh? What are we going to do?'

Beata looked at her for several seconds.

'We're going to get to the truth at last,' she said.

Annika tried to follow the woman's train of thought, but failed. Fear was making her mouth completely dry.

'What do you mean, the truth?'

Beata walked round the table to fetch something. When she straightened up Annika could see that she was holding a noose, the one she had put round Annika's neck earlier. Annika felt her pulse increase, but she forced herself to look calmly at Beata.

'Don't worry,' the Bomber said, smiling. She came over to the mattress with the long rope in her hands. Annika could hear herself breathing faster, and couldn't quite suppress a feeling of panic.

'Calm down, I'm just going to put this back around your neck,' Beata said with a little laugh. 'Goodness, aren't you the nervous one!'

Annika strained to produce a smile. The noose was round her neck, the rope dangling in front of her like a tie. Beata was holding the end of it.

'Good. Now, I'm going to go behind you, just stay calm. Relax, I said!'

Annika watched the woman disappear behind her from the corner of her eye, still holding the rope.

'I'm going to untie your hands, but don't try anything. If you mess me about I'll yank hard on this rope one last time.'

Annika was breathing hard, thinking furiously. She quickly came to the conclusion that there was nothing she could do. Her feet were still chained to the wall, she had a noose around her neck, and dynamite strapped to her back. Beata started to untie the rope holding

447

her hands together; it took her almost five minutes to untangle the knot.

'Goodness, that was tight!' she exclaimed when she was finished. Annika got a sudden itching sensation in her fingers as the blood started to flow properly again. Carefully she brought her hands forward, starting when she saw what a mess they were. The skin on her wrists had worn away, chafed by the rope, the wall, or the floor. Two of the knuckles on her left hand were bleeding.

'Stand up,' Beata said. Leaning against the wall for support, Annika did as she was told.

'Kick the mattress away,' Beata said, and Annika obeyed.

The dried-up vomit vanished beneath the mattress. Then Annika caught sight of her bag. It was six, maybe seven metres away back down the tunnel.

The Bomber walked backwards towards the table, still holding the rope. She put the battery and timer on the floor without taking her eyes off Annika. Then she pulled the table closer to Annika.

The noise of the table-legs scraping along the linoleum floor echoed down the tunnel. When the table was in front of Annika, Beata retreated once again and fetched a folding chair.

'Sit down.'

Annika put the chair behind her and carefully sat down. Her stomach rumbled when she saw the food on the table.

'Try to eat something,' Beata said.

Annika started by peeling the plastic seal from the bottle of water.

'Would you like some?' she asked Beata.

'I'll have a Coke later. You go ahead,' Beata said, and Annika drank. Then she picked out a small cheese and ham baguette, and forced herself to chew properly. She could only manage half of it.

'Enough?' Beata said, and Annika smiled.

'Yes, thank you, that was lovely.'

'I'm glad you liked it,' Beata said happily. She sat down on the other chair. On one side she had the box of Minex, and on the other an open brown cardboard box.

'Well, I suppose it's time,' she said with a smile.

Annika smiled back.

'Can I ask you something?' she said.

'Of course you can,' Beata said.

'Why am I here?'

Beata's smile faded at once.

'Do you really not understand?'

Annika took a deep breath.

'No. But I can see that I must have made you very angry. I really didn't mean to. I'm very sorry about that,' she said.

Beata was biting her upper lip.

'You didn't just lie. You wrote in the paper that I was devastated by that bastard's death. And you humiliated me in public, twisting my words to make it a better story. You didn't want to listen to me and my truth, but you listened to the workmen.'

'I'm sorry. I misjudged your emotional response,' Annika said as calmly as she could. 'I didn't want to quote you in a way that you might come to regret later. You were very upset – you were in tears.'

'Yes, I was upset that people can be so evil. That a pig like Stefan Bjurling should be allowed to live. Why did fate have to use me to put a stop to this misery? Why is everything up to me, eh?'

Annika made up her mind to wait and listen. Beata went on chewing her lip.

'You lied, you spread a false picture of that bastard,' she said after a while. 'You wrote that he was nice and funny and well-liked by his workmates. You let them talk, but not me. Why didn't you write what I said?'

Annika felt confusion growing, but made an effort to sound calm and friendly.

'What was it you said that you think I should have written?'

'The truth. That it was a shame Christina and Stefan had to die. That it was their own fault, and that it was wrong that I should have to do it. I don't think this is fun, if that's what you're thinking.'

Annika steeled herself to play along.

'No, of course I don't think that. I know what it's like to be forced to do things you don't want to do sometimes.'

'What do you mean?' Beata said.

Annika lowered her head, hesitating before saying anything.

'I had to get rid of someone once; I know what it's like.'

She looked up.

'But we're not talking about me at the moment; this is about you and your truth.'

Beata looked at her in silence for a while.

'Maybe you're wondering why you're not dead yet? You're going to write my story first. It's going to be published in the *Evening Post*, with as much fanfare as Christina Furhage's death got.'

Annika nodded and smiled mechanically.

'Here, look what I found,' Beata said, pulling something out of the cardboard box beside her. It was a small laptop computer.

'Christina's powerbook,' Annika gasped.

'Yes, she was very fond of it. I've charged it up properly.'

Beata stood up and went over to Annika, holding the laptop in her right hand. It looked heavy, Beata's hand was shaking.

'There you are. Turn it on.'

Annika took the computer. It was a fairly basic Mac.

She lifted the screen and turned it on. It whirred into action and began loading programs. It only had a few, one of them Word. After a few seconds the desktop appeared. The background picture was a pink, blue and purple sunset.

There were only three icons on the desktop: the hard drive itself, Word and a folder marked 'Me'. Annika double-clicked the Word icon, and the program started up.

'Okay, I'm ready to start,' Annika said. Her fingers were frozen and ached badly, and she rubbed them discreetly under the table.

Beata settled herself on her chair a couple of metres away. In one hand she held the battery, and in the other the yellow-green detonator wire. She leaned against the wall and crossed her legs; it looked like she was making herself nice and comfortable.

'Good. I want this to be as good as possible.'

'Okay, of course,' Annika said, and started to type.

'I want you to write down what I say, in my words, so this is my story.'

'Of course,' Annika said, and typed.

'Mind you, I want you to adjust it so it's good, and easy to read, and in the right style as well.'

Annika stopped typing and looked at the other woman.

'Beata, trust me. This is what I do every day. Shall we start?'

The Bomber straightened up.

'There is evil everywhere. It is eating people up from the inside. Its apostles on earth are finding their way to the heart of humanity and stoning it to death. The battle leaves bloody remnants in space, because Fate is fighting against Evil. But at its side, the Truth has a warrior, a person of flesh and blood—'

'Sorry to interrupt,' Annika said, 'but this feels a little confused. Readers won't be able to follow your train of thought.'

Beata looked at her in surprise.

'Why not?'

Annika thought for a moment. She had to choose her words very carefully now.

'A lot of people haven't done as much thinking as you, they haven't reached the same level of insight,' she said. 'They won't understand you, which would make the whole article meaningless. The purpose is to help people to get closer to the truth, isn't it?'

'Of course,' Beata said, and now it was her turn to be confused.

'Maybe we should hold back a little about Fate and Evil, and take things in a slightly more chronological order instead? That would make it easier for the reader to find the truth. Does that sound okay?'

Beata nodded eagerly.

'I was thinking, maybe I could ask you some questions, then you can answer whatever you want.'

'Okay,' Beata said.

'Can you tell me about your childhood?'

'What for?'

'It lets readers picture you as a child and means they can identify with you.'

'Oh. What shall I say?'

'Whatever you like,' Annika said. 'Where you grew

452

up, who your parents were, if you had brothers and sisters, pets, any special toys, what you thought of school, anything like that . . .'

Beata gave her a long look. Annika could see in the woman's eyes that her thoughts were far away. She started to talk, and Annika shaped her words into a readable story.

'I grew up in Djursholm; my parents were doctors. Are doctors, actually, they haven't retired yet, and they still live in their detached house with the iron gates. I have an older brother and a younger sister. My childhood was a fairly happy one. Mother worked part time as a child psychologist, Father has his own private practice. We had nannies who looked after us, some of them male. This was during the seventies, and my parents believed in equality and were open to new ideas.

'I developed an early interest in buildings. We had a little wooden house to play in, and my sister and her friends used to lock me inside.

'During our long afternoons together, we started to talk to each other, my little wooden house and me. The nannies knew I used to get shut in there, so they would always come and unlock the catch after a while. Sometimes they told my sister off, but it really didn't bother me.'

Beata fell silent and Annika stopped typing. She blew on her hands, it was really cold now.

'Can you tell me about your childhood hopes and dreams?' Annika said. 'What happened to your brother and sister?'

The Bomber went on. 'My brother became a doctor, just like our parents, and my sister trained to be a physiotherapist. She married Nasse, a childhood friend, and didn't need to work. They live with their children out in Täby.

'I broke the pattern in the family, because I trained as an architect. My parents were sceptical; they thought I would be better suited as a nursery-school teacher or an occupational therapist instead. But they didn't stop me, because they were very modern people. I studied at the Royal Institute of Technology, got one of the highest marks in my year.

'Why did I choose to work with buildings? I love buildings! They speak to you in such an immediate, clear way. I love travelling, just to communicate with the buildings in new places, their shapes, their windows, their colours . . . their radiance.

'Inner courtyards give me a sexual thrill. Shivers run down my back when I travel through the Stockholm suburbs, washing hanging out to dry above railway lines, balconies leaning out.

'I never look straight ahead of me when I walk, I look up. I've walked into traffic signs and ventilation units all over the city because I was looking up at the buildings. I find them fascinating; it's as simple as that. I wanted to build a career around my great passion. So I studied for years and learned to design buildings.

'When I graduated I realized that I had made the wrong decision. Buildings on paper don't talk. Sketches of buildings are a mere imitation of the real thing. So I went back to college after just one term out in the labour market. I studied to be a construction engineer instead. That took several more years.

'When I was finished, they were recruiting staff for the state-owned company that was going to build the new Victoria Stadium in South Hammarby Harbour. I got a job there, and that was how I came to meet Christina Furhage for the first time . . .'

68

Beata fell silent again. Annika sat for several minutes, waiting for her to continue.

'Would you like to read what we've done?' Annika eventually said, but Beata shook her head.

'I know you'll make it sound good. I'll read it later, when you've finished.'

She sighed and went on. 'Of course, I knew who she was. I'd seen her in the paper plenty of times, from when the whole Olympics campaign started, then when Sweden won and she was appointed managing director for the whole project.

'Where was I living all this time? Oh, where I live now, in a lovely little house next to Skinnarviks Park on Södermalm. Do you know the area around Yttersta Tvärgränd? It's grade-A listed, so I had to be really careful when I renovated it. My home is very important to me, the house I live and breathe in. We speak to each other every day, my house and me. Exchanging experiences and wisdom. I don't have to point out that I'm the novice in those conversations, do I? My house has stood on those cliffs since the end of the eighteenth century, so our conversations usually involve me listening and learning. Christina Furhage came to visit me there once; it felt right that my house should make her acquaintance. That helped me later on when I had to make my difficult decision.'

The woman fell silent again.

'What did your work involve?' Annika asked.

'Is that really important?' Beata said, sounding slightly surprised.

No, not remotely, but it buys me some time, Annika thought.

'Of course,' she said. 'Loads of people work. They want to know what you had to do at work, what you thought about when you were doing it, and so on . . .'

Beata sat up straight.

'Yes, yes, of course they do. I can see that,' she said.

You egocentric fucking bitch, Annika thought, and smiled.

'I don't know how familiar you are with the construction business? Maybe you don't know how negotiations happen? Well, it probably isn't that important on this occasion, because construction of the Victoria Stadium was such a unique case that none of the usual rules really applied.

'Stockholm was awarded the Olympic Games under Christina Furhage's leadership, as you know. It wasn't an obvious appointment; she had to fight to get the job.

'Christina really was fantastic. She could wrap the old sods in the Olympic movement round her little finger. Us women really enjoyed having a boss like that. Well, I didn't meet her very often, but because she kept an eye on every single detail of the whole project I bumped into her every now and then.

'I admired her immensely. Everyone smartened up their act whenever she appeared, everyone tried their best. She had that effect on people. What she didn't know about the organization of the Olympics and the construction of the stadium wasn't worth knowing.

456

'I was actually employed by Arena Bygg AB. Because I was both an architect and a civil engineer, I was given a number of large administrative responsibilities. I took part in negotiations, I produced sketches and calculations, visited subcontractors and agreed contracts. A general factotum, really, albeit a fairly senior one.

'The actual construction of the Victoria Stadium started five years ahead of the Games. Christina herself appointed me as project manager. I remember very well her asking me. I was summoned to her office, a magnificent room close to Rosenbad, with a view out over the waters of Strömmen. She asked me what I was doing and whether I was enjoying it. I didn't think I performed very well, I was stammering and my palms were sweating. She seemed quite unique, sitting there behind her gleaming desk, big and small at the same time, sharp but still beautiful. She asked if I would like to assume responsibility for the construction of the Victoria Stadium in South Hammarby Harbour.

'I felt giddy as she said those words. Yes, yes! I wanted to shout, but I just nodded and said it would be a great challenge, an exciting responsibility that I felt capable of living up to. She hastened to add that I would obviously have several managers above me, including, at the end of the chain, she herself. But she needed someone to assume operational responsibility of the actual construction, someone to make sure the timetable was followed, that the budget wasn't exceeded, and that the delivery of materials occurred in the right place and at the right time. And of course I would have a whole group of team-leaders under me who would each have responsibility for a particular section of the work, within which they would allocate and organize the work. These team-leaders would report to me on a daily basis, so that I could do my job and keep Christina and the management team informed.

'"I need loyalty," Christina said, leaning towards me. "I need your absolute conviction that what I'm doing is right. That's a precondition for anyone taking this job. Can I trust you?"

'I remember the way she was glowing at that moment, spreading her light over me, filling me with her own power and energy. I wanted to scream YES!, but instead I just nodded. Because I understood what had just happened. She had taken me into her inner circle. She had made me her crown princess. I had been chosen.'

Beata started to cry. She bowed her head, her whole body shaking. The rope leading to the noose lay at her feet, and her hands were clutching the battery and detonator wire tightly. As long as she doesn't cry so much that she short-circuits the battery and sets off the explosives, Annika thought.

'Sorry,' Beata said, wiping her nose with the sleeve of her coat. 'This is very hard for me.'

Annika didn't reply.

'It was a big responsibility, but in actual fact it wasn't that difficult. To start with, the site was cleared, there was blasting and excavation, filling in and levelling. Then the construction crews moved in. It was supposed to take four years. The stadium had to be ready for various test events one year before the Games themselves.

'It went well enough at the start. The workers drove around in their machines doing what they were supposed to. I had an office in one of the barracks by the canal – you might have seen them if you've ever been out to take a look at the site? No?

'Well, I did my job, spoke to the men on site, made sure they did their jobs. The men who did the actual work weren't very talkative, but at least they listened when I told them what needed to be done.

'Once a month I would go to Christina's office and tell her how the work was going. She always received me with great warmth and interest. After every meeting it felt like she knew everything already and just wanted to check my loyalty. I always left the office with a nagging sense of anxiety in the pit of my stomach, as well as a peculiar feeling of delirium and lightness. I was still in the inner circle, I had the power, but I would have to go on fighting to keep hold of it.

'I really loved my work. Sometimes in the evenings I would stay late after the men had left. All alone, I would scramble about the rocky remains of the old Hammarby ski-jump, imagining the finished stadium, the huge stands reaching to the sky, the seventy-five thousand green seats, the perforated steel arch of the roof. I would run my hands over the plans, and I put a big picture of the model on the wall of my office. I talked to the stadium right from the start. Like a newborn child, it didn't answer, but I was sure it was listening. I watched every detail of its development like a nursing mother, astonished at every new change in her child.

'The real problems started when the foundations were laid and the builders arrived. Several hundred men who were going to perform the work I was responsible for. They were led by a group of thirty-five team-leaders, all of them men between forty and fifty-five years old. At this point my duties multiplied fourfold. I was given three deputies to share responsibility with me, all of them men.

'I don't know where it went wrong. I carried on working just the same as I had done before, trying to be clear and straight and precise. The calculations worked, we were on schedule, the materials arrived on time, in the right place, and work went on and kept to the required standards. I tried to be happy and friendly, made sure I treated the men with respect. I can't say when I first noticed things going wrong, but it didn't take too long. Conversations that ground to a halt, scornful expressions I wasn't supposed to see, patronizing smiles, cold eyes. I arranged meetings to share and gather information, and I found them constructive, but my message clearly wasn't getting through. In the end the team-leaders just didn't turn up. I went out and tried to round them up, but they just looked at me and said they were busy.

'Of course I felt like an idiot. The few who had turned up questioned everything I said. They thought I had ordered materials in the wrong order, to the wrong place, and anyway the whole order was pointless because they had already solved the problem in a different way using a different supplier. Naturally, I got angry and asked what right they had to ignore my orders and take decisions like that themselves. They answered patronizingly that if this project was ever going to be ready on time, then they needed someone who knew what he was doing.

'I remember how I felt when I heard those words, how something inside me snapped. I mustn't die, I thought. The men got up and left, derision in their eyes. My three deputies left as well, and went to chat with the men outside. I heard my deputies pass on my orders and the information I had printed on the sheet of paper in my hand, and now the men were listening. They would accept my orders if someone else conveyed them. There was nothing wrong with my work, my judgement or my skills. No, there was something wrong with me as a person.

'After that meeting I called in my three deputies and said we needed to plan our next move. I wanted the

460

four of us to take control of the organization and our employees, to get the work going in the direction we had staked out. They sat round my desk, one at each end and one opposite me.

'"You can't handle this job," the first one said.

'"Can't you see you're getting in the way of the whole project?" the second one said.

'"You're a joke in this post," the third one said. "You have no authority, no legitimacy, and you're incompetent."

'I stared at them. I couldn't believe my ears. I knew they were wrong. But once they had started there was no stopping them.

'"The only thing you're good at is blowing your own trumpet," the first one said.

'"You demand too much from the men," the second one said. "They know you're being unreasonable, can't you tell?"

'"You're going to get frozen out," the third one said. "You're here for the wrong reasons, and you've got the wrong background."

'I remember looking at them, and their faces changed. Their features faded, turned white and shapeless. I couldn't breathe, I thought I was suffocating. But I got up and walked out. I'm afraid it wasn't a very graceful departure.'

The woman sniffed a bit, her head bowed. Annika glanced at her with distaste. *So what?* she felt like asking. *That's what it's like for all of us.* But she said nothing and Beata went on.

'When I was lying in bed that night, my house spoke to me, comforting words whispered through the pink patterned wallpaper. I couldn't go in the next day. Fear paralysed me, gluing me to my bed. Christina rescued me. She called me at home and asked me to turn up at

461

work the next morning. She had some important information for everyone on the site.

'The next morning I went to my office with a great sense of peace. At eleven o'clock we were all called to the north stand. My deputies weren't speaking to me, but I smiled at them so that they would understand. Soon Christina would be there.

'I waited until they were all there before going out, and I made sure I arrived at the stand at the same time as Christina. With her light, clear voice carrying all the way to the back of the stand, she said that she had come to inform us of a change in the leadership of the construction project. I could feel her warmth and couldn't help smiling.

'"Beata Ekesjö will no longer be project leader, and is being replaced by her three deputies," Christina said. "I have every confidence in her successors, and I hope that work will proceed as successfully as it has up to now."

'It felt like the sky had changed colour, all white, sparking with lightning. The light changed, and everyone froze to solid ice.

'My awareness of what I had to do was born that day, but I hadn't yet formulated my goal, even to myself. I left the north stand and the stadium while everyone was still there, listening to Christina's charismatic voice. I had a bag of gym clothes with me, because I had been planning to go to the gym straight after work. I emptied the bag into my locker and took the bag with me round to the back of the barracks. That was where the explosives were kept, roughly a hundred metres away: there are strict rules governing how far away they have to be kept because of the risk of detonation. There was just room for a box of dynamite in the sports bag, it was as if they were made for each other. It was very heavy, twenty-four kilos net, twenty-five gross, roughly

462

the same as the average suitcase. But you can carry it a short distance, especially if you go to the gym three times a week . . .'

'Hang on a moment,' Annika said. 'Aren't there loads of security regulations about storing dynamite? How could you just go in and take it like that?'

Beata looked at her condescendingly.

'Annika, I was in charge of the site. I had my own set of keys for every lock. Don't interrupt me.

'There were fifteen charges in the first box, little weapons rolled in pink plastic, 1,600 grams each, 50 by 500 millimetres. I put the box in the boot of my car and drove home. I carried my treasure carefully inside my house. That evening I stroked them with my bare hands. There were small metal catches at the ends. The plastic felt cold to the touch, my weapons looked and felt like sausages straight from the fridge. They were fairly soft; I used to sit there bending them back and forth in the evenings. Just like sausages, only heavier.'

Beata laughed at the memory. Annika felt sick, partly from tiredness, but mainly because of the other woman's utter madness.

'Can we take a break?' Annika wondered. 'I'd love a Coke.'

The Bomber looked up at her.

'Okay, but just a few minutes. We have to get finished tonight.'

Annika felt herself shiver.

69

'They didn't know what to do with me. My contract specified the construction of the Victoria Stadium and the Olympic village. It would cost them money to fire me, and they didn't want that. Besides, I could do the job, so it made no sense to pay good money to get rid of skills they needed. In the end they made me project leader of the construction of the technical complex next to the stadium, an unremarkable ten-storey building full of control rooms and offices. There's probably no need to say that the building felt dumb and dead compared with my stadium? An empty concrete shell without any real design, and it never learned to talk.

'There was already one manager there, his name was Kurt and he used to go on regular drinking binges. He hated me from the outset, seemed to think I was there to spy on him. The features of his face blurred for me that first day on the job. I could never really see him properly after that.

'Everything on the site was a mess. It was all running late, and was badly over budget. I started carefully clearing up the mess Kurt had created without him noticing. On the occasions when he found me taking a decision, he shouted at me. But after I got there he didn't lift a finger. A lot of the time he didn't even show up.

I reported him the first time it happened, but he got so furious that I never did it again.

'Now I had to make regular site inspections, which I hadn't had to do before. The concrete often changed colour, and sometimes I floated, unfettered and weightless, a few inches above the ground. The men changed shape and look. When they asked me to order more viewpoints, or wondered where the rule of thumb was, I stayed quiet. I knew they were making fun of me, but I had no defences. I tried to be efficient but forceful. I talked to them, but the building refused to talk back. I kept to the schedule and managed the calculations, I walked around the site, and the bell jar around me remained solid. We were ready on time, and only slightly over budget.

'Christina conducted the inauguration. I remember how keen and proud I felt that day. I had done it, I had bounced back, I hadn't given up. I had made sure the technical complex was ready in time for the test events. I hated the actual building, but I had done my duty. Christina knew that, Christina would see it, Christina would realize that I deserved a place in the light again. She would see me for who I was and elevate me to my rightful place again, at her side, as her sister in arms, her crown princess.

'I dressed very carefully that day, in a blouse and freshly ironed trousers and loafers. This time I was the first person out waiting for her, I wanted to make sure I had a place right next to the door.

'I hadn't seen Christina in a long time, just glimpsed her from a distance when she came to inspect work on the stadium. That wasn't going well, from what I had heard. They were no longer sure if it would be ready on time. Now she was here, even more radiant and sharply defined than I remembered. She spoke passionately about the Olympic Games and our proud Olympic organization, and she praised the workers and the people who had helped the work go so smoothly. Then she called forward the manager who had made sure that this building was ready on time and that the result was so excellent, and she called out Kurt's name, and applauded him, and everyone applauded, and Kurt got up and went over to Christina, he smiled and shook her hand, and she put her hand on his arm, and they laughed. But all sound had vanished. Those bastards, those bastards . . .

'That evening I went to the store and got a second box of dynamite, and a pack of electronic detonators. The box was full of little cardboard charges this time, one hundred grams each, little pink cardboard tubes that looked like sweets. In fact, you've got some of them strapped to your back. The box contained two hundred and fifty of them. I've used quite a few, but there are still lots left.'

She sat in silence for a while. Annika took the opportunity to rest her head in her hands. The tunnel was completely silent, apart from the faint hum of the lights in the roof. They're not calling my mobile any more, Annika thought. Have they given up looking for me already?

Beata started talking again and Annika straightened up.

'I was off sick quite a lot during the last year. I'm currently part of the team of project leaders that goes round and inspects the work being done in all the various training centres. For the past two months I've been based out at Sätra Hall, which is where the pole-vaulters will train. So you can see the humiliation I've had to endure, going from leading the construction of the flagship stadium to looking after tiny details in a load of

466

old sports halls. I no longer have time to establish any sort of proper communication with my workplaces. The buildings mock me, just like the men do. Stefan Bjurling was the worst. He was a foreman for the subcontractor looking after the work at Sätra Hall. He would start grinning the moment I tried to talk to him. He never listened. He called me Stumpy, and ignored everything I said. The only time I ever heard him mention me was when the men asked where they should put some rubble. "Give it to Stumpy," he said. He made fun of me, and that lovely building joined in. The sound of that was unbearable . . .'

Beata fell silent, and sat quietly for so long that Annika started to feel uneasy. Her muscles were aching with tiredness, and she had a bad headache. Her arms felt heavy as lead, that paralysing feeling that normally crept up on her at half past three in the morning. She had worked the night shift often enough to recognize the feeling.

She thought of her children, wondering where they were, if they were missing her. I wonder if Thomas will find the presents, she thought. I didn't have time to tell him that I hid them in the wardrobe.

She looked at Beata. She was sitting with her head in her hands. Then Annika turned her head slowly and glanced at her bag, some way behind her. If only she could get hold of her phone and tell them where she was! There seemed to be a signal, even though they were in a tunnel. She could be free just quarter of an hour later. But that wasn't going to happen – not as long as she was tied up, and not as long as Beata was there. Unless Beata fetched the bag for her and covered her ears while she made the call . . .

She started, suddenly remembering an article she had written two years ago. It had been a beautiful early-spring day, and loads of people were out on the ice—

'Are you sitting there dreaming?' Beata asked.

Annika jumped, and smiled.

'No, not at all. I'm looking forward to the next bit,' she said.

70

'A couple of weeks ago Christina organized a big party in the Blue Hall of Stockholm City Hall. It was the last big party before the Games, and everyone was invited. I was really looking forward to it. The City Hall is one of my best friends. I often climb the tower, going up all those stairs, letting the stone walls dance beneath my hands, feeling the draught from the little openings in the walls. Then I stand and catch my breath at the top, and we share the view and the breeze together. It's quite astonishingly beautiful.

'I got there far too early, and quickly realized that I was overdressed. But it didn't matter, my partner for the evening was the City Hall itself, and it took care of me. Christina would be there, and I was hoping that the forgiving atmosphere of the building would help sort out all our misunderstandings. I mingled among the crowd, drank a glass of wine, and talked to the building.

'Suddenly the level of conversation in the hall grew to an excited chatter, and I knew that Christina had arrived. She was received like the queen she was, I stood on a chair so I could get a better view. It's hard to explain, but Christina gave off a sort of aura that made it look like she was always under a spotlight. It was fantastic; she was such a fantastic person. Everyone wanted to say hello to her, and she nodded and smiled. She had time for everyone. She shook hands like she was campaigning to be American president. I was quite a long way back in the room, but she was slowly working her way in my direction. I jumped down from the chair and lost sight of her, because I'm so short. But suddenly she was standing there in front of me, beautiful and elegant in her own spotlight. I felt myself start to smile, from ear to ear, and I think I may actually have shed a tear or two of joy.

'"Welcome, Christina!" I said, holding out my hand. "How wonderful that you can be here!"

'"Thank you," she said. "Have we met?"

'Christina's eyes met mine and she smiled. I could see she was smiling, but the smile changed, and her face died. She had no teeth. There were worms in her mouth, her eyes had no whites. She was smiling, and her breath was dead, rotten. I felt myself pull back. She didn't recognize me. She didn't know who I was. She didn't realize I was her crown princess. She was talking, and her voice came from an abyss, muffled and slurred like a tape being played too slowly.

'"Shall we move on?" she boomed, and the worms crawled out through her head and I knew I had to kill her. You can see that, can't you? You must understand that? That she couldn't be allowed to live? She was a monster, an evil angel with a halo. Evil had consumed her, eating her up from the inside. My house was right: she truly was the embodiment of evil on earth. I hadn't seen it before, the others hadn't seen it, they had just seen what I had, her successful façade and glowing aura and bleached hair. But now I could see, Annika, I could see her real essence, she showed me what a monster she really was, she stank of poison and rancid blood . . .'

Annika felt an almost unbearable urge to throw up.

Beata opened a can of Coca-Cola and took some small sips.

'I really ought to drink Diet Coke because of the calories, but it tastes so horrid. What do you think?' she asked Annika.

Annika gulped.

'You're absolutely right,' she said.

Beata smiled.

'My decision helped me to survive the evening, because the nightmare wasn't yet over. Do you know who she chose to be her Prince, her partner at dinner? Of course you know, don't you? You published a picture of them together. All of a sudden everything fell into place for me. I realized the point of the treasure I had accumulated at home. The big box was for Christina, and the small charges were for anyone who followed in her wake.

'My plan was simple. I started following Christina; sometimes I got the feeling that she was aware of me. She would look round anxiously as she got into her great big car, always with that laptop under her arm. I was really curious about what she wrote on it, if she wrote anything about me, or maybe about Helena Starke. I knew she often went to see Helena Starke. I would wait outside and watch her leave early in the morning. I realized that they were in love, and I knew it would be fatal for Christina if word got out. Which is what made it so simple, at least in theory. Quite a lot of things get messy when you put them into practice, don't you find?

'Well, on Friday night, when I saw Christina and Helena leave the Christmas meal together, I knew the time had come. I went back to my house and got my biggest and best treasure. It was heavy. I put it on the passenger seat beside me. In the footwell was a car battery I had bought at the OK petrol station out in

Västberga. I got the timer from IKEA, they're the sort you usually use to deter thieves from approaching empty summer cottages.

'I parked among the cars over where you're parked. My bag was very heavy, of course, but I'm stronger than I look. I was a bit nervous. I didn't know how much time I had, because I had to get everything ready before Christina left Helena's flat. Luckily it all went smoothly. I carried the bag to the back entrance, switched the alarm off and unlocked the doors. It looked like it was going to go wrong when someone saw me go in, he was heading to that awful underground club. If I'd been left in charge of the project I'd never have allowed an establishment like that to start up so close to the stadium.

'That night the stadium looked magnificent, it was shining for me in the moonlight. I put the box down in the north stand. The text looked almost luminous in the darkness: Minex 50 x 550, 24 kg, 15 pcs 1,600 g. I put the tape down next to the box. It would be so easy to set it up: just press in the metal tag at the end of one of the sausages, and run the wire off towards the main entrance. That's where I put the battery and arranged the timer, just like I'd practised. Where did I practise? In a gravel pit outside Rimbo, in Lohärad parish. The bus only passes through twice a day, but I was never in any hurry. I only set off small charges, one little tube of sweets at a time. There's still plenty left.

'When I had finished my preparations I went and unlocked the main entrance, then I came out through this tunnel. The entrance from the stadium is right at the bottom of the arch, way below the main entrance. The main lift goes down that far, but I took the stairs. Then I hurried across to Ringvägen, I was worried I was already late. But I wasn't – quite the reverse, actually. I spent a long time waiting in a doorway on the other side of the street. When Christina came out I dialled her number on my mobile. They wouldn't be able to trace me, I use pay-as-you-go. They won't be able to trace the call I made to your car yesterday either, by the way.

'It was easy to persuade Christina to come to the stadium. I said I knew all about her and Helena, that I had pictures of them together, that I was going to send them to Hans Bjällra, the Chairman of the Board, if she didn't come and meet me. Bjällra hates Christina, everyone in the organization knows that. He would have been only too happy to have a chance to humiliate her. So Christina came, but she must have thought twice about it. She came on foot, over the footbridge from Södermalm, angry as hell, and it took quite some time. For a while I didn't think she was going to turn up.

'I was standing waiting for her inside the main entrance, hidden in the shadows behind one of the sculptures. I was ecstatic, as was the venue. My stadium was with me, it agreed with me. I wanted to do the right thing. Christina was going to die in the very place where she had crushed me. She would be blown away in the north stand of the Victoria Stadium, because that was what happened to me. When she arrived I would hit her on the head with a hammer, the classic construction worker's tool. Then I would drag her to the stand, wire her up, and, as my pink plastic snakes wound round her body, I would explain why she was here. I would tell her I had seen her monster. My superiority would shine like a star in the night sky. Christina would beg for forgiveness, and the explosion would be the culmination of everything.'

Beata fell quiet for a moment, and drank some more Coke. Annika was ready to faint.

'Unfortunately it didn't turn out like that,' Beata said quietly. 'The truth will out. I don't want to be a hero. I

473

know there are people who think what I did was wrong. That's why it's important for us not to lie. You have to write what really happened, and not try to make it better than it was.'

Annika nodded, quite honestly.

'It all went wrong. The hammer blow didn't knock Christina unconscious, it just made her angry. She started screaming like a stuck pig, saying I was useless and mad and that I had to leave her alone. I hit her wherever I could reach with my hammer. One blow hit her in the mouth, knocking several teeth out. She screamed and screamed, and I just kept hitting her. People bleed quite a lot from their eyes. In the end she fell over, and it wasn't a pretty sight. She screamed and screamed, and to make sure she didn't get up again I smashed her knees. That wasn't nice, just hard work, really difficult. You can see that? She wouldn't stop screaming, so I hit her on the neck. When I tried to drag her up to the north stand she clawed at my hands, so I had to smash her elbows and fingers as well. In the end we got to the stand, to the place where she had stood that day when she crushed me. I was sweating, because she was quite heavy, and she just wouldn't stop screaming. By the time we reached my little armoury, my arms were shaking badly.

'I put her between the pillars and started to fasten the explosives with the tape. But Christina didn't understand that it was time to give up, that her role was now to listen. She wriggled like the snake she was, and managed to get to the nearest flight of steps. She started rolling down the stand, screaming the whole while. I was starting to lose control of my work, it was awful. I got hold of her and hit her in the back, I don't know if I broke it.

'In the end she was quiet enough for me to tie the

sausage-shaped explosives round her. It wasn't very neat. And there was no time for forgiveness or reflection. I quickly pressed the metal plug into one of the sausages, and ran off towards the battery. The timer was set for five minutes, but I shortened that to three. Christina was screaming, she didn't sound human, she was screaming like the monster she was. I stood down by the main entrance and listened to her death song. When there were only thirty seconds left she managed to get two of the sausages off her, in spite of her broken limbs. That shows how inhumanly strong she was, don't you think?

'Unfortunately I couldn't stay and watch the end of the drama. I missed her final seconds, because I had to take cover in my grotto. I was halfway down the stairs when the pressure wave hit, and I was shocked by how powerful it was. The damage was immense; the whole north stand was destroyed. That wasn't my intention, you understand. I didn't want to damage the stadium. Whatever had happened there wasn't the building's fault . . .'

Annika could feel tears running down her face. She had never written anything so revolting in her whole life. She felt on the point of collapse. She had been sitting still on that uncomfortable chair for several hours now, and her legs were aching so much that she wanted to scream. The explosives on her back had started to get really heavy. She was so tired she just wanted to lie down, even if it meant the dynamite blowing up and killing her.

'Why are you crying?' Beata said suspiciously.

Annika took a deep breath before replying.

'Because it was so hard for you. Why couldn't she just let you do the right thing?'

Beata nodded, wiping away a tear of her own.

'I know,' she said. 'Things are never fair.

'It was easier with Stefan, pretty much as I planned. I gave him responsibility for getting the referees' changing-room ready by Christmas. The choice of location was simple. That was where I first met Stefan, and where he told me I would be frozen out by the workers at Sätra Hall. And I knew he'd do the work himself.

'Stefan used to bet on the horses, and took every opportunity to work overtime. He would make sure he was the last one on the site, then would doctor his timesheet. He must have been doing it for years, no one had ever checked up on him. He could work quickly when he wanted to, albeit pretty sloppily.

'On Monday I went to work as usual. Everyone was talking about Christina Furhage getting blown up, but no one spoke to me. I wasn't expecting them to either.

'That evening I stayed behind in the office, doing my paperwork. When everything went quiet in the hall I did a quick circuit and saw that Stefan Bjurling was working in the changing-room at the far end of the building. So I went to my locker and got out my gym bag. Inside was my treasure, the rolls of sweets, the yellow-green wire, the tape, and the little timer. This time I had no hammer; that had turned out far too messy. Instead I got some rope, the sort you use for children's swings, and so on. The rope round your neck is from the same coil. While Stefan was drilling in the far wall, I went in and put the rope round his neck and pulled. This time I was much more determined. I wouldn't tolerate any screaming or fighting. Stefan Bjurling dropped the drill and fell backwards. I was ready for that and used the momentum of his fall to pull the rope tighter. He lost consciousness and I had quite a bit of trouble hauling him onto the chair. I tied him down and got him ready for his funeral. The tubes of sweets, the detonator wire, the timer, and the torch battery. I fixed it all to his back and then waited patiently until he came round.

'He didn't say anything, but I noticed his eyelids starting to twitch. So I explained to him what was going to happen, and why. Evil's time on earth was over. He was going to die because he was a monster. I explained to him that many more would be following him. I still have a lot of treasure left. Then I set the timer to five minutes and went back to my office. On the way there I made sure all the doors were unlocked. That way it was easy for the Bomber to have got in. When the bomb went off I pretended to be shocked and called the police. I lied to them and said that someone else had carried out my work. They took me to Accident and Emergency at Södermalm Hospital. They said they wanted to talk to me the following morning. I decided to carry on lying for a bit longer. It wasn't the right time to tell the truth then, but it is now.

'The doctors examined me, but I told them I felt fine and walked home through the city to Yttersta Tvärgränd. I realized it was time to leave my beautiful house for good. That night was the last I spent in my home. It was a short and dignified farewell. I knew even then that I would never go back. My wandering must end elsewhere.

'Early on Tuesday morning I went back to work to collect the last of my belongings. When I arrived at Sätra Hall I was met with the immediate and unfair condemnation of the building. I was struck by a great and crushing sorrow, and I took refuge in a room where the building couldn't see me. It was in vain, of course, because then you turned up.'

Annika felt that she couldn't write any more. She put her hands on her lap and lowered her head.

'What is it?' Beata said.

'I'm so tired,' Annika said. 'Can I get up and stretch my legs? They've gone numb.'

Beata looked at her in silence for several seconds.

'Okay, but don't try anything.'

Annika stood up carefully, putting a hand against the wall to stop herself falling. She stretched and bent her legs as well as she could with the rattling chain round her ankles. Unnoticed, she glanced down and saw that Beata had used two small padlocks to fasten the chain. If she could only get hold of the keys she would be able to free herself.

'Don't think you can get away,' Beata said.

Annika looked up in surprise.

'Of course not,' she said. 'We haven't finished our work yet.'

She moved the folding chair a bit further from the table to give her legs more space.

'There's not much more left now,' Beata said.

She studied Annika, and Annika realized that she really didn't know what to think.

'Would you like to read it?' Annika said, turning the computer so the screen was facing Beata.

The woman didn't reply.

'It would be good if you read it through, so you can see if I've understood everything correctly, and it would give you a chance to see if I've got the right tone. I haven't written it down exactly as you've said – I've tried to make your story a bit more literary,' Annika said.

Beata looked carefully at Annika for several seconds, then went over to the table and pulled it closer to her.

'Do you mind if I take a little rest?' Annika wondered, and Beata nodded.

Annika lay down and turned her back on the Bomber. She needed to think through her next move.

Two years ago a sixty-year-old man disappeared out

on the ice in the Stockholm archipelago. It had been early spring, sunny and warm, and the man had gone for a walk and got lost. For three days the coastguard and police had searched for him. Annika had been in the helicopter that eventually found him.

Suddenly she knew exactly what she had to do.

71

Thomas got out of bed. He couldn't sleep any longer. He went into the bathroom and relieved himself, then went over to the window and looked out at the Royal Palace again.

There was almost no traffic. The illuminated façade of the Palace and the other buildings, the glimmer of the street lamps, the depth of the black mirror of the water – the view really was quite beautiful.

Even so, he felt he couldn't stand it another second. It felt like he'd lost Annika in this room. It was here that he realized she might be gone for good.

He rubbed his dry, red eyes and let out a deep sigh. He had made up his mind. He was going to leave the hotel as soon as the children woke up, and go out to his parents in Vaxholm. They could celebrate Christmas out there instead. He had to see what daily life without Annika might look like, he had to prepare himself, otherwise he was lost. He tried to imagine how he would react if he was told that she was dead.

He couldn't. There was nothing but an endless black hole. He would have to go on living, for the sake of the children, for Annika's sake. They would have pictures of Mummy everywhere; they would talk about her all the time, and celebrate her birthday . . .

He turned away from the window and started to cry again.

'Why are you sad, Daddy?'

Kalle was standing in the bedroom door. Thomas quickly pulled himself together.

'I'm sad that Mummy isn't here. I miss her, that's all.'

'Grown-ups get sad too sometimes,' Kalle said.

Thomas went over to the boy and took him in his arms.

'Yes, we cry too when things feel bad. But do you know what, you ought to get a bit more sleep. Do you know what day it is today?'

'Christmas Eve!' the boy cried.

'Shh, you'll wake Ellen! Yes, it's Christmas Eve, and Father Christmas will be coming tonight. You want to be awake then, don't you? So back to bed with you for a little bit longer.'

'I have to do a wee first,' Kalle said, struggling free of Thomas's arms.

When the boy came back from the bathroom he asked, 'Why isn't Mummy here?'

'She's coming later,' Thomas said, without a moment's hesitation.

'Donald Duck's on television later; Mummy likes Donald Duck on Christmas Eve. Will she be home in time for the start?'

'I'm sure she will,' Thomas said, kissing his son on the head. 'Now, back to bed!'

As he tucked the boy in under the Grand Hotel's luxurious feather duvet, he caught sight of the clock radio on the bedside table. The red digital numbers were colouring the corner of the pillowcase pink. It was 05.49.

* * *

'This is good,' Beata said. 'Just the way I wanted it to be.'

Annika had fallen into a light slumber, but sat up as soon as the Bomber started to talk.

'I'm really glad you like it,' she said. 'I've done my best.'

'Yes, you really have. People who know how to do their job properly are great,' Beata said with a smile.

Annika smiled back, and they sat there smiling at each other until Annika decided to put her plan into action.

'Do you know what day it is today?' she said, still smiling.

'Christmas Eve, of course,' Beata said with a laugh. 'Of course I know that!'

'Of course, but the days leading up to Christmas go so quickly. I almost never manage to get all my Christmas shopping done. But, do you know, I've got something for you, Beata.'

The woman was immediately suspicious.

'You couldn't have bought me a Christmas present, you don't even know me.'

Annika continued smiling so hard that the muscles in her cheeks ached.

'I know you now. I bought the present for a friend, for someone who deserved it. But you need it more.'

Beata didn't believe her.

'Why would you give me a Christmas present? I'm the Bomber.'

'The present isn't for the Bomber,' Annika said in a steady voice. 'It's for Beata, a girl who's had a really rough time of it. You could do with a nice Christmas present after all you've been through.'

The words hit their mark, Annika could see that.

The woman's eyes started darting about, and she was fiddling with the fuse wire.

'When did you buy it?' she asked uncertainly.

'The other day. It's very nice.'

'Where is it, then?'

'In my bag. It's right at the bottom, under my tampons.'

Beata started, just as Annika had suspected. Beata had a poor relationship with her female bodily functions.

'It's beautifully wrapped,' Annika said. 'If you get the bag I can give you your Christmas present.'

Beata wouldn't fall for that, Annika saw that at once.

'Don't try any tricks,' Beata threatened, and got up.

Annika sighed gently.

'I'm not the one who goes around with dynamite in their bag. There's nothing in there apart from my note-pad, a few pens, a packet of tampons and a present for you. Get it yourself!'

Annika held her breath; she was taking a chance here. Beata hesitated for a moment.

'I don't want to look through your bag,' she said.

Annika took a deep breath.

'That's a shame. The present would have suited you.'

That made up Beata's mind. She put the battery and fuse wire down on the floor and picked up the rope instead.

'If you try anything, I'll pull on this.'

Annika held her hands in the air, face up, and smiled. Beata backed away down the tunnel to where the bag had landed more than sixteen hours before. She took the straps of the bag in one hand, keeping hold of the rope in the other. She walked slowly towards Annika.

'I'll be standing here the whole time,' she said, dropping the bag in Annika's lap.

Annika's heart was beating so hard it was echoing in her head. Her whole body was shaking. This was her only chance. She smiled up at Beata and hoped that her racing pulse wasn't visible in her temples. Then she lowered her gaze to Beata's legs. Beata was still holding the straps of the bag in one hand.

Carefully she put a hand in the bag and found the little parcel at once, the box containing the garnet brooch she had bought for Anne Snapphane.

She quickly stirred the things at the bottom of the bag around.

'What are you doing?' Beata asked, grabbing the bag.

'Sorry,' Annika said, hardly able to hear her voice over the thudding of her heart. 'I can't find it. Let me try again.'

Beata hesitated for several seconds. Annika's heart seemed to stop. She couldn't beg, because that would ruin any chance she had. She had to play on Beata's curiosity.

'I don't want to tell you what it is in advance, because that would spoil the surprise. But I think you're going to like it,' Annika said.

The woman held out the bag again and Annika took a deep breath. She thrust her arm in firmly, felt the present, and right next to it was her mobile phone. Dear God, she prayed, let the hands-free earpiece be attached!

Her top lip was starting to sweat. The phone was upside down, which was good; otherwise the glow of the screen would be visible. Her fingers played over the buttons, found the big oval one and pressed it, quickly and lightly. Then she moved her finger down two centimetres, found the number one, pressed, then moved it back to the big button for a third click.

'Ah, here it is!' Annika said, moving her hand to the gift next to the phone.

Her arm was shaking when she pulled it out, but Beata didn't notice. The Bomber was merely looking at the gold paper and the blue ribbon gleaming in the harsh light. There was no sound from the bag, so the cable must have been attached. Beata backed away, putting the bag down next to the box of dynamite. Annika felt close to hyperventilating, and forced herself to breathe quietly through her open mouth. She had pressed 'menu 1 menu': phone book, news desk, call.

'Can I open it now?' Beata said eagerly.

Annika couldn't answer. She just nodded.

72

Jansson had sent the last page to the printers. He was often very tired the first night of a new shift, but he felt completely wiped out tonight. He usually ate breakfast down in the canteen, a cheese roll with red pepper, and a large cup of tea, but he didn't feel like it today. He had just stood up and started to take off his jacket when the phone rang. Jansson groaned out loud, and almost didn't bother to check the caller-display before picking up. It was probably the printers, sometimes they had trouble transferring colour files digitally, meaning that they were missing the yellow layer. He leaned over and recognized the number at once. Every hair on his body stood up at once.

'It's Annika!' he yelled. 'Annika's calling my extension!'

Anders Schyman, Patrik, Berit and Janet Ullberg all turned to face him from the picture desk.

'It's Annika's mobile!' Jansson shouted.

'Well answer, for God's sake!' Schyman yelled back, and started running.

Jansson took a deep breath and picked up the phone. 'Annika!'

The line crackled and buzzed.

'Hello! Annika!'

The others were crowding round Jansson.

'Hello! Hello? Are you there?'

'Give it here!' Schyman said.

Jansson passed the receiver to the editor-in-chief. Anders Schyman put the phone to one ear and plugged the other with a finger. He could hear crackling and buzzing, and a rising and falling sound that could be voices.

'She's alive,' he whispered, giving the phone back to Jansson, then went into his office to call the police.

'Oh, how beautiful! It's lovely.'

Beata sounded quite overcome. It gave Annika new strength.

'It's very old, practically an antique,' she said. 'Real garnets, and gold-plated silver. It's the sort of thing I'd love to have myself. Those are the sort of presents it's most fun to give, don't you think?'

The woman didn't answer; she was just staring at the brooch.

'I've always loved jewellery,' Annika said. 'When I was little I saved up my pocket money for several years so I could buy a heart of white gold with a border of diamonds I'd seen in a jeweller's catalogue, one of those mailshots you get just before Christmas. When I finally saved up enough money I'd grown out of it, and bought a set of slalom skis instead.'

'Thanks ever so much,' the Bomber said quietly.

'You're welcome,' Annika said. 'My grandma had one like that, maybe that's why it caught my eye.'

Beata unbuttoned her coat and fastened the brooch to her top.

*　　　*　　　*

'This might be just what we need,' the policeman said. 'You can hang up now, the call has come through. We can organize the rest with the operator.'

'What are you going to do?' Schyman wondered.

'We'll head out to the phone network's operations centre in Kista. It ought to be possible to trace where the call is being made from.'

'Can I come with you?' Schyman asked quickly.

The policeman hesitated for a moment.

'Of course,' he said.

Anders Schyman hurried out into the newsroom again.

'The police are tracing the call, you can hang up now,' he called as he pulled on his coat.

'Do you think it would do any harm if we carry on listening?' asked Berit, who was holding the phone to her ear.

'I don't know. If it's doing any harm I'll call. Don't go home, any of you!'

He ran down the stairs to the entrance, his legs aching with tiredness. There was no point in trying to drive, he realized, and jogged over to the taxi rank on Rålambsvägen.

It was still pitch-black, and the road to Kista was completely deserted. They met a couple of other taxis on the way; the driver raised a hand to greet the ones from the same company. They reached Borgarfjordsgatan, and as Anders Schyman was paying for the ride, an unmarked police car pulled up alongside and stopped. Schyman got out and went over to the officer.

'If we're really lucky, we'll be able to track her down from this,' the policeman said.

His face was pale with exhaustion, and his mouth seemed strangely clenched. All of a sudden Anders Schyman realized who he must be.

'Do you know Annika?' the editor-in-chief asked.

The policeman took a deep breath and glanced at the other man.

'Sort of,' he said.

Just then a tired guard came to let them into the building, where the phone companies had their centre of operations.

He led them down several long corridors until they reached an enormous room full of huge television screens. Anders Schyman whistled.

'It looks like some American spy film, doesn't it?' said a man who was walking towards them.

The editor-in-chief nodded and held out his hand.

'There's something of the nuclear power station control room about it as well,' he said.

'I'm operations manager here. If you'd like to follow me,' the man said, leading them towards the centre of the room.

Anders Schyman walked slowly behind the operator, staring around the vast room as he went. There were hundreds of computers, and projectors that turned the walls into huge computer screens.

'This is where we control the whole of the network,' the operations manager said. 'There are two of us here at night. The search you asked for is a fairly simple procedure; I just had to enter the command on my terminal, and the search started.'

He led them to his desk. Anders Schyman didn't understand any of the equipment on it.

'It'll take up to fifteen minutes or so, even though I limited the search to calls made after five a.m. Ten minutes have passed now, so let's see if there's anything so far . . .'

He leaned over a computer and typed something.

'No, nothing yet,' he said.

'Fifteen minutes, isn't that quite slow?' Anders Schyman said, realizing that his mouth was dry.

The operations manager looked at him steadily.

'Fifteen minutes is extremely fast,' he said. 'It's the morning of Christmas Eve and there's not much traffic right now. That's why I think the search will be pretty quick.'

At that moment a series of figures appeared on the man's screen. He turned his back on Schyman and the policeman and sat down. He clattered and typed at his keyboard for a couple of minutes, then sighed.

'I'm not getting anything,' he said. 'Are you sure the call came from her mobile?'

Anders Schyman's pulse started to race. It couldn't go wrong now! He felt himself getting upset; didn't these men know what was happening? Didn't they know how important it was?

'Our night-editor could recognize her number in his sleep. They were still listening to the crackling on the line when I left the office,' he said, licking his lips.

'Ah, that explains it,' the operator said, and typed another command. The information on the screen vanished and it went blank.

'Now we just have to wait,' he said, turning to face Schyman and the policeman again.

'What's happening?' Schyman said, aware that he was sounding upset.

'If the call is still connected, we won't have received any information yet. Details are stored internally in the phone for thirty minutes,' he said, standing up. 'After half an hour the phone creates a record of the call that it sends to us here. Among that information is the A-number and the B-number, the base station and the cell.'

Anders Schyman stared at the flashing screens, getting more and more confused. Exhaustion was making his head thump. He felt he was in the middle of a surreal nightmare.

'So what does that mean?' he said.

'According to what you told us, Annika Bengtzon made a call to the *Evening Post* newsroom just after six. If the call hasn't been cut off, the first information regarding that call will reach us here just after six thirty, which is any minute now.'

'I don't understand,' Schyman said. 'How can you know where she is from her mobile?'

'It's like this,' the operations manager said in a friendly tone of voice. 'Mobile phones act like radio transmitters and receivers. Signals are sent out from a number of base stations, mobile phone masts, all around the country. Every base station has a number of cells which receive signals from different places and from different directions. Any mobile that's switched on re-establishes contact with the exchange every four hours. We conducted our first search for Annika Bengtzon's phone number yesterday evening.'

'You did?' Schyman said in surprise. 'Can you do that at any time, whenever you like, just like that?'

'Of course not,' the operator said calmly. 'In order to conduct that sort of search we need authorization from a public prosecutor. And searches can only be carried out at all if the suspected crime carries a punishment of more than two years in prison.'

He walked over and clicked on another screen. Then he went over to a printer, waiting for a document to appear.

'Well, the last call made from Annika's phone, apart from the one that's still connected, was made at nine minutes past one yesterday afternoon,' he said, studying the printout. 'It was made to a nursery at 38B Scheelegatan on Kungsholmen.'

He lowered the printout.

'The signal from Annika's mobile was transmitted via a station in Nacka.'

The plain-clothed officer spoke up.

'We had confirmation of that call from the manager of the nursery. Annika didn't sound strange, or under pressure. She was just relieved to hear that the nursery was open until five o'clock. Which means she was still free shortly after thirteen hundred hours, and she was somewhere east of Danvikstull, at the far end of Södermalm.'

The operations manager went on reading from the printout.

'The next signal from the phone came at 17.09. As I said, any mobile that's switched on re-establishes contact with the central exchange every four hours.'

Anders Schyman could hardly summon the effort to listen to the operations manager. He sat down on a spare chair and rubbed his forehead.

'There's an internal clock in every mobile that starts counting down every time it's switched on,' the man went on. 'The countdown stops after four hours, and a signal is sent off to inform the system where the phone is currently located. Because these signals have continued throughout the night, Annika must have had her phone switched on. As far as we can make out, she doesn't appear to have moved very far during the night.'

Schyman felt himself stiffen.

'You know where she is?' he said breathlessly.

'We know that her mobile phone is somewhere in the central Stockholm district,' the operations manager said. 'We can only identify the area fairly broadly; and in this case that means the central parts of the city within the old toll gates, plus the closest suburbs.'

'So she might not be far away at all?'

'Yes, her mobile hasn't moved outside that district all night.'

'Is that why we weren't allowed to call her?'

The policeman stepped forward.

'Yes, among other reasons. If there's someone with her and they heard the phone ringing, they might well have switched it off, in which case we wouldn't know if she had been moved.'

'Assuming she's in the same place as her mobile,' Schyman said.

'Surely those fifteen minutes must be up by now?' the policeman said.

'Not quite,' the operations manager said.

They turned their attention to the screen and waited. Anders Schyman needed to go to the toilet, and left the vast room for a few minutes. As he emptied his bladder he noticed that his legs were shaking.

Nothing had happened by the time he came back.

'Nacka . . .' Schyman said absentmindedly. 'What the hell was she doing out there?'

'Here it comes,' the operations manager said. 'Ha, there we go! The A-number is Annika Bengtzon's mobile phone, and the B-number is the *Evening Post* newsroom.'

'Can you tell where she is?' the policeman said expectantly.

'Yes, I've got a code here, hang on a moment.'

The operations manager typed on his keyboard. Schyman felt himself go completely cold.

'Five hundred and twenty-seven D,' the man said.

'What's that?' the policeman said. 'Is something wrong?'

'We don't usually have more than three cells in every base station, A, B, and C. But there are more

493

here. That's extremely unusual. D cells are usually specials.'

'So where is it?' the policeman urged.

'Just a moment,' the operations manager said, quickly getting up and going over to another terminal.

'What are you doing?' Schyman said.

'We've got a thousand codes for stations covering the whole of Sweden, so I'm afraid it's impossible to remember where they all are,' he said apologetically. 'Here it is: base station five hundred and twenty-seven. South Hammarby Harbour.'

Anders Schyman felt his head start to spin, and his neck prickled. Bloody hell, that was where the Olympic site was.

The operations manager checked some more details.

'Cell D is in the tunnel between the Victoria Stadium and training ground A.'

The last traces of colour drained from the policeman's face.

'What bloody tunnel?' he said.

The operations manager gave them a serious look.

'I'm afraid I can't tell you that, only that there is evidently a tunnel between the main stadium and one of the training facilities in the vicinity.'

'You're quite sure?'

'The call was connected via a cell inside the tunnel itself. Cells often cover a large area, but the reception in tunnels is obviously severely restricted. We have another cell that only covers the road tunnel under Södermalm, for instance.'

'So she's in a tunnel under the Olympic site?' the policeman said.

'Well, her phone is certainly there, I can tell you that much,' the operations manager said.

The policeman was already halfway across the room.

'Thanks,' Anders Schyman said, shaking the operations manager's hand quickly with both of his.

Then he rushed out after the policeman.

73

Annika had dozed off, and suddenly felt Beata doing something on her back.

'What are you doing?' Annika asked.

'Carry on sleeping. I'm just checking that the charge is okay. It's almost time.'

Annika felt as if someone had just poured a bucket of ice-cold water over her. Every nerve contracted into a hard lump somewhere near her stomach. She tried to speak, but nothing came out. Instead, her whole body started to shake uncontrollably.

'Whatever's the matter with you?' Beata said. 'Don't tell me you're going to start carrying on like Christina? You know I don't like it when it gets messy.'

Annika was taking quick, shallow breaths through her mouth – take it easy, come on, talk to her, buy some time.

'I'm just . . . I'm just wondering . . . what are you going to do with my article?' she finally managed to say.

'It's going to be published in the *Evening Post*, with as much fanfare as Christina's death,' Beata said happily. 'It's a good article.'

Annika gathered her thoughts.

'I can't see that working,' she said.

Beata stopped what she was doing.

'Why not?'

'How are they going to get the text? There's no internet connection here.'

'I'll send the whole laptop to the paper.'

'My editor doesn't know I wrote it. It doesn't say so anywhere. It's written in the first person. Right now, it just looks like a long submission from a reader. The paper doesn't publish submissions that long.'

Beata was insistent.

'They'll publish this one.'

'Why? My editor-in-chief doesn't know you. He might not understand how important it is that this text gets published. And who's going to tell him if I'm . . . not here?'

That's given her something to think about, Annika thought, as the woman went and sat back down on her chair.

'You're right,' Beata said. 'You'll have to write an introduction to the article, explaining exactly why they ought to publish it, and how.'

Annika groaned inwardly. Maybe it had been wrong to play along with the woman. What if it had just made everything worse? She brushed the thought aside. Christina had struggled, and she had got her face and joints smashed in. If she was going to die anyway, it was better to sit at a keyboard than be tortured.

She got up, her whole body aching. The ground was swaying and she realized that she wasn't judging distances very well.

'Okay,' she said. 'Bring the laptop over and let's get this finished.'

Beata pushed the table towards Annika.

'Write that you're the author and that they have to print the article.'

497

Annika typed. She knew that she had to buy more time. If she had got it right, then the police ought to be fairly close by now. She didn't know how closely the mobile phone would be able to give her location, but the man out on the ice two years ago had been found at once. Everyone had already given up hope for him. His relatives were already grieving when he suddenly called his son from his mobile.

The old man had been completely exhausted, and very confused. He had no idea where he was. He couldn't describe any landmarks; he just said that everything was white.

Even so, the man had been rescued in less than an hour. With the phone company's help, the police had identified an area with a radius of 600 metres, and they found the man within that circle. The phone company had been able to locate him using just the signal from his mobile.

'By the way,' Annika said, 'how did you get into the stadium?'

'That was easy,' Beata said condescendingly. 'I had the codes and my card.'

'But why? It's years since you worked on the main stadium.'

Beata stood up.

'I've already told you,' she said, sounding agitated, 'I worked in the pool of project managers, travelling round to every shitty little sports hall that had anything to do with the Olympics. We had access to the office where all the cards and codes were kept. We had to sign them out and hand them back afterwards, but I managed to keep hold of quite a few. I wanted to be able to revisit build-ings that spoke kindly to me. The Victoria Stadium and I had always got on well, so I made sure I always had a card for here.'

498

'What about the code, though?'

Beata sighed.

'I'm good with computers,' she said. 'The stadium's alarm codes are changed every month, and the changes are tracked in a special computer file that you can only open if you have the password. The really stupid thing is that they never change the password.'

She grinned. Annika started to type again. She had to think of more questions.

'What are you writing?'

Annika looked up.

'I'm explaining how important it is that they give this article as much attention as Christina Furhage's death,' she said cheerily.

'You're lying!' Beata screamed, making Annika jump.

'What do you mean?'

'They couldn't possibly give this as much coverage as Christina's death. Do you know, you were the person who started calling me the Bomber? Have you any idea how much I hate being called that? Do you? You were the worst of all of them, and whatever you wrote always got on the front page. I hate you.'

Beata's eyes were burning, and Annika realized that she had no answer.

'You came into that room when I was struck down with grief,' Beata said, walking slowly over towards Annika. 'You saw me in all my misery and still you didn't help me. You listened to the others, but not to me. That's been the story of my life. No one has ever listened when I cried out. No one but my house. But that's all over now. I'm going to beat the whole lot of you.'

The woman reached for the rope hanging from Annika's neck.

'No!' Annika screamed.

The scream made Beata lose her composure completely. She clutched at the rope and pulled as hard as she could, but Annika was ready for her. She managed to get both hands between the rope and her neck.

The Bomber tugged again and Annika fell off the chair. She managed to twist her body so she landed on her side and not on the explosives.

'You're going to die, you bitch!' Beata shrieked, and at that moment Annika realized there was something wrong with the echo. A moment later she felt a cold draught across the floor.

'Help!' she shouted as loud as she could.

'Stop yelling!' Beata roared, tugging again. Annika was yanked forward, her cheek scraping against the linoleum floor.

'I'm here, round the corner!' Annika yelled, and at that moment Beata must have caught sight of them.

She dropped the rope and spun round, her eyes searching the other wall. Annika realized what she was looking for. In slow motion, she saw Beata head towards the battery and the detonator.

74

The shot rang out a fraction of a second later, blowing a little crater in Beata's back and throwing her forward. Another shot, and Annika instinctively turned her back to the wall, away from the shots.

'No!' she screamed. 'Don't shoot, for God's sake! You'll hit the explosives!'

The last echo died away, she could see smoke and dust in the air, Beata was lying motionless a couple of metres away. It was completely quiet, and the high-pitched ringing in her ears from the gunshots was all she could hear.

Suddenly someone was standing next to her, and she looked up and saw a pale, plain-clothed policeman leaning over her, his weapon in his hand.

'You!' she said in surprise.

The man stared at her as he loosened the noose around her neck.

'Yes, me,' he said. 'So how the hell are you?'

It was her secret source, her deep throat. She smiled weakly as he pulled the rope over her head.

To her own great surprise, she burst into floods of tears. The policeman took out his radio and gave his call sign.

'I need two ambulances,' he said, looking up and down the tunnel.

'I'm fine,' Annika whispered.

'It's urgent, we have a gunshot injury,' he called over the radio.

'But I do have a bomb strapped to my back.'

The man let the radio fall to his side.

'What did you say?'

'I've got a bomb on my back. Can you take a look at it?'

She turned round and the policeman saw the pack of dynamite on her back.

'Oh fuck, don't move!' he said.

'Don't worry,' Annika said, wiping her face with the back of her hand. 'It's been there all night and it hasn't gone off yet.'

'Evacuate the tunnel,' he yelled back towards the door. 'Wait by the ambulance! We've got an explosive device here!'

The policeman leaned over her and Annika closed her eyes. She could hear that there were several people nearby from the sound of footsteps and voices.

'Just relax, Annika, we'll get this sorted,' the policeman said.

Beata groaned loudly from where she lay on the floor.

'Make sure she can't get hold of the detonator,' Annika said quietly.

The policeman got up and looked along the fuse wire. Then he took a couple of steps and grabbed hold of the yellow-green wire.

'Got it,' he said to Annika. 'Now, what have we got here?'

'It's Minex,' Annika said. 'Small, pinkish red.'

'Yes,' the policeman said. 'What else do you know?'

'There's about two kilos of it, and the detonating mechanism can be a bit unstable.'

'Shit, I'm not much good at this sort of thing,' the policeman said.

In the distance Annika could hear sirens wailing.

'Are they on their way here?'

'Yep. Bloody good thing you're still alive,' he said.

'It was touch and go,' Annika said with a snort.

'Right, stay absolutely still now.'

He looked intently at the explosives for several seconds. Then he took hold of the end of the fuse wire, where it was attached to the dynamite, and pulled it out. Nothing happened.

'Thank God,' he muttered. 'That was just as easy as I hoped it would be.'

'What?' Annika said.

'This is a very basic device, the sort they use on building sites. It wasn't a bomb. If you just remove the metal plug from the charge, the device is no longer primed.'

'You're joking,' Annika said sceptically. 'Do you mean I could have pulled it out myself, whenever I felt like it?'

'Pretty much.'

'So what the fuck have I been doing, sitting here all night?' she said angrily to herself.

'Well, you did have a noose round your neck as well. That could have killed you just as effectively. You've got some pretty nasty marks on your neck, by the way. And if she'd let the wire touch the battery, even slightly, it would have been curtains for both of you.'

'There's a timer as well.'

'Hang on. I'm just going to get the dynamite off your back. What the hell has she used to stick it on?'

Annika sighed deeply.

'Duct tape.'

503

'Okay, so there's no metal thread woven into the tape, then? Good, I'll just tear through it here . . . There, all gone.'

Annika felt the weight on her back vanish. She leaned back against the wall and pulled the tape off her stomach.

'Anyway, you wouldn't have got far, would you?' the policeman said, pointing at the chains. 'Do you know where the keys are?'

Annika shook her head and pointed at Beata.

'She must have them in her pocket.'

The policeman took out his radio again and called the others back in now that the device was disarmed.

'There's more dynamite over there,' Annika said, pointing.

'Okay, we'll take care of that as well.'

He laid the taped bundle of sticks on top of the box, then went over to Beata. The woman was lying on her front, completely still, blood pouring from a hole in her shoulder. The policeman checked her pulse and lifted her eyelids.

'Will she make it?' Annika asked.

'Who cares?' the policeman said.

And Annika heard herself say: 'I care.'

Two paramedics appeared in the tunnel, pushing a trolley between them. With the policeman's help they lifted Beata onto the stretcher. One of the men went through her pockets and found the keys to the pad-locks.

'I can do that,' Annika said, and the policeman tossed them over to her.

The paramedics checked Beata's vital signs as Annika unlocked the chains. She got up, her legs trembling, and watched the two men push Beata back towards the entrance to the tunnel. The woman's eyelids fluttered open and she caught sight of Annika. It looked like she was trying to say something, but her voice was too weak.

Annika watched the trolley until it disappeared round the corner. More police came into the tunnel. The air was soon full of chatter, voices rising and falling. She put her hands over her ears, feeling that she was close to collapse.

'Do you need a hand?' her source asked.

She sighed, and felt as if she was going to start crying again.

'I want to go home,' she said simply.

'You ought to go to hospital and get checked out,' the policeman said.

'No,' Annika said firmly, thinking of her shit-stained trousers. 'I have to go to Hantverkargatan first.'

'Come on, I'll help you, you're still really groggy.'

The policeman put his arm round her waist and led her towards the entrance. Annika suddenly realized something was missing.

'Wait, my bag,' she said, stopping. 'I want my bag, and the laptop.'

The man said something to a uniformed policeman, and someone passed Annika her bag.

'Is this your computer?' the policeman said.

Annika hesitated. 'Do I have to answer that right now?'

'No, it can wait. Let's get you home.'

As they got closer to the entrance Annika caught sight of a wall of people in the darkness beneath the training ground. She stopped instinctively.

'There's only police and medical teams out there,' the man beside her said.

The moment she stepped out of the tunnel a flash went off right in her face. For a second she was completely blinded, and heard herself scream. When she could make out shapes again she saw the camera and the photographer. In two strides she had reached him, and knocked him to the ground with a powerful right hook.

'You bastard!' she yelled.

'Bengtzon, for fuck's sake, what's got into you?' the photographer exclaimed.

It was Henriksson.

She asked the police to stop at the corner shop, and bought some conditioner. Then she climbed the two flights of stairs to the flat, unlocked the front door and stepped into the silent hall. It felt like another age, as if several years had passed since she was last there. She pulled off all her clothes and let them fall in a heap in the hall. She took a towel from the toilet and wiped her stomach, backside and groin. Then she went straight to the shower and stood under it for a long time. She knew that Thomas was at the Grand Hotel, he would be home as soon as the children woke up.

She put on fresh clothes. She bundled all the old ones, including her coat and shoes, in a big, black, plastic bin-bag. Dragging it behind her, she took the bag out and threw it in the bins down in the basement.

After that, there was only one thing left to do before she got some sleep. She switched on Christina's laptop. The battery was almost exhausted. She found a USB stick and copied the article she had written from the computer's desktop. She hesitated for a few seconds, then double-clicked on Christina's folder, the one marked 'Me'.

There were seven files, seven chapters which all started with a single word: Existence, Love, Humanity, Happiness, Lies, Evil and Death.

Annika opened the first one and started reading.

She had spoken to all sorts of people who had worked with Christina or were close to her. They had all contributed to the image of the Olympics boss that Annika had in her head.

But in the end, Christina had chosen to speak after all.

Epilogue

Towards the end of June, six months to the day after the last bombing, Beata Ekesjö was found guilty in Stockholm City Courthouse of three charges of murder, four attempted murders, murder by arson, malicious damage, destruction constituting a public danger, theft, and driving without a licence. She didn't say a word throughout the entire trial.

The recommended sentence was that she be kept in a secure psychiatric hospital, and that strict conditions be set for her eventual parole. There was no appeal, and sentence was passed three weeks later.

No one seemed to pay it any particular attention, but during the whole five weeks of the trial, the accused always wore the same piece of jewellery.

It was a cheap, old garnet brooch of gold-plated silver.

The article about how a civil engineer, Beata Ekesjö, became the serial killer known as the Bomber was never published.

THE END

Liza Marklund on *The Bomber*

Early in 1995 I decided I needed to become a boss. It was a purely political decision. I was a reporter and columnist on the recently established newspaper *Metro* in Stockholm, and as usual I made it my business to track down stories about violence against women, child abuse, feminism, and other forms of oppression.

One of the articles I wrote was a sarcastic piece entitled 'Funny How There Are Never Any Women Around', in which I poked fun at the fact that there never seem to be any women involved whenever there's a promotion or a pay rise in the offing, or some other sort of official recognition.

While this was all going on, the management of the *Metro* were trying to persuade me to accept the job of news-editor for the paper. I kept saying no. I explained that I was very happy to have power and influence over my own work, but that I had no ambitions to decide what other people should do. Most of all I wanted to write thrillers and grow strawberries.

'Oh well,' my bosses eventually said. 'We'll just have to find a bloke instead, if there are no women around this time either . . .'

That made me think. If I was going to continue writing about women never being given the opportunity to get ahead with any credibility whatsoever, I had to accept the consequences of my own demands.

So I became the news-editor.

The following year I was appointed editor-in-chief.

A year after that I was head-hunted to become the head of daily news broadcasting at TV4 in Sweden.

Being a boss was much more fun than I had imagined, and also a great deal harder. It made me appreciate the very powerful forces at work within any organization: that people are prepared to do pretty much anything in order to gain power.

During my years at TV4 I signed a contract with a publisher to write a series of crime novels featuring a central character called Annika Bengtzon: Annika after my eldest daughter, and Bengtzon after my favourite boss at the *Expressen* newspaper. I wanted my heroine to combine the innocence, sensitivity and beauty of my daughter with the professionalism and thick-skinned attitude of my former editor. Scared, vulnerable, caring and loving, but also ambitious, clumsy, aggressive and intelligent. Because that's what women are like – because women are people, even if we aren't always treated that way.

I was planning to write five books. I had been gathering ideas over the years and I had various sketches and outlines on my computer, waiting to grow into books.

Rather naïvely, I imagined that I would somehow be able to write crime novels alongside my normal work, at the same time as looking after three children and a husband who was the head of programming at a rival channel.

It didn't work out terribly well.

To be honest, the job at TV4 wasn't going terribly well either. Within the tough, male-dominated environment of the Stenbeck Group, which owned the *Metro*,

I had never had any problems being a female boss. The only thing that mattered was the quality of my work, not what gender I was.

At TV4 I wasn't just a boss, but specifically a *female* boss. Which was considerably messier. I was the only woman in a management team of six, I was ten years younger than anyone else, and the only one who had been recruited from the enemy (the Stenbeck Group, in other words).

There was a lot of discontent in the organization at that time. There were a number of self-appointed grandees swanning around like lords of the flies, and these individuals set out to sabotage things for the new management team. You didn't have to be a genius to see that I would be right in the firing line, seeing as I seemed to be the weakest link in the chain.

I was aware of all this and I thought I would be able to avoid taking their attacks personally, but that wasn't a long-term solution. I resigned after just a year or so to devote myself to writing my books full-time.

Everyone thought I was mad. There were crazy rumours about me getting the sack, because no one would be stupid enough to leave one of the most prominent jobs in Swedish journalism out of choice, just to sit in their bedroom writing novels.

Well, once I *was* sitting there the next problem presented itself: could I actually write a novel? I'd never even tried before. I may have had a book published, based on the true story of a woman who had been forced to go into hiding because of the terrible abuse she had suffered, but that wasn't the same as writing a novel from scratch.

To make things easier for myself I decided to start writing about the subject that was closest to my own experience at the time: the book where Annika Bengtzon became a boss. Admittedly, this was the fourth in the series I had sketched out, but back then I didn't even know if I'd be able to finish *one* book, so that was where I started.

And things turned out okay in the end.

The Bomber went on to spend eighteen months at the top of the Swedish bestseller charts.

The management of TV4 bought copies to give to the employees of the newsroom as a Christmas present.

British-Swedish film director Colin Nutley made a film adaptation of the book, which turned out to be one of the most successful Swedish movies during the decade.

It has been translated into 30 languages, and the rights have been sold to 115 countries.

I'm glad I'm no longer a boss.

Having read *The Bomber*, you'll understand why.

Liza Marklund
Stockholm, November 2011

Author's Acknowledgements

This is a work of fiction. Any similarities between the characters in this novel and real people are purely coincidental.

The newspaper the *Evening Post* does not exist either. It may reflect elements of many actual media companies, but is entirely the product of the author's imagination.

Locations and places visited by the characters in the novel are, however, described as they appear in reality, or would have appeared. This also applies to the Victoria Stadium and the Olympic village.

Finally, I would like to thank everyone who has helped make this novel possible with their help and advice. They are:

Arne Rosenlund from the Stockholm 2004 Olympic bid team, who explained the organization needed to apply for and host the Olympic Games.

Per-Axel Bergman, project manager of the Hammarby Sjöstad development, who described plans for the Victoria Stadium and the Olympic village.

Bosse Daniels, explosives expert with Frölanders Järn AB in Breds-Skälby outside Enköping, for advice and demonstrations of various sorts of explosives, detonators, fuse wires, timers, etc.

Gunnar Gustafsson, head of operations at Comviq, for information about mobile phone signals.

Lotta Wahlbäck, civil engineering student, for her insights into attitudes towards women, education and hierarchies within the construction industry.

Lotta Byqvist, for descriptions of sales analysis at an evening newspaper.

Lotta Snickare, of the Swedish Association of Local Councils, for introducing me to the work of the Association.

Stefan Wahlberg, producer of the Swedish television programme *Efterlyst* (roughly equivalent to the BBC programme *Crimewatch* in the UK), for information about police radio channels.

Robert Braunerhielm, managing director of MTG Publishing, and Annika Rydman, union representative of the *Expressen* newspaper, for advice about employment regulations and redundancy practices.

Thomas Hagblom, of the Stockholm Klara sorting office, for explanations and demonstrations of the work of the Post Office on that site.

Conny Lagerstedt, for information about growing organic tomatoes.

Niclas Salomonsson, my literary agent, and his staff at Salomonsson Agency for all their fantastic work.

And, above all, Tove Alsterdal, who read every line and commented, listened, discussed, analysed and provided invaluable advice and suggestions.

Thank you, all of you!

Any errors which may have crept in during the writing process are all my own.

Liza Marklund

Name: Eva Elisabeth Marklund (which only the bank statement calls her. To the rest of the world, she's Liza).

Family: Husband and three children.

Home: A house in the suburbs of Stockholm, and a town-house in southern Spain.

Born: In the small village of Pålmark in northern Sweden, in the vast forests just below the Arctic Circle.

Drives: A 2001 Chrysler Sebring LX (a convertible, much more suitable for Spain than Pålmark).

Five Interesting Facts About Liza

1. She once walked from Tel Aviv to London. It took all of one summer, but she made it. Sometimes she hitchhiked as well, sometimes she sneaked on board trains. When her money ran out she took various odd jobs, including working in an Italian circus. Sadly she had to give that up when it turned out she was allergic to tigers.

2. Liza used to live in Hollywood. Not because she wanted to be a film star, but because that was where her

first husband was from. In the early 1980s she had a two-room apartment on Citrus Avenue, a narrow side-street just a couple of blocks from Mann's Chinese Theatre (the cinema on Hollywood Boulevard with all the stars' hand and footprints). She moved back to Sweden to study journalism in Kalix.

3. She was once arrested for vagrancy in Athens. Together with fifty other young people from all corners of the world she was locked in a garage full of motorbikes. But Liza was released after just quarter of an hour: she had asked to meet the head of police, commended him on his work, and passed on greetings from her father, the head of police in Stockholm. This was a blatant lie: Liza's father runs a tractor-repair workshop in Pålmark.

4. Liza's eldest daughter is an actress and model. Annika, who lends her name to the heroine of Liza's novels, was the seductress in the film adaptation of Mikael Niemi's bestseller *Popular Music from Vittula*. Mikael and Liza have also been good friends from the time when they both lived in Luleå in the mid-1980s. Mikael was one of Liza's tutors when she studied journalism in Kalix.

5. Liza got married in Leningrad in 1986. She married a Russian computer programmer to help him get out of the Soviet Union. The sham marriage worked; he was able to escape, taking his brother and parents with him. Today the whole family is living and working in the USA.

Liza's Favourites

Book: *History* by Elsa Morante

Film: *Happiness* by Todd Solondz

Modern music: Rammstein (German hard rock)

Classical music: Mozart's 25th Symphony in G-minor. And his Requiem, of course.

Idols: Nelson Mandela, Madeleine Albright and Amelia Adamo (the Swedish media queen).

Liza's Top Holiday Destinations

1. North Korea. The most isolated country in the world, and the last iron curtain. Liza has seen it from the outside, looking into North Korea from the South, at the Bridge of No Return on the 38th parallel.

2. Masai Mara, Kenya. Her family co-owns a safari camp in the Entumoto valley.

3. Rarotonga, the main island in Cook archipelago in the South Pacific. The coolest paradise on the planet.

4. Los Angeles. Going 'home' is always brilliant.

5. Andalucia in southern Spain. The best climate in Europe, dramatic scenery, fantastic food and excellent wine. Not too far away, and cheap to fly to!

Turn the page for a sneak preview of
Liza Marklund's next thriller,

VANISHED

Prologue

Time has stopped, she thought. *This is what it's like to die.*

Her head hit the tarmac, and she blacked out momentarily. Fear vanished, along with all sound. Only silence remained.

Her thoughts were calm and clear. Her stomach and pelvis were pressed against the ground, ice and gravel against her cheek and in her hair.

How strange, the way things turn out. How little you can actually predict. Who could have guessed that it would end up like this? A foreign shore, far away in the north.

Then she saw the boy in front of her again – his outstretched arms – and her fear returned. She heard the shots, the sobbing that went with them, and felt helpless.

'Sorry,' she whispered to the memory of her brother. 'I'm sorry I was so weak, so pathetically useless.'

Suddenly she felt the wind again. It tugged at her bag, hurting her. Sound returned. One foot was aching. She became aware of the damp and cold coming through her jeans. She had simply fallen, she hadn't been hit. Her mind went blank again, but one thought remained: *Get away from here.*

She struggled onto all fours but the wind forced her back down. She tried again. The buildings were making the squalls unpredictable, sweeping in mercilessly from the sea, and along the road.

I have to get away from here. Now.

She knew the man was somewhere behind her. He was blocking the route back to town. She was stuck.

I can't just stay here in the glare of the headlights. I've got to get away. Anywhere but here!

A fresh gust of wind took her breath away. She gasped and turned her back to it. More headlights, bright yellow, turning the grey, grimy surroundings into gold. Where could she go?

She picked up her bag and ran with the wind behind her towards a building by the water. A long loading bay ran the whole length of it. There was a mass of wreckage that had blown to the ground, what on earth was it? A staircase? A chimney! Furniture. A gynaecologist's chair. A Model T Ford. An instrument panel from a fighter plane.

She struggled onto the loading bay, dragging her bag behind her. She wove between bathtubs and schooldesks, finally crouching down behind an old desk.

He's going to find me, she thought. *It's only a matter of time. He's never going to give up.*

She curled herself into the foetal position, rocking and breathing heavily, covered in sweat and filth from the tarmac. She realized she had walked right into the trap. She wasn't going to get out of this. All he had to do was walk up to her, put the revolver to the back of her head and pull the trigger.

She peered cautiously under one of the sets of desk-drawers. All she could see was ice and warehouses, bathed in the yellow of the headlights.

I have to wait, she thought. *I have to work out where he is. Then I must try to escape.*

After a few minutes her knees began to ache. Her thighs and calves grew numb, her ankles were sore, particularly the left one. She must have sprained it when she fell. Blood was dripping onto the quay from the cut in her forehead.

Then she saw him. He was standing by the edge of the loading bay, three metres away, his harsh profile dark against the yellow. The wind carried his whisper with it.

'Aida.'

She shrank back and screwed her eyes shut, now a small animal, invisible.

'Aida, I know you're here.'

She was breathing through her mouth, silently, waiting. The wind was on his side, silencing the sound of his footsteps. The next time she looked up he was walking along the other side of the road, beside the fence, his weapon discreetly concealed under his jacket. Her breathing accelerated, coming in irregular bursts, making her feel giddy.

When he vanished round the corner and went inside the warehouse she got up, jumped down onto the tarmac and ran. Her feet were thudding, louder than the wind, her bag bouncing on her back, her hair blowing in her eyes.

She never heard the shot, just sensed the bullet as it whistled past her head. She started running in a zigzag pattern, making abrupt, illogical twists and turns. Another whistling sound, another turn.

Suddenly the ground stopped and the raging Baltic Sea took over. The waves were enormous. She hesitated for just a second.

*　　*　　*

The man went over to the place where the woman had jumped and looked out at the sea. He peered intently, his gun poised, trying to see her head among the waves. Hopeless.

She'd never make it. Too cold. The wind was blowing too hard. Too late.

Too late for Aida from Bijeljina. She had overplayed her hand. She was too alone.

He stood there for a few moments, the wind coming right at him, firing crystals of ice into his face.

The sound of the Scania truck starting up behind him was carried away, never reaching him. The vehicle glided off into the yellow light and disappeared silently.

Sunday 28 October

The Securitas guard was alert. The chaos left by the previous evening's hurricane was everywhere – toppled trees, sheets of metal and plastic from the roofs and walls of the warehouses, their contents scattered by the wind.

He braked sharply as he entered the Frihamnen port area. In the broad, open space facing the water lay the innards of a fighter-plane cockpit, some medical equipment and sections of a bathroom. It took him a few seconds before he realized what he was looking at: wreckage from one of Swedish Television's props stores.

He didn't see the dead bodies until he had switched off the engine and undone his seatbelt. Rather oddly, he didn't feel fear or horror, just genuine surprise. The black-clad corpses were lined up in front of the wreckage of a staircase from some cancelled TV series. Before he had even got out of the car he knew they had been murdered. It didn't take great powers of deduction. Parts of the men's skulls were missing, and a sticky substance had run out of their bodies onto the icy tarmac.

Without a thought for his own safety, the guard got out of his car and walked over to the men. They were no more than a couple of metres away. His reaction was one of astonishment. The corpses looked extremely odd – their eyes had partly popped out of their sockets, and their tongues were hanging out a bit. *Like Marty Feldman's younger brothers*, he thought. Each had a small mark towards the top of his head; each was missing an ear, and, as he'd already noticed, parts of their skulls were missing.

The living, breathing man stared at the two dead ones for a while; he was later unable to estimate for how long. His stare was broken when a lingering gust of the storm swept between the grain silos and knocked the Securitas guard to the ground. He put his hands out to break his fall and one of them landed in the spilled brain tissue from one of the bodies. The feeling of the cold, sticky goo between his fingers made him immediately, violently sick. He threw up on the bonnet of his car, then tried frantically to wipe off the mess from his fingers on the material of the front seat.

Read the complete book – *coming soon*